CON VICT ION

OTHER BOOKS AND AUDIO BOOKS

BY ROBBIN J. PETERSON

Going Home

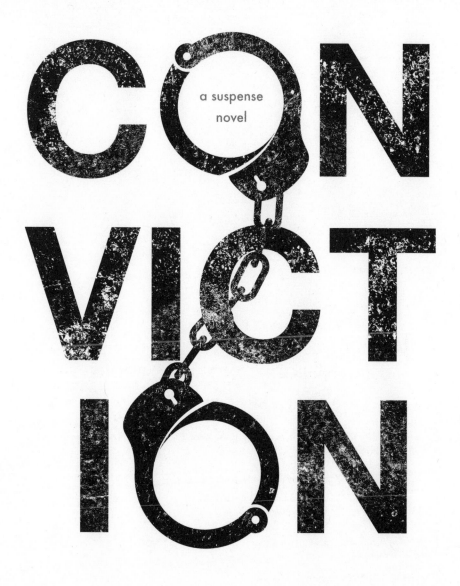

CON VICT ION

a suspense novel

ROBBIN J. PETERSON

Covenant Communications, Inc.

Published by Covenant Communications, Inc.
American Fork, Utah

Printed in the United States of America
First Printing: June 2018

22 21 20 19 18   10 9 8 7 6 5 4 3 2 1

978-1-52440-328-7

This book is dedicated to missionaries who serve everywhere, even if it's just down the street. Thank you for your service. You are touching more lives than you realize. You are doing more good than you know for people now and for future generations.

ACKNOWLEDGMENTS AND PREFACE

UKRAINE IS A UNIQUE COUNTRY that has experienced great changes, some volatile, since September 1991, when it first opened its borders as an official mission for the preaching of the gospel. Some of the stories from missionaries ten years ago are different from stories of missionaries who are serving there today, and some are the same. To honor past missionaries and current missionaries, I've blended some of their experiences while trying to stay true to actual mission borders for the year 2013, as well as the people's cultural and political climate during that time. Also, in the book, the city Kramatorsk resembles the city Kharkov more, which is bigger and farther north and used to be part of the Ukraine Donetsk Mission.

That said, this is a work of fiction. Any similarity to people, names, or situations is coincidental, unless you're Bryt Christensen, and then I totally named my character after you. Bryt, thank you for sharing your exciting mission, which gave structure and color to my imagination. Rachelle and Nathan Vanbuskirk, thank you for sharing Ukraine with me through funny stories and Instagram! I used some of the jokes you shared with me; see if you can find them. Also, a big thank-you to Stephanie Lacy at Covenant, who shared her missionary knowledge—this book would not be as strong without you. Angela Piccolo, thank you for the beautiful cover! And to my editor, Sam, who balances her talents and motherhood like a boss, thank you for trusting and believing in me. Also, thank you to the entire Covenant team who read or edited, made suggestions, and gave words of encouragement. President Miskin, thank you for caring enough to take time to answer questions. Katy Nielsen, Karen Aston, Tara Nielsen, Jodee Packer, Bonnie Jensen, Rachel Mceachran, Emily Scott, and Liz Christensen, thank you for reading my unpolished words and for cheerleading. You pushed this book to where it needed to be. Julie Ann Carter, your whole life should

be a book; thank you for helping me with ranching facts and for all the
fun memories we've made with you and Tyler. Mark Jensen, thank you for
listening to me talk about imaginary people and telling me why they stink
and how to make them unstink. To my dad and Jack-Dad, thank you for
serving missions in Thailand and Tennessee—your experiences are in this
book too. And Seth Peterson, you are my relentless fan, and I can never
thank you enough for it. Sorry for ruining high council talks because people
have already read similar (ahem, your) mission experiences in my books.
Kids, thank you for enduring our own type of Ukrainian Terror Famine and
letting Mommy write.

September 2, 2013

I STARED DOWN FORTY THOUSAND miles and tried to swallow the dread that had lodged itself in the back of my throat. Brett's large shoulders bumped mine as he shifted to get the middle seat to lean back more. We'd been in the air for over two hours, and although my legs weren't nearly as large or long as Brett's, they were beginning to feel cramped.

"Are you nervous?" Brett asked.

I shrugged. For someone who had pretty much ignored me my whole life, he was sure chatty now that we were missionary companions. He'd let me have the window seat because it was my first time on an airplane, and he'd found a place for my heavy backpack in the overhead. It made it hard to pretend he wasn't there, forget where I was going, and who I was with.

"Why? Are you nervous?" I asked, still staring out the window.

"Sure," he said. "Ukraine is the real deal. What if we get with companions who are jerks? What if people don't want to listen to us? What if"—he paused dramatically—"all the girls are ugly?" He grinned. "Admit it. You're also afraid of that."

I didn't answer or even smile. My fears had nothing to do with girls.

It had been easy the past twelve weeks in the MTC to go along with Brett's energetic charisma that plowed over everything in his path, but today, I couldn't do it anymore. Maybe it was because today, leaving for Ukraine, being alone for the first time with Brett, everything had finally come to a head. He didn't know anything about me or what I'd done; if he did, he'd probably tackle me right here and leave me to die. Sometimes I wished he would just so I wouldn't have to face the guilt that constantly tore at my insides when he was around.

For what had to be the tenth time, he asked, "Don't you think it's weird we're serving in the same mission, leaving the same day?"

"Yeah." This time, I gave a small chuckle and looked at him. His head was back, and he was staring at the ceiling. I knew what he really meant was it was weird that two people in our tiny ward, from our small town of Standish, were leaving to serve a mission on the same day. Not that it was weird that he was serving with *me*.

But really, it was more than weird that he was serving with me.

The fact that it was him out of the fifty thousand other elders serving around the world was more than crazy coincidence. My original decision to put my papers in had had as much to do with escaping him as pleasing my mom. It was as if the Lord had sifted through a bag of really good punishments, pulled out Brett Tyson's name, and said, "Ah, yeah, this is gonna be good."

God knew what I'd done. He'd inspired Salt Lake to put me with Brett. I knew how Jonah felt when he was swallowed by the whale. The second Brett's call came to the same mission I'd been called to, I knew there was no running from my problems, there was no running from the Lord.

He'd find me.

Brett was my whale.

But to be honest, which was not one of my strengths, it wasn't totally God's fault I was here. There were a thousand moments I could have refused the mission call. But for reasons I still couldn't explain, I was in an airplane rocketing toward Ukraine. I was like one of our cattle, voluntarily getting on a truck that would take me to my death. Maybe it was because not going would mean seeing the hurt on my mom's face, something I'd successfully hidden from since last November.

The pilot interrupted my thoughts, announcing we were beginning our descent into Chicago. I felt for the belt buckle and tightened it, pressing myself into the back of my seat. There was a tug on my stomach and pressure in my ears as we circled around and came lower.

Brett leaned his large frame forward and rested his head against the seat in front of him. "Hey." He waited until I met his eyes. "You doing okay?"

I rubbed my prickling thumbs together. "Sure."

He looked past me and out the small window. "You thought Salt Lake was a big city? What do you think of Chicago?"

I stared outside as we descended even lower. I could see buildings as tall as mountains in the distance, surrounded by dark clouds and layers of smog.

The plane touched the runway, and my heart rate sped up with the thundering sound of the airplane braking. I gripped my hands in front of me and waited for the bumpy ride to end. When it finally did, my head swam with the lack of motion. A ding sounded as the seat-belt light flicked off and people came to life around us, standing and grabbing luggage from the overhead.

Brett stood and stretched up and over the sleeping man on the end to get our bags. "Should I wake him?" I asked, pointing at the man.

Brett tugged the bags down and handed me mine. "Nah, that guy was drinking some expensive stuff. I wonder why he wasn't sitting first class." He stretched his legs out into the aisle. "I'd use my money for more legroom rather than booze."

An image crossed my mind of Brett as a pro-football player, sitting in first class instead of learning Russian. Maybe what he'd said at seminary graduation was true. Maybe getting kicked off the football team had pointed him in the right direction. Maybe he could be forgiving.

Hope lit up inside me like a small match, but just as quickly, it disappeared. I'd destroyed Brett's dreams, and he didn't have a clue it had been me. There would be no mercy.

Instead of waking the man, I stuck an I'm-a-Mormon card in his front breast pocket. Brett grinned at me as we half crouched in our seats, waiting until everyone in front of us filed off the plane. When it was our turn, Brett slung his black leather bag over his shoulder, and I followed him down the narrow aisle with my backpack.

The Chicago airport felt much bigger than the Salt Lake airport. We had a two-and-a-half-hour layover, which I learned was really just enough time to find the international flights, wait in line to go through security, and run to our gate so we wouldn't miss our eleven-hour flight to Turkey. When we got to our gate, people were overflowing around the desk and the seating areas, speaking languages I didn't recognize. A flashing sign said a different time than we'd been told. It looked like the plane would be taking off late.

Brett pasted a smile on his face and told me late flights were typical. But the busy airport and fear of the unknown were making me feel unusually stressed. What if we missed our next flight from Turkey to Kiev? I'd heard stories of missionaries having to spend the night in airports. I didn't know enough Russian yet to ask where a bathroom was, let alone Turkish.

We found some seats on the outskirts of the terminal, our backs to the constant flow of traffic behind us. Brett graciously took the inside next to an older woman and her daughter, leaving me to be an introvert on the end.

The two women were on their way to Israel but knew English well. They seemed intrigued by us, and Brett kindly and smoothly told them about our belief in Jesus Christ as the Savior of the world. I listened mostly as a spectator, watching Brett already in motion as a real, live missionary. While he had been attending football practices and away games on Sundays, I'd been at church, suffering in a shirt and tie. Yet, here, being a missionary came as naturally to him as being a football player.

Somewhere in the conversation, I felt something bump against my leg, where my bag was resting. I glanced over. No bag.

I jumped up and searched the crowds of people. Someone looked back at me. A kid in black, two large circles pulling on his earlobes, and he was wearing my backpack.

"That kid has my bag!" I yelled.

But Brett was already jumping over the tops of the seats. I followed in his wake as we ran past several shops and restaurants, the way becoming a gradual upward incline. Near the top, I saw the kid turn once more to look at us, and his eyes went from narrow to wide as he watched Brett running toward him.

Before the kid could even turn to sprint, Brett full-on tackled him. The backpack slid across the black-and-white checkered tile, and the kid let out an angry sling of cuss words.

I grabbed my backpack, but Brett stayed on top of him. "Why did you steal my friend's backpack? Do you need money? Help? No, I'm not getting off of you until you give me some answers."

Two security guards pulled up on standing motor vehicles, a white man with a wide black mustache and a stern, older black woman with a sagging chin. The man said loudly through a megaphone, "Sir, get up. Both of you stand where I can see your hands."

The woman seemed to notice that Brett and I were together, with our similar clothes and name tags. She turned her stern eyes on me. "What happened?"

"This guy took my backpack, and then my companion here, Elder Tyson, tackled him. He played football, you know."

She gave a sideways glance at Brett, who was now standing, out of breath, brushing the dust off his black pants. "No kidding," she said without smiling.

Brett gave her a nod, then turned his attention to the red-faced kid who was being handcuffed by the male security guard. I checked through my bag; everything seemed to be there. The guards didn't question whether the bag was mine or not, and when I pulled out an English Book of Mormon and offered it to them, they said a simple, "No, thank you," and left.

Brett rubbed at a tear in his shirt, among other dirt stains covering his pants.

"Thanks," I said, carrying my bag rather than putting it on my back.

Brett put his arm around me as we walked back down the hall toward our gate. "Who knew the Chicago airport would be so exciting? Nothing a couple cowboys from California can't handle though, right?" He dropped his arm and punched my shoulder lightly.

I breathed out. "I don't know about that—I didn't even have time to find some rope to reel him in."

He laughed. "Yee-haw! Ride 'em cowboys."

I laughed too but more because my body was craving a nervous release from all the stress I was feeling.

We reached our seats, and I put my backpack on, too hyped up to sit. "Thanks," I said again to Brett as he slumped in his chair.

"You'd do the same for me," he said, winking.

"There's no way I could have done that."

He brushed my words away with one hand. "But you would have if you could."

Again, I shook my head, the ache in my throat growing by the second because I knew I wasn't the type of person someone could count on or trust. I was the opposite of everything I should be, everything I pretended to be.

Brett thanked the women who had watched his bag, and when he dug through it and handed them a pamphlet on Christ as a gift, they even accepted it with looks of gratitude. The speakers announced it was time to begin boarding. Slowly, we made our way to the end of the line. The women waved at us before they walked through the corridor.

"Good job," I said for lack of anything better to say. "You saved the day *and* taught someone."

Brett frowned slightly. "I was kind of worried about giving them that pamphlet. They told me they were Muslim, and I just don't want to cause any problems, you know, once they get home. But they seemed excited about it."

I nodded. "Yeah, it's hard to know who to teach and who not to."

Brett shrugged. "I guess just go with the Spirit? The Lord knows who needs the gospel, so you just have to grab on to those opportunities and let the Lord do the work. It's His work, not ours, right?" He patted me on the back, and I smiled, even though inside I felt like turning around and looking for the first flight heading back to Reno—the closest airport to home.

I stared at a spot above the doorframe we'd be going through and didn't look away. As long as I didn't think about what I was doing, I could do this.

At last, it was our turn to get on the plane. It was crowded, and space in the overheads was limited. We were at the back of the plane, but it was our luck that no one joined us on our row of three, so just before the plane took off, I slid over next to the window, and Brett sighed contentedly, able to fully relax in his seat with more elbow space.

As we pushed through the air over Chicago, I stared down at the sea of never-ending buildings and the great expanse of Lake Michigan. I wondered if we'd see New York or Washington D.C. or Paris. All I knew was we'd be arriving at 10:00 a.m. Istanbul time, when it was midnight in California.

Brett fell asleep before the sun was fully set. I knew I should sleep too. Our plane was catapulting through the sky, hurrying to meet the sun, which would make a very short night. The inside lamps were turned down, encouraging rest, but I stared out the window instead. There were times in the flight when the earth was completely black, void of all lights, and I wondered if we were passing over clouds or water. Then I would see some scattered lights below us and realize it was simply nothingness.

I stared at the blackness, my heart torn between right and wrong, searching for an in-between, but all I could see was Brett jumping over the terminal seats, sacrificing life and limb to get my backpack. He deserved to know, but it would take someone more courageous than me.

Ten Months Previous
November 5, 2012

IT WAS NO SECRET THAT Brett Tyson had dumped Angela Bell two days before Homecoming.

The whole school knew. Some people felt bad because they knew her dad had said she could drive his new silver Ferrari, and they knew how much she'd paid for her dress. But I felt bad because while Brett found it easy to find a new date, most of the other guys who were part of that scene already had dates.

I wasn't part of that scene, meaning the cool kids. I was part of the Future Farmers of America and drove down Main Street with pieces of hay flying out of the back of my truck. In all honesty, if I had to choose between spending an eternity with a herd of stampeding cows or a crowd of loud teenagers swinging their bodies to music, the cows would win. The only exception was if Angela Bell was one of those bodies.

It could be a joke that she'd asked me to Homecoming. I'd thought about that. But she'd driven the forty miles outside of Susanville just to pick me up at my ranch in her dad's silver Ferrari.

In reality, maybe it was because she knew I'd never say no. And she needed a yes.

I hadn't said no to her in kindergarten when she'd asked me to cut her pigtail. Not in junior high when she made me do all the work for our joint science project. Not in high school when she'd dropped a stack of cheerleading fliers off in my beat-up Chevy truck and begged me to stuff them in envelopes, which I'd done in the shed that night after feeding my new calf, my fingers

numb and sticky from the formula. Not in the hall at school when she asked
me if she looked pretty.

So when she asked me to Homecoming, she got her yes. Without hesitation. An automatic response she'd conditioned into me.

I stood by her at the dance, awkwardly drinking punch, and even held
on to her waist and danced a couple slow songs. She placed her head on
my shoulder when Brett happened to dance near us. I was grateful when
she asked if I wanted to get some fresh air.

She shivered and sat on one of the stone benches lining the student walk-
way once we got outside. I tried to appear casual as I placed myself on the end
of the same bench, my body chilled more because of nerves than the cold.

"Neal, really?" she asked, smiling as she looked at the empty bench between
us. "Most boys would take advantage of the cold and sit closer to a girl, not farther away than they would in class. Is this how Mormon boys stay so chaste?"

I cleared my throat and shot a quick smile at her, my face hot. I didn't
say the first thing that came to mind—an image of her kissing Brett near
the football field. Clearly not all Mormon boys were very chaste.

She got up and scooted closer to me on the icy bench, her dress sequins
sparkling like moving diamonds under the yellow streetlamp. She sat there
in silence before asking, "Are you going to serve a mission for your church?"

I stared at the circles of light on her dress and wondered what her reaction
would be if I told her I didn't know. It seemed like something a guy should
know. A month ago, I thought I had almost a year and a half to figure all that
out. But then general conference happened, and the prophet announced that
elders could serve missions at the age of eighteen instead of nineteen. There
were less than a handful of LDS seniors in my school, but the news had
spread, and even nonmembers in our small town were talking about it.

I had counted on an extra year to earn money, to help my dad on the
farm. And I could still take that year—there was no law saying you *had* to
serve at eighteen. But the look on my mom's face, the way it lit up like it was
an answer to prayer, the tears that kept falling through the duration of the
meeting—I knew from that moment what her wishes were. We came home,
and she told my dad, the look of hope still fresh on her face. He had looked
from her to me and back to her and said, "Neal will make a fine missionary."

That was all. My nonmember father, who needed his son to put food on
the table, had said I'd "make a fine missionary." And I was left to feel like a
giant rubber band stretched toward my mom, the farm, and the fear of the
unknown.

Through the nearby gymnasium door, I heard the steady beat of Taylor Swift and a loud group of girls screaming along the words.

I blew out, my breath hit the cold air, and I watched the fog swirl in front of me before I finally answered, "Probably. I always planned to."

"When?"

"I turn eighteen in March, so I guess I can this summer. If that's what my dad wants."

Angela hugged her white dress coat tighter. I stared at the flower holding her corn-silk, blonde hair to the side in a bun and wondered for the hundredth time how I was lucky enough to be her date tonight.

She turned her big blue eyes on me. "Brett is in your congregation too, isn't he?"

I swallowed and nodded.

"And is he planning on serving a mission?"

I shrugged. I didn't really feel like talking about Brett and his activity levels at church.

She scrunched up her face and looked away. "I asked him the same question not long ago. I asked him if he would stay for me."

"Really? What did he say?" I hadn't known a mission was on Brett's radar. He already had universities checking him out for football scholarships.

"He said he wouldn't be around either way next year. He's looking at playing football at Boise State." She pursed her lips together and narrowed her eyes up at me. "I guess that told me enough. Football or mission—I'm not in his plans." She suddenly cocked her head. "What would you say?"

"About what?"

"What would you say if you were in love with the perfect girl and she asked you to stay home from a mission for her? Would you tell her no?"

I opened my mouth, but nothing came out. I could only stare at Angela's long eyelashes and the way her soft lips turned from a pout to a smile in perfect unison and think that Brett was a much stronger man than I.

She grinned, showing the tips of her white teeth and whispered, "Do you want to get out of here?" at the same time she touched my hand. My heart rate began to skyrocket as she pulled me to my feet. She dug through her purse and pulled out a set of keys.

I stumbled after her as we headed away from the gymnasium. At the edge of the parking lot, she jingled the keys in the air. "Do you want to drive?"

I stared past Angela to her parents' Ferrari. Its sleek body stood out next to the family minivans and generic four-door cars. I looked back at the school.

"What's wrong?" she asked. "Cowboys only know how to drive monster trucks?"

"No, I can drive it," I said quickly. "Are you sure your parents won't mind?"

She smirked and threw the keys. I caught them midair and stared at the cursive *B* hanging off the key chain.

"What about Chad and Tina? Should we tell them we've left?"

She shrugged, unconcerned. "It's not like they're stranded—they have a car."

We stepped next to the passenger side, and I stared at the way the body curved outward around the wheels, screaming of money and sophistication in such an off-the-path California town that didn't even know what style of jeans was popular.

Angela hopped up and down on the toes of her high heels. "Are you going to open the door?"

"Oh." I fumbled with the key chain, and she reached over, took it from me, and clicked one of the buttons. The vehicle purred to life, and she waited outside her door and cleared her throat. I grasped the door and opened it so she could climb in.

My heart hammered louder than the distant music as I walked around the front of the car. Not only was I going to drive a real-life Ferrari, but Angela was also with me tonight. Me. Alone. I opened the car door, and she shot me a warm smile that made me pretty much melt into the front seat.

She gave me a quick lesson on where the gears were and made sure the headlights and heated seats were on. We left the parking lot and traveled down Susanville Main Street at twenty-five miles per hour. The engine purred quiet as a kitten, so unlike my beast of a truck. We hit the last light by the McDonald's, on the edge of town.

"Keep going," Angela said at the light. "Toward Janesville."

When the light turned green, I pushed the gas. The engine accelerated, and we were flying at sixty in less than four seconds.

"Wow!" I hooted.

She laughed a high, tinkling laugh in response. I slowed down at the curve, and the car responded smooth as leather. It was complete freedom I'd felt only riding my horse alone in the mountains. We drove in silence the five minutes it took to get over Bass Hill, then over into the smaller town of Janesville, past pine trees and fields of harvested alfalfa that marked Northern California's high desert.

"Take this road," Angela directed, pointing at the sign for Janesville Main. I slowed and turned down the wide, two-lane road. It was dark; there were no streetlights. The only lights on the road came from houses lining the street. Thick pines blocked the stars and lights from the distant highway.

Again, Angela directed me to turn down a road that wrapped around a small elementary school. I followed it until she said, "Turn here," pointing to what was known as Dirt Pine, an unpaved, uphill, bumpy road, where a couple dozen homes dotted the uneven mountainside. It was littered with rocks and mini-boulders.

I hesitated, the Ferrari humming. "You want to take *this* up there?"

"Sure. There's a great view."

I knew plenty of better views, ones that were all smooth road. "Are you sure?"

She rolled her eyes and crossed her arms. "I thought you country boys weren't scared of dirt roads."

"Not scared of the *road*," I said, gripping the steering wheel tighter, imagining what her dad would say when Angela showed up with his pristine tires soiled and muddy, pebbles imbedded in each ridge. "It's just— this car deserves to be on a road where it can really fly."

Her lower lip pushed out, and she continued to cross her arms. "I'll drive if you can't handle it."

I sighed and turned the steering wheel to the left. We would do it Angela's way, like we always did. We'd gone only a quarter mile and a few houses in when she said to pull into a rock-paved driveway. I did, relieved that she'd finally decided to turn around and get back to better road. The headlights revealed a white manufactured home, the lights completely off.

I put the car in reverse, but Angela reached out and touched my hand. "Wait," she said. "I need to do something here. Put it in park."

My heart gave an uncomfortable lurch, and I knew inside that I shouldn't. We needed to leave this place. I couldn't think of a logical reason why, just a feeling in my gut I'd learned to trust as the Holy Ghost. Again, Angela placed her hand on top of mine and moved the gearstick into park for me, then reached over and turned off the car. All the lights went off.

My heart began to hammer, and I was blinded in the complete darkness. I heard Angela get out of the car.

"Come on, Neal," she whispered. "Follow me."

I fumbled around, trying to find the handle, but Angela opened the door from the outside for me, her cell phone lit up like a flashlight.

"What are we doing here?" I asked, pulling myself out of the car. I glanced down the road, but the only light was from the millions of stars overhead peeking around clouds and pines and the outline of Thompson Peak.

Angela didn't answer, but I could see her flashlight directed at the back seat of the Ferrari as she pulled out a Styrofoam egg carton. She placed it on the hood of the car, then pulled out what looked like an actual egg.

"Here," she said, placing it in my hands. "Principal Mengham won't be home for at least three more hours. I'll let you throw the first one." She dug around in her purse and pulled out a can of spray paint. "I'll use this."

"Wha—Angela," I said, the egg cold in my hand. "We're egging his house?"

"Is it a first for you? I thought cowboys did this sort of thing."

"We eat our eggs. I only throw eggs at Easter."

She laughed, her voice echoing off the quiet house. "You're funny, Neal." She moved quickly in front of me and kissed my cheek, stroking my other cheek with the tips of her icy fingers. "Then do this for me. No one will ever know it was us, I promise. We have the perfect alibi."

I grabbed her fingers. "But why?"

She slipped her hand out of mine and took a step back. "Really, Neal? I thought you of all people would want to throw eggs at Mengham's house. Mengham is the one who told your friend Steve he couldn't run for junior class president because he's a Mormon."

I shook my head. "That was Mrs. Kesler. Not because he's a Mormon. She said it was because his grades weren't good enough."

"No," Angela said firmly. "Steve gets good enough grades. What are you talking about? I was there. I was working on signs for the Halloween carnival. It was Mr. Mengham. He made Mrs. Kesler say that. You know Mengham's church hates Mormons."

I clenched my jaw. I'd heard things said around our small community over the years, gossip about what other churches said about ours, but I never thought our principal would take sides like that. I shook my head, my heart pounding. I suddenly felt dizzy and sick.

"Mengham took ag business out of the curriculum for next semester," Angela said.

"What? I need that class. Why?"

"Because of your mom."

My grip on the egg tightened. "That doesn't make sense."

She took a step closer. "Brett's mom told me about her, how everyone at church looks down on you guys because of what she did. But I don't judge her."

"It's not like that at my church," I said louder than I should have—my voice echoed off the silent trees. I lowered it to a harsh whisper. "Brett's mom thinks there's something wrong with ranching. It's not because of my mom."

Angela crossed her arms. Even in the dark, I could see her eyes were narrowed to angry slits. "Well, Mengham asked your mom out in high school. Apparently, he had a crush on her, but she told him no because he wasn't Mormon. He said she pretended to be a good girl until Mr. Rebel Motorcycle came around. He was your dad—right?"

I heard the egg hit the side of the house before I even decided if I should throw it or not. Angela stopped talking, and I took in deep breaths of air, clenching my empty fists. She smiled up at me and reached for my right-hand knuckles. My tight fingers instantly relaxed, and I grasped her hand instead, a feeling somewhere between liberation and terror at what I'd just done. She turned my hand until my palm faced up, and she placed another egg in the middle of it.

September 3, 2013

It was dark, and then a light began to glow outside. Beneath us were miles of ocean. I drew the shade most of the way down so as not to annoy everyone else on the plane, then picked up my scriptures, hoping to find an answer there.

I opened to 1 Nephi 10 and began reading. When I got to verse eighteen, I read it more carefully. "For he is the same yesterday, today, and forever; and the way is prepared for all men from the foundation of the world, if it so be that they *repent* and come unto him.

"For he that diligently seeketh shall find; and the mysteries of God shall be unfolded unto them, by the power of the Holy Ghost, as well in these times as in times of old, and as well in times of old as in times to come; wherefore, the course of the Lord is one eternal round."

He that diligently seeketh shall find.

What was I seeking? It was something—or I wouldn't feel so empty, so void of light inside. My eyes kept landing on the word *repent.*

I didn't want to think about the possibilities that word suggested or what it would cost.

I'd mostly repented. I'd prayed and asked God to forgive me. I hadn't spoken to Angela Bell since November of last year. I would *never, ever* do it again. Wasn't that enough?

I rubbed my eyes, tired but too upset to sleep. I knew it wasn't. Where the MTC had failed to teach me Russian, I had learned a bit about the repentance process. It wouldn't be a true confession without telling Brett. And telling him at this point was too much—I couldn't think about it. But how could I teach people about Christ and repentance if I refused to do it myself?

Again, I saw Brett tackling the kid for my backpack. He'd called me his *friend*. He'd shown me nothing but kindness our entire time in the MTC. Not that he'd been *unkind* to me before we'd served. I just hadn't been on his radar, which had made the last seven months of high school that much easier to keep flying under.

It was painful, but I tried to allow my brain to think about what I hadn't before: what I had to do to fully repent.

My heart racing, I imagined myself telling the mission president what I'd done. I'd seen President Meyers's picture in my mission pamphlet. In my mind, his smile turned to a frown, his eyes filled with instant distrust and disapproval.

What if I got sent home after all the efforts to save enough money to buy new suits, scriptures, shoes, and even luggage? We'd never get that money back. I rubbed my face. It made me physically sick.

Why had I waited so long? I could have told Bishop Hendricks in my interviews. I could have told Mr. Mengham right away. I could have asked my parents for help. I thought not telling was simple self-preservation. It would all blow over and disappear after I left high school and Lassen County, and the sun would come out again like it did after a bad storm. I never expected it would be more like a snowball that turned into an avalanche.

Was vandalism *really* a sin you could get sent home for?

But I knew it wasn't the vandalism. It was the lie. Brett had paid the price for my actions, and I had let him.

I closed my eyes and again thought of Jonah from the Bible. I saw myself in the dark belly of the whale. I could feel I was starving, death and the unknown stretching infinitely before me. I'd failed the Lord. But worse, I wasn't alone. Brett was shackled to me, his plans altered, our futures intertwined.

Why, God? Why? It was hard enough to decide to serve a mission. Why did you have to send me here with Brett?

Brett's words came strongly and firmly to my mind. *"You just have to grab on to those opportunities, and let the Lord do the work. It's His work, not ours, right?"*

Opportunities?

I turned the word over and over, unlocking possibilities I hadn't seen before. Was the whale a punishment? Or an opportunity to change?

Had God put me here where I couldn't run because He *wanted* me to repent? Not because He was punishing me but because He was offering me a chance to finally lift my burden? The idea of being cursed to serve with Brett had made total sense, a just punishment from God. But the idea that God *loved* me and was so full of mercy that He had actually arranged my mission to be with Brett so I would repent was mind-blowing. That He cared enough about my own personal salvation and peace of mind was humbling in a way I could barely fathom. He cared about *me*. Not just the people I'd be teaching.

Waves of love from the Spirit washed over me. Tears streamed down my face that I quickly wiped at. I was grateful Brett was asleep. God, with His infinite love and abilities, had cared enough to not let me get away with hurting Brett.

Maybe like God had needed Jonah to serve, He needed me to serve now, and He couldn't have made that happen unless I'd been here on this plane with Brett at this time because now I would finally do what I should have done all along. And it made me wonder if I hadn't gotten called to this mission with Brett, would I be thinking I'd gotten away with it? How would that have affected me on my mission? Or for the rest of my life? What if I'd decided to repent, but I was in Africa and Brett was in Ukraine? And I couldn't tell him. The idea of holding on to the secret finally felt unbearable.

"One hour," Brett muttered hoarsely, making me jump. He pointed at his watch.

I cleared my throat. "One hour," I repeated.

BRETT LEANED BACK, HIS SCRIPTURES open on his lap. His eyes looked far away, deep in thought.

"Brett," I said.

He looked over.

I forced it out of my mouth. "I have a confession." I searched his face, still free of judgment. I knew this was the last time I would see him look at me like that, and for a brief second, I held on to our new friendship, knowing I was about to rip it apart, and I considered once again not saying anything. But then I felt the pain of never being free.

"I—I threw the eggs."

Brett yawned. Then he said, "You threw the eggs." His eyes looked dazed. I nodded, and he stared blankly back at me.

Then he sat up straighter. Understanding lit his eyes. Confusion distorted his features. "You aren't talking about Mr. Mengham's house?"

I swallowed but didn't look away. "Yes."

"No, man. There's no way." His narrowed eyes were sharp, angry. "That couldn't have been you."

My heart hammered into my head, but I pushed myself. "I was with Angela Bell."

He set his jaw. "You have to be lying," he whispered.

"I didn't know Angela was going to pin it on you. I didn't find out what she'd done until after you'd been suspended from the team."

"Yeah, but you never told anyone it wasn't me, or did I miss that part of high school?" His face had changed, and even in the dim airplane lights, I could see splotches of purple growing on his cheeks. He growled and slammed a fist on the top of his scriptures.

Terrible Tyson the Football Player had held the record for breaking the noses of two opponents in the same game his junior year. His senior year, he'd broken only the captain of the opposing team's collar bone. Confessing while we were both missionaries was actually a pretty genius move now that I thought about it.

He inhaled deeply and smoothed the top of his scriptures with unsteady hands, as if just touching them could calm him. "You're not joking, are you? Because seriously, if we were still in high school, I'd probably kill you."

I felt my own hands shaking. "I know sorry isn't enough."

"Why didn't you say anything sooner?"

I looked away, desperately staring down the seat in front of me to steady my thoughts. "I should have. I've wished every day I had. Angela threatened me, of course, but that shouldn't have stopped me."

"How can you live with yourself, man? I would never let someone take the fall for me like that. How could you do that to me?"

"I regret not saying anything. I regret hurting you now. I need to repent of it, and telling you is the first step."

Brett shook his head. "Football was my life. I lost all trust with my team, all credibility. My mom didn't speak to me for a month. Even now, I'm like the biggest disappointment in her life."

"She didn't believe you?"

"No one did!" he said loudly. I flinched, and he glanced around us before saying quieter, "Sometimes I think it'll never be the same between her and me."

I'd seen his mom, Peg, at games. She'd been as much or more invested than Brett.

I tried to help him see what I did. "Football *was* your life. Look at you now. You're serving a mission. You're better than you were before. You're doing what the Lord wants you to do."

"You think I couldn't have done both? A football scholarship *and* serve a mission? Since when is serving the Lord limited?"

"You bore your testimony about how it changed your life and perspective," I said, feeling less sure. "The entire school loved and respected you for the way you handled everything."

"The entire school? I don't know who you hung out with, but none of my friends were congratulating me. More like enjoying my failure—it meant more opportunities for them." Brett jumped up. "I can't sit here anymore. I'll be back." He stood in the aisle and pointed a finger at me. "Don't follow me."

Technically, we were supposed to stick together, but I didn't want to test his threats to kill me. I took a deep breath and ran a shaky hand through my hair. I felt like a schmuck and rehearsed in my mind what I could have said differently, but there was nothing. Now he knew the truth, much too late for it to benefit him.

I'd taken the selfish way out. I'd gotten out of trouble in high school, and now I'd ruined his mission just so I wouldn't feel guilty anymore. I'd left Chicago with a friend and would arrive in Istanbul with an enemy.

Several long minutes later, Brett returned. He sat, visibly calmer. I didn't try to start a conversation with him, and he didn't with me. The pilot announced we would be landing in thirty minutes and to stay seated and buckled. Brett leaned over his fold-down table, his scriptures open across the top, hands on either side of his face, as if to block me. I stared out the window, my face burning with shame.

It wasn't until we had landed and everyone was standing and grabbing luggage that I heard him say, "Neal." Again, he flexed his jaw. "It took a lot of courage to admit what you did to me. Not as much as if you had admitted it right away and saved me a lot of trash, but you could have said nothing. And I guess I appreciate knowing the truth." He sighed. "I thought you were a cool dude, but now I just don't know. I'm going to need time. I thought I was all over it, but now I'm reliving the nightmare." He tapped his scriptures in a restless rhythm and glared at me. "Do you know what it feels like to be wrongly accused of something? It's the worst feeling in the world."

He clenched his jaw and looked away. "I wish you could feel that and know what you put me through."

It was seven in the morning, Ukraine time. People pressed against our backs in front of the airline desk as I stood in a sleep-deprivation fog. I had fallen asleep in the airport in Turkey and on the two-hour flight to Donetsk, and now, rather than being rested, my body craved more.

"Our bags . . . uh . . . *Moi khvatayet* . . . uh . . . *sumki*." Brett looked at me for help, but I knew I wouldn't do any better than he was communicating that our luggage hadn't been on the moving belt. A woman from our same flight was behind us somewhere in line, crying. I wanted to cry too.

"Eh?" the man asked again.

Brett ran a hand through his hair.

A voice behind us said, "I speak English and Russian. Do you need help?" We turned to see a man in his thirties, with shoulder-length hair and a black leather jacket. Many people rolled their eyes, muttering under their breath things I didn't understand, most likely thanking him for saving us from our own stupidity.

"*Da*," Brett said. "Thank you. We lost our bags."

The man came to join us and explained in Russian our situation to the man at the desk. The man handed us two papers, and the deskman yelled for the next person in line.

"This form is so they will ship your bags to you once they are found," the man explained. "Do you have an address?"

Brett reached into his bag and pulled out his planner that had the address to the mission home in Donetsk.

"Is this your home address? Where you'll be living?"

Brett shook his head. "We don't know that information yet. But it should get to us through this address."

The man helped us fill out the form, which took several minutes, then handed it back to the desk workers.

"Buy you a coffee?" he asked kindly.

"No, thanks," Brett said. "We don't drink coffee. How do we get out of this place?"

"Follow me. I'm headed that way too. I'm Dan, from just about every-where, but I call Canada home. Where are you both from?"

"Dan?" Brett repeated, as if clarifying. Dan nodded, an amused expres-sion on his face. "Um, nice to meet you. I'm *Stareyshina* Tyson, and this is *Stareyshina* Christensen. We're from California."

He led us to another long line. "California? I've been there. Palm trees, the beach, eh?"

Brett chuckled. "Not where we're from. Think skiing and volcanos." He grinned at me, then choked suddenly the second he met my eyes, as if just looking at me caused an involuntary gag reflex. My face burned, and I looked away.

We had to go through customs to enter the country. Having fewer bags made it slightly quicker for us, but still, they went through everything and questioned us. Dan made the process a bit easier, helping to translate. While we waited, he asked us questions about the Church. Brett handed him a Book of Mormon in English, and he accepted it before he left us standing outside on the sidewalk among hundreds of other people.

The sun was muted, covered by a thick cloud cover, the air hot and sticky. I had expected it to feel cooler in Ukraine. Sweat dripped down my back as we searched through the sea of people for anyone resembling two *stareyshiny*. Several minutes went by, and my legs began to feel weak. Brett must have felt the same because he led us to a wall, where we sat on the ground with several feet between us.

Twenty minutes later, two missionaries walked near the entrance, searching. Brett and I quickly stood and waved to them.

"You're the newborns?" the tallest one asked, his accent slow and Southern. "I'm Stareyshina Little, from Texas. And this is Stareyshina Erickson."

"Hi." Stareyshina Erickson adjusted his glasses. "I'm from Baltimore. Where are you boys from?"

I nervously held out my hand. "I'm Stareyshina Christensen. From California."

"And I'm Stareyshina Tyson. From California."

"Two Californians?"

"Yup," Brett said without looking at me.

"It's a big state," I said.

"Not big enough," Brett muttered.

They looked between us, and an uncomfortable silence settled, broken only when Little asked, "Where's your luggage?"

Brett explained what had happened.

"The same thing happened to Stareyshina Tomson a few months ago. He said it showed up a week later," Little said.

That gave me some peace of mind.

"Let's go find us a *marshrutka* bus," Little said.

We followed them across the street to where other people were gathered. A short purple bus resembling a van pulled up, and the missionaries climbed through the open door, settling on a seat near the back.

"We got you covered this trip," Little said. He pulled money out of his wallet and handed it to the people in front of them, who then passed it up to the bus driver. He put his wallet back in his pocket and said, "Tell us what's going on in the US of A."

"Yeah," Erickson said. "How are the Ravens doing?"

Brett shook his head. "No one cares. But the 49ers were doing well last I checked."

Little laughed and thumped Brett hard on the back before they launched into a discussion on who would play in the Super Bowl. I listened, not really wanting to be a part of the conversation about football. Not that I didn't like football—it was fine—but with Brett, it felt like I was ripping off a bandage and staring at a green pustule, and I didn't want to look.

Little yelled something and raised his hand, and the marshrutka bus stopped. He grinned at us. "Well, boys, this is it. You ready?"

I grabbed my backpack and followed the other three missionaries out onto the sidewalk and watched as other people climbed in and took our spots, already passing their money through others' hands to the driver. We walked across the street and up to a tall building where President and Sister Meyers were standing ready to greet us. They looked very much like their picture. President Meyers was tall and narrow, with graying thick hair. His wife was dark and short, with a wide smile.

I had read that the Meyers were graduates of the University of Utah, had a family of five daughters, mostly married now, and some grandchildren. He'd started his own successful computer business that had eventually gone overseas. He'd traveled all over Europe and had even studied Russian before getting called as a mission president. He seemed capable in every sense of the word.

"Stareyshina Tyson and Stareyshina Christensen, welcome." President Meyers's hands were not large, but they were firm. His brown eyes were warm but intent, like he knew what I was thinking before I did. It made me uncomfortable, and I tried to avoid them as much as possible.

He greeted Erickson and Little similarly, and after a few minutes of conversation said, "Thanks for helping these two new missionaries get here. We'll see you tomorrow at transfer meeting."

We said our goodbyes, then President looked around at the ground. "Where's your luggage, Stareyshiny?" I stupidly looked around at the ground too, exhausted from our travels.

"It got lost," Brett said. "We filled out some paperwork with the mission home address. Someone helped us."

President nodded. "It should get here all right, then. We might have some extra clothes at the mission home, and your companions might be able to lend you some until it shows up. If it doesn't, well," he rubbed his chin, "we'll figure it out later if that happens."

I sure hoped they weren't permanently missing. Too much money and sacrifice had gone into those bags to be lost before I'd even started my mission.

We followed the Meyers to an open, white, covered structure I decided must be a bus stop.

"The first order of business is to go to the hospital and get you tested for infectious diseases," President said as we stood there sweating in the heat.

"You're joking," Brett said.

President didn't smile. "I don't really joke much."

"Didn't we get checked for that back at home?" I asked.

"Well, you had your shots. But your visa shows you'll be living here for two years, and they want to make sure you didn't pick something up from wherever you've come from. It's a new policy taken from old policy. Probably for a few months, and then it will change. It's happened before, and we've dealt with it. It will not be very invasive, and I will be there the entire time to make sure it's not."

I yawned. All I wanted to do was find a bed and sleep for three days.

A long, blue double bus clambered around to where we stood, its middle an accordion, the top connected to a large electric wire, like I'd seen in pictures of cities in the '30s and '40s in America. We waited for several people to climb out, then joined the surge of waiting people.

It was standing room only. President found his wife a seat, and the three of us clustered near her. I kept my eyes glued to the world moving in a flash behind the crowded windows, occasionally searching the glum faces of the people around me.

It was several stops before President indicated we should get off. We walked a block until we reached an aged tan building three stories high.

Inside, it felt several degrees cooler, possibly because it was so much darker. We sat in some metal chairs near a large window—the room's only source of light.

When it was our turn, we walked down a hall into another dark room. It reminded me of when the electricity went out sometimes during school and everything was left in shadows. It was hard not to view it as a sketchy place when I compared it to America and even our small hospital back home. The nurse led us to a small room with a cracked wooden bench. Brett and I sat side by side and leaned our heads against the concrete wall behind us.

"The last two stareyshiny I brought here passed out. Are you the fainting type?" President asked. Again, he didn't smile.

Brett snorted and rolled his eyes. "Bring it on," he said.

I balled up my hands in tight fists and swallowed hard as I watched the large, sterile needle the nurse prepared next to me. It looked like the type we used to vaccinate calves—the type I'd accidentally shot myself with in the hand before. I looked up at the ceiling instead.

She picked up my arm, turned it over, and began pressing on veins.

I heard Brett whisper under his breath, "Ladies first."

I fought the urge to jump when I felt the sting of the needle and began to count. By the time I'd reached fifteen, she'd handed me a cotton ball and instructed me to do something in Russian that I didn't understand. I pressed the cotton against my arm.

Relief flooded through me now that it was over, and I glanced at Brett, who looked more serious and pale now that it was his turn. She began rubbing his arm, checking his veins. Curious, now that it wasn't me, I watched as the needle went into his forearm. He watched the whole time—something I knew I couldn't have done.

The vial was nearly full when the nurse began to shake her head, and then she pulled out the needle and said something loud and frantic in Russian over her shoulder. I wasn't sure what was going on until President Meyers crossed the small room in half a second and caught an unconscious Brett. The nurse made a *tsk* sound and said something to me, which I didn't know whether to take as a compliment for not fainting or as an insult. Her expression could have said either.

As she left the room, President rubbed Brett's shoulders. "Stareyshina Christensen, wet your hands in that sink." I immediately stood and did as I was told. "Rub your hands on his face. Let's try to wake him." The water worked, and Brett came to with unfocused eyes.

"I'm sorry, coach," he slurred. "Burke didn't throw me the ball. Neal tackled me from behind. I didn't even know he played football. He just took me down." Then he began to sob deep, shaking sobs that made my throat shut and eyes burn.

THE EVENING GREW DARK, AND the lights of Donetsk seemed never ending. We traveled by taxi this time. Brett sat up front, still uneasy from the hospital experience, while President, his wife, and I took the back seat. The city shone through hazy clouds, making it look a smoky rust-orange, as if the buildings were smoldering. The taxi dropped us off under the flood of a lonely streetlight near a tall apartment complex.

We trudged up the steps to the second floor. President unlocked his door, and we entered the apartment. It was nice, with a more modern feel than I would have judged from the outside of the building. There were wood floors with rugs, as well as a decorative rug on the wall. There was plenty of room for us to sit in the living room or at the large dining table.

We ate rolls and some sort of vegetable soup while President Meyers told us about Ukraine. "The first missionaries arrived in Ukraine in June 1991. That was twenty-two years ago. Before that, people were told what to believe. Now they get to choose. There are millions of people here—millions—who haven't heard the gospel. You have an opportunity to find them and share your convictions about Jesus Christ."

My head ached. I was so tired, but I listened as President explained rules and some of the dangers. "If someone's holding a knife or a gun, don't be stupid; give him what he wants. You're not invincible. And carry your papers with you at all times. Sometimes the police will stop you and want to see them. Also," he hesitated and played with his napkin, "there has been some political unrest. Nothing to worry about, but try to avoid any large gatherings. I've heard rumors of riots in Kiev, some bullying of people in government offices, and I don't want any missionaries getting hurt."

We both nodded to show we understood, but really, I wondered what a large gathering looked like, because everywhere we went, there were so many people. I was used to me, a horse, a hundred cattle, the sky, and the earth. Anything more than that was too many.

"Don't eat meat prepared by members—or any meat if you can avoid it—and be home by curfew every night. There are more things you'll learn and your companions will tell you. It's hard to cover everything. Tonight, I want to have a private interview with both of you separately before bed. Tomorrow, there will be too much going on with meetings and other missionaries to interview. It will be brief. Is that all right?"

Brett and I both nodded silently.

President said "brief," but I knew mine would be the opposite of that. True repentance would mean confessing to my mission president. I felt it inside. This was bigger than just what I could fix between the Lord and me. It made me fidget, and I became inattentive as I silently rehearsed what I would say to him.

"You both must be exhausted—although Stareyshina Tyson here had a nap," President said, winking, proving he did joke sometimes. "Let's get this over with." He looked at me. "Stareyshina Christensen? Would you like to go first?"

Brett met my eyes, and I saw something that resembled pity before he looked away. I followed President down a short hall to a small room set up like an office. The first thing I noticed was a medium-sized picture of the Savior on the wall. There were only two chairs. I sat in one of them.

"So, tell me about yourself, Stareyshina Christensen," President said as he shut the door. "I read that your parents own a ranch? Did you play any sports in high school?"

I shook my head. "I was too busy working."

He sat across from me in the other chair. "Your mission must be a sacrifice for them."

"It's something we've prepared for," I automatically responded.

"They sound like good people." He said it like a statement and a question and waited, as if opening up the airways for me to talk.

"Yeah," I said, blowing out. "Really good—the best." I didn't do small talk well, especially when I was dreading what I needed to say. Also, part of me didn't want to talk about my family. I had seen and heard plenty of judgment in Susanville over the years, my bishop included.

"Tell me about them." He met my eyes, and I stared back, but he just watched and waited until I knew I would have to say something. Telling President about my family wasn't scarier than telling him about Brett, but I was worried it would taint his opinion of me when it was time for me to confess.

But I was determined to be 100 percent honest tonight. I could start by being honest about my own family. I licked my lips, dry and cracked from all our travels. "My mom's name is Marlene. I have a younger sister, Sarah; she's fourteen. She's actually my half-sister." I felt along the cuffs of my sleeve and tugged at the fabric. "My dad, Jeff, isn't a member."

"Is he your biological father?"

I wanted to ask, "Does it matter?" but instead, I said, "My biological dad left when my mom was pregnant with me and died in a car accident a year after I was born." I didn't feel it necessary to say the other things the Quincy Stake members seemed to spread as if the gossip were still breaking news. That they'd never been married. That my mom, who was Laurel president at the time, had made a mistake. "My dad now is the only dad I've ever known." I stared at a dry patch of skin on my hand. "He's the best."

"And you said he's not a member?"

My eyes shot up and searched President's face, but I saw only warm brown eyes that showed he was listening. I nodded slowly.

"He's supporting you on your mission?"

"Well, yeah—it was always what my mom wanted. And he'd do anything for my mom. She doesn't ask for much." I felt my face burn with talking so much about myself.

He smiled. "You're blessed to have them."

I nodded and swallowed the lump in my throat, trying to push away the pit that had settled in my middle since I'd left home. President had no idea how blessed. *I'd* had no idea until I'd left.

Dad had taken two days off from farming to drive me to Provo with my mom. I think we had all hoped when I submitted my paperwork at the beginning of May that I would have a few months of work before it was time to leave. Two weeks later, it came back that I was leaving the seventeenth of June. I'd had to scramble to get my doctor's appointments and mission clothing, and then I'd left them empty-handed right before all the big work had come.

It was probably better I hadn't had so much time to think before my mission. I might not have gone through with it.

"Do you have a girlfriend waiting back home for you?"

I didn't smile. I was too nervous. "Just a dog named Pal."

President laughed loudly and hit his knee. "That's good to hear." He stood. "I like to ask about family because it helps me see *why* you're serving, where you're at in your testimony. The fact that as a family you planned and sacrificed to serve, with a nonmember dad's support, speaks volumes about where you've come from. I'm not surprised a hardworking cattleman was sent here to Ukraine. This is not an easy mission. The Lord always knows what He's doing."

I put on a poker smile, but I knew if he'd heard my dad's final words to me, he wouldn't be so sure about my upbringing. He'd put both hands on my shoulders and said I could come home whenever I wanted. "This mission is for you, Neal. Not me, not your mom. But for *you*. If that doesn't suit you, come home. You're always welcome at home."

I couldn't think about that. When I did, it seemed to knock all the wind out of me. I knew going home would not make my mom happy, even if my dad had said it was my choice; it wasn't just about me.

I switched my attention to President Meyers, who sat on the edge of his desk. "I have only one piece of advice for you. The older I get, the more trials I experience, and as I've prayed to know what the Lord wishes me to learn from those trials, it all comes down to one thing: love. Love is always the answer. When I've struggled with wayward children and I've asked *how*, it's love. When I've asked *why* I have to serve in a particular calling or move to a certain place . . . or even lose a grandchild"—President looked down and swallowed, and I felt the emotion in the room shift.

This was him talking about *his* family now, and my heart opened in response. He met my eyes and smiled kindly—"the answer is always *love*. The Savior wants us to learn to love like He does. He wants us to *choose* to love, to feel His love, to share his love. The Lord sent you to be a missionary here to *learn* to love. Through service, you'll find it. There are about as many members in this whole country as the small town you and Stareyshina Tyson come from. But you'll discover that the Lord loves the people here very much.

"I've told you of some of the dangers, the drunkards and violence, the muggings that can happen, the police and others who might want to target young American missionaries for money. Just be smart, listen to the Spirit, and be obedient—strictly obedient. Then leave the rest up to the Lord."

I nodded. It was quiet for several seconds, and in that small amount of time, my nervousness quadrupled. The Spirit inside me burned with a prompting. *It's time.*

He stared at me, and his expression changed. Instead of telling me we were finished, he moved from leaning casually against his desk to sitting in the other chair. His mouth opened, then closed before he spoke. "I always ask missionaries how their companionship is going. I don't *usually* ask missionaries that question as soon as they arrive. It's not as though you'll be with Stareyshina Tyson much longer." He cleared his throat. "I have noticed some coldness between you. You come from the same town; I assume you knew each other before the mission?"

"Yes."

He nodded but didn't say anything. I could feel the consequences of telling him pressing on my chest. It would change everything. He'd send me home. He'd mark me as a bad missionary. He'd tell my parents—that part scared me the most. And even if he didn't send me home, the judgment would radiate from his eyes the rest of my mission. I wouldn't be able to escape him—or Brett—for two years.

But I could see the consequences of not telling him too. God was showing me a path to find peace. Would I walk away from that because of fear? I'd already gone halfway by telling Brett. I was almost there.

"To be honest, sir"—my voice shook—"I wanted to talk to you about my relationship with him—with Brett." I swallowed. Where was my memorized speech? "Brett and I knew each other in high school. We weren't friends, exactly, but it was a small school." I took a deep, steadying breath. "This is hard. But I need to tell you this."

He blinked and gave me an encouraging, silent nod.

I launched into my planned discourse. "I did something that hurt Brett. About nine months ago, we had a mutual acquaintance, and I let her influence me to vandalize our principal's house. And then she pinned it on Brett, and I never told anyone. I let him take the blame, and as a result, he was kicked off the football team and lost any scholarship opportunities that were coming. And they were definitely coming. He was the best thing that ever hit our small high school." I stared at President, waiting for the storm to fall. For the shock he probably felt, knowing a missionary had come this far only to be sent home because of a disregard for the repentance process. I expected a reaction like the nurse in the hospital when Brett had fainted, a shaking of his head, along with a *tsk*.

Then he would call my parents.

He nodded. "Continue."

I hadn't rehearsed anything else. "Well," I wet my lips, "of course I regret—I wish I had said something before. I was afraid and embarrassed. At first, everyone criticized Brett, but then it's like Brett just worked harder to prove to everyone he wasn't that person, and in the end, I don't think there was anyone more liked in our class than him. He doesn't see it that way. He says his mom still won't talk to him. But his example, the way he handled all of it, well, he deserves to be here. And . . . I don't." I sniffed hard to keep my emotions in check and stared at my hands. "I didn't want anyone to know. And each day"—my voice caught—"each day I didn't tell, it was just more evidence of what a jerk I was." I wiped my eyes with my sleeve.

When I finally looked at President, he didn't look angry—more like touched. "Fear can be a powerful motivator to do the wrong thing," he said softly.

"The worst part is how much I've hurt Brett. I didn't know we would serve a mission together. I didn't know how much I'd come to respect and like . . ." I closed my eyes and held my breath for a second. "I told Brett on the way here. I told him I was sorry. But I think it's too late."

"It's never too late." He reached out and patted me on the knee. His eyes held mine. "I'm glad you took the opportunity to finally tell Stareyshina Tyson, even though it was hard. Jesus Christ is full of mercy. He wants us to succeed." He paused. "I'm glad you told me this. I know it wasn't easy. I'm sure you've already talked this over with the Lord quite a bit too?"

I nodded numbly. "Yes, and I expect I will for some time."

President Meyers leaned forward, elbows on his knees. He waited until I made eye contact, then said, "This isn't something you need to beat yourself up over anymore. We all make mistakes, some bigger than others. Vandalism is serious. Hurting people is serious. But *you* are also part of the equation. *You* matter too. The Lord doesn't want you to suffer for this your entire life. This life is about *changing* through our experiences. That's why the Savior's Atonement was absolutely necessary, because it wasn't about *if* we made mistakes but *when* we made mistakes. You are not a failure; you are in the midst of this earth, living the life God intended for you to learn from. It's a failure if you *don't* learn."

His words were so different from what I had expected. I began to feel hope for the first time.

"This is what I want you to do. I want you to write three letters: one to the principal—tell him what really happened. I want you to confess to your parents and tell them you are learning what it means to repent and your mission president is helping you. Then I want you to write to Brett's mom. Tell her what happened and how you feel now. Tell her how you feel about her son—all those things you told me. Then move on."

Move on? After opening all those cans of worms? I took a deep breath. Confessing to all those people would be harder than hard. I guess when I'd assumed President would send me home, I'd just planned to show up and say my mission hadn't worked out. I didn't think I'd actually have to directly confess to Mr. Mengham, my parents, and Peg Tyson.

"So you're not sending me home?"

He smiled. "Were you hoping for that?"

I let out a shaky laugh. "No, sir, I want to be here. I just thought that might happen."

"Then I'm even more impressed you decided to tell me about it. That takes a lot of personal strength. How are you feeling about what I've asked you to do?"

I fidgeted with my tie. "It's not going to be easy. I sort of wish I didn't have to."

"You have to—if you want to repent. Part of repentance is confessing. Not just to me but to those you've hurt." He picked up a set of scriptures behind him on the desk. He turned a few pages. "Doctrine and Covenants section 58 talks about how to repent. Can you read verses 42–43 out loud?" He handed me the book.

I looked down at the verses marked in red pencil. "'Behold, he who has repented of his sins, the same is forgiven, and I, the Lord, remember them no more. By this ye may know if a man repenteth of his sins—behold, he will confess them and forsake them.'"

The word *confess* stood out like a chore on a list of things I didn't want to do.

"Does this help you understand better?" he asked. "I'm pretty sure you've forsaken your sin because it doesn't sound like you've made vandalizing and lying a habit. But the Lord has asked that we also confess our sin. Can you think of why this might be? What good comes from confessing our sins?"

"It makes us suffer?"

President Meyers's face broke into a small grin. "I don't think Christ really wants us to suffer—that's what He did for us. This life is about choosing *good* over evil. Acting against God—making a poor choice, like vandalizing—is showing God we don't choose Him. Confessing our sins is a way of openly showing God we are choosing Him over evil and that we humbly acknowledge and love Him. It's a recommitment. It also helps us show love for others. The greatest commandment is to love God; the second is to love others. True repentance does both of these things."

"I've never thought of it like that," I said.

He nodded. "So, are you willing to write three letters to confess your sins openly before God?"

I blew out. "Yes."

"Just curious, but what did Brett say when you told him?"

"He was really angry. I don't think writing these letters will change that."

President stood to show our interview was over. "They say time heals everything. I'm sure he'll find a way to forgive you. Remember, the secret is *love*. Pray and ask God how He sees your companions. You find love through prayer and service. The biggest challenge on my mission is companionships—and that is *not* a secret."

THE NEXT MORNING CAME TOO early. After a quick breakfast of eggs and toast, the four of us traveled by bus to the mission office. President wanted to be early, so we left at 7:30 a.m. While we sat on a less crowded bus than the previous day, President Meyers told us how a car was a luxury most Ukrainians did not own. He said out of the branch of one hundred twenty people there in Donetsk, only one person owned a car. Sometimes they could be rented, if needed, but otherwise cars would not be our main method of transportation.

When we reached the church building, President Meyers led us down to the basement, where the mission office was located. A Stareyshina Baxton from Connecticut was there, making sure all the documentation for registering the transferring missionaries to new cities was in order. He spoke quickly as he shuffled and filed through papers, letting me know I was registered in the city of Kramatorsk and everything was taken care of. President Meyers let me know that Stareyshina Kaufman, from London, would be my trainer.

At ten o'clock, we met in the chapel up top and sang "The Spirit of God," followed by a prayer given by Stareyshina Little. President Meyers spoke briefly, then turned the time over to the district leader and assistant to the president to say a few words. We closed with a song and a prayer.

While the missionaries had their interviews with President, the rest of us broke into groups and worked on role-playing, teaching English, and conducting better companionship studies.

President Meyers told the missionaries in their interviews who their new companions would be and where they'd be serving. Those who would be transferring had been notified ahead of time to bring their belongings to the conference. Suitcases and extra bags lined the back of the room.

I joined the group I was assigned to, which was working on role-playing, and thankfully, I wasn't with Brett—I was nervous enough. It wasn't long until I spotted Stareyshina Kaufman in our group. He stood out in both appearance and energy level. He was around six feet, thin, with blond hair and white eyelashes framing translucent blue eyes.

"May I play the investigator?" he asked. His British accent was strong and sounded similar to some of the English flicks my mom and sister had forced me to watch.

I noticed people grinned as Kaufman passed them and sat up front in one of the metal chairs. He faced Stareyshina Erickson, held a pen as if it were a cigar, and said he couldn't understand why smoking wasn't allowed by Mormons. "It's not as if it's more pollution than we get from the air we breathe here, now is it? Just look at Chernobyl."

Several of the missionaries snickered.

"No other church outlaws smoking. And how else am I to maintain my lovely figure? I'll start eating chocolates, Nutella, and such, and then where will I be?"

Erickson buried his nose in the scriptures, trying to find one on smoking, no doubt. I wondered how I would answer that question. Some of the other ranchers and cattlemen we had contact with smoked or chewed tobacco. I wondered what I would say to someone like them.

Erickson finally explained the Word of Wisdom, as outlined in the Doctrine and Covenants, which Kaufman kept asking why about until Erickson finally resorted to the First Vision. When I thought about it, every question about the Church, I could either answer with the story of the First Vision or the plan of salvation. I took note.

Transfer meeting lasted a couple hours, and then it was time for a quick lunch. Kaufman came and sat next to me, his plate full of the same steaming, white, half-circular pockets I had. "I hear we are to be companions. Stareyshina Christensen, is it?" He reached out a hand, and I shook it. "That will be a mouthful for these Russian speakers here. I'm Kaufman, from London. And you are from the same place as Stareyshina Tyson? California?"

"Yeah. Same place." My eyes drifted to where Brett had his back to me a few tables away. We hadn't been within twenty feet of each other all day.

"Well, it's lucky he will be in Kramatorsk too. You'll get to see each other once in a while. A bit of home to make you realize how far away you really are." He took a bite of the pockets and said, "Have you ever had *varenyky* before? Some call it *pierogi*." I shook my head. "What are you waiting for, then? Eat up. It's best hot, son."

I cut into the piece and blew on it. Inside were mashed potatoes, mushrooms, and something else that tasted like cabbage.

"Good?" he asked.

I nodded and took another bite. While we ate, Kaufman talked of Kramatorsk. He was quick to smile and always had something funny to say. He exuded a confidence that made me feel instantly accepted and alienated. Confident people often affected me like that.

After lunch, someone rented a van to give missionaries rides to the train station, and we parted from President Meyers and the other missionaries. When President Meyers went to shake my hand, he clasped it with both of his and gave me a heartfelt "Good luck, Stareyshina." It filled me with love, and I began to feel the stirrings of the peace that came with being forgiven.

Everyone was in good spirits on the way to the train station, Kaufman more than anyone. We were dropped outside the train station—a tall dome-shaped building that resembled a gigantic white barn. But inside, it looked more like a cathedral with large windows and large chandeliers. People spilled out of it on stairs and escalators, and others were standing in lines. Kaufman helped me use a kiosk to purchase a train ticket.

We didn't wait long before it was time to board the train. Some of the trains were white on the outside, but ours was blue. Four sisters in our area went first, followed by three more elders and Brett. I followed Kaufman up the stairs, holding tightly to the metal rail to keep from falling.

The inside resembled a city bus but with wooden benches sitting back to back down the whole length. The train was crowded and shook with each of our steps. We found a spot where the four of us could sit facing each other, while the sisters moved farther ahead and sat across from a woman and her young son. Brett sat on the opposite seat from me, and we stared silently out the window, at the ceiling, everywhere but at each other.

Some musicians stood at the back with a violin and a type of horn, and Kaufman got out his camera and took a few pictures of us, as well as the men with instruments.

"Have you ridden on a train yet, Christensen?"

I shook my head.

"Well, I'll tell you how to do it proper, like a true Ukrainian. You look out the window, make this face." He furrowed his eyebrows. "And you think about how miserable your life is. See? Look around you, watch, and learn."

I stared at the people around us and noticed that what Kaufman had said was somewhat accurate. Even with the music playing, there was no laughter or positive chitchat going on, only dark, thoughtful masks. I gave

Kaufman a slow smile and shook my head. He laughed heartily and hit me on the back. Brett grinned back at him. Probably because Kaufman had hit me.

When the train finally began to move, the musicians sat down. I relaxed, the noise from the train too deafening to talk or even think. The train swayed and clattered noisily over each section of track. Soon, I found myself leaning forward, slumped over the backpack on my lap, and I felt myself falling asleep.

It was hot and still light outside when we arrived in Kramatorsk. We walked up the stairs and into the main body of the train station.

The Kramatorsk station was cavernous, like the one in Donetsk, with a very tall dome ceiling, this one holding an intricate gold chandelier with dozens of white lights. Large circular paintings covered the ceiling, with rich reds, browns, and yellows.

We passed a large waiting room with white pillars and another chandelier, chairs all facing an ornate painting that took up nearly the entire back side of the room. It was of a pale and gray city, at the center a dark statue of a man staring at the large buildings in the distance as if he approved of them.

Voices echoed around us as I stared at the large electronic signs with names of trains and times. It was like the modern world had met an old, medieval one and was trying to coexist.

We followed the sidewalk and said goodbye to the sisters. Then six of us guys walked a few blocks farther to a nearby restaurant to eat together before going our separate ways.

The restaurant had a distinctly rustic feel, with wood ceilings and floors, while the walls were made of decorative stone. We sat at a long, black, rectangular table and looked through the menu, which was pretty much useless to me.

I glanced across to the other end of the table to see how Brett fared. He kept his head down, staring at the menu. His hair was disheveled from the long trip, but other than that, he looked perfectly at ease—like he always did.

"Have you eaten here before, Murray?" Kaufman asked the elder sitting across from me from Payson, Utah. Out of all the missionaries, I felt I related to him the most. He looked as though he'd be more comfortable in cowboy boots. His companion, Stareyshina Osborne, was from Florida and was the only one who seemed okay with the heat.

"No. You?"

"Johnson and I came here a few weeks ago with Berg and Sloan. The *shashliki* is very good. It won't make you sick."

"Da," Berg said, "*nezavisimo ot togo, naskol'ko sil'no vy poprobuyte byk nikogda ne budet davat' moloko.*"

Everyone but Brett and I burst into laughter. Brett met my eyes for a brief second, then looked away just as quickly.

Kaufman wiped his eyes and said, "Sorry, Christensen. Berg is always educating us with local colloquialisms. *No matter how hard you try, the bull will never give you milk.* Did I do it justice in translation?"

Berg grinned. "Da, Kaufman. The lame man always laughs at the blind."

Again, the guys erupted in laughter. I faked a smile but didn't find it all that funny and buried my head in my menu. As if the language weren't hard enough, speaking in Ukrainian proverbs was more than my brain could handle. The server came, and Kaufman ordered shashliki for me.

Soon, raw vegetables, bottles of Coke, and steaming meat on kabobs—the shashliki—were brought out on white ceramic plates.

"Johnson and Sloan are the missionaries we replaced, right?" Brett asked.

Kaufman nodded. "Da. Johnson was my companion, and Sloan was Berg's. Berg and I were together until you got here, and Murray and Osborne have been together longer than either of them have had steady girlfriends."

Again, there was laughter.

Stareyshina Osborne said, "Christensen, we never thought they'd let Kaufman be your trainer."

"Not after his last companion." Murray snickered.

I met Kaufman's clear, blue eyes before he looked away. "What can I say? The girls can be quite a problem here."

"What was he out? Like, five months?" Murray asked with a crooked grin.

"He seemed a good man," Osborne said. "I was surprised he got emergency transferred. Weren't you?"

Kaufman gave a short nod. "Da."

"How long have you been out?" I asked.

"Two." He watched me with a hint of a smile, clearly enjoying my discomfort.

Berg snorted. "Don't believe him. He's going home soon."

"You're going to make him distrust me, Berg." Kaufman gave me a careful look-over. "I will be watching this little chap so he doesn't run off with some lovely Ukrainian. The most important reason, of course, being that beautiful Ukrainian girls grow into babushkas. Although, a grandma would have a fine time fattening you up. Did you not get as much as your friend there in California?"

Brett laughed loudly, along with the others.

"It's proper he has you, Kaufman. Perhaps you might be his babushka?" Murray said in his best British accent, which came out sounding like a Southern belle with a cold.

They all laughed some more. I was still stinging from being called a *little chap*. My five-foot-ten was definitely dwarfed by Brett, but I wouldn't say I was scrawny. While he'd been beefing up and chasing balls, I'd still been driving tractors and lifting bales.

I pursed my lips together. "I didn't come here for the girls."

Kaufman was amused. "Stareyshina, never underestimate the girls here. It can be a dangerous mistake."

"Da," Berg agreed. "Speak highly of the lake but stay on the bank."

Again, the missionaries lost it, crying, hitting the table with their fists— even Brett. This was probably what Joseph Smith was talking about when he'd warned against loud laughter. I was glad to see our bill arrive and wondered if the owners of the restaurant were just as eager for us to leave as I was.

"Stareyshina Christensen," Kaufman said. "Shall I thank you in advance for buying my supper? New bloke always treats."

"You'll get used to Kaufman," Murray said. "He likes to kid around." I tried to send him a grateful smile before I sipped my Coke. "Hope you're not anti-caffeine," Murray continued. "Once in a while, you can find a Sprite, but mostly, we're just lucky we can find something without alcohol."

"Oh, I don't think Christensen is a stickler for rules," Brett said.

I felt my face grow hot as all the missionaries looked at me.

"We can't all be fat-heads like Tyson," I said under my breath, but Brett's glare showed he'd heard.

"And we can't all be liars like you," he hissed. An uncomfortable silence settled around the table. I watched Berg look from Brett to me and back again.

So this was how it was. No more silent treatment. Brett would make me pay for what I'd done.

I wanted to go home more than I ever had in my life.

Kaufman told me dinner was his treat after all. I was relieved I could postpone learning to use Ukrainian money for at least one night. I noticed he paid for Brett also, which Brett looked sincerely grateful for.

We stepped out of the restaurant. The sun had set, but the heat hadn't left. We lingered on the sidewalk while I questioned all the pictures I'd seen of winters in Ukraine with snow, fur hats, and boots. I held my suit coat draped over my arm; my white shirt stuck to my wet back.

"Time to go," Berg said. "Are you ready, Stareyshina Tyson?"

Brett grinned. "Absolutely." He tipped his hand from the top of his head. "So long, boys." He didn't so much as glance at me, but I knew he was as grateful as I was to finally be out of each other's presence.

By twos, everyone departed. I slung my backpack over my shoulder. For a good part of an hour, we threaded through hurrying people before boarding a bus so crowded my head hit someone else more than once. Then it was walking again. Sometimes Kaufman asked me questions, but often, we walked in silence, the busyness of the day finally catching up to us both.

There was a glow from city lights trapped under the canopy of clouds, allowing me to see some of our surroundings. I had little experience with anything more than two-story buildings, but high apartments were the norm in Kramatorsk. Walking outside at night made me feel vulnerable, and I began to think about what President Meyers had told us about following the rules.

Everyone on the street scared me. Half of them looked like they could be drunk, yelling or laughing as loudly as the missionaries had in the restaurant. Before I'd come, I'd looked up information on traveling to Ukraine on the internet and found stuff on a U.S. government website. I'd read how once you were in Ukraine, you were pretty much on your own. American laws could

protect you only so far, so travel at your own risk. Then I'd made the mistake
of reading stories and blogs about people put in jail, their lives threatened until
they forked out enough money.

I was relieved when we finally reached our apartment building, which,
on the outside, seemed about a dozen stories high. Kaufman led me to a door
on the side that took us inside the apartment complex. I stared at the colorful
wall—the top half white, the bottom half green. Kaufman stopped outside
what looked like a regular wooden door. "This," Kaufman tapped the door
with his hand, "is a lift. But they never work, so we take the stairs."

Five flights later and halfway down a hall, we were standing in front of
our door. I stared at a spot in the middle where the gray paint was peeling,
sweat pooling on my forehead, while Kaufman unlocked the door with a
key.

Inside, it was dark until Kaufman switched on a swinging bulb from the
ceiling. I mopped my wet face and stared at the overly warm studio apartment. Two twin beds lined a corner of the room, a tall fan near the window.

Kaufman hung his suit coat over a wooden chair tucked under a small
rectangle table in the middle of the room. He threw his bag on one of the
beds—the one with blankets on it—so I set my backpack on the other one,
which was a plain mattress. There was no couch, so I sat on my bed, next
to my backpack, and stared at the ugly yellow-flowered wallpaper covering
most of the apartment.

"Would you like a tour, mate? Let's start with the kitchen, shall we?"

I forced myself up from the bed and followed Kaufman to the far
side of the room. Exposed gas and plumbing pipes ran up and down over
turquoise-squared wallpaper, above a small oven. There was no counter
space between the tiny oven and the kitchen sink, which looked more like a
bathroom sink—the kind at rest stops along the freeway—not big enough
to wash dishes in. There was also a really big blue thing that looked like a
mini hot-water heater with pipes running through it.

Kaufman opened a short white box. "This is the fridge." He moved to
the stove. "This is the stove and oven. It's all gas, not electric, so you have to
light a match after you move this knob. I'll show you when it's time. Also,
the two back burners don't work."

I nodded. "I've used gas heat before."

"Jolly. I'll show you the toilet, then." I followed him to a door on the
side of the kitchen. Inside, there was a similar sink to the kitchen's, a toilet,
and a showerhead hanging on the wall and a drain in the floor.

I stared at the faucets on the wall and at the sink. "Which direction is hot?" I asked.

He smirked. "You Americans think everything is so easy." He motioned for me to follow him back to the kitchen. "See this?" He tapped the large blue box. "When you move into an apartment and see this, you know the Lord is smiling down on you, because not all places have them. It's called a hot-water heater, which means hot—not cold—showers. It works like the oven: you have to light a match, and then you get hot water. Understand?" He shook his head. "Of course you don't, but you will. Did you bring the filter from the mission home?" Kaufman held out his hand, as if waiting for it to materialize.

"Yes." I returned to my backpack on the bed and pulled out the white cylinder Sister Meyers had given me. I watched him bend over and pull a similar-sized cylinder out of a tube at the back of the sink. He exchanged it for the new one.

My eyes were starting to droop when I heard Kaufman say, "We now have—somewhat—drinkable water." He grinned and leaned his arms against the back of one of the kitchen chairs. "So sorry, but I forgot about an appointment. We'll need to run. Do you think you can?"

No. I didn't think I could. Was he serious? But I stood like a zombie and prepared to go anyway.

He straightened and pulled on his suit coat. "Now, there's a good boy. I'll train you to be a good son. And while we walk, I'll tell you a story." He walked over to a box on the floor and dug through it until he pulled out a long black Maglite. "Here is your torch, issued from the mission home."

I crossed the room to take the heavy flashlight. "Why?"

"I believe it is for several reasons. You know the big holes in the streets? I think you call them 'manholes'—that's what President Meyers calls them anyway. They are often missing covers. You could fall in—very treacherous— so best be aware where you're walking, with this," he said, tapping the light against his palm.

"Missing manhole covers?"

"People pinch them for the metal; it's worth quite a bit. I know a missionary who got sent home with a broken arm because he fell in one." Kaufman opened the door, then turned to wait for me. "Do you have your paperwork?"

I nodded, and Kaufman closed the door behind me and locked it. He began the promised story before we'd even finished going down the stairwell.

"Once upon a time, a missionary with a long white beard and charming manners—we'll call him James the Wise—was told he must go on a journey. Part of this journey was training a shorter hobbit missionary to become a strong keeper of the ring."

He held the door open for me to go outside, and I raised an eyebrow. "Hobbit?"

"You are kind of short."

"Hobbit short?"

He shrugged. "It's just a story."

"Let me guess, your first name is James?"

"You are very intuitive for a hobbit."

"Can I add to this story?"

"You can *always* add to the story."

I turned my eyes to the cracked sidewalk. "I'm not much of a story-teller. What else happens on this journey?"

"Well, let's see, it's a very long journey, about two years."

"Does it involve sleep? Ever?"

He chuckled. "Of course. But only between the hours of 10:00 p.m. and 6:00 a.m. It also involves things like reading ancient records translated through the gift of God and learning to speak in foreign tongues."

"Like British?"

"The' might be a spot o' that."

I shoved my hands deep into my pockets. "I think this hobbit is in way over his head."

"Ah, yes, but he was short, as I mentioned."

I gave a tight smile. Kaufman was clearly a very intelligent, articulate person, but I was tired of being teased so much tonight.

He seemed to notice and frowned slightly at me. "It can definitely feel confusing and dark in the beginning."

"Was it that way for you?"

"Yes, it's like that for everyone. You think it will last forever, but it won't. You'll make it through this like a champion." He stopped walking and patted my shoulder. "This is our stop."

We walked into the apartment complex and hiked up to the third floor. The door was on the end next to a large window. I leaned against the wall, stared out the window, and waited as Kaufman knocked several times, with no answer.

Even in the dark, I could see that the city below us was full of trees. The lights on buildings peeked through and around the darker foliage. Something bright caught my eye. It was a fire next to what looked like a giant statue.

After what seemed like a full minute of knocking, I finally said, "Maybe they forgot."

"Da, maybe." Kaufman stopped knocking and turned around. He looked at me, then rolled his eyes and shook his head. "Every stareyshina must learn not to touch the walls here."

I immediately straightened, and Kaufman pointed out the white chalk-like dust covering my black jacket and the top of my black pants. "The white comes off?"

"Stareyshiny wear so much black, they must be careful. Except in the winter. People will just think it's snow." We went downstairs and outside.

Kaufman stood outside the door a moment, shoved his hands in his pockets, and blew out. "I wish someone somewhere would keep an appointment."

As we walked near the parking lot, I craned my neck in the direction I'd seen the fire and giant statue. I could see pieces of it hidden behind the thick trees. I stopped walking and pointed it out to Kaufman.

He turned to see what I meant. "It's a statue of Lenin. Most cities have one."

"Can we go see it?"

He shrugged. "I thought you were tired, mate. But all right."

We walked around the trees, and I saw a three-foot brick wall surrounding the base. The giant statue was of a stern-looking man wearing a long jacket, his hand on his heart. Even in the heat, a small fire burned at the base. On the wall, there was an inscription Kaufman read out loud. "The eternal flame, for all those who have died in war."

"In California, this kind of thing would be outlawed during fire season."

"Fire season?" Kaufman seemed amused. "Is there an extra season in America I've not discovered? Like autumn and summer?"

I smiled. "Sort of. So, why is this here?"

"It's symbolic of Ukraine lasting forever. This fire is fueled by gas year-round."

I stared at the flame and marveled that a country would go through so much effort to keep a symbol like fire going when all around me, I saw chipping paint and elevators that didn't work. Nearby, a group of young men gathered under a tree. They appeared to be around our age and older.

"Come on, mate," Kaufman said.

We walked across the grass rather than along the sidewalk that ran near their tree. They didn't say anything, but I felt them watching us.

The walk home seemed to go faster than the walk there. There were people out in the streets, probably enjoying the five-degree difference since the sun had gone down. A group sat on the steps of our apartment building, laughing loudly and drinking large bottles. They called out hello to us, but Kaufman gave only a slight wave and kept walking.

By the time we reached the top step to our floor, I felt like crawling. I couldn't wait to drop into bed. Kaufman propped the only window open and turned on the tall rotating fan that sometimes blew toward his bed and sometimes toward mine.

I half listened as Kaufman called our district leader, Stareyshina Murray, to report on our day. My sheets and blanket were with my lost luggage, so Kaufman handed me a spare blanket from the closet. He also lent me one of his clean T-shirts and gym shorts before going to brush his teeth. The blanket smelled of mildew. I draped it across the mattress, then wadded up my dirty white shirt for my pillow and lay across the blanket—it was much too hot to need a covering.

Back home, we didn't have air conditioning in our house, even though there were two weeks out of the year I always wished we did. But even then, I'd never felt this hot at night before—ever. I closed my eyes, knowing that despite the heat, I would sleep hard tonight.

"Christensen?"

"Huh," I muttered, my eyes closed.

"Companionship prayer."

I rolled halfway up and saw that he was kneeling in front of his bed. It took all the effort I had to kneel on the hard floor. He offered the prayer, thanking God for our safety that day and praying for individuals with names I couldn't repeat even if I tried.

After the prayer I got back into bed, my last conscious thoughts reflecting on how long it would take before I was no longer a hobbit.

THAT NIGHT, I DREAMED OF the lost man.

I'd seen him twice in my dreams before. The first was April 14, the day I'd turned eighteen. The second time was the night before I left Susanville to drive to Provo, Utah, to attend the MTC. He had hungry, empty, light-green eyes, wore a thick coat and black boots, had a heavy backpack, and traveled roads.

In previous dreams, he didn't see me. But this time, he did. His pained eyes looked directly at me, through me, begging me to find him. But he wasn't lost anymore. He was in a cage.

I couldn't move. I could barely breathe.

I woke up to the sound of Kaufman's blaring alarm. While he pounded snooze, I dragged myself out of bed to use the toilet. When I came out, I stood by the window and let the warm air from the fan blow across my borrowed T-shirt while I thought about the dream. Was there someone waiting for me, someone in this country?

From five stories up, I could see a parking lot below us filled with a handful of cars, a strange metal jungle gym that looked more like something from the movie *War of the Worlds*, and a horizon of never-ending trees. The feeling of urgency I'd had in the dream wouldn't leave me, and I stared out the window, wondering where he could be.

The alarm clock went off again, and this time Kaufman yawned and rolled out of bed. My quiet presence near the window seemed to startle him awake. He stood and jumped up and down a few times. I watched him walk over to the kitchen, open a bottom cupboard, and pull out a match. He struck it, then moved a knob on the blue box and lit the burner. "Mind if I take the first shower, mate?"

"Go ahead," I said, turning back to the window. The clouds were moving in the distance. Back home, I would suspect a cloud cover by the afternoon, but I didn't know with Ukraine.

Kaufman wasn't in the bathroom long, and when it was my turn, I remembered how to work the showerhead. The water felt comfortable, not very warm, but I was sticky from a night of sweating, so the cooler water was refreshing. I dressed in my same pants, but Kaufman lent me some extra garments and a clean white shirt. I hoped I wouldn't have to wait long for my clothes to arrive.

I opened the bathroom door, and the smell of breakfast met me. The same smell from home. Kaufman stood by the stove with a pan, making what looked like scrambled eggs. Some homemade bread was cut in slices on the table, along with two plates, two forks, and two bottles of water.

Maybe it was the stress of everything, but watching Kaufman make me eggs was just too much. My eyes stung as I watched him dish the hot eggs onto my plate as well as his. It was like being home for a brief second, eating eggs with my mom. But everything was different here. Homesickness swept over me.

He paused when he saw me watching. "Do you object to eggs?"

"No." I cleared my throat and moved toward the table. "Thanks for breakfast."

"No problem. You're my son. That's what dads do."

I smiled. "My dad never cooked for me."

"Really?"

"Did yours?"

"Yes—well, when he was at home. He had a rigorous job."

"What does he do?"

Kaufman sat down. "He was an investigator."

"Like Sherlock Holmes?" I pulled out one of the wooden chairs and sat in it. "Sorry, that's the only English investigator I could think of."

"Sure, just like him. At least you didn't say Dr. Who."

"Or Inspector Gadget? Or Psych?"

"I don't know them. Would you like to pray?"

After the prayer, I took my first bite. "This is great. Thank you."

"Not a problem." He stood and rummaged through the fridge until he pulled out a jar of dark-colored jam that he slathered on his bread. He handed it to me, and I put some on my own bread. It tasted like blackberries.

"How many missionaries have you trained?" I asked, spreading more jam on my bread.

"Just you and Stareyshina Johnson. You are most likely my last, since I'll be going home in less than three months. I doubt President Meyers will move you before then. He tends to leave people in one place for a long time." He paused and looked up. "Unless there is a need to move you."

I thought about what Brett had said, the jerk.

"So, was Johnson at the transfer meeting?" I asked to distract myself. "He was the one they were talking about last night, right? Emergency transferred?"

Kaufman's blond eyebrows knit together, and he picked at his food. "He ended up going home. President told me yesterday in our interview."

I waited for more, but Kaufman stood and dumped his remaining eggs in the trash. I quickly finished eating, then helped clean up so we could use the table for companionship study. We sat across from each other, scriptures open.

First, we read from *Preach My Gospel*, starting from the beginning, and discussed, "What is my purpose as a missionary?" That took about twenty minutes. Then we got out our Russian language books and studied together. Kaufman was patient, but I could tell it was boring for him. After fifteen minutes, he told me I could study the rest of the time on my own while he pulled out his Russian *Bibliya*—Bible.

I tried to pronounce the words softly under my breath, but I knew I was saying them wrong. After thirty minutes, I couldn't take any more. When Kaufman stood to get a drink, I slid the book away and stood too. I stretched my back and moved my arms up above my head, then bent down and touched my toes.

"Twenty more minutes, then we're leaving," Kaufman said behind his water bottle.

"Okay."

He sat back down at the table and, this time, pulled out a picture. I tried not to stare, but it was of four people standing next to a giant water fountain: Kaufman, another missionary, a guy in jeans and a black jacket, and a girl in a colorful sweater. She was very pretty, with long dark hair. Kaufman was standing close to her—too close.

Kaufman tucked it inside his journal.

I looked up and met his eyes. "Who was that?" I asked.

"My last companion and our housekeeper, Jinya."

"I thought you said our housekeeper was a dude."

Kaufman smirked. "He is. His name's Jinya."

I waited for more, but Kaufman only shot me a sly smile, pulled out a piece of paper, and began writing a letter. It reminded me that I too had letters to write.

But I didn't want to write them. The idea still scared me. I opened my scriptures randomly and began reading silently at the top of the page in Moroni 7:13: *But behold, that which is of God inviteth and enticeth to do good continually; wherefore, every thing which inviteth and enticeth to do good, and to love God, and to serve him, is inspired of God.*

Do good and love God. It reminded me of what President Meyers had said about choosing good and loving Christ and about serving and loving my companion. I thought of Kaufman making me breakfast. Had he received the same advice? Whether he had or not, it had worked. Just that small act of service had made me think for a few minutes that I could be a missionary. My homesickness ebbed away slightly, and I tried to focus on how good things would come.

***

The first place we went after our study time was a fish market where President Kuznetsov, our branch president, worked. I couldn't understand most of what he said, but he shook my hand a lot, which smelled like fish for the rest of the day.

Kaufman told me he'd suggested an area we could tract in, so we found the apartment building, started at the top, and moved down to the bottom. No one answered their door, although they did yell through it. Kaufman was good at yelling what I assumed were clever replies. He taught me one of them, which was "Have you heard? The gospel of Jesus Christ has been restored!" He tried to get me to yell it once, but I gave up halfway through, and the person on the other side told us to get lost.

I learned when Kaufman took us by a member's home that everyone had nice rugs hung *on* their walls—probably to cover their ugly wallpaper—and tattered rugs covering the floors. He told me there were no vacuums and that most apartments had a metal bar outside to beat your rugs on. But with no working elevators, I suspected the people on the top floors didn't beat their rugs all that often.

The next day was Saturday. I took my turn making breakfast, which didn't end well. But Kaufman said that was one more reason why we had windows and fans.

By Sunday, I felt like I knew less Russian than when I'd arrived in Ukraine.

We held church in a government building the branch rented on Sundays and Mondays. President Kuznetsov greeted us when we arrived. We finished helping him set up the sacrament table, and he asked if we would be willing to help bless and pass it.

Kaufman said one of the prayers; the branch president said the other, sparing me from having to pray in Russian. I passed the bread and water, like a good deacon. I counted fifty-seven people in attendance. Fifty-one were women. Six were men, counting President Kuznetsov, Kaufman, and myself. Kaufman made sure we sat by the one person he didn't know and was able to set up an appointment with her before she left.

I counted the meeting a success because I only had to say the word *yes*, which was "da," and nod my head. Only Kaufman told me later not to nod my head so much because then people would think I really understood.

After sacrament meeting, one of the older babushkas was standing near the sacrament table, taking all the leftover pieces of bread and tying them in a napkin. She wore a tight scarf over her gray head, like the rest of the babushkas. Her tanned face was deeply lined.

Kaufman walked over to her and said, "*Nyet*, sister, please don't."

She seemed to insist Kaufman give her the rest of the loaf of bread. He shook his head, and she seemed very angry with him, leaving in a huff to join Sunday School.

"What was that about?" I asked.

He sighed. "Every week she wants to feed the birds. I'm taking this bread to President's home. The birds can go hungry, crazy babushka."

He wrapped the bread tightly and put it in his bag. "Babushkas are the biggest reason to stay away from Ukrainian girls. Remember what I said at the restaurant? Pretty Ukrainian girls turn into babushkas. Probably within one year of taking their vows. They go from lovely to seventy. No in between."

I laughed, but for once, Kaufman looked serious.

Sunday was the only day we ate at a family's home. Kaufman told me President Meyers had asked us not to eat at members' homes for several different reasons. The first was because he didn't want there to be favorites and jealousy among the members.

The second was because the people were poor compared to American money standards. Kaufman told me President Kuznetsov made around ten dollars a day. Many of the missionaries donated generously from their monthly stipend to the fast offering fund to help the branch feed those in need.

Families who fed missionaries were willing to go hungry for days to make sure the missionaries were well fed. A loaf of bread was about twenty cents American money, not much for us. But for them, that was a significant amount. This was why Kaufman made sure we brought a lot of food with us to dinner, insisting to President Kuznetsov's wife that it was the mission president's rules we had to keep.

And the third reason, I learned the hard way.

The stir-fry had been delicious at the branch president's home, and the meat sauce that Kaufman hadn't touched, I'd had third helpings of.

"Everyone gets sick at first, totally normal," Kaufman yelled through the bathroom door Monday morning while cooking himself eggs and humming much too loudly.

"Why?" I croaked, my head leaning against the toilet. "Why did you let me eat it? You didn't eat it. I thought you were my father. You're supposed to teach me these things."

"No better teacher than experience," he said from the other room. "It will pass quick enough."

At around three o'clock, a knock sounded on the door. I peeked out from my blanket that, despite the heat, I had wrapped tightly around my head and body.

"Come in, Jinya," Kaufman said. "We missed you yesterday at church."

I poked my head out and watched a clean-shaven young man about our age, with dark hair, walk inside. He was the man with the black jacket I'd seen in the picture. Kaufman had told me a housekeeper was a coveted position because of the good pay. He told me not to tell people at church that Jinya was our housekeeper. If word got out, there would be problems. Kaufman said President actually encouraged us to have a housekeeper, to give someone a job, but they had to have a temple recommend and be trustworthy. Jinya was a returned missionary. He'd grown up near Kiev and served his mission in Donetsk.

I understood only some of what they said in Russian. Jinya spoke quickly and rather softly. He paused midsentence and I understood as he looked at me. "Is your companion sick?"

"He ate something," Kaufman said in English. "You know how the new ones are. Did you ever get sick on your mission?"

"Nyet," Jinya said but then switched to English. "I had American companions who did." Then he asked something about cleaning in Russian.

Kaufman answered him, then paused and said in English, "You might want to clean the bathroom last."

Just his saying the word was enough to make me rush to the bathroom again. Several minutes later, I ran my hands under cold water and touched my face and massaged my temples. *This too will pass*, I told myself again and again.

Kaufman and Jinya offered to give me a blessing, which I accepted.

I sat on the edge of my bed, and they put their hands on my head. Kaufman offered the prayer in English and told me my suffering would not be long and I would make a full recovery, but all of my trials and experiences were here to teach me wisdom.

If the wisdom I needed to grasp was never to eat meat from a member's home again, then it was a lesson I had absolutely learned.

Jinya was leaving when Kaufman said, "Hey, Christensen's clothes haven't arrived yet—they got lost. Do you happen to have any dress pants and shirts he could purchase or borrow? You look like you're both the same size."

"Da," Jinya said, then in English, "I'll see what I can find."

***

Wednesday, late morning, I woke to Kaufman nudging my foot. "You were speaking in your sleep again." He grinned. "Shall I tell Sister Alkaev what you think of her, then?"

I wasn't sure who Sister Alkaev was; blearily, I sat up and rubbed my head.

"Do you feel any better?"

I nodded and yawned. My stomach was no longer tied in knots, and I felt like I could eat.

"Your luggage arrived this morning. It looks as though you can wear your own things again, mate."

It was around eleven o'clock when we were ready to leave the apartment. It had been less than a week since I'd arrived. The streets were a little cooler today, at least not as humid. Kaufman handed me some fliers for us to post on various buildings, advertising our weekly English class.

We stopped at a grocery store at the bottom of an apartment complex. While I stapled a flier to the board outside, Kaufman pointed to a different advertisement. "There's a basketball tournament. We should sign up with Berg and Tyson."

"No, thanks," I said, handing him the stapler.

He began walking, and I followed. "You'll have to get over your anger with Tyson sometime."

"I have. But I stink at basketball."

Kaufman clicked his tongue and muttered, "That's un-American."

He handed me a stack of fliers, and we found spots to distribute them, covering several blocks. We were down to a few when we turned a corner and saw an older babushka standing at a bus stop, an olive-green scarf covering her head. She shot us a toothless grin, so Kaufman started up a conversation with her. I caught words like *day* and *coffee*.

No, that was probably wrong. I shook my head, which drew her attention to me.

She asked Kaufman a question and pointed in my direction.

I cleared my throat. "*Dobroye utro*." Good morning.

She stared blankly at me.

"He's not from here," Kaufman said in Russian.

"Where?" she demanded.

"America," I said, trying to redeem myself.

She spit on the ground near my feet and pointed a gnarled finger. "We beat you in the war." The rest of her heated words were lost on me but not their intent to insult.

I didn't say anything, only stared dumbly. She stalked off, and I told myself to breathe. "What did I do wrong?" I asked.

"It's *utra*," Kaufman said.

"*Utra*," I practiced several times, Kaufman finally pinching my cheeks together with his fingers to force a better "oo" sound. I pushed his hands away. "What was she mad about? Is she still angry about the Cold War?"

"No." Kaufman snickered. "Not the Cold War, World War II."

"*World War II*? Was she even alive then? She said, 'We beat you.'"

"Yes, Ukrainians, Russians, they think they won World War II. That's what some of the monuments stand for too, like the one of the missile near our house."

I stared at him, astonished. "Is that what you learned in your history books too?"

"Not exactly. I imagine England's history books differ from yours"—a snide smile—"but we probably both agree on who won World War II. Ukraine thinks they won because they beat Hitler. They resisted him from taking control of their country. Yes, they were murdering Jews and raiding countries like Poland, but they stayed Russians."

"Ah. That's just lovely."

Kaufman began walking. "But not all Ukrainians feel like that. Some of the older generation still harbor some anti-foreign sentiment, but most Ukrainians

I've met are educated and actually love America. You made *American Idol* and Hollywood and Facebook. Where would the world be without America?"

"There wouldn't be Super Bowl Sunday."

He snickered. "True."

"Why wasn't she angry with you? Your country sided with the Americans."

"She didn't know I was from England."

I stared at his translucent eyelashes and blue eyes that contrasted with the generally darker Eastern European complexions we met with. "She thought you were from here?"

He smiled. "One day you'll sound like a native too."

I shook my head. Not in the next two years—there was no way. My mood turned pessimistic as we walked in silence down crumbling sidewalks. I stared at the spaced trees, each planted above the ground in a circle of grass, surrounded by brick. I ran my hand along an iron fence painted orange. Behind it were gray cement buildings, acres and acres of gray cement buildings. Buses and cars drove noisily in the street, and I imagined myself getting on one of the buses and not stopping until I reached the airport.

It was past one when Kaufman steered us in the direction of Makanan Pizza. I stared at the menu and wondered how much a train ticket would be to get home while Kaufman ordered us calzones and sodas.

We ate in silence until Kaufman said, "If you don't mind me asking, what did happen between you and Stareyshina Tyson? It's pretty obvious you don't care for each other."

My chewing slowed.

He grinned. "Was it a girl?"

I swallowed and washed my food down with a swig of Coke. "Not everything is about girls."

"Da, but it *should* be."

"Well, it wasn't," I said too quickly. Kaufman pressed his lips together as if he didn't believe me. His mention of Brett reminded me I still hadn't done what the mission president had asked me to. I'd had plenty of excuses, like hugging the toilet for two days. I shifted in my seat. "There might have been a girl involved, but it wasn't like what you're insinuating. It was more about revenge than love."

He whistled. "Ah, yes. Now that sounds like a story worth hearing. Revenge is a powerful force. Tell me, what motivated it?"

I didn't feel like telling this story. For one, because I wasn't the good guy in it, and another, I didn't need Kaufman to have more fodder to tease me with. So I chose to try to leave myself out of it. "The girl wanted revenge on Tyson because he snubbed her."

"So she came to you. And you helped her get revenge. It was a tragedy, then, not a romance." I made a mental note to not say anything personal in front of Kaufman again. "And now you despise each other."

"I like him just fine. We had a disagreement on the way here."

"About a girl." He grinned.

What planet did Kaufman hail from? England couldn't be that different from America. But sometimes I was truly afraid Kaufman might suddenly sprout a wand and a broom and yell "Stupefy!" at passersby. He was that weird.

"I'm not the type to go looking for future babushkas, just so you know. I'm not like your last companion."

Kaufman frowned. "He didn't go looking—it just happened. When I said never underestimate the girls here, I meant it."

We didn't say anything else. I hadn't meant to shut Kaufman up, but talking about Johnson had done it. Whatever had happened there, Kaufman still seemed pretty upset about it, and I could feel from the way he drew circles absently on the table that there were stories he didn't want to share with me either.

THE COLD CAME ON GRADUALLY at first. The humidity was the first to dissipate, leaving comfortable breezes and chilly mornings. But that only lasted a couple weeks. By the second week of October, it had cooled off drastically, and an inch of snow covered the ground. The windows were shut and locked, the fan pushed into the corner. We began holding companionship study in the kitchen next to the open oven door. The government decided when the heat should be turned on. Kaufman said last year in Horlivka it wasn't until mid-November.

But the cold was easier for me to deal with than the heat. I had spent nights camping on cattle runs with my dad. For nine months out of the year, we wore coats or jackets, and the other three months, we still kept them handy. Cold was something I could understand. The Russian language, however, after five weeks, was still something I could not.

I dropped a few *Kniga Mormona* in my backpack before buttoning my black coat. I topped it with a scarf, then grabbed a furry fox hat Kaufman had bought me. The gift sounded more thoughtful than it was. Really, Kaufman was tired of random babushkas stopping me to lecture on the dangers of not wearing a hat in the cold, as if it were their duty to advise me. I'd seen similar ladies henpeck a mother on the proper way to wrap her baby too.

I flipped the ear coverings of my hat up, not because it was warm out but because it kept people from thinking I was drunk.

Today, it was Kaufman's turn to choose what we did for our preparation day. He elected for lunch around the corner at a restaurant called Waffle Café, which was located underneath some apartments we'd been tracting in.

My stack of waffles was covered in chocolate and raspberries, with two scoops of whipped cream on top. It was the best thing I'd eaten probably ever. I grinned at Kaufman and took another bite.

"Good?" he asked.

I nodded and closed my eyes. I had found my purpose in coming to Ukraine.

I opened my eyes to see him rummaging in his bag. Seconds later, he pulled out two pieces of paper and two pens. "We're going to write stories."

"Stories?" I asked, my mouth full of my last bite of waffle.

"Yes, and don't be a stick in the mud. You need to write a fictional story about you as a missionary. You get ten minutes."

"Can I eat first?"

He gave a pointed look at my empty plate. I returned the pointed look in the direction of his, which still had half a waffle. He pushed it toward me and sighed. "You'll catch up to Stareyshina Tyson in no time."

I didn't reply. Kaufman knew I hated talking about Brett. I had seen him twice now, at district meetings. It was always the same. Either I didn't exist, or he had something rude to say. I preferred being invisible.

And each time I saw him, I was reminded of the letters I still hadn't written. President Meyers hadn't asked me about them, but I knew one day he would.

I stuffed the last bite of waffle in my mouth and took a long swig of Coke, which did not complement the taste of the waffles.

"You're stalling," Kaufman said.

I crossed my arms.

"Stareyshina Hobbit, do it, or I won't show you where they play football."

"When you say football, do you mean American football or everyone else's football, which is really soccer?"

"What do you think?"

"Probably soccer because that's all they care about here."

"Stalling."

I picked up the pen and grumbled. "This feels a bit too much like high school English class."

"When you say 'English class,' do you actually mean a grammar class where you learn to pronounce things in gratingly horrible accents and spell things less accurately than your ex-motherland? Or is it a class on Britain's superior history, culture, and civilization?"

"Um, neither?"

"Do you mean *neeether* or *nyther?*"

I shook my head. It was never-ending with Kaufman. "You know, we speak English in America too."

"That's debatable." He bent his head and began writing. "You may begin."

I hit my pen against the paper. "A fictional story?"

Kaufman nodded.

I stared out the window, not sure how to start. It was almost picturesque, this warm café, out of the snow. They even had candles lit in several corners that made it feel cozy. My stomach was full, and I felt comfortable, almost content. The feeling surprised me. Kaufman glanced up and raised a stern eyebrow. I knew he meant business, so I picked up my pen.

I thought about rehashing his *Lord of the Rings* bit. I stared at the raspberry juice and chocolate smeared across my plate, reminding me of Alfred Hitchcock movies and how they used chocolate syrup for blood. Blood, snow, ice. There had to be a story in that. I picked up my pen.

Being a missionary in Ukraine is a lot like pretending to be a Viking— without the muscles, without the beard. Take me, for example. I'm five foot ten and haven't grown very much facial hair. But I eat fish, like a good Viking. And while I'm on this journey far from home, surrounded by large, bearded men, I can only think of going home. But every day, I must pick up my ax and sword and arrows and sit on the side of the ship to wait and watch while others battle and fail. One day, it will be my turn, but I know I will die, and when I do, the waves will come up and take me down into their depths, and I will swim as fast as I can with all my strength until I'm free.

It had taken me ten minutes to write. After rereading it, I decided it was, number one, trash, and number two, without a doubt the best thing I'd ever written. Aside from that, it was really bad. It was like spilling my insides across the table for Kaufman to poke at with a stick.

I was about to wad it up when he reached out and grabbed it. "Time," he said. He shoved his story at me, which was three pages front and back. I stared helplessly as he began to devour my piece without delay.

He frowned up at me. "This is pretty dark, you know?"

I shrugged. "It's all I got."

"I thought farmers were industrious, no-nonsense types, but you're more like a dark diva."

"A dark diva?"

"A drama queen." He snorted a chuckle, and something about it made me laugh too.

"Oh yeah? I'm going to finish yours, see what kind of Shakespeare or J. K. Rowling you are. Doesn't everyone in England write, the whole *lot* of you?"

He shrugged. "Of course."

It was an absurd story that I would have expected from Kaufman. The main character was a prince on a quest for a treasure to appease a fair maiden. The maiden had one blue eye and one brown and hobbled because when she was thirteen, she had reached for a cookie in a bowl on the top shelf and it had fallen and bashed her foot. I smirked and coughed, which made him laugh, causing people to stare. There was a dragon and a sword fight where the prince won but only after his best mate turned into a frog and was devoured by the dragon. Then it ended.

"I'm surprised," I said, handing it back to him.

"Why?"

"It didn't end with a stomach-churning kiss."

He laughed. "Well, it's not finished. I could always add that. We'll see what my publisher says. I meant it as a type of allegory, like yours."

"An allegory?"

He nodded. "A parable."

"Hmm, mine was a parable?" I tried to look impressed instead of bored.

"Most definitely. Much more parable than mine was."

"So what was mine saying?"

"You're tired of waiting and watching me fail at missionary work. You know one day you'll have to actually talk to someone in Russian—probably when I go home—but you're afraid that you will flop at missionary work."

I opened my mouth. I could see how my story could be taken like that, but I hadn't meant to say any of that. "No—it wasn't about you," I said. *"Really.* I don't think you're failing. Sister Fyodorovych started to cry when you taught her about Christ's Atonement. Just because she's already baptized doesn't mean you aren't winning the battle."

"I haven't baptized anyone, Hobbit. Not one person on my mission."

I swallowed. How would it be to give your mission your all and have zero baptisms to show for it? I remembered my recurring dream about the lost man. What if I never found him? I made an attempt at positivity for Kaufman's sake. "Maybe you're doing good in other ways? Your English classes are so full people have to stand."

He gave me a crooked smile. "It's true. People here are starved for entertainment."

"That's the spirit," I said, patting his arm. Then to distract him, I asked, "I'm curious, who is the frog?"

"You."

"I get eaten by a dragon? Wow. That's not passive aggressive or anything. I presume you're the prince?"

"Only if he gets the girl."

"Who's the dragon that eats me?"

He pursed his lips together and looked more seriously. "Perhaps it's Stareyshina Tyson."

I shrugged, sensing Kaufman had more to say on the subject. "If you let your dark, brooding anger continue, it will conquer you, Stareyshina Hobbit."

I met Kaufman's eyes and tried not to be offended. Maybe I had been dark and broody at times, but it wasn't all because of Brett. It was because I didn't measure up as a missionary. It appeared Kaufman and I both had insecurities in that area.

"I apologized to Brett, but I don't think forgiveness is in his plans."

"That's his choice," Kaufman said matter-of-factly. "What's yours?"

I didn't answer. If I was honest, I was angry at Brett because he hadn't forgiven me and he'd said hurtful things. That was probably the biggest reason why I hadn't written the letters yet. Part of me didn't feel like he deserved it. "I guess I need to try harder to move past it," I said to the table.

"Good answer," Kaufman said, packing up our stories, "because we're going to go meet him at a museum now, and I don't want you ruining our afternoon."

"Hey, you said we were going to go see a football stadium."

"You mean *soccer*. We're going to go see a *photograph* of where they used to play forty years ago."

"I think that qualifies as bearing false witness."

"Believe me, it's better than a muddy pitch. C'mon, now. You'll love it."

I was feeling a bit put out as we paid for the food, then walked outside. The sun was behind the clouds, and the wind had picked up. We hurried to the bus stop, hugging our coats tightly as we walked.

The museum was across town, bordering our zone area. It was a large building made entirely of clear glass sitting on about a half-acre cement pad. Out front were several statues of political figures. As we came nearer, we could see the outline of four missionaries waiting, three waving wildly through the glass wall. I could guess who wasn't waving.

Kaufman opened the large double door for me. Murray and Osborne walked up to us and started talking about a new fossil exhibit. Berg silently joined them, but Brett stayed apart and stared at a nearby display. I thought of Kaufman and his silly stories and realized he'd been setting me up for this all along, with the frog and the dragon. No wonder he'd been able to write three full pages. I shoved my hands into my pockets. His mischievous mind had probably been plotting this for days.

I stayed on the opposite end from where Brett stood, making sure several missionaries stood in the space between us.

The glass building was an outer shell covering another five-story structure inside made of tan stone. We entered this building to see most of the exhibits. It was not crowded, and I welcomed its quiet halls and dark corners. Staying within eyesight of the others, I wandered over to some display cases, not really seeing any of the things inside. We went up one hall and down the other. I pretended to be fascinated by the paintings of Ukrainian agriculture, mostly so I wouldn't have to talk to anyone.

After awhile, my waffle coma wore off. Staring at antique armor sets, I began to think, *This is wrong. This museum is wrong. This city. The work I'm not a part of. It's all wrong.*

Even doubly wrong because Brett was here too.

Maybe those who had sent me had made a mistake. Maybe I was supposed to go to Alaska or Canada, where there weren't as many people. Ukraine was kind of close. Well, not really.

I stopped next to Kaufman. He was speaking with a balding museum worker in a dark suit about the lit-up glass cases nearby. My eyes rested on a brilliant gold ring with brownish-red gems set in the sides.

"He doesn't understand. Sorry," Kaufman said.

I looked up, saw the museum worker was watching, and realized he must have been speaking to me. Embarrassed, I tried an apology in Russian, but I could tell it failed.

He shook his head as if he hadn't understood but said in accented English, "Two million American dollars. Ah, you understand. You know Nicholas II?"

Brett came up behind. I moved aside so he could see and to put some space between us. The museum worker continued, speaking to both of us now. "The ring belonged to Nicholas. He was murdered in Russia. But he loved his summer home in Livadiya. This ring was found there, among his belongings. We had to trade for a Kazimir Malevich painting." He laughed.

"A small one, of course." He looked away and stared at the ring. "A truly honored guest." He sighed as if it were not an object but a real person. He turned his eyes on me with a stern expression, as if I'd disagreed with him.

"It's beautiful," I stammered, then used the word *beautiful* in Russian.

He gave me one stiff nod, then walked on.

Kaufman gave me one of his teasing smiles behind the museum worker's back, glanced at Brett, then went to stand by another display case with Berg. I knew Kaufman was giving me alone time with Brett, which was absolutely unnecessary. I watched from a distance as Berg held out a piece of paper and Kaufman glanced at it before shoving it in his pants pocket.

I stared at the glass case, awkwardly aware of Brett. I began to think of the prince in Kaufman's story, the treasure, the dragon . . . and the frog.

I heard Brett walk up closer to the display case. "They don't have this kind of stuff where we come from, do they?" he said.

I shook my head. "No. They don't."

"How have you been?" he asked quietly. "Are you homesick?"

"A little bit," I answered, surprised he was actually talking to me. A wave of nostalgia made me swallow hard. "Are you?" I asked, still staring at the ring.

"Da and nyet. The language is hard. Being a missionary is harder. But it is coming together." He said *da* and *nyet* naturally amongst the English words, as though he had spoken them every day of his life. Proof it was coming along much better for him than me.

The security guard at the door announced something in Russian. I looked at Brett and shrugged. Brett leaned forward and said quietly, "Closing time."

So, he understood. Of course he did.

He chuckled behind his hand and joined Berg. They both glanced at me, then Berg said something in Russian, and the two of them laughed loudly.

I decided I liked Brett best when he ignored me.

I DIDN'T SAY ANYTHING AS Kaufman and I took the bus home. The sun was beginning to set, and I was hungry. I'd eaten all the snacks I'd brought in my backpack, plus some of Kaufman's. I knew Jinya would probably have dinner waiting for us at home, so we shouldn't stop somewhere. On Mondays, I got a home-cooked meal, clean laundry, and a clean apartment. It was becoming my favorite day, as long as I didn't have to see Brett.

The marshrutka bus was full. Kaufman and I passed our money forward through several hands until it reached the bus driver. I glanced around at the people—a mother and her children, a businessman, a few older men and women—all quiet, wearing the same somber expressions. As Kaufman usually joked, "This is where we sit, stare out the window, and think about our miserable lives."

But today, he wasn't joking. He sat unsmiling, deep in thought, his eyebrows low. He had seemed different since we'd left the museum, despondent, which wasn't like him. The gray buildings and skies swirled by among skeletal trees that clung on to bits of red and amber.

For once, it was me trying to search for a topic of conversation. "Where was your favorite area?" I asked.

Kaufman's eyes focused on me, but his expression didn't change. He sat up a little straighter and said, "Here."

"Here?"

"Isn't that what a missionary is supposed to say?"

I shrugged. "Or you could be honest."

He paused, then said, "There was this place in Horlivka. Our branch of twenty people met in a fish market. Truly, I am not joking; it reeked of fish. It was closed on Sundays, and that is where we held Primary, Relief Society, and sacrament meeting. I was there four months, and my companion, Stareyshina Nekrasov, was the branch president. We even had a branch choir."

I chuckled. "Only in Ukraine." Kaufman smiled and nodded in a fond way. "And you liked that place better than here?"

"No." His smile faded. "I'm just showing you how much worse it could be. Even worse than being with Stareyshina Tyson."

I stared up at the cracks in the ceiling of the bus. "I'm not so sure about that. Did you hear what Berg said when they were leaving? I didn't understand."

"It wasn't nice."

"Yeah. I gathered as much."

"I'm sorry, mate. Sorry you have this trial."

Kaufman's sympathy made me feel a little lighter inside, enough that I remembered why Brett was angry with me in the first place. I sighed loudly. "I probably deserved it." I avoided Kaufman's eyes. Kaufman loved a story like a dog loved a bone. When I did finally look at him, his eyes were burning with unasked questions. "Don't worry," I said. "I won't let the dragon eat me."

That made him smile, and I was happy I'd successfully lightened his mood.

Our apartment smelled of food cooking, and Jinya was setting bowls on the table when we walked through the door.

"Ah, home sweet home," Kaufman said.

Jinya smiled and said in broken English, "It was good come home on mission to food. Woman with five children, she cook good *banosh* for stareyshiny."

"Did you ever serve here in Kramatorsk?" I asked.

Jinya shook his head. "Nyet." He switched to Russian. "But jobs were better in Kramatorsk than other places I served in my mission."

"Was she your maid?" Kaufman said in Russian. "The woman with five children?"

Jinya switched to English. "She taught me to cook. She taught me well, yes?"

"Yes," Kaufman said, giving him a reassuring smile. He opened the drawer with silverware and began helping set the table. I set my stuff down by my bed, then returned to the kitchen and collected three cups from the cupboard.

Kaufman set out another bowl. "You know you are eating with us, Jinya. Why don't you ever set a bowl for yourself?"

Jinya shrugged; his face turned pink. "I don't want to intrude, in case you are busy and need to run. I know the life of a missionary."

"Well, we always have time for you. This looks delicious," Kaufman said. He sat in one of the chairs, and we joined him. "I'll say the blessing."

After the prayer, Kaufman said, "I look forward to your borsch every week."

Jinya laughed. "They say no Ukrainian girl will marry if she doesn't know how to make borsch. I'm just learning so I am prepared if she does not."

Kaufman and I laughed. I took a bite of the dark-red soup and let its heat warm me to my shoes. The first time I tried the beet soup I wasn't sure if I liked it. Now, I couldn't imagine life without it.

"Johnson especially liked borsch. Maybe he knew Anya was a poor cook," Jinya said, chuckling. His brown eyes searched Kaufman, but Kaufman stared at his soup as if he hadn't heard. "How is Anya?" Jinya continued. "Do you ever hear from her?"

Kaufman looked up and said a bit gruffly, "Nyet, should I?"

"Sorry, I was not trying to offend you."

"You didn't," Kaufman said, his tone softened.

"We were all good friends, da? I thought she might write. But maybe she only stayed in contact with Johnson?"

"Perhaps," Kaufman said, his eyes on his borsch again. "Although, I doubt it. Did you get a haircut, Jinya?"

Jinya touched his dark hair, which was much shorter now and combed to the side like we wore ours. "Da, do you like it?"

"It looks nice. Like a stareyshina again, da?" Kaufman said.

Jinya returned Kaufman's smile and finished his soup. Kaufman stood and rinsed his dishes at the sink. I followed his example, and then it was time for us to leave again. I slipped my coat on. Jinya stayed to tidy up, and as usual, Kaufman left him some money on the table.

The temperature dropped even more as we walked the dark streets. Monday nights were when we held English class. The government building the Church rented was very accommodating in letting us store pictures and chairs and allowing us to use the chalkboards.

Usually, Kaufman was happier than a momma cow with her calf on the nights we taught class. It was his natural element, a live audience of fifteen to twenty-five people, all watching and listening to him act out words. And he didn't let me sit in the corner like I wanted to. He didn't let anyone sit in the corner. He was the only person I'd ever seen who could make every word in the English language an action word—didn't matter what it was: apple, post office, the days of the week . . .

But tonight as we walked, he didn't smile. He walked with his hands shoved deep inside his pockets and stared more at his feet than at the starless sky.

"Are you feeling all right, Kaufman?"

He looked over at me sharply. "Da, of course." Then he sighed loudly and lapsed into silence.

We arrived at the building, and Kaufman tried the door. It was unlocked. The branch president held interviews on Sundays and Monday nights, but he also liked to attend the English classes and usually came early to open the building and get the classroom ready.

Sure enough, we found him setting up chairs, the chalkboard already wiped down.

Kaufman greeted him warmly, and after about ten minutes, when it looked like we had enough people, we began with a prayer.

We often picked about twenty words and, through skits and games, made sure they were re-used again and again. Tonight, the plan was for me to say the words—with my very poor cowboy accent, as Kaufman said—then he would act them out. Kaufman began serious, but by word five, he was back to his old self, overdoing it and getting plenty of laughs in return.

After about an hour, we ended with a prayer. Someone had brought cookies, so we all stood and ate them before saying goodbye.

"Good work tonight, stareyshiny," President Kuznetsov said in English, locking the door. " Are you taking the bus home?"

"Da," I said.

But Kaufman said, "Not quite yet. One more stop, then we'll head home."

President smiled, shook our hands, and left in the direction of the bus stop.

I was unaware of any more appointments. It was after eight thirty now, curfew was in an hour, and it would take half that to get home. Kaufman began walking down the sidewalk.

"Where are we going?" I asked, keeping pace with him.

He stopped walking and pulled a folded piece of paper out of his pants pocket—the one Berg had given him. He handed it to me, and I read over the message written in Russian. It looked like someone wanted to meet us. Kaufman took the note back and said, "Do you remember that girl Jinya was talking about? Anya?"

"The girl from the picture."

"What?"

"The girl in the picture you have with Jinya and Johnson."

"Da." Kaufman cleared his throat. "She wants to meet me at 9:00 at this address. She says she needs to talk to me."

"Talk to you? What about?"

"I don't know. I thought about ignoring it—but now . . ." He bent the paper back and forth between his fingers. "I'm just not sure what to do." He took a deep breath. "I don't think she would ask if it wasn't important."

"Why meet her? She knows where you go to church. She probably even knew we had English class tonight. If she has something to say, why didn't she just come to us? Why pass a message through Berg?"

"I don't know," Kaufman said. He set his hands on his hips, as if unsure where to go. "It is rather confusing. But maybe she's in some sort of trouble?"

"Kaufman." I stood in front of him and forced him to look at me. "You're not a prince. Anya is not a princess in distress. This part of the story is not where you rescue the girl. This is where you serve your mission faithfully and go home in three months to girls who will not grow into babushkas before age thirty." I expected a smile, but all I got was another sigh.

Kaufman stared at the ground for several seconds, then said, "What Jinya said was true. We were all friends. They used to come with us on p-days to museums—Jinya, Anya; Berg and his companion, Sloan; and Murray and Osborne; and my companion, Johnson. I knew, well, I suspected Johnson liked her. We all *liked* her."

"*You* like her?" I asked. "What about locking your heart?"

"I'm not in love with her. Of course there's some level of attraction, but I'm committed to being a missionary. Johnson was committed to being a missionary. It was all so out of character for her and Johnson, and I just want to know, to understand. Will you go with me?" he asked quietly. "Will you keep me safe from her? I don't want anything to be reproached with. But I just need to know. I just want to see her again."

I blew out. "How far away is this address?"

"Half a kilometer, I think. We could be there in ten minutes."

I nodded. What else could I do? Kaufman was strange, but he'd been a good friend. He'd shown sympathy on the bus after the museum. And President had said to love my companion.

We walked in silence. I felt uneasy and tired. But Kaufman was the senior companion, and I made a choice to trust him. It wasn't long before I recognized a shape in the distance: a large gray statue with a fire burning next to it. I'd been here once before, my first day in Kramatorsk.

I stopped walking. "This isn't the first time she's told you to meet her here."

Kaufman turned around, his eyes pleading. "No. This is the first time she's asked me. The other time"—he looked away—"that was just me. This is where she lived."

I shook my head. This was looking worse and worse. But somehow, the familiar building made me feel less afraid. The small parking lot held a handful of typical Ukrainian cars, which, by American standards, were very outdated, eighties-looking. But one car stood out from the others: a shiny, silver Mercedes.

I pointed it out to Kaufman, who shrugged and said, "Mafia."

"Mafia? Like cigars and killing-people mafia?"

He opened the door. "Don't worry, Christensen. We're just missionaries. We leave them alone; they'll leave us alone. I heard California has a gang problem—same thing, right?"

"Not my part of California," I muttered, following him through the door.

We walked down the long hall, past several closed apartment doors, until we reached the stairwell.

"Shall we try the lift?" Kaufman smirked.

I leaned against the wall and yawned as Kaufman opened the elevator door and looked around inside. "Amazing," his muffled voice said. "I really don't know how you could fit a full-sized adult in this anyway."

"You know," I said, "the MTC could have prepared us better for Ukraine by disabling the elevators and forcing us to run stairs."

Kaufman stepped out of the elevator and rolled his eyes at me.

I shrugged. "What? I thought it was funny."

Placing both hands on the front of my coat, he pulled me forward off the wall. "Didn't I tell you so?" he asked as he dusted off the white residue now on my dark coat.

"Why don't people just wear white around here?" I asked, brushing the backs of my sleeves.

Kaufman laughed. "Wear white? Like ready for baptism? You're full of jokes tonight."

Kaufman's laugh was proof his mood was lifting and he was returning to normal. Maybe it had been a good thing we'd come after all.

The door we'd entered at the end of the hall opened, and we watched a balding man step inside, wearing matching black exercise pants and a jacket, with a red stripe up each leg. He grinned, as if he'd found what he was looking for. I could smell the alcohol from where we stood. My feet felt frozen to the cement floor as I watched him walk toward us.

He slowed to a stop when he was between us and the stairwell door. His eyes stared at my name badge. "Stareyshina Christensen." He laughed, his breath heavy. "Stareyshina? Who's elder are you? You are so young!"

This joke was not new to me, but it had never sounded more menacing. I glanced at Kaufman, his face hard.

"We want no trouble," he said loudly in Russian.

"Trouble?" the man staggered slightly. He glared at Kaufman, then swung wildly. Kaufman punched the man soundly in his ribs. I heard a crack, and the man doubled over, yelling words I knew weren't G-rated, even in Ukraine.

Kaufman looked at me. "Take the stairs."

"The stairs?" I was still in shock. "Let's get out of here."

"We've come all this way. Hurry."

Adrenaline pumping, I followed Kaufman, taking the stairs two at a time. My parents had taught me that you obeyed first and asked questions later. It could mean the difference between life and death on the ranch.

When we reached the top, his knuckle was bleeding. He held it tightly against the inside of his coat. Casually, he asked, "Will you be our knocker, then?"

He moved to walk, but I grabbed his shoulder roughly and pushed him hard against the wall. He shoved me away with his unhurt hand. I didn't touch him again; we just glared at each other from opposite sides of the hall, each breathing heavily.

"What the heck was that, Kaufman? You probably broke that guy's ribs! What if we get in trouble? What if he sends for the police?"

He shook his head. When he spoke, his voice sounded calm, even if his face looked the opposite. "The police? Really? That man probably won't even make it home without passing out."

"Why did you punch him?"

His mouth gaped open. "What should I have done? Invited him to tea?" He stepped away from the wall and dusted his coat.

"Is that what the Savior would do? Fight people on the streets? I should have brought my boxing gloves instead of my scriptures."

"Boxing gloves?" He held his aching fist. "Da. That would have been a good idea."

I shook my head. "I can't do this. I can't do this anymore. I'm going home. Tomorrow—tonight." I bent over my knees and breathed in deeply; the world glowed prickly yellow.

After a few seconds, I felt Kaufman's gentle hand on my back. "Christensen, don't be a quitter. That's no fun."

I straightened and glared at Kaufman. "We almost got killed because you came to see a *girl* as a missionary. I'm leaving now." I trudged down the stairwell.

After one flight, I turned to see I was alone. Kaufman hadn't followed me. I didn't care. I wanted to be far away from this place. I reached the bottom. No one was in the hall. I stopped and hesitated in front of the door to the outside. Abandoning Kaufman upstairs was different from leaving the building.

I couldn't make myself go back toward the stairwell though—I didn't want to feel trapped again if someone came in. A few minutes later, Kaufman appeared at the end of the hall. His face held no expression, and he made no eye contact. I stepped outside alone onto the concrete slab and blinked against the cool night breeze.

Headlights turned on in the parking lot and then off again. Kaufman joined me outside. A man got out of the shiny Mercedes and slammed the door.

The sound made me jump, and I was off. I sprinted as fast as my legs could take me around the side of the building and through an alley, and then I turned and took another. I could hear Kaufman out of breath behind me. I ran until I spied a large metal dumpster. I didn't even hesitate before I jumped inside. I moved over to make room for Kaufman as I heard him clamor in after me.

"Did you see them?" I whispered, holding my coat sleeve over my nose to cover the odor.

"See who?" Kaufman whispered back. And I heard the humor in his question. He was amused by this.

"This isn't a joke," I hissed.

"We're sitting in a large pile of filth in a dumpster late at night. Of course this isn't a joke."

"I saw a man get out of the Mercedes. He was staring at me."

He paused as if processing. His next question held no humor. "What? Did he see you?"

"Da—how could he not?"

Kaufman whispered a curse word. "That's what this is about?"

I flicked what felt like his face.

"Ouch, that was my nose."

"Watch your language."

"Steady on, Christensen, don't you think you're being a bit rash?"

"You said they'd leave us alone if we left them alone, that I didn't need to worry!"

He grunted as if checking his patience odometer and swore again.

Again, I flicked him. This time he pushed my face. "Knock off," he said.

"You knock off."

"In England, those words don't mean the same."

"Yeah, and I'm the queen."

Kaufman shifted in the dumpster. "Well, it's late, and I'm ready to get out of this bin, if you're finished being afraid."

"How did your meeting with Anya go?" I asked.

"She didn't answer. Does that make you happy?"

"No," I said. "And what would have happened if she had?"

Kaufman was quiet for several seconds. "I don't know." Then he shushed me.

We froze. Outside, we could hear footsteps echoing off the buildings. I held my breath, which wasn't hard since the garbage reeked. The sound came within inches of us, and I closed my eyes, praying. But they never stopped; the person continued walking until we could no longer hear the echo of steps.

Kaufman swore. But this time, I didn't bother flicking him.

WE STAYED A FEW MORE minutes before we couldn't take the smell of decomposing trash any longer. Kaufman climbed out first, then helped me. We could hear dogs barking in the distance and the sounds of traffic, but we saw no one. We took a different route home and didn't speak. The adrenaline from the evening left me drained, and Kaufman looked more down than ever.

We passed a small train port. It was late, but Kaufman stopped. "I need to check schedules here. Do you mind if we go in briefly?"

The train station was no larger than a medium-sized restaurant, with a few benches and kiosks to purchase tickets. There was also a restroom, which I really needed to use.

I stood near Kaufman as he studied a map on the wall. He wrote down some information in the small notebook from his bag, shaking his hand a few times as if it hurt.

I kept my eyes on the kiosk nearby.

I had money in my pocket. Flying out of Kiev would be cheaper than flying out of Donetsk. I could get a train ticket to Kiev, and once I was there, I could purchase a plane ticket to America. No more thugs, no more language barrier, no more Brett. The thought filled my entire chest with relief. When would I ever get a chance like this again?

I turned my back to the kiosk, afraid Kaufman would read my thoughts. And then as if it were a miracle, he said, "I need to use the loo." I turned my head in the direction of the restroom. "Okay. I'll just stand near the door," I said, trying to sound casual despite my aching bladder. Technically, we were supposed to stick together, but the bathroom was a gray area.

"Do you need to go?" he asked.

I shook my head.

He stopped just outside the door, worry etched on his face. "Are you sure?"

"I'll still be here when you get back. I'm not taking off with some babushka tonight."

He narrowed his eyes and gave me a tight smile, probably still smarting from my girl lecture. He stuffed his notebook in his bag and walked in. I leaned against the wall and counted to five, then walked the thirty feet to the kiosk. It took only ninety seconds to purchase a ticket, and one hundred twenty for Kaufman to go in and out of the restroom.

I was breathing heavily when he returned but tried to hide it by walking a little ahead of him at a faster pace. The ticket was safe in my pocket. I could feel the papery edge of it with my fingertips.

I shined the Maglite for us as we walked the couple blocks home, since Kaufman's hand was still hurting. The sky was a hazy black-orange above the city lights. There were no stars, only clouds, and the air felt full, pregnant with unseen snowflakes waiting to fall.

We were ten minutes late by the time we reached our apartment building. I hurried up the stairs, the urgency to use the restroom extreme now. Kaufman held out the key so I could open the door for us. I inserted it, but saw it was already unlocked. I turned the knob and looked at Kaufman. "Do you think Jinya forgot to lock it?"

"Maybe," he said.

I pushed the door open and hurried to the bathroom in the dark.

A couple minutes later, I came out. Kaufman was sitting at the table under the yellow hanging bulb, and I could tell I'd startled him. He slid something under what looked like his journal and stood.

"Everything okay?" I asked.

"Da," he said, shoving his hands into his pockets. "Nothing seems out of place—no harm done. We'll have to tell Jinya to be more careful. I think I'll use the loo now too."

I moved so he could walk past me. Once the door was shut, I casually walked to the table and flipped the book over to see what was hidden underneath. It was the picture I'd seen before, with Jinya, Johnson, and Anya. Her note was sitting underneath, opened, as though Kaufman had been rereading it. I pushed the book back in place and walked over to my bed, which was covered in lumps of freshly washed laundry. Jinya had laid out my white shirts, as he always did, near my pillow, so they wouldn't get wrinkled before I could hang them up.

Kaufman came out. He walked over to his own pile of laundry on his bed. We didn't say anything. Tonight had put a wedge between us—I wasn't sure how big yet. How much would it crush him if I took off tomorrow? And did that matter to me?

I heard his footsteps behind me as he reentered the bathroom and closed the door. I heard the shower running a few seconds later. I picked up the last pair of my garments to put them away and noticed a large Russian Bible and Book of Mormon underneath. The scriptures looked older and used, unlike our stack of new scriptures near the door to give away to people. I knew they weren't mine. Kaufman's had probably ended up on my side of the room somehow. I set them on the floor by my bed—*let him pick them up.*

When Kaufman finished, I got in the shower to get the smell of garbage off. After brushing my teeth, I knelt on the dirty rug between our beds to show Kaufman I was ready to pray. He joined me, his hand wrapped in a white kitchen towel, a piece of lunch meat sticking out at the top.

I nodded at it. "Nice."

He adjusted the wrap. "It's feeling better, thanks for asking. How about you pray?"

I glared over at him. "How about you?"

"I'd prefer you did," he answered, holding up his hurt hand.

"That's your hand, not your mouth. Besides, I said dinner prayer."

We locked eyes, and I could see neither one of us would concede, both of us feeling less than worthy to pray, for different reasons. He held his good hand out, and we did rock, paper, scissors. I won. He sighed and gave the shortest prayer I'd ever heard him give.

He stood, but I stayed on the ground, my arms still folded. Inside, I was angry. It was Kaufman's own fault his hand was hurt. He'd chosen to meet a girl when we should have headed home. He's the one who had punched that guy instead of running away or giving him what he wanted. Ending up in a dumpster, hiding from mafia, was not my fault.

I stared hard at the back of Kaufman's knees as he cleaned off his bed. "What if it was all a setup tonight?" I asked. "Just so we'd get hurt? You know you can't trust girls, right?"

Kaufman turned but didn't meet my eyes. He ran a hand through his hair, his face red. "You know so much, do you, Hobbit?"

I felt my own anger build but tried to stay calm. "I've been deceived by a girl before too. It's not a new thing for me. But come clean; you put us in danger. President Meyers told me he trusts you."

Kaufman slumped down onto his bed. "I know." He mumbled, "It was stupid."

I got up from the rug. "What happened with Johnson wasn't your fault. Sometimes people aren't who you think they are."

He looked up, and I saw worry in his clear eyes. "I've been a poor father to you, haven't I?"

I sat on the edge of my bed. "Fathers aren't perfect." I shrugged. "At least, mine never were." A look of pity crossed his face that I didn't like, so I added, "You need to move on. No more worrying about Johnson and Anya. Think forward, not backward. Let's find someone for you to baptize."

He stood, pulled down the covers, and got into bed. Slowly, I walked across the room and turned off the light before settling under my own blankets.

"It's not that easy, mate," Kaufman said in the dark.

I stared at the black ceiling long after Kaufman's breathing became rhythmic and steady, the events of the day weighing on me. My mind kept going to that moment in the hall when the drunk man had attacked us, and then it took darker turns, wondering what would have happened if things hadn't worked out. What if we'd died? Life was short and unpredictable.

Was I ready to die?

I thought about the train ticket in my coat pocket that I wouldn't use. I thought about Brett and about my attempts at repentance. I still hadn't done what President Meyers had asked and written those letters. Trying not to squeak my bed too much, I got up and turned on the bathroom light. I found a pen, three pieces of paper, and three envelopes, then sat next to the toilet and began writing.

13

"CHRISTENSEN! WAKE UP!" KAUFMAN WAS shaking me. It was then I heard the pounding, as if our front door would burst. I sat up in the semidark room and scrambled to get out of bed but ended up wrapped in my blankets and falling to the floor. I stared at the clock. 4:00 a.m.

"Hurry!" Kaufman was throwing things into a bag. The pounding kept up an angry, steady rhythm. I rolled away from my blankets and began to mimic Kaufman's movements, grabbing random clothes and stuffing them in the empty bag I kept under my bed.

"No!" He kicked his bag to the side. "We don't have time. Grab your wallet and passport!"

Trembling, I pulled on my slippers and grabbed my name tag off the nightstand. I dumped the contents of my backpack on the bed, digging for my wallet and passport papers in the mess. I shoved them in the now-empty backpack, my heart jumping with each blow against the door.

Kaufman crossed the room and threw me my coat. I struggled into it. I tripped on some scriptures on the floor, picked them up, and tossed them into the bag too.

"Hurry!" Kaufman hissed.

The pounding had turned to bashing. I zipped up my backpack and quickly slipped it on. Kaufman pulled open our small window five stories above the ground and leaned out. I watched, horrified. What was he planning to do? The sound of gunshots ricocheted off the building, and he pulled himself in quickly.

With one final crash, our door exploded, and dark-clothed figures spilled through it, holding large guns in front of them. They yelled that they were the police. I thrust my hands into the air and felt several sets of hands grab me, pulling me down into a crouched position as they tugged my hands behind my back and locked them in handcuffs. I couldn't see Kaufman, but I heard him struggling behind me, saying things about his innocence and asking questions, but one of the men told him to stop talking or he'd be shot.

"It will be okay, Stareyshina!" I choked. "The Lord will protect us!"

Something hard hit my mouth. I tasted iron and knew it was blood. Hands yanked me up by my shoulders, and they shoved me through our broken front door and into the dimly lit hall.

I tried not to panic and said a silent prayer as we were marched down the stairwell. We hit the cold night air, and I saw several white police cars with blue stripes parked near the sidewalk.

Someone shoved me into the back seat of one, then I watched helplessly as Kaufman was escorted out of the building and pulled toward a different one. He craned his head and struggled, his eyes wildly searching the other police cars. I wanted to let him know where I was. I tugged against the handcuffs behind my back, wishing I could open the door.

We had to stay together. But there was nothing I could do. When two officers got in the front seat, I didn't say or do anything. My mouth still stung where I'd been hit, and fear forced me into silence. Maybe if I cooperated, they'd see this was all just a big mistake.

I SQUINTED AND TRIED TO avoid looking at the large bright bulb blinding me. Metal cuffs dug into my wrists. Footsteps, a snapping crunch, then coarse laughter. For a brief second, someone moved between me and the light, giving me a second of relief before the flood of brightness covered me again.

Someone held something up to my face.

"Yours, I think, Stareyshina Christensen?"

It was something flat and small, broken in two pieces, but if I tried to look directly at it, I saw only spots. He tried to pin it on my shirt, sticking me in the process.

"Your name badge fits you better now—broken and dirty—like you." He laughed, along with other male voices in the room. "Bah, he does not understand me, I'm sure of it. American. It says in his papers he's only been here six weeks."

I ducked my head to give my eyes a break. Then he was in front of me. His breath smelled of old shoes. "You took it, Stareyshina," he said in a low growl. "Tell me where it is and I'll let you go. Or maybe I will send you to prison forever anyway." The men laughed and jeered, but they all spoke too quickly. My head hurt and stomach churned, beads of sweat pricked my forehead. "Well?" The Ukrainian guard growled several words in Russian that I couldn't understand.

I shook my head and said in Russian, "*Oshibka!*"

"Mistake? Da, you are right about that."

The light shifted to darkness where he stood in front of me. I felt something hard hit the side of my face, and my head reeled from the blow. Tears of pain pricked my eyes. My ears rang, the laughter sounding distant.

I took in a deep breath, then was yanked to my feet so hard my teeth hit each other.

"Where is it, Stareyshina?" the guard yelled.

"I don't know. I don't understand," I tried again in Russian.

"No more lies," he hissed in my ear. His fist connected with my stomach. I leaned forward. I couldn't breathe. "Weak," the guard mumbled. "A religious preacher who steals? You deserve what you get. Take him out of my sight."

Two officers grabbed me and forced me through a door at the back of the room. I'd fallen off a horse more than once. I'd broken my foot when a cow had stood on it. Those had been painful times, but they had felt more natural, the hurt understandable. They hadn't tested my endurance or sense of justice like this. Waves of panic, fear, and anger coursed through me.

I half-walked and was half-dragged through halls of white cages. The lock clicked on one; the door slid open. My legs buckled as I fell into it. My knees hit the cement ground first, followed by my left shoulder.

Then something hit my back, like a rock. I flinched, wishing I could curl up and cover my head with my hands, but they were still handcuffed behind me. The guard laughed. "You'll have nothing to do but read your Bibles here."

"If you can turn the pages," the other said. I heard a loud thud next to my head where another object landed.

I didn't move. I didn't dare, even if I could. The lock clicked, footsteps echoed down the hall, and all voices grew silent. I closed my eyes and let the cool cement press against my aching jaw, my arms numb behind my back.

15

MY HORSE BUCKED NERVOUSLY UNDER me each time I reached out for the stray cow. I knew if I could just touch it, let it know it was going the wrong way, it would turn, but each time I tried to grab its stubborn head, my horse knocked me away. Then the cow would thwack me in the face with her tail. It was an unusually long tail, with spikes and something metal. It finally knocked my face so hard I fell off my horse, landing on my stomach.

I rubbed my middle, the pain throbbing, then settled into the cool, firm ground. It was dark, rich soil that smelled of home.

***

I shivered and reached for my blankets, but my arms wouldn't move. They were numb and wouldn't cooperate. I tried to roll over, but that resulted in searing pain radiating from my stomach to my shoulder. I forced my eyes open, and the blurriness became objects. I was on a very cold, hard floor in sweatpants and a Lassen High Future Farmers T-shirt, facing a peeling white wall.

And my hands were cuffed behind my back.

Pain radiated through my arms, my chest, my abdomen. I rolled to my shoulder, groaning involuntarily. I would have to use my stomach muscles to sit up. I gasped in pain at first but worked through it until I was in a sitting position. My head throbbed, and I was tempted to lie down again. I wished I could touch my body to see with my hands what the damage was. My eye felt swollen, and I had pain on both sides of my face.

I looked around for some kind of bed or place to sit but froze when I saw someone watching me. Only a few feet away was an elderly man sitting on one of two cots, his back against the wall. His face was a full gray-and-white beard. Long, greasy, gray hair lay plastered to his head. His eyes were black and as aware of me as I was of him.

His Russian came out mumbled. "They beat you up pretty badly."

I didn't move. He pointed at his face then at mine and winced.

I squinted at the small cell and the empty cot. A blanket was folded on top of it. A small window with bars was a few feet above it. I could see it was light outside. A toilet sat in the corner, next to my bed.

"You were laughing." The old man's voice was deep, gravelly, as if he hadn't used it in quite a while. "In your sleep."

I hesitated, afraid of what this man might do. He could have kicked me a few times while I'd been sleeping. Maybe he had. My body ached.

The man continued to stare at me, his face curious. I could see how thin he was and weak. I stood so I would be ready to fight him. A look of fear briefly crossed his face as I stood, and guilt swept through me. Hadn't I told Kaufman last night that fighting wasn't the answer? But perhaps I'd been wrong.

Clearly, I'd been wrong.

President had been wrong—*love* wasn't the best teacher; it was *pain*.

Standing made me feel sick. I backed up until I was leaning against the wall, and from there, I watched the man.

He lowered his chin. "I'm not going to hurt you. My name is Egor."

I stared at his weathered face, his eyes filled with caution. "I am *Stareyshina* Christensen."

His face broke into a hint of a smile. "Stareyshina? How old are you? They don't even call *me* stareyshina here." I didn't respond; my mouth hurt too much from the effort of saying my name. "Oh, you are serious? I'm sorry. I assumed you were joking." He seemed sincere.

I responded the best I could in Russian, "It is fine."

He nodded.

My knees began to ache, and my body shook. I sank to my knees, my head against the cold wall.

I heard the bed squeak, and the man was soon next to me. "You need help, Stareyshina. Here, come with me." He grabbed my shoulder gently and helped me to my feet. He didn't let go until I was on the empty bed underneath the window.

This was my bed.

I sat on the edge. "Thank you," I said.

He turned back to where one of my slippers had fallen off at some point and picked it up. He slipped it on my foot over my white Nike socks.

"You are not from here," he said, sitting on his bed.

I was surprised I understood him so well, and though I was still unsure if I had heard correctly, I answered. "Nyet—America."

His eyes widened, and he seemed momentarily at a loss for words. "America?"

I nodded, and he cleared his throat and pointed at my face. "You have a black eye." He made a clicking sound with his tongue. "The guards are brutal here."

"Guards hurt you?" I asked.

"Not now. When I first came, they pushed me around a bit, but look." He pulled up the sleeves of his dark-blue prison uniform. "This keeps them away." Both arms were covered with red-and-white, dry, scaly, peeling skin. He smiled at me. "They call me *Shramy.*" Scars. "Don't worry. I've had it many years now. But I do not tell the guards that." He smirked and covered it back up.

I pointed at his arm. "Pain?"

He shrugged. "It is uncomfortable. I think it means I am sick. How did an American like you get to be here?"

I shook my head, amazed I was communicating in Russian. "I do not know. They say I steal."

He nodded. "Many people steal in this country."

"Nyet. Not me. I not steal."

He looked at me closely. "I would probably doubt your words, but I see your books, and it makes me wonder." He reached underneath his cot and pulled out two books: a Russian Bible and Book of Mormon. "Are you a preacher? I recognize this book"—he held up the Bible—"but not this one." He held up the scriptures with *Kniga Mormona* written across the front.

I didn't answer, feeling the vulnerability of the situation. Egor hadn't done anything to hurt me yet—but that didn't mean he wouldn't. I was to stand as a witness of Christ at all times. I swallowed and kept my eyes on his. "Da, I'm a Mormon missionary."

"Eh, Mormon? What is a Mormon?"

"A believer in Christ. We believe in the books you're holding, that they come from God."

He set the Bible down and began to thumb through the Book of Mormon.

I felt myself relax a little, enough to think to say a small prayer to keep me safe. Safe from the guards, safe from Egor and whatever disease he carried. And

I prayed for President Meyers to know where we were. Last night, Kaufman had said the line was busy when he'd tried to call Stareyshina Murray. We were supposed to report on the woman we'd been teaching, the one who had come to church my first Sunday. Maybe they would try to call us this morning, and maybe they would get worried when no one answered.

And I prayed for Kaufman. I hadn't seen him.

"Missing," I said. "A man, like me. Preacher same like me. Did you see?"

Egor shook his head. "No, only you."

IT FELT VERY LATE IN the morning when we heard someone yell, "Food!"
A guard slid the food through a small opening in the prison door, then
locked it.

"Are you going to un-cuff him?" Egor asked. I shrank into the wall
behind me and stared between Egor and the guard. "Or how will he eat?
He is to eat, da? Or are these both mine?"

The guard growled something under his breath and called to someone
nearby. Another guard came and opened the door with some keys, then got
his gun out where we could see it. The other guard walked toward where
I sat on the bed. He pushed me forward roughly and, with a key from his
belt, unlocked the handcuffs. As they disconnected with my skin, I resisted
the urge to yell in pain.

"Religious hypocrite," the guard growled, pushing me back up hard
against the wall.

I narrowed my eyes at the accusation. When would the brutality stop?
When would I be released?

He laughed. "You understand me? Good, good. How about you try
to hit me? You want to, da?"

I glanced at Egor, who shook his head once. I kept my eyes on the cell
door across the room.

"Trus"—*coward*—he whispered in my ear. He waited there, his breath
on my face. It was as if my heart had stopped. It took all my willpower not
to flinch or push him away.

"Okay, fine," he said after a length of time. "If you will not fight me, I
will go find someone to abuse in your honor. How do you like that, religious

preacher?" Again, he waited. "What is your choice? Take your beating? Or have someone take it for you?"

Someone else? That couldn't be what he'd said, what he meant. Again, I looked at Egor for help. He firmly shook his head. I felt my mouth twitch, to ask a question, to find a way out of this, but inside, I felt a small voice tell me not to move. I pursed my lips together.

"Very well." He chuckled. "You shall hear it." He exited the cell; the door slid squeakily shut, and locked. His footsteps went only a short distance before I heard a new cell door open.

Then a whimper. Then a scream.

Fear pulsed through my veins. Another scream. My hands flew to my ears. I squeezed my eyes shut and began to pray.

After several long seconds, Egor touched my shaking arm. Reluctantly, I dropped it.

"It's over," he said.

I wiped both my eyes and breathed in deeply.

The guard came back, glanced in at me, then laughed. He said a slew of words in Russian I didn't understand to his guard friend, and I heard their boots as they tromped off.

My body felt tight, like I was a wound up ball of string. "Will he be okay?" I whispered.

Egor shook his head as if he didn't understand.

"Will the man . . . pain? Will he be okay?"

"I—I think so," Egor said. "You are worried about him? About the other man?"

"Da," I repeated, "Is he okay?"

Egor scratched at his beard. "The guard probably picked someone weak, who he knew would call out so you would hear."

Someone weak. I remembered last night, the feeling of helplessness, confusion. I had cried out too.

"Excuse me," Egor said, "but many people would not be worried about someone they don't know. You are safe. That's all you care about—all you should care about."

But I wasn't safe. Not here. I rubbed a shaking hand across my forehead. "The man—he is not safe. He is hurt. Because of me."

"Nyet," Egor said sharply. "Not because of you. Because of the guard." He raised a gnarled finger and emphasized each word. "Not because of you."

I nodded. Understanding Egor was becoming easier.

He picked up our bowls of food and spoke slowly. "You did well not to fight with the guard. You might not have lived. Da, he would let you hit him enough to leave a mark. Then he would beat you until you were beyond hope. He would claim you attacked him first. It is their way."

I swallowed, again remembering the night before.

"You are lucky," he continued. "I've never heard anyone get a choice before. Maybe they are careful because you are American. There are people worried about you? Asking questions? Willing to pay money?"

I didn't say anything. My eyes filled with tears, thinking about my parents and how worried they would be. It made the wedge in my chest a thousand times thicker than those nights in the MTC.

I held my hands out in front of me. Deep ridges on both wrists burned red where the metal had rubbed my skin. Tenderly, I touched them. "*Spasibo*"—*thank you*—I said, hoping Egor would realize how grateful I was. Most likely, I'd still be wearing the cuffs if he hadn't said anything—and maybe nearly dead if he hadn't guided me with the guard.

I breathed in a shaky breath and squeezed my eyes shut.

I heard the bed squeak. Egor sat next to me and handed the plate to me.

I took it. "Why are you in prison?" I asked.

He frowned and took several bites of food. Had I asked the right question? Had I offended him? He didn't answer, and I didn't say anything else.

I stared at the meat stew in my own tin bowl. It was like my dog, Pal's, dish at home; it even smelled like dog food. This meat had to be against mission rules. I poked at it with the metal spoon, rusted in some spots, and remembered the days I'd spent running to the toilet after eating at the branch president's home.

I heard a sob come from somewhere in a nearby cell. With shaking hands, I set my food on the bed next to me, sure I might vomit if I stared at it any longer.

Egor looked down at my uneaten food. "You are not hungry?"

I shook my head. "Nyet." I held it out to him, indicating he was welcome to it. Slowly, he took it from me, an ashamed look on his face. "Rules," I said. "I am a missionary. I can't eat the meat because of how it is prepared."

"Can't eat food? How will you live?"

It was a good question, one I couldn't answer.

He dumped the stew in his own bowl. "How long have you lived in Ukraine?" he asked.

"Six weeks."

He raised both eyebrows, clearly surprised. He took a bite of my food and sadly shook his head. "You know very little about this country."

I sighed and stared above us where the small window revealed a dark, cloudy day. Egor finished the food, then placed both bowls near the cell door. He came back and stood next to my cot, slipped out of his boots, then, with his bare feet, stood on my cot. I stared at his brown, sore, gnarled feet covered in splotches as he stretched to see out the window.

He hopped down and slipped his boots back on. He bent behind his cot and pulled out a small dark rock that he used to mark a line next to several other tally marks in the corner between our cots. Carefully, he circled the line and said, "To show the day you arrived."

"How many?" I asked.

"Two hundred eighty-nine. Who knows how many lines will be there when I leave?" He glanced hesitantly at me, and I knew he'd thought, *Or you.*

I noticed another circle a few tallies from the top and pointed at it.

"That is the day the man who was here when I arrived died."

"How did he die?"

"I don't know. It was in his sleep. But the guards are sure it was because of the disease I carry." Egor sat on his cot and fixed his blanket to comfortably cover his legs, his boots sticking out at the end. "They must not care much for you to put you in with me."

I pondered that until Egor, staring at the blanket, said, "I stole some food." He met my eyes. "You asked me my crime, why I am here. That was my crime. I stole some bread. I lived on the streets several years. My skin prevented me from getting a job as I got older. I had no family. My wife had died. I became tired. I thought at the time perhaps prison would be easier than the streets, da?

"It is warmer here, but maybe not easier, like I thought. I feel I do not have much longer to live in this life." I stared at the dark-purple circles surrounding his aged eyes. *Humble. Honest.* I knew it without knowing how, and the fear of him left me.

"Read to me, Stareyshina," he said. "Read from your books." He pointed to the scriptures near me on the bed.

"I don't know if I can," I replied meekly.

"You can't read these books?" Suspicion entered his eyes immediately.

"I love those books," I replied, my face hot. "But I do not read Russian well."

"Ah. Well, maybe I can help you. Come, let's begin."

I picked up the Book of Mormon and opened it to the first page. There was no name on the cover, but its worn edges weren't mine.

I realized I must have grabbed Kaufman's.

THE DINNER MEAL WAS AN unattractive gray porridge, I passed my bowl to Egor. I had no appetite. I stretched out on my cot and stared at the cement ceiling. Egor finished eating and started to read. My brain barely registered the words as I watched the black sky.

Footsteps neared our cell. The gate slid open, and three guards walked in.

"Get up!" one yelled, holding a gun.

The other two guards grabbed my arms and yanked me to a stand. My heart seemed to freeze in my chest; I didn't resist them. They shut the cell door behind us, and I moved with the men down the white-cage-lined hall until we reached the same door I had come out of the night before.

I held my breath as one of them pushed me through the door, my adrenaline pumping, fists clenched, ready to protect myself. My apprehension took a different form when I saw President Meyers sitting in the same spot I had before but without the interrogation lights.

He stood as I walked in, and the guards dropped their hold on me.

"Stareyshina Christensen," President said. He crossed the room and threw his arms around me.

I began to shake; relief coursed through me as I clung to him. I was safe. The nightmare was over. He stood back, his hands on my shoulders, and stared at me. I wiped my eyes quickly, taking in deep breaths.

He rubbed his thumb just under my eye. The pressure caused me to wince. "What happened? Did they hurt you?"

I didn't know if the guards understood English or not. I glanced hesitantly over my shoulder at them. Bad things happened when they didn't like what I said. I worried about President's safety.

President frowned, his face red, visibly upset.

"Have you come to get me?" I asked.

He covered his mouth with his hand, then let it fall down his chin. "I—I need to know what happened, Stareyshina."

"Police came in the night. They broke down our door. They keep asking me where it is, this thing they think I stole. What do they think I stole, President? Why am I here? Where is Kaufman?"

He put both hands on my shoulders. "Stareyshina Christensen—Neal—I'll try to answer your questions, but we don't have a lot of time. I need to know. Did you steal it?"

"Steal what?" Inside, I felt myself cracking. I stumbled backward. President grabbed my shoulders again but this time guided me to a nearby chair—*the interrogation chair.* President wasn't here to get me; he was here to question me. I bent forward, wrapping my arms around my head.

President took one of my arms off my head and tugged on it. He examined it and felt the deep grooves in my wrists, his face dark. With narrowed eyes, he said something in Russian that sounded like a reprimand to the guards. They looked down like kids caught stealing cookies.

He turned back to me. "The Church is looking into it, but it's complicated. The government is convinced by money, of course, but the Church doesn't operate that way. We have to be careful. *You* have to be careful."

"I don't understand. Why am I here?" I asked.

President Meyers sighed heavily and looked away. When he met my eyes again, he said, "I might as well let you know. There is hard evidence against you."

"What? What evidence? What do they think I did?"

"There are tapes, videos of you from a surveillance camera in the museum in Kramatorsk. I've seen them. There was a ring on loan from Russia in the museum. They think you stole it."

"A ring?" I repeated. "In a museum?" I searched my brain, and then I saw it. "King Nicholas's ring, on loan from a museum in Livadiya."

President's eyebrows furrowed. "How do you know that?"

"We went there for p-day. Murray, Berg, Osborne, and Brett were there, looking at the ring too. All of us were there. Nobody stole it. Didn't you see them looking at it, too, in the video?"

He shook his head. "The video wasn't of you looking at it. It was of you *stealing* it last evening."

My mouth opened, but no words came out, my breath quick.

His tone turned pleading. "Are you saying you didn't do it?"

"How could I steal a ring? I don't even know how to take a bus by myself!" I dropped my head in my hands, helplessness pouring over me. When I'd first seen President Meyers, a part of me had hoped—*knew*—he was here to save me. Another part feared he was a prisoner too—that we were all prisoners—because it made just as much sense for him to be here as me.

"I have agonized over this, wondering if you were guilty or not, pleading with the Lord what to do." I looked up and allowed President's eyes to search mine. "I want you to understand. I have fought this ever since Kaufman called and told me you were in prison—"

"Kaufman! He called you?"

President sat wearily on the floor in front of me. "Yes, he called me around five hours ago." He glanced across the room before saying quietly, "Did Stareyshina Kaufman say anything to you? Did he take anything with him? Did he tell you anything?"

I searched my memory. "We both panicked. We grabbed our passports. They separated us." I briefly thought of the drunk man in the hall, us hiding in a dumpster, Kaufman trying to meet a girl. But those things had nothing to do with my getting thrown into prison for stealing a multimillion-dollar artifact. It was Kaufman's job to tell President about those things.

"I have called anyone I thought would be able to help. The United States embassy is aware and doing what they can. We have lawyers from the Church on their way to Ukraine to try to figure this out with me. But prisons are violent, overcrowded, with poor medical care. I have done my research, especially tonight. This is a pretrial detention facility. They are sometimes worse than actual prisons. If you are convicted, you could spend years in prison—here in Ukraine. But even without being convicted—" He rubbed his gray hair. "Who knows how long it will take for your case to come to trial. People spend years just waiting—whether they are from Ukraine or not. And there is much unrest right now politically."

"Are you saying—are you saying I could be here years? Here in this prison? Even being innocent?"

He stretched up and grasped my shoulder. "Let's not focus on that. What do you need? What do you have? Are you safe? Do you have food? Water?"

I swallowed, the weight of everything he'd said crushing me. I forced my brain to answer his questions. "I am in a cell with an older man who is good. We have two small meals a day. I gave him my meat. We have water brought to us once a day."

President mopped his face with his hand. "The meat is a problem. And the water, does it seem safe?"

I shrugged. "It tastes the same as we had at our apartment."

He seemed satisfied with that answer. "Is there anything else? You're still in your own clothes. I will see if you can keep your garments."

I hadn't considered that.

"Can you have reading material here? I could get you some scriptures."

"I have my scriptures—well, Kaufman's." I shook my head. "Why is this happening to me, President?"

His eyes filled with tears, and he cleared his throat. "I don't know. There's nothing I want more than to leave you with comfort, but I have more bad news. There is more evidence against you than just the video. They found a train ticket in your coat pocket, scheduled to leave today. Was it yours?" he asked quietly.

I'd confessed lying to Brett, and now this. He'd never believe me. "Yes, sir. I did buy that ticket."

"Were you planning on going home?"

I fidgeted with the bottom of my T-shirt. "I hadn't decided." But the train ticket was solid evidence otherwise.

"Why?"

I swiped at the tears on my cheeks and couldn't look at him as I said, "I was giving up."

"Does Kaufman know you bought it?"

I shook my head. "No."

He stared at me, disappointment in his eyes.

I wanted to explain. "I'd had a really rotten day, then Kaufman and I had a fight. I guess it was the last straw. But then before bed, we talked about it, and I told him we were going to find someone for him to baptize before he goes home. We both made mistakes, and we apologized." Confusion filled me, and I felt the tears swell again. "But, oh, forgive me—I wish I'd already used it and gone home." I crouched forward, my knees pressed against my forehead.

President patted my back for several seconds. "I won't blame you for that thought. Neal. Look at me. I don't have a lot of time."

I sat up and used the bottom of my dirty shirt to mop my face.

"I want to leave you with some comfort. Do you remember what I said when we first spoke? Do you remember how I told you it's all about love? Life is about *becoming*, changing, remember? The Spirit directed me to tell you that for a reason. Pray—I know you are—but *pray* to become a converted individual to Jesus Christ. Pray to know who in this prison needs you. And pray for deliverance."

President stood and brushed off his pants. "I had to make a decision today about whether or not I should release you as a missionary. I'm going to put off that decision. The evidence is there, but"—he reached out and touched my shoulder—"after talking to you, I think they have the wrong man." His smile was sad. "You are under a different set of rules here. It would be difficult to shower daily, watch what you eat, stay with a companion. But maybe you should think about the reasons why you are asked to keep those rules as a missionary, and maybe you should choose to still be obedient to some. But you are the judge now. Keep the Lord as your constant companion. Maybe this is not the end of your mission but the beginning of what God wants you to learn."

"Yes, President," I said automatically. His words did not bring comfort; they brought sheer terror. I didn't want to learn whatever lessons the Lord had in store for me here. President's speech had sounded like I might be here for quite some time, a fact that made me feel completely helpless.

"Do you understand the language? Are you having trouble understanding directions?"

I shook my head, the full realization of that fact hit me. I stared wide-eyed at President. "I have understood."

He nodded, relief filling his features. "A blessing. Truly. Six weeks and you can understand the language? Sounds like the gift of tongues to me. The Lord is truly with you."

I nodded, still scared but also finally comforted with that thought.

"*Pora*," a guard said gruffly. It was time to go.

I stood, but I had more questions. "Are you going to see Kaufman now? Is he here? Did they hurt him too?"

President squinted at me as if gauging his next words carefully. "They let him go."

His words were like a kick from the guards; they were unexpected and harsh. *They let him go?* The guards walked toward us and grabbed my arms.

"President, tell my mom and dad I love them. Tell them not to worry. And—the letters. I wrote the letters, but I didn't mail them. They are in my journal. Will you mail them? Please?"

"Yes, Stareyshina." President's voice caught, tears in his eyes. "I'll take care of it. I'm so sorry."

I'D WORRIED WHAT THE BACKLASH would be once President Meyers was gone. I hadn't understood all he'd said to the guards in Russian, but I'd understood his tone. As I walked back to my cell, I waited for the guards to tell me my mission president had no power here, that they could do as they pleased—but there were no harsh words as we made our way to my cell, nothing but the echo of boots against concrete, mingled with the whisper of my slippers.

My cell door was open, and they waited for me to enter before shutting it—that was all. Egor looked up from his cot, and I watched him hastily set aside the *Kniga Mormona*.

I listened to their footsteps fade away and took in a deep breath, saying a small prayer of gratitude that I had arrived unhurt. If I could just focus on being grateful, maybe I wouldn't lose it. I gestured toward Egor and the discarded book. "You were reading?"

He nodded, a bit red-faced. "Only a little. There is not much else to do here."

That was definitely true. I sat heavily on my cot.

"Where did you go?"

"My mission president. He is trying to help." I blew out and shrugged to show I didn't know what would happen, whether he could help. The action alone made me feel depressed—and afraid.

He nodded a silent response.

I pulled my knees up to my chest. I was still shocked from President's last bit of news. Kaufman was free. I knew I should feel relieved. I'd been so worried, and now I knew he was okay. If our situations were reversed, I'd be worried sick about him. I tried to picture Kaufman in a frantic state, worried about me.

But I couldn't feel worse for him than me. I just couldn't make myself do it. Not when there were things like calzones and waffles and even eggs and toast that he could eat right now. And he was close to going home. And I was looking at an indefinite amount of time here now.

The thought was crippling.

How had Kaufman walked away unscathed? We'd never left each other's side. If I was on that video, he should have been on it too. Someone had framed me.

I sucked in a deep breath of air and held it in my chest. I couldn't give up hope. The Church would find a way to help me. Maybe I'd get a fair trial. Maybe people would come to my defense who knew me personally—

Like Brett?

My hope deflated just as quickly as I'd built it. Brett wouldn't defend my character. Wasn't this what he wanted for me? To feel what it was like to be wrongly accused?

He was right. It was the most horrible feeling in the world.

Emptiness closed around me, and I curled up in a ball on my mattress.

God was punishing me. It wasn't just Brett I'd injured. What about the helpless man I'd sent the guard to beat instead of me? I'd hurt someone to protect myself. It was a self-preservation cycle I couldn't seem to break.

I held on to the words President Meyers had said the night I'd confessed about Brett. God didn't want us to suffer for our sins. That was why Christ had come—to atone for us—so we wouldn't have to suffer.

"*Otboy*"—*lights out*—the guards yelled, then switched off the main breaker, leaving the cell dark. A bluish-tinted light poured in from the hall.

I hugged my thin blanket to my body and poured my soul into a silent prayer.

***

The next morning after breakfast, I tried to ask Egor what a pretrial detention facility was.

He shook his head as if he didn't understand.

"Did you ever go before a judge or have a trial for your crime?"

"Nyet. I was put in here as soon as I arrived. I didn't know I was to receive a trial or go before a judge. I thought this was how it was done."

His answer troubled me. I glanced at the tally marks near his bed. He'd been here almost three hundred days with no trial.

Egor handed me the scriptures. "Come, read."

I took the scriptures from him but felt the heaviness of his situation as much as my own. I stared at the closed book in front of me.

"Every disadvantage has an advantage, Stareyshina. It does no good to dwell on what can never be. Come, read."

I could see absolutely no advantage to being in prison. I opened the book at random and began to read in Alma 37.

"35 O, remember, my son, and learn wisdom in thy youth; yea, learn in thy youth to keep the commandments of God.

"36 Yea, and cry unto God for all thy support; yea, let all thy doings be unto the Lord, and whithersoever thou goest let it be in the Lord; yea, let all thy thoughts be directed unto the Lord; yea, let the affections of thy heart be placed upon the Lord forever.

"37 Counsel with the Lord in all thy doings, and he will direct thee for good; yea when thou liest down at night lie down unto the Lord, that he may watch over you in your sleep; and when thou risest in the morning let thy heart be full of thanks unto God; and if ye do these things, ye shall be lifted up at the last day." I stopped reading. I remembered Kaufman's blessing he'd given me when I'd been sick, how he'd said I was here to *learn wisdom*. I never told Kaufman, but that was a line from my patriarchal blessing.

"Egor, what does *learn wisdom in thy youth* mean to you?"

He scratched at his beard. "I suppose it means learn while you are young. Then there is time to modify the future. Learning when you are old—well, sometimes it is too late to change. There is a saying, 'Wisdom is in the head, not the beard.' Now that I have a very long beard, I know that to be true."

That made sense—unless you were stuck in a prison cell for the rest of your life. Then there was no future to modify, nothing to learn. "I was always taught that those older than me were wiser," I said.

"Hmm. I don't think that is a popular belief here," he said. "At least, it wasn't my experience. Ukrainians are good at giving advice but maybe not at receiving it. Myself included."

He smiled a slow, thoughtful smile. Seeing a Ukrainian smile was such a rare gesture—it hit me what a gift it was. It was a sign that Egor considered me a close friend. I returned it, a silent prayer of gratitude for him. Then I stared back down at what we'd read. "According to this verse, *learning wisdom in thy youth* is learning to keep the commandments of God."

Egor nodded. "Da, that would definitely change the future of a young man."

I thought of the commandments. Which ones had I struggled with? To *not bear false witness* popped in my head. How much easier it would have been for everyone if I'd kept that commandment in high school. Or if I'd just told Angela to throw her own eggs. Maybe God had put those words in there to keep me from making that huge mistake—and I'd never noticed until now when it was too late.

"I like those verses," Egor said. "Read them again."

I read them again and again until I could hear the words and meanings in my head almost as well as English.

Egor sighed. "Maybe *learning wisdom* is trusting the Lord will guide us in the right direction. You pray to God every night, Stareyshina? Not just at mealtimes with me?"

I nodded. "Every night."

"And every morning?"

"Da."

"Then maybe it is more than just my poor skin that is protecting us. Keep praying. Maybe I will pray too. It's not too late for me, even though I am not young?"

I swallowed a lump in my throat. "The Lord says it's never too late." I looked down at the verses again and repeated them again and again until I could almost do it from memory.

That night, I explained to Egor how to say a personal prayer, and I watched him fold his arms, and kneel on the floor beside his cot, his head bent, his lips silently moving.

I climbed onto my cot and repeated the words to the scripture verses in my mind, even though I already had dozens of times. It kept thoughts of Brett and Kaufman, and hopeless thoughts that I may never get out of prison, at bay.

The verses were my new white handbook: relying on the Lord. I said a prayer of gratitude for them and apologized for not being wise in the past, wishing with all my heart I'd prevented the stupid things I'd done.

The Spirit filled my mind and heart, and I felt a powerful surge of peace and joy. A singular thought filled my mind and heart: *the plan never was to be perfect.*

I thought about what President Meyers had said about how this life was for *becoming.* He'd said I was only a failure if I didn't learn.

An image of companionship study came to mind, with Kaufman and I next to the oven, reviewing the plan of salvation: where we came from and where we were going. In the middle of it was earth life. We had drawn a big circle that represented the earth and a big heart in the middle with a line attaching it to a stick figure meant to represent Jesus Christ.

But now I felt we should have drawn the heart bigger. *Christ* was the plan. God already knew I wasn't going to be perfect. Maybe the verse should have read: *learn wisdom* from *your youth*, I thought. Maybe those words weren't just to caution me about Brett—which clearly I hadn't heeded. Maybe the Lord knew I would desperately need that phrase, and those verses, *now*.

The lights switched off, and I could hear the voices of other prisoners echoing and bouncing off the walls; someone sobbed loudly.

Move forward, not backward. That was the advice I'd given Kaufman. I tried not to think about the ways he was moving forward while I sat helplessly. Instead, I repeated the verse again and held it close inside my heart like a fire to warm me in the cold.

"FOOD," THE PRISON GUARD YELLED.

I bent down to pick up the two metal plates. They were cold, just like I knew the gray lentil concoction living inside them would be. I carried one over to Egor, who sat on the cot, wrapped in his blanket. I wrapped my blanket around me and sat next to him on his bed. The days had turned colder, and the nights had become almost unbearable. It was the beginning of November now. We heard coughing almost incessantly, echoing down the white halls.

There were twenty-five tally marks behind my circle now. President Meyers had come to visit me three times. I put a dot at the top of the tally marks on those days. He had no good news, although he was hopeful my trial would happen soon.

I didn't think about the food's texture or flavor; I only ate.

Egor's dish, however, sat untouched next to him. He stared at the open scriptures, a crease between his eyes. After a few minutes, he looked up. "This King Benjamin is not like the kings I know," he said. "Listen. 'Learn wisdom that ye may learn that when ye are in the service of your fellow beings ye are only in the service of your God.' There it is again. 'Learn wisdom.'" He set the scriptures down and rubbed his arms as if they hurt. "He thinks being a king is about serving people. Ha! That is not wisdom! That has never happened! It is a child's tale." He picked up his bowl and scowled as he took a bite.

I knew responding might agitate him more, but I did it anyway. "Sometimes putting someone else's needs above ourselves is better. Sometimes we should face the pain ourselves instead of sending it to someone else to take for us."

"You're still wishing you'd taken the beating instead of that other prisoner? Still? Regret, regret. Maybe next time you hear someone screaming, you should call out for the guards to get you instead! Bah! You're just as crazy as King Benjamin."

He dropped his spoon in the bowl, splashing a bit of soup. "He says when we serve others, we are serving God. But he says if we serve God, we are still *unprofitable servants*. What is the point of serving God if it gets us nowhere?" He shook his head and scrunched up his face as if the thought itself were sour.

I had never seen Egor this restless. I tried to tread lightly. "We aren't perfect; therefore, we are always in God's debt. Jesus Christ is the answer. He paid that price for our sin."

"For everyone? He paid for everyone's sins?"

I nodded, not quite sure where Egor was going.

"Then why do we work hard and serve others? What good does that do us if everyone is already sin-free through Christ?"

Sometimes Egor gave me such a headache. "They aren't free of sin unless they repent. The Atonement is for everyone, but we must ask for it. He asks us to keep His commandments. We show our love and devotion to Him when we follow those commandments. And then he blesses us."

Egor stopped eating and stared. "Do you try to follow the commandments?"

"Da, of course I try."

"And has He blessed you?" He gestured to the cell.

"Da," I said firmly.

He shook his head. "And does He curse us when we do not obey His commandments?" Egor asked. This time I wasn't sure how to answer, but Egor had more. "You have tried to live a good life, yet you were put in this prison cell by mistake. *A curse*. It's as if you've been *cursed* for obeying commandments rather than blessed. So why keep the commandments if it will bring a curse?"

I stared at the last drops in my dish, my appetite gone. My mind had spun similar circles, like Egor's, wondering why—why. It never did any good; it only left me feeling bitter inside, and the darkness could more easily engulf me.

Egor was quiet. He knew his words had affected me. Too many thoughts had been weighing on my mind, unresolved. President hadn't been to see me in eight days. Was I forgotten? Cursed?

I stood and took the plates back to the cell door so the guards could pick them up later, but this time I returned to my own bed. Egor continued to say nothing. We did not always need words to know when we needed a break from each other.

I lay on my bed and stared at the ceiling. Absently, I rubbed the thick stubble on my face. It was easy to feel neglected. I hadn't showered. I was still wearing my FFA T-shirt, my gym pants becoming worn and falling loose around my diminishing waist. To say I smelled awful was an understatement. When President Meyers said it would be hard to follow the mission rules, he wasn't joking—especially when it came to being clean.

I looked at my life like a balance. Was life a tally sheet? Just as long as those good things outnumbered the bad, I'd be blessed?

I sighed, remembering what President said all lessons in life pointed to: *love.*

I turned my head and watched Egor. He was lying on his cot, but I could see his eyes were open, staring at the nothingness above us. "Life is about becoming," I said. "Not about earning blessings."

Egor turned his head toward me. "What?"

I rolled over and up onto my elbows, my cot squeaking. "God doesn't think we should be only a little more good than bad, then rewards us or curses us. Life is not a scale and if you are a little more good than bad, you are safe and won't ever have hardships. Life is about changing into something different, becoming something better. That is what Jesus wants. He wants us to need Him, love Him."

I put a hand on my chest. "It's about love. Jesus wants us to let Him inside and allow Him to change us. That's why we have the commandments, to help us know *how.* That is why we serve, like King Benjamin, to show love, increase love. That is how we let Jesus inside, by choosing to love other people. Then God changes us—not what is happening around us—but what is happening inside us."

Egor stared at me as if I were speaking a different language. Maybe I was. "Do you understand?" I asked.

"Stareyshina, where did you learn to preach like that? Your ideas— I've never heard them before. Are all Mormon preachers like you?"

I wasn't sure what to say. "I guess so. Except—well—they shower more."

"Da! But the showers here are not a thing to look forward to!" He laughed a coarse laugh until his eyes were streaming. Then a fit of coughs forced him to stop and breathe. He shook his head. "Laughing is the best medicine. I feel cured of my grumpy mood."

I repeated the verses I'd memorized from Alma 37 out loud. When I finished, I looked at Egor.

"Your favorite," he said. "I think you have learned much *wisdom,* Stareyshina. And your accent is becoming very good."

"It is my teacher," I said, smiling at him.

"Ah, yes, the scriptures are a good teacher." He grinned. "And they never shower."

THE NEXT DAY, TWO GUARDS approached our cell. They opened the doors, their guns out and ready. The sun was barely rising through our barred window.

"*Dush!*"—*shower*—they yelled. "Stand up. Hurry. We don't have all day."

We scrambled off our cots and followed the guards out to the line of men gathering down the hall outside a door. Egor and I took our place in the back of the long line of navy-blue jumpsuits. I stared at the shaved heads, which contrasted with Egor's stringy, long hair and my shagginess.

Some of the men stared back at us as we stood in line—I'm sure we were a sight.

"Have you done this before?" I whispered to Egor.

"Da," he said. "A month ago."

"And they didn't shave your hair?"

"They call me shramy, remember? They don't want to touch me."

"Egor," I said quietly, "it is necessary I keep my underclothing. It is holy."

He looked at me, surprise on his face. "Your underclothing is holy?"

"Da. What do I do?"

"There is so much to Mormons I still don't understand." He turned his back to me, but I could tell he was thinking, processing.

We inched forward in line as two men exited the bathroom area, their heads wet, their clothes fresh. Two guards accompanied them down the hall. I counted the men in front of us. Twenty-two. How long until it would be our turn? Mere minutes went by before two more men exited the bathroom, their heads wet. Again, we moved forward.

"*Sotrudnik*,"—*officer*—Egor said. "My prison mate here tells me his underwear is holy." Then he chuckled.

I felt my face turn red, embarrassed. What was Egor doing? The guard stepped closer to us, and fear shot through me.

"Holy?" The guard smiled. "I have never heard of holy underwear."

"Have you heard of Mormons?"

"Da, old man, but Mormons are American preachers. They do not end up here."

"Well, this one has—probably by mistake. He has the holy underwear Mormons wear."

The guard was quiet before he whispered, "By mistake?" His question was a threat.

I did not move a muscle or breathe.

Egor didn't seem to notice. "Are there rules about wearing holy underwear in prison?" Now some of the men in line who were listening laughed. My concern shifted from myself to Egor. "Is there place for religion in prison? He has scriptures to read—but his underwear?" Egor smiled at the men in front of us, including them in the joke.

The guard took several steps toward Egor and held up a large cross tattooed on the back of his wrist that moved up his forearm. "Old man," he sneered, "holy relics are not a joke. Do you believe in God?"

My legs quaked under me, and I made a conscious effort to stop them from shaking. I wished Egor had stayed quiet. I wished I'd never told him.

Egor rolled up his sleeve, revealing his splotchy, red rash. "I do not wear a cross, only sickness. I *should* believe in God since I may see Him soon."

The guard recoiled in disgust and took several steps back. "No wonder your hair looks like you're dead. Your atheism and shramy skin will make very fitting company for your Mormon cellmate. Keep your underwear—both of you. And get to the back of line so no one has to share your water."

Others moved in front, shooting us looks of disgust, but no one dared touch us. The guard moved away, but my eyes would not leave him, and my heart would not slow. I would have taken my garments off and handed them over before ever doing what Egor had.

***

The water from the showers had been ice cold.

When we got back, I tried to warm myself by running in place and doing jumping jacks. "You were right." I breathed. "A shower here is nothing to look forward to."

Egor wrapped his blanket around himself and yawned. "You're making me tired just watching you."

"Come," I motioned with my hand. "I want to show you American push-ups and sit-ups. We have been lazy here."

Egor rolled his eyes. "Heaven help us. The young chicken fears he'll never be a rooster if he doesn't strut and cluck and flap his wings."

I laughed. "The movement helps fight the cold. And it makes me feel happier—less depressed. Try it."

"Depressed? This is you depressed?"

I ran in place again. Then I stopped and rubbed the fabric on my arms. "This new suit is much warmer than my T-shirt."

"All right." Egor stood slowly from his cot. "Your depression is killing me. Show me how to do an American push-up, which I fear is the same as a Ukrainian one."

I grinned, then dropped to the floor to demonstrate a push-up. I could do only a few before my arms protested. Had I really become so weak in so little time? Panting hard, I moved to sit-up position. Egor got down and mimicked me. Then we ran in place for a while. Egor stopped before I did and sat on his cot and watched.

When I felt sufficiently tired, I stretched my body, remembering from gym class all the ways I could stretch my legs, torso, arms, and back. Egor seemed to think it looked acceptable, so he joined me. We took our time. It was almost like having a purpose—but not quite.

I finished and sat on my cot. The exertion had done wonders. "Don't you feel more alive now, Egor?"

"Nyet." He huffed. "I feel deader." He went to laugh, but it turned into a cough. After a minute of coughing, I started to worry that it might be more than just a shortness of breath. We heard the sickness surrounding us in the cells night and day now. Maybe Egor and I would be next.

He took several breaths, then sat on his own cot. "Your depression seems cured now. You are almost too happy for someone who is stuck in prison for a crime you didn't do. Maybe you really did steal that ring."

"You know I didn't."

"Da," he said after a moment. "I know you didn't. You're not smart enough."

"Ha."

"Maybe you are starting to like prison life?"

I blew out. "It could be worse."

His eyes widened. "Really? How?"

"Well, you are good company, Egor. What if I'd been stuck with some-one . . . weak?"

"Weak? The shower made you crazy. I'm probably the weakest man in this prison."

I shook my head. "That's untrue. You spoke to the guards so I could keep my undergarments—I was afraid, and you were brave. Why did you approach him like that? I thought you'd gone mad."

Egor sighed. "I saw his tattoo. Prison guards take pride in their tattoos. Like a relic to ward off evil spirits. And he likely needs it, as he's beating helpless prisoners for fun. They say the devil likes to hide behind a cross. I've found that's especially true here."

"How did you know he wouldn't beat you?"

"I didn't. I just made sure it wasn't you."

I swallowed, all humor gone.

"Nyet, Stareyshina, I won't have you feeling bad again, like for that poor man who took your beating. My chances were higher of avoiding it, with my skin. And as he said, I am punishment enough as a cellmate." He pushed his bony fingers together at the tips and stared at them.

"You told me the guards prey upon the weak here, but they leave you alone. *That* is proof you are not weak. Strength is not always physical."

His eyes went moist, and he covered them with his hands. He took a deep breath, then said, "You are my only friend left in this world."

His reaction surprised me.

"My wife and children are dead. I had a brother, but I don't know where he is. I thought several times about finding ways to leave this life myself, but I was a coward—not brave, like you say. Then you came. With your book. It has changed how I think, how I feel. I'm not afraid anymore of being alone."

He moved his hands from his face to his chest and looked at me. "I feel inside, like you said, that Christ is in me, changing me. I'm not afraid to be alone because He is with me. Maybe it is not too late for an old man to change?"

"Never too late," I said, my voice thick with emotion.

He looked up at the ceiling. "One day I know I will meet God. He will ask me what I did with my life. He will ask me what I did with one of his servants from America, sent to preach. I want to tell Him"—he swallowed, emotional—"I want to tell Him I did all I could. Those were my thoughts in the shower line. I know I said King Benjamin was a fool, but I guess I have adopted his ways."

I smiled, then reached out and patted Egor on the knee.

He wiped his face with the sleeve of his shirt. "You have saved me. There is another saying, 'Who gives in need, gives double.' That is what you have done for me, Stareyshina."

21

THE COUGHING AROUND OUR CELL grew in magnitude, heard at all hours of the night and day. Around a week after our shower, Egor developed a fever. A few days later, I too began coughing. Then came aching joints and sore lungs. No doctor was sent for; no one asked how we were. Just like our hair, we were left alone. And not just by the guards. It had been three weeks since I'd seen President Meyers.

Egor seemed especially ill. Every day, his cough got worse, not better. I took his bowl from him after the evening meal and set it inside mine next to the slotted door. Then I retreated to my cot and blanket. Egor looked like he was asleep again. He hadn't asked me to read to him all day; he had only slept. I had forced him to eat every meal.

At what point did I demand a guard get him to a doctor? Would they listen to me? Surely prisoners had some sort of rights. But then I feared the guards would be the fastest route to death. Sleep was probably the best thing for Egor—that was what I told myself anyway—but I was terrified I'd soon be sharing a cell with a dead man.

I'd seen corpses of cows before. I'd seen them through their different stages of decomposing. I'd seen them bloated to twice the size they were in life, but I'd never seen a dead human. I'd never been to anyone's funeral. Death and sickness were something I thought about only in terms of head of cattle and whether it meant I'd be able to afford gas in my truck.

Here, death was a smell, a temperature, an absence of sound. I heard it sometimes in the night, a silence where there was once a wheeze, and then I'd crouch in a ball in my cot and worry. What would happen if Egor died? It was too scary to contemplate. He was my safety net.

I'd spent six weeks with Kaufman as a companion, struggling to learn the language. Now I'd spent almost an equal amount of time with Egor, and he'd taught me more Russian than the MTC and Kaufman combined times ten. Although, I was more aware every day that it wasn't just Egor; it was the Lord. It was the scriptures. It was feeling so desperate my brain had homed in on the language like a lifeline. Something I'd never had to do with Kaufman.

Egor coughed in his sleep, his body shaking in his attempt to get air. I sat up, ready to help him. Egor rolled over. "Stareyshina," he whispered, "can you pray with me?"

"Da." I got out of bed and knelt in front of him on the hard ground and waited, but he had fallen asleep again. The thought came that I could give him a blessing; that was what he needed. But fear instantly filled me with doubt. I'd never given anyone a blessing. I'd never even stood in the circle or assisted anyone.

I rubbed my aching head and shivered. I was missing so many life experiences.

I'd been given blessings before. Not by my dad but by bishops and home teachers, the patriarch, my stake president. And Kaufman. Maybe I could remember how it went.

Slowly, I set my shaking hands on Egor's head. He didn't stir. I decided I would just say a prayer that sounded similar to a blessing and hope it worked. I stated his first name only and told him that with the priesthood I held, I wanted to give him a blessing. Then I prayed to my Heavenly Father and asked Him to spare Egor, to help him heal, to give him comfort and peace, and to bless him with increased conviction and faith. The words entered my mind and heart, and I knew all would be well.

With tears streaming from my eyes, I closed the prayer and climbed back into my cot.

Egor continued to sleep, but inside, I felt different. Peace settled over me for the first time in days.

I woke the next morning to a guard hitting our bars and yelling for us to get up.

I pushed my blanket off and scrambled over to Egor's cot. Shaking him, I said, "Egor, wake up." His eyes fluttered open.

"Nyet, not the old man," the guard said. "Just you. Bring any possessions you have."

The guard walked out of eyesight, probably waiting for an assistant to unlock the gate. I grabbed the scriptures from under my cot, my heart thumping. I shook Egor by the shoulder. "Egor—Egor." He opened his eyes again and focused on me. "I think I'm leaving."

I helped him sit up, his thin shoulders shaking. I couldn't leave him like this—but what could I do? "Here," I said, handing him the large Bible. "We haven't finished. You keep it."

He reached out and clutched it with both hands, his knuckles as ashen as his face. "I don't think I will live to read it."

"Nyet," I said firmly, "You will. You need to."

"God bless you, Stareyshina. I will miss you."

When the guards opened our cell, I squeezed his hand, then stood. They didn't handcuff me. I looked back at Egor from outside the bars. He waved a feeble hand, and I had to blink several times. I swallowed my emotions. I didn't want the guards to see me cry.

We entered a part of the prison that looked very unlike a prison. I couldn't stop staring at the foyer with large windows, cushioned chairs, even a potted plant. The room gave no hint of the suffering that went on beyond the metal door I'd just come through.

We stood outside a large wooden door, and I held my book as a guard handcuffed my hands in front of me. It was uncomfortable, and I knew I wouldn't be able to hold the book for too long. I prayed it would not fall. I doubted anyone would pick it up for me.

They opened the door to a large room. There was a platform containing one long table, where three men sat. Below the platform were more chairs. I recognized President Meyers sitting in one. He stood as I walked in, his face etched with worry. Next to him was a man I didn't recognize but who wore a similar suit coat, white shirt, and tie. And then there was a third person, a middle-aged woman wearing a bright-colored sweater and dark pants.

At the back of the room was a large black cage.

No one had to tell me who it was for and why I was here. My day of trial had come.

I looked at President, his expression somber. I was nervous under his gaze. He'd stayed away so long. Was it because he doubted my innocence? Did he see me as a prisoner now? I'd been a prisoner for more time than I'd been a missionary in Ukraine. My beard was scratchy, and my greasy hair fell in my eyes.

The guards guided me to the cage. Next to it was a familiar person, wearing a black uniform and fur hat. I recognized his build and the sneer plastered on his face. He was the same guard who had beat me my first night in prison. He opened the door of the cage. I tried not to tremble as I passed him. He patted his gun and glared at me before locking me in.

The man seated in the center stood, his chair scraping against the floor. His large belly hung out over the table. "My name is Vadik Mikhailov. I will be running the proceedings of Neal Christensen. These two are my associates." He pointed to a tall, thin, balding man on his left and said, "Abbas Fedorov," then to his right, "and Dakarai Lebedev." The man on his right—Dakarai— glared out underneath bushy gray eyebrows.

My hands were still handcuffed, and there was no place to sit. I felt the book begin to slip. The sound it made when it fell made everyone jump and look at me. The heavy-set man glared from across the room and cleared his throat loudly.

The woman stood and said in Russian, "I'm Anna Kozlov, an ambassador with the American embassy. This is President Conrad Meyers and Elder Jonathan Todd, both from America. Do we have an interpreter for Mr. Christensen?"

The man sat back in his chair. He gave a small smile. "You may interpret if you wish."

"I was called here as a representative for this American, as administrator in international public affairs. Not as an interpreter. You should have one as part of this court."

"We all know Russian, *miss.*" He emphasized the word as if it annoyed him.

Her back tensed, and I watched her angrily whisper something to President Meyers. President twisted in his seat and looked back at me. "Do you need an interpreter, Stareyshina?"

In Russian, I said, "I think I can understand the general idea." Then in English, "But perhaps you can give me a rundown at the end?"

My mission president repeated what I'd said to the men at the front of the room, who all looked unconcerned and rather bored.

The heavy-set man waved a hand. "As you wish, of course. Anything for the American who comes here and insults our country."

"Or is wrongfully accused by your country," President Meyers retorted. His neck and ears had turned borsch-red.

The woman gave President Meyers a sharp look, then turned toward the three men at the table. The man with bushy eyebrows glared even more, and the thick man in the center shook his head as if to say, *You should not have said that.* I wished very much President hadn't said it either.

The thin bald man on the end stood and began telling the details of my case. How I'd been captured on surveillance camera stealing the priceless ring and how it had not only angered those at the museum but the Russian government it was on loan from, a very precarious relationship as it was. He then asked if my church was trying to start a war. This could be considered an act of treason, which would be thirty years minimum in prison.

I waited for the woman to contradict him, to tell him there was no way I was trying to start a war, but she didn't. She only listened. A coldness crept into my chest as thoughts of being in prison for thirty years pulsed through me. I was a foreigner. This was not America, a place where I was innocent until proven guilty. There was no jury here. This group would determine my fate.

"This also was found in his possession the night he was captured," the man said, holding up the train ticket. "Further evidence of his guilt."

President Meyers did not turn back to look at me. Elder Todd said next to him, "Conrad Meyers questioned Stareyshina Neal Christensen as to why he was in possession of the train ticket. He was honest and told him he had planned to use it to return home early from his mission. His family are cattle ranchers and are in need of his help in America."

The thin man standing let the ticket drop and glared at Elder Todd. "*Honest.*" He smirked. "Tell me, as a cattle rancher, did he know how to tie knots then, Conrad Meyers?"

President Meyers hesitated. "I don't see why this information matters."

"Answer the question."

"Da, I suppose he did. It is not unusual to know how to tie knots. Is it? Neal?" He looked back at me.

I didn't answer.

"Why is this relevant?" President asked the man next to him in the suit and then the woman, but neither answered.

The tall man on the end stood and moved toward a small TV. He pushed play. A fuzzy scene showed someone with short, dark hair, putting some sort of nylon netting over his head. He wore a white shirt with a black rectangular name badge on the breast pocket. He cut through the glass case and removed the ring. He turned toward the camera once as he was escaping. The camera slowed, and although his face was distorted, I caught sight of what looked like one of my ties and my name badge.

I reacted. In Russian, I yelled, "What? That's not me!"

The guard smacked my bars with his weapon, growling a warning. I moved away from him to the opposite side of the cage and squeezed my lips together, forcing my face to be expressionless, my heart pounding.

"Have you seen this?" the heavier man in the middle asked President Meyers.

"Da," he answered. "I have seen it."

"The guards were drugged, tied up with rope and knots."

President Meyers sounded frustrated. "How can a knot condemn a man?"

"The rope was from America, the packaging thrown in the wastebasket. You should not have been so careless, Neal Christensen."

"Do you have any proof of that?" the woman asked. She shook her head, frustrated, and again whispered angrily to President Meyers.

"There are other Americans in Ukraine. There are others who could have purchased rope from the United States," Elder Todd said.

"Well, what about the name tag? How do you disprove that? That is Neal Christensen's name badge, is it not?"

No one said anything.

"Black souls wear white shirts, Neal Christensen," the man sitting in the middle said. "I think there is no point in going on with this case. Are we ready to make a verdict?"

"I would like to know if Neal could be taken home to the United States." President Meyers looked at the woman for support. "He could serve out his sentence there."

She nodded. "Taking this man home to finish his sentence in America would save our country money, it would rid us of this man, and foil any other designs he has on the country. It would be a good move internationally in our relationship with the United States. I am in favor of sending him home to a prison there."

"Where he can be freed? The United States government would put this man in prison and pay for him to be jailed for a crime he committed here?"

"Da," she answered simply.

"Nyet, I think that would not favor this country. We are still searching for the ring; it has not been recovered, and until it is found, this thief will not be going home."

"What about the prison camp in Donetsk? Is it possible for Neal to go there?" President Meyers asked. "It would be closer for me to visit him. He is a good, strong worker."

The large man pinched his lips together, then conversed with the other men in hushed tones. The silent man with bushy eyebrows nodded.

"There is not a lot of room in Donetsk, but the other prisons are certainly just as full." He smiled, revealing a wide space between his front teeth. "We can always squeeze in one more. He seems strong and would be more useful to our country making shoes than rotting here. As it happens, we have a van leaving for Donetsk within the hour and a vacant seat." He looked at each of the men seated next to him. "Are we agreed?"

"I move to convict Neal Christensen as guilty to the charge of stealing priceless artifacts in a country not his own," the thin man said.

"I second that," the man with bushy eyebrows said in a gruff voice.

The large man in the middle nodded. "Then we are agreed. The sentence is twenty years in Donetsk."

I felt all of my breath leave at once. President Meyers stood and mopped his face with his hands. I was a prisoner—condemned. *Twenty years.* No more waiting.

No one needed to explain to me what had happened. I'd heard every word. Like an animal, I began to pace from one side to another, overcome with anguish, hatred, fear. President Meyers and the man in the suit approached the cage. He stuck a hand through the spaces between the bars, and I stopped.

"Neal," he beckoned for me to come to him. The guard took a step forward, but President glared at him. "I'm going to pray with him," he said firmly. He placed a hand on my shoulder, and the other man in the suit placed a hand on my opposite shoulder. In English he said to me, "This is Elder Todd. He is the area authority over Ukraine. He came to support you today. You must be strong. No matter what."

"But, President," I sputtered in Russian, "you heard them; you saw that video. That wasn't me!"

"Neal, be calm. Don't do anything stupid," President said.

"Anything stupid?" I said in English, but it didn't feel right. I switched to Russian again. "Do you know what I've been through here?"

President's face went white. "What has happened? They said they would leave you alone."

"Oh, da, they left us alone. My friend—he's dying. He might be dead already. He is sick with no care—and now I will be gone. He will die. Is that what you wanted, President? For us to be abandoned?"

President dropped his hand and turned to look at the administrators up front.

The man laughed. "More lies? He can say whatever he wants. It will not hurt me."

"Egor needs me!" I pleaded. "And you have sent me to Donetsk. Why?"

"Neal." He put a hand on my head and smoothed it like he would a wild colt's. "I'll take care of it; don't worry. I'll help him." He rubbed my shoulder. "You must be calm, Neal." He repeated my name, as if to reassure me. "Stareyshina," he said sadly. He looked me over and shook his head. "You're skin and bones." He glanced at Elder Todd, then back to me. "They would not have kept you with Egor. This place is not where you need to be. Transfers are always hard. We learn to love the people we serve."

My eyes filled with tears, but I couldn't wipe them. I dropped my head to my chest.

"Donetsk will be better for you than here. They will keep you busy. Have you heard 'a dog in the chase doesn't notice the fleas'? I have spoken to people and made arrangements there."

I looked up. "You already planned for me to go there? You knew this would happen?"

"Nyet—of course I didn't know—or want—this to happen, but I needed to have a plan just in case." Lower and in English, he said, "This is not a good prison. It is not a safe place. You probably know this better than me."

My eyes stung. Da, I knew.

"I will help Egor, I promise. There are things I've learned I can do. I'm sorry, Neal. I did my best. Believe me, I did all I could. In Donetsk, I will not leave you alone. I know you've been through so much. The Lord loves you. We will not stop fighting for you."

I nodded at him, filled with hope by his last words.

President nodded to Elder Todd. Their grip on my shoulders tightened, drawing me closer to them, the bars between us. Elder Todd gave me a blessing. He told me the Lord was pleased with my friendship with Egor and that the Lord was aware of him. He said to continue to stand as a witness of Christ and to cleave to my scriptures. That I'd been sent to Ukraine for a special mission at this time and that I would learn about it little by little. I needed to have patience and endurance.

And then, at the end, I heard the words that I was released as an official LDS missionary in the Ukraine Donetsk Mission.

I STEPPED INTO THE VAN, still handcuffed. There were seven of us sitting side by side. I didn't know how long it would take to get to Donetsk. I didn't ask. I really didn't care.

President had let me down. The Church had let me down. I had even left my Book of Mormon, forgotten in my cage—so much for *cleaving* to my scriptures, like Elder Todd had said to do in his blessing.

My assigned seat in the van was in the middle of the second row, sandwiched between two other prisoners. We were all handcuffed. There were no seat belts, not even for the driver. The man to my left, next to the window, shoved me roughly for more space, knocking me into the man on my right and causing him to slip partway off the bench. He pushed himself back on, which shoved me into the man by the window, and so it continued. The two of them spat and snarled at each other, with me in between as a weapon, until the guard threatened to shoot us all.

I wished he would.

Inside, I was dead. I could not fathom being sentenced to live as a prisoner in Ukraine for twenty years, released as a missionary. Things like this weren't supposed to happen to LDS missionaries. This wasn't how missions were supposed to end.

It began to snow outside; large flakes covered the van windows, as well as fog from the warmth of our bodies. Hours later, we arrived in Donetsk. The van pulled into a gated courtyard, and we were pulled one by one from the van and marched at gunpoint through another courtyard and into a white cement building.

Once inside, a new process took place. I was taken to a prison doctor, who checked my entire body for everything from tuberculosis to lice. I passed, but she did say I was experiencing a nutrition deficit. She fed me a warm meal and gave me some vitamins. I didn't feel like eating very much, but she insisted I eat it all.

She then sent me down the hall with a guard, who instructed me to line up next to a group of around fifteen men standing along the hallway. I wasn't sure what we were waiting for at first, but then I saw one of the prisoners going down the line, shaving heads. When each man finished getting his haircut, he entered a nearby door.

When it was my turn, I leaned forward as the other men had and watched as large chunks of hair fell onto the cement floor. I was the last man, and when the prisoner finished, he immediately began sweeping up the piles of hair. When it was my turn, I opened the door and walked through it as the others had.

The room, several degrees cooler, was of the same cement floor as the hall, but it smelled damp and sour. Showers covered the back half of the wall; toilet stalls missing doors covered some of the side wall. There was one sink. A man stood at it, shaving, staring at his reflection in the cloudy mirror.

One of the prisoners was collecting clothing from the other men. I watched him walk into an adjacent room filled with laundry machines, and when he came out, he wore only a towel around his waist.

He approached me. "You're new? Take off your old uniform and put it in that bin there." He pointed to a container near the door.

I swallowed. "I want to keep my underclothes. They're important to me."

He glared. "Of course. Do you think underwear is free? Wash them yourself. Washing day is assigned with the rest of your cell."

I wasn't sure what he meant but did as he said and threw my old uniform in the bin near the door. The man at the sink was finished shaving, and he walked over and handed me the razor before entering one of the toilet stalls.

I rinsed the blade under the sink faucet, then stared at my reflection in the blurry mirror. I wouldn't have recognized myself. My jaw, even under the beard, looked much narrower, my cheeks sunken in slightly. There was a large scar near my left eye, and there was something different in my expression that wasn't there before my mission. Something that said a smile was foreign and that life was about hardship, not joy. I looked like the people who rode the buses.

I looked Ukrainian.

It scared me.

I took several deep breaths, refusing to lose it. I shaved as well as I could with the unfamiliar blade, which reminded me more of my Scout pocketknife than any razor I'd used. When I finished, a guard took it from me, and I found a vacant shower. The water was the same shocking cold I was used to. There was no soap. Maybe that was something that wasn't free either.

My new uniform was gray-blue and white striped, immediately reminding me of Holocaust movies. I was also given a pair of thick boots that fit loosely, and a heavy, utility-like gray coat. No socks.

When I finished, a guard took me to a desk where another prisoner was working. "Check him in, Duma," he said.

Duma appeared to be in his midtwenties. A black tattoo covered one side of his neck, his hair a dirty-blond stubble. Intense green eyes met mine.

He was familiar, but how?

"Name," he asked, along with a slew of other questions, like my birthdate, nationality, religion, etc. When I said LDS, he gave me another sharp look-over.

"Mormon," I said.

"Da, I know what *LDS* means. Crime?" He stared at me, waiting.

I swallowed. "They say my crime is stealing."

"You are American, LDS, eighteen years old? It can't be. A *stareyshina* from America?"

I nodded.

His eyes pierced mine, and he whispered, "Unbelievable."

A guard came forward. "Where am I taking him?"

Duma cleared his throat. "Cell 518. Upstairs five flights and . . ."

"Da, I know my way around the prison, *dog*." He grabbed me by the arm. Another guard took up the rear with a gun.

I turned once to look back at Duma and saw he was still watching me with those light-green, familiar eyes. How had he known about missionaries?

Up five flights of stairs and down several hallways, I began to see the belly of my new prison. It was so different from what I'd seen in Kramatorsk. The halls had dark-blue walls and yellow lights, the cells marked with a single, private metal door instead of the giant white cages.

We stopped near one of the doors, and the guard put in his key, swinging it inward. Inside, there were three sets of bunk beds, enough for six people, but there was only one man in the room. I heard the door shut behind me, and the lock clicked in place.

The man looked down at me from the top bunk closest to the door, his hair a flaming red. "Are you going to be living here?" he asked, frowning.

I stayed by the door. "It looks that way."

He made an impatient sound. "We are already full. Where do they think you'll sleep?"

I looked around at the empty room, unsure what he meant. "Full? Where are the others?"

"Working, idiot. Why did they send you here? Who was it that sent you?"

I thought of the man with the green eyes and tattoo again. "I think his name was Duma."

"Duma? Are you serious? We are already bulging like a mother pig! And for what? What did you do? Steal potatoes? Insult a police officer?"

I stared at him, trying not to show how nervous I was. I had very little practice communicating with other prisoners, besides Egor. I was sure I'd say the wrong thing. He glared, then turned his back on me.

Several coats hung against the wall, and one pair of boots sat on the floor underneath. I left my own boots on but hung my coat among the others. Carefully, I sat on the bottom bunk farthest from the other inmate. I had no book to read, nothing to do but stare, and after several long minutes of him ignoring me, I was lulled into a secure boredom. It had been a long day, and my belly was fuller than it had been in weeks, so it didn't take long until I was asleep.

I woke to what I first thought was thunder. I sat up and heard something similar to a stampede of cattle moving past our cell door. The lock clicked, and four men clunked through the door. Behind them, I saw the hall filled with others. They dragged their feet and rubbed their necks.

I immediately scrambled off the bed and moved to the back of the room by the window. Three sat on bottom bunks and, without a word, removed their boots and stretched their feet. Two wore socks, one did not. The fourth one went to use the toilet in the corner of the room.

The man without socks sat on the bunk I'd just left. His short, buzzed hair matched his coal-black eyes. Every part of him but his face and ears seemed covered in black tattoos. Even his feet were covered in small pictures. He looked up at me. "What do they call you, eh?" His question startled me but didn't sound angry, like the redhead's had, more just genuinely curious.

"Neal," I said.

"Nil," he repeated. "That is an uncommon name. I am Sergei. Are you staying with us?"

I nodded.

"Where did you come from?"

"Kramatorsk."

"And before that?"

I hesitated. "America."

"Ah, I wondered. You have an accent like an American I met once. Why did they send you here? We have no bed for you."

"*American.*" The redhead sat up and grunted. "I should have known. You're all the same. Pushing your way into places you don't belong. Even here." He spit on the ground. "Russia lovers."

Sergei sighed. "Boris, you are lucky that didn't hit me, or I would have made you eat it. Only you can turn everything into a political argument. I would say it's because you're from Kiev, but I don't want to insult our capital. Will you be back to work tomorrow?"

Boris lay back down on his bed. "Most likely. There is no hiding now that my temperature is gone."

"You could put the thermometer under hot water. I read a book once about a person who did that." Sergei winked at me.

"*Hot water.*" Boris rolled his eyes. "I don't know the last time I felt hot water. Duma is the one who sent this American here."

A boy who looked too young to be in an adult prison hopped onto his top bunk and glared at me. "I won't share—not this time. Not with an American."

"No one said you had to, Gavriil," a large man said, his hair so white and shorn he looked bald. "Maybe you can sleep on the ground and give him your bed instead." He pulled his shirt off, his muscles bulging across his chest, shoulders, and abs. He took a seat in the middle of the floor and flipped through a deck of cards.

Another man joined him on the floor. Although smaller in stature, he had the same muscular bulges in his arms and back. His shaved hair was dark; a tattooed snake slithered up the back of his neck.

The door opened, and Duma walked through, a guard escorting him. Again, the door shut, the lock clicked, and with that one more person, I saw why Boris had grumbled. We were crammed inside like cattle in a truck.

Boris sat up. "Well, Duma? What's the meaning of a seventh person? Have you noticed we only have six beds?"

Duma didn't look at me as he hopped onto the top bunk next to where I stood. Again, I had the impression I knew him from somewhere. He undid his boots and dropped them on the floor. They made a loud thud, which made the card players jump.

"All the cells are full, not just ours. If it weren't him, it would be someone else. And I figured it might as well be him. They're bringing a mat in tonight."

Boris sputtered a string of words I'd never heard before.

"Boris, take a nap. You're so grouchy—like a baby," Sergei said.

Boris stared down Sergei from his bed. "Sergei, I will kill you if I ever get the chance."

"If you did not say that every day, I might actually be afraid," Sergei said.

"There have been pro-Russia demonstrations in Kiev ever since Yanukovych rejected the European Union association agreement," Duma said, as if to change the subject. "Rumor is he pursued a Russian loan bailout to be closer to Russia. Now there are riots everywhere. People have been shoved in here for causing trouble in the streets."

Everyone was quiet for several seconds, as if processing what Duma had said, then Sergei said, "If only it were football season. Then everyone would have something else to think about."

"Da," the big bald man on the floor said. "Then we could listen to the game."

Boris glared. "Riots? How would you know, Duma?"

Duma picked up a magazine and began turning the pages. "I check people in all day and ask them their crime, remember? Plus, I read."

Boris mumbled something about making shoes all day and rolled his eyes.

"Ah," Gavriil said, "the people finally see they should have put Tymoshenko in office instead of that trash Yanukovych."

"Tymoshenko," Sergei muttered like an oath. "The blonde-braided demon."

Boris turned red. "*Angel.* You mean *angel.* She should be our leader! Then she would have stopped giving money to the big bully-brother Russia. We are *Ukrainian*! When will we stop being Russian?"

Sergei shook his head. "She cries and whines, but she can't represent this divided country. She should have stayed in jail."

"You Easterners are all the same," Boris growled. "What about the Russia that has oppressed us? Starved us? Don't you remember the Terror Famine that drove people to cannibalism? Russia denies it even happened. It was to stop our independence! And they continually stop us again and again!"

Sergei clicked his tongue. "You're being dramatic again. All full, Duma? Is that possible?"

Duma looked up from his magazine. "It's a popular place to be."

"Yes, making shoes to please the government. Slave labor," Gavriil said.

"I personally would rather be doing *something* than nothing," the man with the snake tattoo said. "And arguing is a stupid waste of time." He turned to look up at me. "Are you really from America?"

"Of course he is," Duma said, setting his magazine aside. He sat up and dangled his feet off the bed. "Most stareyshiny I've met have been American. Only they wore shirts and ties. How in heaven did you end up here, Stareyshina?" His eyebrows pinched upward with the question, almost like he was in pain, almost like he needed help . . .

He was the lost man from my dreams.

My mouth opened, and I almost shouted it to him, but I stopped myself and swallowed. He existed. He was here in Ukraine. And I had found him.

"Do you speak Russian, American?" Duma asked slower.

I nodded numbly. "Da. A little."

"Did they send you here to find me, then?" He chuckled.

I felt my face turn hot. He couldn't mean God. Had he had the same dreams? "What do you mean?" I asked.

"The tithing money." He smirked. "Those stupid stareyshiny made me a branch president, their religious leader."

The big bald man looked up from the floor, grinning. "They made you their religious leader?" He looked over at the man with the snake tattoo, and they burst out laughing.

I stared at Duma. "You stole the tithing money?"

"Da," he said smugly.

"That's why you're here?"

He laughed as if I'd told a joke. "No. This country does not care about the pitiful tithing money I took. They feel as I do. Any church that makes a man like me president and then hands him money deserves what they get."

The room erupted in laughter.

I wanted to punch Duma—make him stop. There was one woman I knew in our branch in Kramatorsk who regularly went without eating two meals a week just to pay her tithing. I thought of my own parents who had struggled, sometimes years on end, but my dad still paid an honest tithe so my mom could have the blessings of the temple.

"You're a hypocrite," I said.

"A hypocrite, Stareyshina? Have you looked in a mirror lately?"

Again, there was laughter. I had nowhere to sit, nowhere to hide. I ran a hand across my newly shorn head. Duma picked up the magazine again, a pleased smile plastered on his face.

I stood there several minutes, not knowing what to do with myself. I finally sat on the floor, my back against the wall. My mind wandered to that first night I'd had dinner in Kramatorsk with the elders, how Brett had made fun of me and I'd felt that overwhelming feeling of not belonging, that feeling of insecurity, the possibility of being hurt. That seemed so minor, so insignificant compared to what I felt now. If I were to go back to that dinner, I would have no complaints. I would be so grateful and cheerful to be eating, to be warm, safe, and clean. Brett could glare all he wanted. I was ashamed how much I'd taken for granted.

"What was it like in the outside world?" Sergei asked, interrupting my thoughts.

I treaded with caution. "I just came from Kramatorsk, where I stayed in a small cell with another man. We didn't work like you. We never left. But before I was in prison, Ukraine was . . ." *Crowded, impoverished, hard, a bit scary, with a few very kind babushkas.* "Cold. It had gotten very cold." I swallowed, hoping they wouldn't ask me anything else, sure my vision of Ukraine as a foreigner wasn't the Ukraine they were familiar with—but it was all I knew.

"Did you play cards in Kramatorsk?" the big man asked from the floor.

"No. Just read scriptures. The Bible—and the Book of Mormon. But I left my scriptures."

Sergei nodded. "The Bible is the best book in the world."

Boris snorted. "It's for people with no logic."

I was beginning to see Sergei and Boris always took a side, and it was always opposite from each other.

The prison guards laid my mat on the floor at dinnertime, and one of the guards asked, thick with sarcasm, if we'd like some Easter cakes and vodka with that. My cellmates were silent, and I took note. There were a lot of things different here in Donetsk, but some things did not change.

That night, I stared at the dark ceiling from the scratchy mat and thanked God for my blessings. I thanked Him for cellmates who had in all civility not tried to kill me yet. I thanked him for a bed. I prayed for my family. I tried not to think about how my mission had ended, and how the next twenty years would go. Would I ever go home again?

My eyes drifted to the dark figure of Duma sleeping on his bunk. *Duma.* If he hated the Church so much, why had he chosen me to be in his cell? Was he really the same man I'd dreamed about? The Lord couldn't have meant for me to come here and find this thief—this thug—who stole the Lord's money. He'd been baptized, he'd had the gospel, and he'd refused it. I was supposed to teach him? That had been done. His job was to accept or refuse—again, done.

There was nothing left to do but rot in prison together.

MAKING SHOES WAS NOT VERY difficult, just painful and long and hot. It took muscles, repetition, and sometimes hours of sitting or standing. That first week, I learned that sometimes we got dinner—sometimes we didn't. Lunch was some kind of porridge or soup. Every night, we came back exhausted. The nights we didn't get dinner were the hardest nights to sleep. Those were the times I had the hardest time thinking of blessings, and I began to murmur and petition the Lord while my stomach gnawed at itself.

After work, there were around four hours before lights went out. It took about fifteen minutes to walk back to our cell, fifteen minutes to eat, and then I had three and a half hours to stare at the wall. Often, we were asleep before lights out.

I missed my scriptures. I worried about Egor.

We worked six days a week. I heard every group of workers varied on their one day off so the factory was constantly running. Our cell worked Monday through Saturday, with the blessing of the Sabbath off. That was the day we showered and washed our own laundry.

During work, there were times where we talked. I learned Gavriil, the smallest, was my age—eighteen—and had only been there for six months. He was there for stealing a car and setting fire to it. He seemed the most gangster to me but was constantly being laughed at for it, so it didn't do much for the tough-guy reputation he seemed to be going for. He avoided talking to me. Once I heard him mutter religion wasn't in style.

Ivan was the largest of our cellmates, at about six foot three. He was thinner than he should be, but his bones were big, while the rest of us looked like our bones were dissolving. He never said what he'd done to end up incarcerated, but he hated being idle. He always had a deck of cards in his hands, or he was doing push-ups with Trofim, the man with the snake tattoo.

Trofim did everything Ivan did. Trofim had robbed a store years ago
when he was my age and was still angry he'd been caught.

Boris went out of his way to avoid me in the assembly line. Sergei said
not to worry about him; it was just his Irish temper. That earned Sergei a
shove, which Sergei seemed more than happy to return. Boris, I learned, was
not remotely Irish, and was the oldest in our cell, about thirty-five. He was in
prison for vandalizing at an election over ten years ago. His red hair was such
a giveaway that he was the only one caught and sent to prison from his small
pro-Ukrainian group.

Then there was Duma. I learned from the others that he was twenty-six
and had been here three years. I heard the crime that had landed him in prison
was embezzling funds from a small company through a computer system he
helped set up. He had such a clean slate in prison and a quick knack for
picking things up, they'd given him an office job when short-staffed, working
on computers—the very thing he was in prison for. As Sergei put it, "The
thief who stole an *altyn* is hung, and the one who stole a *poltinnik* is praised."

We didn't see him very much, not even on our days off. The others
treated him with respect, laughed at his jokes. I suspected he must wield
some sort of power, working in the office.

I couldn't figure him out, and that bothered me. Often, he kept the
peace between Sergei and Boris in the evenings just by a few words behind
his magazine. He always had a magazine. The front desk lent them to him.
Duma checked one out nightly, dutifully returning it the next day. Often,
he shared knowledge from the outside world.

Out of all my cellmates, Sergei was the one I connected with the most.
He was always kind and never condescending toward me. I wondered at
times if it was because Boris had taken such a decided dislike to me, so
Sergei contrarily liked me.

Sergei was the second oldest in our cell, thirty-one. He had been an artist,
some paintings but mostly tattoo art. He'd also been an alcoholic. About eight
years ago, he had run over a woman with a borrowed car. He said that he
deserved every year he served and would yet serve. Prison had changed him
and his addiction.

When Sunday came, he showed me where the chapel was.

Sundays, after showering and laundry, we could go outside, stay in our
cell, or go to church. I could hardly believe this was true when Sergei first
told me and invited me to go with him. There was a Christian minister
who came and held services for anyone wanting to attend. I learned out
of our small group of attendees, there were Jews, Eastern Orthodox, and

other types of Christians—anyone who wanted to be spiritually edified and uplifted.

Father Michael was a short, balding man who reminded me of Friar Tuck from Disney's *Robin Hood*, only he didn't wear a robe. He wore a black button-down shirt or sometimes a white shirt with a black jacket.

A simple wooden cross adorned a podium at the front of the room, a large Bible open on top. The chapel was small, and Father Michael's voice boomed strong. "Jesus Christ taught all to love God first, then our neighbor. But that is not all," he said. "Christ also taught us to love our enemies. In Matthew chapter 5, it says to 'love your enemies, bless them that curse you, do good to them that hate you and pray for them which despitefully use you, and persecute you . . . For if ye love them which love you, what reward have ye?' It is easy to love those who love us, but those who hate us? Very hard."

The scriptures were like music settling deep into my soul. I had been in Donetsk for six days now, six days without scriptures, and I had missed them so much. The Spirit was there when Father Michael spoke, as if somehow this small room were exempt, separate from the caged world I trudged through daily.

It was my second Sunday when Sergei introduced me to Father Michael after the meeting. The preacher grasped my hand with both of his. "You are most welcome, Nil. In fact, I have been told about you already. It is Stareyshina, isn't it? I have met your Brat Meyers. I'm so pleased you have come."

The sincerity and kindness made my eyes go moist. "Thank you, Father Michael," I said, trying my best to sound respectful.

"I have something for you." Father Michael went over to his podium; the back side was a small bookshelf. "President Meyers couldn't make it himself today, but he gave me this." He pulled out a black book—my *Kniga Mormona*.

I clutched it close to my chest and swallowed my emotion. "Thank you."

He smiled and patted my arm. "I'm to report on how you're doing. And how are you?"

"Better now that you've brought me this," I said, holding up the book. "Tell him he was right." I swallowed. "Things are better here."

"I will tell him," Father Michael said. "He wanted to be here himself, of course, but he is occupied at the moment. There have been riots, the Berkut and other police have been attacked, and a missionary near the south border was caught up in something just last night that left him injured."

His news startled me. "Who was it? Is everything all right?"

"I don't know his name. I hope so," Father Michael murmured, his eyebrows furrowed. Again, he patted my arm, then moved on to talk to Sergei and some of the other men.

We were escorted to the outside common area, which was about half the size of a Church gymnasium. Snow was shoved to the side across the concrete. The cold bit our faces as around fifty of us stood against fences and walls or walked in circles, leaving enough breeze between us to fill our lungs with air that did not stink of leather, factory steam, or ripe men. Instead, there was the smell of homes and fireplaces outside our world and exhaust from cars going places mingled with the stench of prison-made cigarettes.

An open wooden crate sat on the ground, and the churchgoing men immediately went to it and began digging through what looked like letters. Tobacco was bartered for; discarded envelopes and letters were ripped up and shared among the smokers.

Sergei immediately took up his place as tattoo artist with primitive instruments he stored outside and that somehow the guards didn't care about. It was during this time that Sergei turned giddy. He threatened to unleash his creative talent on me in the way of a cross or some religious Mormon symbol.

I didn't bother telling him getting a tattoo was generally frowned upon in my church. Or about diseases I didn't want to catch. I only shivered in my industrial coat and said, "No, thank you."

As I watched the men receiving their brand of choice, I couldn't help but think of back home. Branding time had always marked the change of seasons. The men held back their sounds of discomfort with big talk, but the cows had said how they'd really felt, with their deep bellows of pure pain. I missed those sounds from home.

I took in a deep breath of the smoky Ukrainian winter air and imagined the scent of singed hair and hide instead. Those times had always made me grateful not to be a cow.

But now, here in this freezing enclosed court, miles from home, how I wished I'd been made a cow. Maybe I would have received a curved shape of a *C* intertwined with an *H*—my family's brand. It would have shown where I belonged, who I was. Maybe I would have been returned home instead of shoved in here, where I didn't belong, lost to my family. Was my dad worried about his lost cow? My eyes began to sting as moisture hit the icy air.

A scripture came to my mind, from Alma. *Have ye received his image in your countenances?* Thoughts turned from my family—too hard to contemplate—and I focused on the scripture.

Had Christ branded me His?

I thought about the idea of *becoming*. Egor had said the gospel—*Christ*—had changed him inside. Was that what it meant to receive Christ's image? I imagined myself branded as Christ's, and that would mean I wasn't lost—not to Him anyway.

My eyes grew moist again, but this time, it was because of a sweet feeling of joy. I felt a physical shift inside me, as if all my sadness and burdens were being lifted, carried by someone else, making me feel lighter and loved.

Duma was suddenly leaning against the wall next to me.

"Someone wrote me about you," he said, holding up a letter. "Do you want to know who?"

I nodded warily, the feelings of peace slowly ebbing away.

"Someone from England named James Kaufman. Do you know him?"

"Kaufman?" I stood up straighter. "My last companion was Stareyshina Kaufman from London."

Duma frowned. "Then why did he write me?"

I shrugged. "Do you know him?"

"Nyet. He wants to know if you're here. But why didn't he just write you himself?"

"I don't know." Kaufman could have asked President Meyers. Why would he write a complete stranger like Duma?

Duma handed me the letter. "He said someone wants to kill you, and it's important I let him know if you're here. He also asks if you have your scriptures. Does that seem strange to you?"

"Da," I sputtered. Of course it seemed strange that someone wanted to kill me. I opened the letter. It was brief and said just what Duma had told me. The handwriting looked like Kaufman's. I remembered reading his silly story about the prince, the frog, and the dragon.

I handed the letter back.

"Is that your book?" Duma asked.

I held up my *Kniga Mormona*. "I left it in Kramatorsk. But my mission president delivered it to me today."

He leaned forward. "May I see it? Just for a moment?"

I handed it to him, and he flipped through several pages, back and forth as if searching for something, then stopped and began reading. He looked up. "Do you have a Bible too?"

I shook my head. "Not anymore."

"It doesn't matter." He shook his head and handed my book back to me. "One needs both." He stood straight, away from the wall. "I'm going to tell this Kaufman that I don't know you, and you'd do best not to contact him either."

He walked a few feet away, then turned back again. "Eh, Stareyshina, what did they say you stole?"

"A ring."

He rubbed a hand across his face, pushed his collar up farther on his neck, then sauntered away without a word.

Two guards began yelling that it was time to line up, so I made my way to where Sergei stood, my legs numb from the cold.

"Look, Nil," Sergei said, holding out the arm of the man next to him. It was an eagle holding a branch.

I smiled. "You are quite the artist, Sergei. It's beautiful. And to think you did all that with those crude instruments."

"I can do one for you next week. We can put it on your chest. See?" He grabbed a piece of an envelope and a pencil and wrote: Нил. "*Nil.* You know, like American Superman? No one will see."

"If I wanted to be branded, I would have done it when I was five with my dad's hot iron."

He made a face. "A hot iron is *not* the same as a tattoo. Besides, it's disgusting to hear you talk about branding cows. It's inhumane. If I ever get out, I will start up a save-the-cows campaign."

"Or you could design brands for cattle so they look nicer."

He brightened. "That's an idea."

I smiled and shook my head. "No cow campaign, then? You're that easily dissuaded?"

He laughed, and I did too until I caught Duma's eye closer to the front of the line, and then thoughts of Kaufman filled me, and I wondered who might want me dead.

Sunday, December 13, was the coldest I'd been yet in Ukraine. Ice covered our cell window. It had been two weeks since Duma had shown me the letter, and in that time, there had been no attempts on my life—nothing out of the ordinary at all—and I began to feel less jumpy. I still didn't know how or why Kaufman had written Duma. Maybe some Church records showed Duma was at the same place as me? But then, why not just write to me? It didn't make sense. If I hadn't seen the letter myself, I wouldn't have believed it.

More people showed up at church simply to avoid going outside. I walked into the warm room and noticed President Meyers talking with Father Michael. It was the first time I'd seen him since my trial—Father Michael assured me he would come when he could. I stared at the stand where they stood talking and waited for him to notice me.

But he didn't.

Now I blended into the sea of shaved heads and tattoos. And I was no longer a missionary. The realization spread through my veins like ice water.

When the room held nearly thirty men, President Meyers looked around for the first time, searching the crowd. His eyes flickered recognition as they met mine, and surprise. Maybe because of how changed I'd become in prison, or maybe he'd assumed I would approach him, not stare at him from a chair. It would make sense for me to go up to him. Why hadn't I?

I didn't know. I only knew I felt disconnected from him. He was no longer my mission president. I felt suddenly young and old at the same time. Young like I had the first time I'd walked into his office and had felt like I needed to tell him about Brett. Old because now I knew things

President would never know. He'd go home to his house in L.A., swim in his pool, kiss his grandkids.

Grandkids I'd never have.

I looked down at my hands—black, blistered, calloused, cracked.

That would never be my life now.

He approached where I sat and, with something like a sigh of relief, said, "Neal." He reached a hand out and shook mine.

"Hello," I said solemnly in Russian, shaking his hand.

I had just showered, but my garments were drying, so I'd had to go without until I could get them tonight. It was Ivan's job to do the linens and uniforms today.

There had been days with my dad when I'd worked all day herding cattle on horseback, slept under the stars, and worked the next day. But it was different here in prison. I didn't own deodorant. I was clean for now, but I would work, sweat, freeze, and sleep in these same clothes for the next week. And I would smell like a man who had. Next to President's pressed, clean suit, I felt underdressed and unworthy.

When I met his eyes, I watched his relief at seeing me fade to worry. "Are you doing all right, Neal? I asked Father Michael if he could contact you for me. I was so glad to hear he had."

I tried to deflect the attention away from me. I looked to the right. "This is Sergei, my cellmate. He introduced me to these meetings."

Sergei looked at us and nodded at President without much expression.

"This is, uh, my friend, religious Church leader—we call him President Meyers," I explained.

President Meyers smiled sincerely, and Sergei shook his hand. "Nice to meet you," President said. "Thank you for taking care of Neal."

"Of course," Sergei said simply.

I wanted to ask about Egor, but I was also afraid to hear that maybe President had forgotten about him or maybe Egor wasn't doing well. So I avoided it. Instead, I answered questions. Yes, the prison was better than Kramatorsk. I did not tell him about the long hours of making shoes or that my garments were worn and I had calloused blisters from wearing no socks.

President seemed to know what I wanted to hear despite my not asking it. "Egor is doing better. He has pneumonia. He is being watched closely at the prison infirmary, and they say he has a good chance of surviving."

I reached out and grasped President's hand and shook it.

"And I have this." He reached into his pocket and gave me two letters that looked like they had come from the United States.

I didn't recognize the writing on one of the letters, but I couldn't stop staring at the familiar curves and lines on the other. "My mom."

He nodded. "I spoke to her on the phone yesterday. She said to tell you not to worry and she loves you. You are constantly in all their prayers."

I wiped my streaming eyes and nodded, taking in deep breaths. *My mom.*

"What do you need, Neal? There must be things you need here."

I shook my head. All I needed was that letter.

"I'm bringing more scriptures. I've ordered them and have permission from the prison."

"That's wonderful," I said, taking in another deep breath. He patted me on the back and went to the front.

The service was about to begin, and President Meyers was teaching us. Father Michael introduced President in a respectful way. There was no jealousy, no need to prove he was the better preacher. Maybe living in a world with so much division, hate, atheism, and control for power, he saw the value in love, like President Meyers did. Maybe he believed in the things he preached.

Feeling sufficiently humbled, I tuned in to President Meyers. I nervously moved my fingers across the knees of my prison pants. I knew his Russian was adequate, but it would not be the same as Father Michael's. I prayed silently that he'd have the gift of tongues. President met my eyes and smiled before staring down at the large Bible in front of him.

"There is a word in the scriptures that comes up again and again: *if.*" He paused. "After Christ fasted forty days and forty nights, it says Satan came to Him, to tempt Him. Matthew 4:3 reads, 'And when the tempter came to him, he said, if thou be the Son of God, command that these stones be made bread.' Satan used the word *if* to challenge the Savior. He wanted the Savior to prove who He was. That He wasn't truly the Savior unless He could do the things Satan wanted Him to.

"Then, when Christ was hanging on the cross, it says in Matthew 27, 'They that passed by reviled him, wagging their heads, And saying, Thou that destroyest the temple, and buildest it in three days, save thyself, if thou be the Son of God, come down from the cross.'

"Again, *if.* If you truly are the Savior, you will do *my* will, what I ask you to. Are we not also that way? Do we often tell the Savior we will believe only *if* He shows Himself how we want Him to? Do we ask Him to prove Himself to us?

"Christ did not come down from the cross. It was God the Father's plan for Christ to die, to save us all. If He hadn't followed through with the Atonement, all would be lost. Christ knew that. Do we know that?

"Do we ask God to take away our personal crosses we are forced to bear, even though God knows the bigger plan?

"I can't imagine how hard life is in this prison. I can't imagine what you go through daily, weekly, year after year, but I do know there is a God in Heaven who loves you, who is aware of you, and He doesn't take away your crosses, your trials, because He knows they will *save* you. They will lead you to Christ if you allow them to. They will help you grow into someone you can't become without them. He is wiser than any of us. When we choose to submit, choose to grow, choose to *love*"—President paused and looked at me—"He will not leave you comfortless, directionless. He will give you what you lack.

"Satan may count it a silent victory that you are trapped in a prison, that you must endure hardships. But he is wrong. He doesn't know the secret. It is through those hard experiences that we find Christ. These trials will work for your good. If you *choose* to let them."

President looked down. "There is a scripture in Matthew 5: 'Blessed are they which do hunger and thirst after righteousness: for they shall be filled.'" President glanced back up, and I saw him search each man's eyes individually. "Christ has the power to *fill* you to overflowing, if you seek Him."

I heard several sniffs around me, and I could feel the Spirit there, filling all who listened.

It wasn't until we were preparing to leave that I saw a pair of familiar green eyes on the back row.

Duma had joined us for the sermon.

He gave a silent nod, his face expressionless, but instead of comfort at seeing him, I felt distrust and worry. He'd stolen tithing money. What kind of trouble would he cause here?

***

That night, there was no dinner. My cellmates grumbled loudly, but the guards told us to stop complaining; we were not the only Ukrainians to go to bed hungry, and some of those people had actually worked today.

I didn't pay much attention to their protests. I had letters from home.

I read the letter from my mom three times, and the one she'd included from my father, I'd lost count how many times. I could feel my mom's despair in her cheerful list of possibilities. When life got tough, she could kill reality with optimism. It was a quality that had always bothered me, but now I held on to it like a lifeline. Maybe she would fool herself through positive thinking enough to not feel the pain.

My dad spoke of cows, mountains, weather, and alfalfa as if I were only at Scout camp and would be home any day. But he also said he was praying for me. That was how I knew he was worried, because I'd never heard him say a prayer my entire life.

The other envelope President had given me was from George Mengham. He'd received my letter and had written that he forgave me. The community as a whole was praying for my safe return. I tried to imagine the towns and wards and other Christian congregations throughout our rural area praying for me. It was shocking and extremely humbling.

I picked up my Book of Mormon, leaned against the cool stone wall, and stared in front of me at the nothingness. It would be lights out soon.

"Blessed are those who hunger after righteousness, eh, Nil?" Sergei winked at me. "For they shall be filled."

I smiled and chuckled. "Da."

"What does it mean?" he asked. "How can righteousness fill your belly when it is gnawing angrily at you?"

I wasn't sure if he was teasing or serious. I waited for Boris to protest with a growl, but there was no sound from anyone. I couldn't tell if it was because they, too, were waiting for an answer or were simply beyond caring for the day.

"Blessed are those who hunger and thirst after righteousness, for they shall be filled," I repeated, almost to myself. I looked up and met Sergei's eyes. He was staring intently back at me. I knew then that he did want to know. "I think it is a different kind of hunger than from food; it's an emptiness you feel deep in your soul. Seeking Jesus Christ—*righteousness*—can fill that void."

Sergei's voice was barely a whisper. "And how do we find Jesus Christ to fill that void inside us?"

A scripture came to my mind, and I opened the Book of Mormon to 1 Nephi 10:18–19. I read out loud, "'For he is the same yesterday, today, and forever; and the way is prepared for all men from the foundation of the world, if it so be that they repent and come unto him.

"'For he that diligently seeketh shall find; and the mysteries of God shall be unfolded unto them, by the power of the Holy Ghost, as well in these times as in times of old, and as well in times of old as in times to come; wherefore, the course of the Lord is one eternal round.'"

I looked up at Sergei. He had that look that said he was working things out in his mind. I stared at the tattoos on his arms and his neck: a prisoner.

Sergei was a man searching for an anchor. He'd made poor choices, like we all had, but that was not who he was to me or to God. I remembered how President had told me to pray for my companions—to pray and ask God how He feels about them.

I looked around the room at all the other men, lying on their beds, all prisoners, but they were people who came from somewhere; they were souls who had worth.

The lights were switched off, and it was quiet.

I lay on my mat and thought about how many times I'd judged these men—all the prisoners—wondering what good learning about the gospel was for any of them. They lived in this dark world of hardship, evil, violence, sin. They participated in it. They would never get baptized, never join the Church. Then why would God send them a missionary?

The thought shamed me now. God didn't want to lose any of His children. He loved these men in here as much as everyone else in Ukraine. As much as He loved me.

I imagined Christ walking through the cities and people bringing their sick to Him. He healed all of them, turning none away. There was a saying I remembered that hospitals are for the sick not the healthy, just as churches are for the sick in spirit.

I couldn't picture a place more downtrodden and spiritually sick than a prison in Ukraine. Why *wouldn't* God send them a missionary? Why didn't He send all prisoners missionaries?

I'd been released as a missionary. I swallowed down the emotions that always came with that thought. But Elder Todd's blessing had said I'd been sent to Ukraine for a special mission at this time, that I'd find out little by little.

Now that I thought about it, it didn't sound much like a release blessing. More like a reassignment.

Not released, the Spirit said, filling me. *Just a transfer.*

OUR BREAKFAST THE NEXT MORNING was gray and runny, but it was food. A guard also dropped a package inside our cell. It was obvious it had been opened and searched, but we could still read on the outside of the box: *To the occupants of cell number 518.*

I looked up from my mat and met Duma's eyes where he stood eating his breakfast. His eyes narrowed, mirroring my thoughts. Was this box meant to harm me? Still holding his tin bowl, he cautiously stepped up to the box and poked it with his bare feet. It did nothing.

Boris stood near him. "Duma, you act as though it holds a bomb."

"I hope it does," Sergei said, setting his bowl aside. "I would eat it over this stuff."

"Let's make Nil open it," Boris said. "It's probably for him anyway. Isn't someone trying to kill him? I won't take the bullet."

I scrambled up from my mat. "I don't want you to get hurt. I can open it." Duma shot me a critical look. "How bad could it be?" I asked him. "It passed inspection."

"Clearly, you don't understand the prison system well. But go ahead, if you insist," he said.

It was quiet as I opened the box, then I gasped. Several of the prisoners backed away.

"What? What is it?" Sergei yelled.

I held up one soft, clean, stark-white sock, and their gasp mimicked mine. I opened the box wider and showed them it was full of white socks. At the bottom were two pairs of brand-new garments, still in the package. I ran my finger across the blue English letters on the clear packaging from the Church Distribution Center. It was the most beautiful thing I'd ever seen.

Sergei picked up one of the socks. "Who are these for?" He held it reverently as he rubbed it through his hands, ran it across his face, and inhaled it deeply.

"They are for us." I laughed. I couldn't believe it. "They must be from President Meyers."

I folded a pair of socks until it resembled a round snowball, then threw it at Gavriil, who was standing near the window. He called out, surprised, then dropped to my mat to retrieve the ball. He pulled them over his hands and rubbed them across his face. I made more sock balls and threw them to the other men, who eagerly took off their boots and slipped them on their feet and hands.

I aimed one at the back of Sergei's head. It hit him lightly, and when he turned, I lobbed one at his face. He laughed, surprised, slipped the socks off his hands, and threw them back. Soon men were grabbing socks by the handfuls and hiding behind beds, making their own sock-balls. It caused a mass reaction, similar to what I'd experienced once in the middle school lunchroom. Only this time it involved socks, pillows, hats, and dishes, as well as food.

A guard opened the door, and we went instantly motionless. I glanced at Boris, who had food smeared across his shoulder, probably from Sergei. The guard looked from one face to another. "What is going on in here?"

I didn't know this guard, if he was kind or violent, but I made a decision to take the blame for my cellmates before I let fear stop me. I had started it, after all. "A sock war," I said.

He looked confused. "Sock war?"

Duma stepped in front of me. "Sergei hit Boris first, then we all got involved. It won't happen again. We will clean up the mess."

"Yes. And then *he* will clean up the hall and stairs after that," the guard said, pointing at me. "All of you get ready for work."

The cell door slammed shut, and Duma pushed me against the wall. "Stareyshina, are you trying to get yourself killed?" He stepped away and shook his head angrily. "A *sock war*? Were you not tortured enough in your last prison? That guard could make you wish you were dead."

"He still might," Gavriil said. The others muttered an agreement.

Duma turned to face me. "The rule is the leader speaks. *Always*. I'm the leader. *Remember* it. You're invisible. *Stay* invisible."

My voice sounded gruff. "Da, I understand."

But I didn't understand why Duma would want to protect me.

THE HALL AND STAIRS TOOK me an hour to mop. A different guard watched me from the one who had broken up the fun in the cell. This one seemed more interested in his newspaper and cigarette than picking on me, which was a blessing from God.

I was late to work. I had to work an extra hour to make up for it, as well as do hand stitching, which was the worst job. I did not complain. My life had become fragile. Perhaps it had always been, but now, I was suddenly aware of it in a way I never had been before. The screams from Kramatorsk still haunted me in my sleep.

I arrived back at my cell just before dinner that night. It was cold stew, but no one minded. We ate without speaking. Then we stacked our tin plates near the door slot and lounged on our beds. I noticed several of the men's hands were covered with socks, including Boris's.

Sergei held up his feet and admired his still-mostly-white socks. "My feet have never felt so warm. How did the punishment go?"

"Mopping?" I asked. "Not as bad as it could have been, thanks to Duma." I sighed loudly, exhausted.

Duma looked down at me from his top bunk behind his newspaper. "You'll learn. And then the rules will change and you'll relearn."

It was quiet, as we all stared at the ceiling, tired from a full day's work.

"What are you thinking about, Nil?" Sergei asked. It seemed an odd question, but sometimes Sergei just needed to talk.

"I was thinking about something my mission president said—'A dog in the chase doesn't notice the fleas.'"

Sergei chuckled quietly.

"I didn't get it at the time, but now I think I do."

"What a bunch of moldy borsch," Boris growled from his bed above us. "I notice the fleas. Every day here feels like a year. Maybe it's a holiday for you school girls but not for me."

"Ah, Boris, with you here, how could it not feel like a holiday?" Sergei asked. "And may I suggest washing better on Sundays to get rid of the fleas?"

"Will you read to us again, Nil?" Ivan stopped all conversation with his remark.

My heart thumped hopefully. "Da, if you wish."

"I prefer listening to it over Sergei and Boris's matrimonial disputes," he said.

Everyone chuckled but Boris, who said, "Religion is for the unpatriotic and simple-minded."

A story came to my mind of Alma, when he was imprisoned. I opened to it and began reading.

THE DAYS DID NOT MOVE as quickly as a dog in the chase, but they moved faster than they had in the detention facility in Kramatorsk. Our reading from the Book of Mormon continued every night. Interestingly, it was always Ivan who requested it, and he was the first one asleep as I read. I decided he wasn't lying when he said he preferred it to Boris and Sergei's bickering. It seemed to have a calming effect on the entire cell. I found myself thinking about our nightly discussions as I hammered soles on shoes or moved the leather through the hot steam machine. I discovered I thought less of home and more about the men in my group. My prayers for them increased and became more individualized.

Christmas passed without much thought. Father Michael gave a sermon on it the Sunday before and brought us all a piece of hard candy.

It was Sunday, mid-January. After breakfast, we lined up with our worn linens and clothing outside the shower room. Boris carried a laundry basket down the line, and we dumped our sheets, blankets, and uniforms into it.

Sergei and I lined up together to walk to church services. I saw President standing near the podium, talking to Father Michael as I walked into the room. He had not come since he'd spoken last time. Duma hadn't come again either. This time, I did not wait for President to approach me. I walked to the front, Sergei with me. Father Michael shook our hands, then moved to the chairs to speak with the other men walking in.

President smiled, but his eyes looked pinched, as if forced. He was more enthusiastic as he shook Sergei's hand, especially when Sergei said, "Nil mentioned you might be able to get me a Book of Mormon?"

"Of course. In fact—" He turned and showed us a large box behind him on the floor. It was completely full of scriptures—Bibles and copies of the Book of Mormon.

Sergei and I knelt on the floor and turned the new books over in our hands.

He picked one up and smelled the new pages, then stood and grabbed President's hand again. "Thank you, sir, thank you. And for the socks." He gave President a giant hug and kissed him loudly on the cheek.

President laughed. "I am touched," he said. "Truly, I am." Then in English, he said to me, "That's the most gratitude I've ever received for giving socks to someone."

I laughed, and President wore his smile, but as he watched me, it faded and left his eyes, and I saw worry there, as if it had been etched there permanently. Perhaps it had.

"What's wrong, President?" I asked.

Sergei patted me on the back as if to say he understood and went to save us a seat.

President cleared his throat. "I have some unpleasant news."

I prepared myself for the worst. Had he heard about the threats to kill me? Maybe he knew more information? Or maybe it was my family back home. Panic started to fill my chest. *Please don't let it be my family.*

"Egor died six days ago, in the infirmary."

I took a sharp breath in. "Egor? I—I thought you said he was getting better."

He looked away. "It looked that way, but he didn't make it." President cleared his throat. "I know how much he meant to you. When I went in to see him Monday, they told me he was gone. They gave me this." He shuffled over to the podium and picked up a hardback copy of the Bible.

"It was his only possession." He placed it in my hand. It felt heavy, thick, and sad.

I stared at the Bible in my hands until I couldn't see it anymore. I wiped at my eyes.

"I'm sorry, Neal. He was so very sick. He's in a better place—you know that. You prepared him to meet his Father in Heaven. One day you'll see him again."

I nodded. I did know. I thought of how sick he'd been when I'd left him and drew in a shaky breath. "Thank you, President, for bringing me this piece of him."

He rubbed my shoulder with his hand, hugged me tight, then released me. The gesture was very fatherly. I wiped my eyes with my sleeve.

"I also brought you this." He handed me more letters from home. "Hopefully it softens the blow a little."

I took them, along with some paper and a pen from President. "Write your letters, and bring them to me next week or give them to Father Michael if I'm not here."

"Thank you," I said, searching President's eyes, waiting for the worry to leave now that he'd told me about Egor. But it didn't. Maybe it would always be there. Some things couldn't be erased with a good night's sleep.

He shook his head and whispered, "I'm amazed by you, Stareyshina. You don't know how well you're doing. You don't see it. But I do." Again, he squeezed my shoulder. "Releasing you as a missionary was a hard decision and not just mine to make; I hope you realize that. When I left you that first day, I'm embarrassed to say I still had my doubts. I wanted to believe . . . but there was such substantial evidence to convict you." He swallowed, fighting emotion. "I read your letters, the ones I asked you to write. The Spirit testified of your innocence—the letters themselves were evidence of your deep love for the Savior, for your family, of your conviction to the gospel of Jesus Christ. And yet here you are"—he took a deep breath and rubbed his forehead—"despite your innocence, despite everything I tried to do."

He paused, searching my face. "I need to know, is there anything you can tell me that might point me in the right direction? Anything strange? Has anyone tried to contact you?"

I cleared my throat and tried to think back to before prison, but it was hazy—too many things had happened since then. It was like sifting through memories of a different person. But I thought of something more recent. "Kaufman wrote a letter to one of my cellmates, asking if I was here. Duma said he doesn't even know Kaufman. Kaufman said someone wants to kill me. It was a warning."

"Stareyshina Kaufman?"

"A James Kaufman from London. It seemed odd he didn't just write me—or ask you."

President Meyers rubbed his chin. "That does seem odd. Kaufman went home in November, a month early. He was understandably shaken after you went to prison."

I nodded, an empty feeling engulfing me as I remembered our last conversation. He was worried he'd failed me as a trainer, and I'd promised I'd help him find someone to baptize. Then everything had come to a screeching halt. I'd failed him. Abandoned him. I swallowed, thinking how much worse he probably felt.

"Is Kaufman doing okay?" I asked.

President sighed. "I actually haven't spoken with him. His parents said he moved to Bolivia. He's helping refugees. They said he wanted to lose himself in service."

"That sounds like something Kaufman would do. He always had a lot of energy. Although I thought he might use it on the stage." I grinned.

President patted me on the back and gave a small chuckle. "I do miss that kid."

It was time for the meeting to start. Sergei saved us a seat on the front row. I listened to Father Michael's sermon, but my mind was full of things I hadn't done. And I kept thinking about Egor. I couldn't believe he was gone. My only convert. I'd never baptized him or taken pictures and sent them home to my family. I would never mention him in a homecoming talk.

I was the only one left on this planet who cared about him.

Would that be me one day?

I thought of President's kindness, but one day, he would be gone. Like Kaufman, he would go home.

What would happen then? Would I still get letters from my family? For the next twenty years, would a mission president come to visit me, even after I was no longer missionary age? I was only President Meyers's stareyshina. One day, I would be off the records, abandoned, and forgotten.

Fear, like a small piece of thread, began to unravel my peace, tempting me to tug on it and destroy the firmness of mind I'd been building. Through a miracle, I had met Duma, the one I'd come to Ukraine to find and teach. But he was already a member, and he hated the Church.

Mine was the most messed-up mission there ever was.

I didn't go outside after the sermon. I went upstairs to my cell and read the letters from home. They were full of details about my family's daily life. My sister was old enough to go to church dances now. My father wrote about how a dozen cows had refused to get water from a nearby pond and died of dehydration. "Stupid cows," he wrote. And I agreed.

It was as if I was just on a mission in Ukraine, and I realized that as long as my family kept writing me, kept remembering me, someone would always bring me their letters. I wouldn't be forgotten by them.

And I was on the records of The Church of Jesus Christ.

I was branded a member of the Church—a very great blessing. I still felt empty though. I picked up my Book of Mormon, which I did out of habit whenever I hurt too much to go on.

I opened to Lehi's dream about the tree of life. It wasn't until I stopped reading somewhere in chapter 13 that I realized the Lehi in my mind had a long beard with pieces of silver and gray and fuzzy white near his temples. His eyebrows were full of coarse silver strands above kind eyes on a face of hard lines etched into his skin like tree's bark. His smile was yellow, and his face held years of worry, worn by the weather, dried by the cold, burned by the sun.

He was Egor.

I imagined him and me eating the fruit from the tree of life together, like we had so many times in that small cell.

I picked up his Bible and ran my hand over its cover and the outside of its pages. *Please, God, guide me to where I'll find comfort this day.*

I scanned through the title page and then the table of contents. The next page was an explanation of abbreviations. I was about to turn the page again when something caught my eye. I squinted between two paragraphs where the word *ring* was written very tiny in black ink, along with Genesis 41:42.

Curious, I turned to the reference and read silently. "*And Pharaoh took off his ring from his hand, and put it upon Joseph's hand, and arrayed him in vestures of fine linen, and put a gold chain about his neck.*"

The verse below had the *b* cross-reference above the word *ruler* circled. I glanced at the bottom and saw the reference: 1 Nephi 3:29. I reached down and picked up my Book of Mormon from under my mat, where I kept it. I turned to the reference and was amazed to see the small *c* above the word *deliver* circled.

I'd never paid much attention to any markings in Kaufman's scriptures while I'd had them in prison. Not that they were noticeable; they were so small and black they blended in perfectly with the other ink. I'd been too distracted by learning the language and feeling the message of the words to care about them.

But now I was being led somewhere. I scanned through the verse. It was where the angel came to Nephi's brothers to tell them to quit beating Nephi with a rod and to go back to Jerusalem, where Laban would be delivered into their hands. I could see no correlation between the two verses.

I looked up the next cross-reference: 3 Nephi 3:21. I read through the verse about Gidgiddoni. In verse 22, the *b* above *place* was circled. I glanced at the cross-reference and turned to Mormon 2:7.

The next verse had the *b* next to *robbers* circled. I read the verse and through the next two. There was nothing in verse 46 marked, but in the next two verses, the numbers 47 and 48 were circled in a different color, this time blue ink. "And it came to pass that after three hundred and five years had passed away, (and the people did still remain in wickedness) Amos died; and his brother, Ammaron, did keep the record in his stead.

"And it came to pass that when three hundred and twenty years had passed away, Ammaron, being constrained by the Holy Ghost, did hide up the records which were sacred—yea, even all the sacred records."

That was it; my trail was done. There were no more marks and absolutely no correlation. Why had Kaufman marked those scriptures? I opened it up and started again at *ring*. There was the word *ruler, deliver, place,* and then two verses circled. I thumbed through the Bible's pages, searching for more markings. It was such a large book, but nothing stood out. I reached the index and Bible Dictionary and kept going until I finally reached the hardback cover.

And there, inside the back cover of the book, was a box. It was a two-inch by two-inch standing black block. It looked as though it had been glued to the inside of the cover. On top of it was a tiny dial with numbers. I twisted it and saw that it moved, like some kind of combination lock.

How had I never noticed?

The pages at the back of the Bible were cut into perfect black, square holes to fit the block so when I closed the book it disappeared into its pages. The holes began in the middle of Romans and went to the end of the book. I opened and closed the book several times and managed to get some of the pages stuck a bit around the box.

The fact that we had not seen this was proof that we had read the Bible so little, focusing on reading and rereading the Book of Mormon.

I moved the combination to several different possibilities, trying to figure out how it worked. There was a line at the very top, like any combination lock, to align the numbers with, but I had no idea how to open it, and I was afraid of what could be inside. The scripture about a ring was setting off an alarm in my head, making me feel paranoid.

My hand shook as I closed the book. My brain didn't want to consider the possibilities that a ring could be in this Bible. That made absolutely no sense. I hadn't stolen it. Kaufman hadn't stolen it. Egor hadn't done this. There was no way it would be with me in prison.

I hid the book under my mat before anyone came in. I didn't sleep well that night, my mind going in circles. I stood with everyone else the next morning, preparing to work, making sure my Bible was still hidden under my mat. I tied my boots and put on my coat, but I couldn't stop worrying about what was in the locked box.

THE DAYS BLURRED TOGETHER, AND the Bible stayed safely hidden under my mat, never completely forgotten. I rarely found a moment alone to try to discover its secrets, and at night, I didn't dare pull it out in case someone saw or heard.

One night, mid-February, I was reading in Alma 36:3, where it said, "Behold, thou art in thy youth, and therefore, I beseech of thee that thou wilt hear my words and learn of me; for I do know that whosoever shall put their trust in God shall be supported in their trials, and their troubles, and their afflictions, and shall be lifted up at the last day."

I stopped reading. I could hear Ivan's soft snoring, even though the lights were still on.

"Every night, we read," Sergei said, "and I am filled with an indescribable good feeling, but I am still troubled inside. God says He will support us in our afflictions if we put our trust in Him, but what about the sinner? And eternal damnation? I am worried I will never be with God, that I will burn in torment for my sins. What can I do to repent? Is it even possible?"

Sergei's question touched me, and I set the book down. "I had an experience before I came to prison, and I had to repent of something I'd done that hurt someone else. I believe in the Atonement of Jesus Christ. When I was young, I was taught to repent. We first pray and ask for God's forgiveness. Then we try to do what we can to make it better. And third, never do it again. For more serious sins, it takes confessing to someone with proper priesthood authority."

Sergei nodded, but his eyebrows were still furrowed. "Mine is a serious sin. How will I be able to confess to a priest with proper authority?"

"I don't know. I will ask President Meyers if he has an answer."

Sergei nodded. "I would appreciate that."

Duma rolled over to face me. "It's useless. Repentance is well and good for someone who isn't in prison for breaking the law. We can't change here or make it better—we are stuck."

"You still have choices," I argued back. "You can choose if you are cruel or kind. You can choose to thank God or ignore Him."

"Ignore Him? And why not? That's all He's done for me."

"What about blessing you with an office job, with magazines? And a shelter from the cold? What about the fact you are alive and not dead? Even after you stole His money, He still gives you these things."

"Da." Duma turned his back on us. "That is how I know He is not there, or He would not have."

Sergei sat up, his eyes wide. "Are we too far gone? Is he right?"

"Do you feel you are too far gone, Sergei? What does your heart tell you? God speaks through our hearts and our minds. He doesn't speak through our doubts and fears. You can apologize to those you've hurt; you can turn your back on sin and embrace Christ. You've already done this."

Sergei was quiet for a long while, then said, "I will pray and see what the Lord tells me."

"I will pray for you too," I said.

"Thank you, Nil. You are a good friend."

"*Otboy*," the guard said, and the lights turned off. I rolled onto my side. The Bible poked me in the ribs, reminding me of its presence under my mat. I scooted myself back a few inches and re-adjusted my blanket.

I tried not to let Duma's comments make me angry. Everyone was in a different place, had a different time frame, but inside, I felt afraid for Duma. I remembered the dream I'd had of him behind bars. Even now, after seeing him in an actual prison, I still felt his chains were more spiritual and emotional than physical. There had been such a feeling of urgency.

I had been in Donetsk prison three months now, and Duma seemed as much a mystery now as he had when he'd only been the lost man from my dreams.

It was mid-March. I stood in the assembly line, wrapping the hard shoes with leather and passing them to Sergei so he could hammer the holes on the bottoms to fit it to the soles. Mondays were always the most difficult days to work.

"Did you hear?" Boris came up behind us, out of breath. "They have ousted Yanukovych. He is no longer president of Ukraine."

"Really? Why?" Sergei asked, not looking up.

"Because he was too Russian, as I told you. He was giving money to the bear next door. Money that this country needs."

"I don't like it," a man across from us named Andrei said. "There could be a rebellion."

"Rebellion?" Sergei asked. "Here?"

"We are close to Russia. It makes sense, doesn't it?" Andrei said. "There is only talk."

Sergei looked up at me, and I could see a flicker of concern before he went back to the shoes.

"What would it mean to have a rebellion?" I asked.

Andrei shrugged and looked to Boris.

"I don't know," Boris said. He rubbed his smooth chin. "At least, I don't want to think about it."

We glanced around uncomfortably until a guard told us to get back to work.

***

It was a couple days later, Wednesday, after work, when we saw what a rebellion might mean. Duma wasn't back yet, and we were taking off our boots, standing around in our cell. Ivan and Trofim had begun a game of cards.

"Look," Sergei said, standing near the window.

Ivan stood and leaned to see what Sergei was pointing at behind our makeshift sheet curtain. "Look there. Do you see them?"

"Those are military tanks," Ivan said.

We all moved to the window. The sun was low in the horizon, but we could still see through the skeletal trees the military tanks and trucks driving past the prison.

"Are they Ukrainian?" I asked.

"No," Duma said. We had not heard him come in. "They are Russian, Pro-Russian Separatists. Donetsk is under attack." All of us stared at him. The shock felt unreal. What did he mean? Duma, who was always cool, took a deep breath. "I fear we may no longer be in Ukraine."

"Then where are we?" Boris whispered.

"I don't know," Duma said. "We must wait to find out, I suppose."

"They've stopped," Ivan said. Sure enough, the line of green-camou-flage trucks had halted across from a large field next to the prison.

"Is the war to be here, then?" Gavriil asked.

No one had any answers.

It was very quiet that night. It was as if every person in the entire prison was holding their breath, listening, waiting. The calm before the storm—we all knew it. I held my Book of Mormon to my chest, too nervous to read. The lights were turned out early, and we hardly noticed when dinner wasn't served. Everyone lay on their cots, everyone but Ivan. He was continually leaning over me to see out the window. Watching, almost hypnotized.

Around what must have been 3:00 a.m., we heard it. Loud explosions and repeated gunfire. Ivan kneeled at the edge of my mat and yelled, "Get down! It's hitting the prison walls!" Duma, Boris, and Gavriil hopped off the top bunks and crouched on the floor next to the rest of us, and we all held our heads. We stayed that way until the sun came up. The guards brought no breakfast. They opened our door and shouted orders to get downstairs, then led us to the outside courtyard. We could hear only scattered sounds of shots now, and not close. Several military men stood in a line, holding guns in front of the chain-link fence. There was no talking, only the sound of crunching gravel echoing off the buildings as two hundred of us prisoners neared them.

"Are there any of you loyal to Eastern Ukraine? We are finished with being ruled by a Western government who wants to be European. We are more Russian than Ukrainian. We are tired of being run by leaders who can't and won't protect us, who can't provide for us."

I watched Sergei put an arm around Boris's shoulders in an attempt to placate him.

"We are asking for volunteers. You don't need to know how to shoot a gun. We will train you. And for this, you will receive freedom, food, and some pay."

"What about those who won't fight?" a voice asked loudly from somewhere in the middle.

It was very quiet as the man in charge looked at each of us as if trying to distinguish where the voice had come from. Continuing to scan us, he said, "You will stay here, where you are most comfortable—behind bars. No telling what will happen to you. No one can guarantee the safety of this prison. The boots will continue to be made and sold, I'm sure. The factory here has some value." He stepped back. "I will wait here for any who desire freedom and want to join our numbers."

Ivan brushed past us, followed by Trofim. "Rather do something than sit here and rot," he said. Gavriil hesitated, then also followed. A lump formed in my throat. How long would he last in a war? I stared at the stern Russians with guns. To join seemed a new prison—I didn't even consider it an option.

Slowly, those of us who would not join were pushed to the back, and a messy line was formed for those who wanted to be recruited into the Russian army. When it was clear those of us in the back were not part of the line, we were sent back to work on shoes.

The next day was like before, only this time we were rushed into the small chapel, with a new regiment up front. They looked less official but no less fierce. Father Michael stood silently at the back of the room, drinking a cup of coffee.

A large man stood, a gun slung across his front. His voice was deep and carried in the medium-sized room. "We are asking for volunteers to defend our home against invaders. It will be volunteer only. There will be no pay. But for those of you who can take up arms and help our city and join our community to fight these invaders, join us." They looked around the room, pleading. Only a few men came to the front. This time Boris joined them.

"For Ukraine," he said as he passed Sergei.

I looked at Duma and Sergei, the last of our cell. "What will happen?" I asked.

Duma took up chewing a nail, and Sergei shook his head and heaved a great sigh. "We will stay prisoners for our own safety. Which is not very safe."

Father Michael tapped me from behind, and the three of us turned. "Nil," he said, "I have been waiting until I could see you. I have a message. Your church pulled missionaries out of Donetsk days ago, for obvious safety reasons. I will be leaving too, along with most of the city, I imagine. President Meyers wanted you to have this." He handed me a small folded note, barely the width of two fingers. "Read it quickly."

I unfolded the paper until it was its full size, a messily torn quarter sheet of paper covered in black ink.

"The Church is pulling all missionaries out of Eastern Ukraine. I fear for your safety. Legally, in situations where two countries collide like this, prison files can go into limbo indefinitely. Evidence has surfaced pointing to your innocence. If you find a way to escape, I'm leaving my contact info with the stake president in Kiev. Follow the Spirit. All of my love and prayers are with you and your cellmates, President Conrad Meyers."

I read over the words again while Duma and Sergei read over my shoulder, but it was in English so I doubted they could understand.

My innocence? I looked up at Father Michael.

"Are you finished reading it?" he asked.

I nodded. He took it from me, folded it until it was small again, and dropped it in his cup of coffee. He mopped his face, looking worn and stressed.

"Father Michael, what will happen?" Sergei asked.

"It seems we should all try to escape while we can," Duma mumbled.

"And where would you go?" Father Michael asked sharply. "And to which country? You have no release papers, no identity. The ex-convicts won't be able to find work. Maybe *you* don't remember starvation, but there are many in this prison who do. They know there is food here—for now, at least. Those who have gone to fight will either die because they don't know how to shoot a gun or come back here and choose bars because they can't fire on their brothers and destroy this land they love. Eastern Ukraine has overnight become a war zone." He ran his hand through his hair. "Prisons have already begun to fill with new political prisoners who are not treated well. There are 17,000 inmates in twenty-eight prisons just in the areas Russia is openly taking over. Who will care about them? You are lucky, Nil. Lucky to have a church who cares what happens to you. Lucky you are more than a number."

He placed a hand on my shoulder. "I tell you this not so you give up hope but so you understand. I know you were trained to be a religious missionary, that you know the scriptures. You must take my place here and help these men find light in darkness."

A stern look from the guards who had entered to take us to the factory cut our conversation short. This time Duma joined us. He said he was no longer needed at the front office.

We showed him how to hammer the nails, and Sergei and I worked on connecting the soles to the shoes.

"I don't want to be out there in the fighting," Sergei said, lining up the holes. "But it seems unavoidable. Even making shoes, we are in the line of fire. I have no money. I have nowhere to go. No one wants to hire a criminal artist. I mean, look at me. I'm covered in criminal art."

It was true. Sergei had more tattooed skin than bare skin. He'd never thought past prison. His life plan was to pay restitution for a crime he would never forgive himself for. "Are you going to leave, Nil?"

"I don't know," I said. "I want to go home—back to America. I keep hoping God will provide a way."

"Stareyshiny are all the same." Duma squinted at the shoe in his hand. "You come, and just as quick, you leave, just as long as you have enough baptisms to make it worth your time."

I clenched my jaw. "Really? I came, was starved, beaten, wrongly accused of a crime, and can never leave. How does that fit your reasoning?"

"Sounds like you achieved Ukrainian citizenship. Congratulations."

"And would that be Western Ukraine or Eastern? Or Russia?"

Sergei straightened next to me. "Fighting will not do either of you any good. Are you going to escape, Duma? Do you have somewhere to go?"

Duma stared at the same shoe, trying to get the nails just right. "I have a sister in Horlivka, but who knows if she will still be there." Then he glared at me. "Maybe the Mormons got to her."

"Maybe they did," I said, not ready to let it go. "There are worse things than joining the true church on earth."

Duma glared at me. "She's already a member of the Mormon Church, or, as you put it, *the true church on earth*. As am I. And for me, there was nothing worse."

Sergei and I exchanged a look. "I don't understand where all this hatred comes from, Duma," I said, my tone softer. "I haven't done anything to hurt you."

Duma glanced up at us, then back at his shoe. A guard walked by who I hadn't noticed before, but Duma had. He was always aware, always cautious. Sergei and I gave our work better attention.

Lunch came, and the three of us huddled near each other, eating the cold broth with chunks of veggies. The machines were momentarily stopped for the break, and I wondered if it was my ears ringing or if I was hearing gunshots. Our eyes were continually drawn to the windows.

That night, Duma moved to Ivan's bed on the bottom bunk, and I took Trofim's spot on the other bottom bed and moved the Bible with me. Sergei stayed where he was, and we distributed the extra bedding among ourselves. The cell felt empty and colder with them gone. The lights were turned off early. We listened to the gunfire, sometimes close, sometimes farther away.

I couldn't sleep and knew they couldn't either.

Duma broke the black silence, not bothering to ask if either of us was awake. "I was baptized with my sister. And my mama. We were baptized in a chapel in January in water colder than I've ever felt here in prison. I told the stareyshiny it would be foolish to get baptized in that cold water. They told me God would bless us. That *He* would provide, just like you said.

"My mama told me as we walked home she had never felt warmer in her heart. She died less than two weeks later. The stareyshina I had argued with against the baptism had already gone home by then—to America. Replaced by new stareyshiny. They didn't care about us. He just wanted one more baptism before he left my country. One more conquest. The new stareyshiny didn't attend her funeral.

"Da," he said, his voice thick. "I played the Mormon game. I waited until I could get revenge. That tithing money didn't even compare to what it cost to bury my mama. The other things I stole made a better living for me. So you say your life is in God's hands? It sounds like a dangerous place to be. God has a strange way of supporting those who believe in Him. You are perfect proof of that."

Understanding and sadness pierced my heart. "I'm sorry for your pain and for your loss."

"Let me guess, God makes it all better?" His words cut through the darkness.

"Those missionaries did not do things how Christ would have wanted them to. That is not God's fault. God cares about you, not just for the baptism numbers. He loves *you*."

I could see the outline of Duma lying on his back five feet away from me. "How can you say that, Stareyshina? You have done nothing wrong, and God has thrown you in here. How can you defend Him?"

"God didn't throw me in here. Man did. And those men will be judged someday. God doesn't take away the source of the pain, but He makes it so it doesn't hurt so much.

"There is a scripture—'Wherefore, ye must press forward with a steadfastness in Christ, having a perfect brightness of hope, and a love of God and of all men.' I could not have endured what I have without Jesus Christ. He has guided me, kept me safe, brought people into my life who have helped me. Like you. Focusing on what He *hasn't* done for me will never bring peace. It will not change what has happened. But when I take my pain to Him, He lifts it, He takes it on Himself."

No one said anything for a long time, and I was worried Duma had closed his shell, but then he said, "Da, I admit it. I am in pain—but you are too late. Much too late. I have sold my soul to take revenge on those stupid stareyshiny. To God, I must be dead."

"God loves who He makes. He made you. He made your mother. He made those missionaries who hurt you. He only wants you to let Him inside. If you can do that, it's never too late."

"How?" he asked quietly. "How do I let Him in?"

"You pray that He will forgive you for your past wrongs. You pray for the Lord to make your heart bigger."

"Shh," Sergei said. Outside, the sound of firing had stopped. "Is it over?" Sergei asked.

Duma, lying on his stomach, whispered, "Nyet. Who knows if it will ever be."

LIGHT STREAMED THROUGH THE CURTAIN. I immediately sat up, not used to having the sun wake me up. There were no lights on in the room, no light in the hall through the door window.

I got up and used the toilet, and after I flushed, no water returned.

No lights, no water. No sounds of guns.

Faintly, I heard in the hall, "Get up!" The guard was finally making his rounds. "No breakfast! Get up!"

We put on our boots and grabbed our coats, but I didn't put mine on. Something made me quickly wrap both my scriptures in my coat and hold it in a bundle. Sergei looked over at me, a look of panic in his eyes.

We joined other prisoners walking down the dark hall, each with a hand out to hold the wall. I was in front, followed by Sergei and Duma. The guard was in back, holding a flashlight. I wondered how we would make shoes if there was no electricity or water.

Halfway down the stairs, without warning, an explosion sounded somewhere above us. I heard the building shudder, and I lost my balance. I tried to brace myself, holding my bundle close to my body, but landed hard in the dark against several steps. Someone landed on my legs, and I grabbed what felt like their back as I tried to stand. We stumbled around in the dark, bumping into each other, yelling, trying to find the wall.

My hand touched what felt like cool, hard concrete, but I hesitated, confused about which direction to follow. Then a pool of light filled the cramped area, and I made out Duma's shape. He'd found the door.

We hurried through the doorframe and stood in the dimly lit hall, our hearts racing as people began running in different directions. Another explosion sounded somewhere away from the building.

Sergei dropped to the ground. "We are being bombed!"

"Come," Duma said, pulling Sergei to his feet.

Duma led us down the hall to another set of dark stairs. This stairwell had a small window in it, and we could see much better. My leg ached, but I managed to keep up. When we reached the floor below us, there was smoke and yelling. A guard was dragging another guard, who was either unconscious or dead.

"Move!" the guard yelled because we blocked the door.

We jumped out of his way.

"Do you think there are many injured?" Sergei yelled through the smoke.

I coughed. "How will we find anyone?"

Duma sounded panicked. "We need to get out of here. Now! We need to leave."

We retreated into the stairwell and moved down the stairs inch by inch, holding the wall for support in the dark. When we reached a landing, a deafening blast sounded above us.

"Keep going," Duma yelled in the darkness, my ears ringing from the explosion.

We continued down several more flights of stairs until there were no more to go down. Duma opened a door, and we stared at more darkness in front of us. The temperature had dropped significantly, the smell of dampness and mold permeating the emptiness around us.

"Where are we?" Sergei whispered.

I could hear Duma's steps moving in front of us. "The basement," he said.

We inched along the wall. I didn't know what I was touching, but the cool, porous surface felt like concrete. We turned a corner, and it became a bit brighter. After several feet, we could hear faint voices. Slowly, we moved toward the light until we were standing in a room as wide as an entire floor of the prison. Large, discolored, rectangular pillars held up the ceiling. Small windows let some light in above us.

A large crowd of men stared back at us, all in stripes, wearing the same worried expression, some holding injuries. Behind us, we heard more coming, making their way to the spacious room.

Duma began walking around, asking the men questions about which cell they were in, what they did in the prison for work. His years of organizing the prison cell occupants on the computer had prepared him for this. He began to give orders and assignments. He never seemed hurried or overly aggressive, but a leader was what the prisoners needed. They were not used to fending for themselves or thinking independently. Duma had the closest thing to a leadership position that these men knew.

He assigned two men who had worked at times in the infirmary to assess those who were hurt, and Sergei and a few men who had worked in the cafeteria to go upstairs to see what was going on and find some food. He asked a group of around ten men to grab as many blankets upstairs as they could. And he asked me to get a good layout of the basement. All the while, he continued to greet men who were making their way to the basement to escape the smoke-filled halls of the prison.

Cautiously, I walked the perimeter of the large room, poking my head through doors. I found a closet full of random supplies—extra boots, some coats and hats, and a stack of dark pants. I found some candles but no matches. I brought the candles and some of the coats and hats I'd found to the large room. One of the men had some flint he used for cigarettes. Duma sent me down the hall again, this time with a burning candle.

There were some boxes, a bathroom, and a lot of broken, rusted things. There were no weapons. No food. The way things were thrown about, I wondered if someone had already been here and taken what they wanted.

I did find a large barrel full of liquid. Duma sent several men to help me bring it back. Then he smelled some of it and tasted it. "Alcohol," he said. The men cheered, but Duma and I didn't smile, only exchanged one long, concerned look.

I knew why I was apprehensive, but Duma's reaction confused me, so I asked him. "Alcohol always brings trouble," he answered.

Sergei returned with the three other men several hours later, each looking worn but carrying a couple of big burlap bags. Sergei set his down next to us. "Lentils and some kind of potatoes, maybe turnips? Also, look." He held up several stacked tin dishes—twelve in all.

"Did the guards give you trouble?" Duma asked.

"No guards. We could hear guns, fighting on the north side of the building. The windows in the kitchen are shattered by bullets. All the water is off and the electricity. The plumbing—everything."

Duma sighed. "Did you see any others?"

Sergei shook his head. "Nyet. We're going to need water. Is there any down here?"

Duma looked at me.

"None that works," I said.

"We're going to have to make that top priority," Sergei said.

The three of us nodded.

"We'll probably have to leave the prison to find it," Duma said.

"I found a stack of pants in one of the closets," I said. "It would be less obvious than striped uniforms."

"That could work," Duma said. "There is a man named Maxim who says he has family locally in Donetsk. They often bring him packages. He thinks they can help. I'll ask him if he can get a couple men together and see what supplies they can find."

By the end of the day, one hundred three prisoners had made their way to the basement. Maxim agreed to go out with two other men to find more supplies. I made the dark pants fit by tying rope around their waists, and once it got dark, the men slipped out a cellar door.

Only six out of the ten men who had gone upstairs looking for bedding came back. Each held a makeshift blanket bag full of ten to fifteen blankets. They hadn't stayed together, as looking independently had seemed safest. They also informed us that the floors had a few military men raiding the prison. All prisoners were either dead or had joined forces. Four of the prisoners looking for supplies had been forced at gunpoint to leave with separatists.

"Hopefully they don't tell them where we are," Sergei said.

"Maybe they won't care that we are here," Duma said. "This place is its own kind of death."

We all stared at each other grimly.

Duma directed how much food to prepare. Before we began to pass it out, Sergei asked if I would say a prayer. As I did, people bowed their heads and grew silent. I thanked the Lord for what we had found, prayed for our safety and those friends and family who were affected by the fighting, and as I ended in the name of Jesus Christ and looked up, I saw several people wiping their eyes.

I thought about what Father Michael had told me to do and realized the people desperately needed spiritual strength.

It was cold in the basement, and there was nowhere to sit or sleep. Duma devised a plan of each man going with a partner to find their own mattress. We would take turns. Night would surely be safest, and there was no time to lose. He volunteered to go first—with me.

After I hid my scriptures, we held the walls as we passed through halls and up the dark stairwell. My body and mind were tired, but I was grateful my stomach wasn't completely empty. Duma kept making us pause to listen. We went out onto the first floor and heard no sounds of gunfire or any signs of people. We found only one cell door that would even open. We took two of the six mattresses in there, dragging them down the stairwell in the dark.

When we arrived back, Duma instructed eight more eager men to go upstairs, telling them where we had found the mattresses. The night continued that way until the first rays of morning came through the windows. We had a total of forty-seven mattresses. We lined them up to make one big one. Most of the beds also had blankets, so we increased our supply of those too.

I curled up on the edge of a mattress, wrapped in a blanket in the back corner, while men kept warm passing tin bowls of alcohol.

Sergei sat near me. "Nil, I need help. Keep me strong. I can smell that drink. It's been ten years since I've had any of that poison—and I hate it—but I find it continually calling to me."

"Come," I moved over. "Let's try to get some rest." He climbed down next to me, and I threw a blanket over him. Dusty light rays poured through the room, and I felt my eyes grow heavy until I found escape through sleep.

I woke up to a man rolling across my feet, and Sergei was gone. Around me, people were yelling. A man barreled into another man, using his head as a weapon.

"Stop!" I stood up. "Do you want people to find us? Do you want to get killed?" I tried to pull the man away, but he turned and swung at me. I ducked and moved away from them. Again, he came at me, but this time I didn't duck but punched. I felt his bones against my fist, and images of Kaufman swam through my mind as I watched the man double over and crawl across the mattresses. It grew quiet around me, and I realized I'd made a spectacle of myself.

"Stop yelling," I said firmly. "Stop drinking! Stop fighting! There is a war going on above us. If you want to be a part of it, there's the door." I took a deep breath and pointed to the side of the room where the stairwell to the outside was.

No one said anything. Instead, they moved away and laid on mattresses. I leaned against a pillar, breathing heavily. How long would we have to stay down here? How long would we last?

Sergei came up to me with a cup. "It's water," he said. "Maxim came back. I figured those of us who have had *nothing* to drink should have the first share."

I took it gratefully, even if it wasn't nearly enough to quench my thirst. "I am proud of you, Sergei," I said, placing a hand on his shoulder.

He patted my hand. "You were right. Christ can help us through our trials."

Duma had sent the other two men with Maxim in case he decided not to come back and stayed with his family instead, but that wasn't the case. The three returned with a large barrel full of drinkable water his family had given them, and he said there would be more in a week. All the power and water was out, but his family said there was a water source outside of town. They were willing to barter shoes for it.

But we would have to make that barrel last a week.

Sergei was put in charge of food and water rations. And I was put in charge of reading. It was self-assigned. At first it was just to myself. I found a corner where the light from the windows was best and opened the Bible randomly to the page marked *ring*. It was as if my scriptures naturally wanted to turn to that page now.

Sergei leaned against the wall next to me. "Will you read out loud?"

"Da," I said. I turned to the beginning of the chapter. "'And it came to pass at the end of two full years, that Pharaoh dreamed: and, behold, he stood by the river.'"

I had read eight verses of Pharaoh's dream and Joseph's interpretation of it when I heard Sergei say to others nearby, "Come, come listen."

They sat on mattresses, leaned against walls, stared up at the light or at nothing at all. Not all wanted to listen, but twenty or thirty did, even Duma. We read all day, finishing Genesis, moving into Exodus. We read about Joseph's freedom from prison, about a people in bondage to the Egyptians, and about them being freed.

The light in the windows faded, and I stopped reading when I could no longer see the words. We hadn't eaten or moved, but now, with the night, I stretched. Someone lit a candle, and I marveled at the Spirit I felt. The men were quiet, contemplative. We ate some hard potatoes and lentils that had been soaked several hours in a little water. Then we all went to sleep.

The sound of a bomb woke me. It didn't sound like it had hit us, but it was near enough. I could make out shapes in the shadows; it was early dawn. I stood in the dark and made my way down the hall to where the bathroom was. We didn't know when the electricity or plumbing or water would be back on, but we had no other choice but to use the now-very-foul-smelling room and its drain on the floor.

I found my way back to the large room, no longer tired, only cold. I stood in the corner near the windows, where I had read earlier, and saw

Duma across the room. He made his way over until he leaned against the same wall as me. For several minutes, we said nothing. Just stood there, listening. We could hear gunfire and sirens in the distance.

Life had changed so much in such a short amount of time.

It was strange, but here in this damp dungeon, I finally felt Duma and I were allies.

I had seen a different side of him our last night in our cell when he had told me about his mother. He was logical, structured, stubborn, and held grudges—but he did care, probably too much.

"You're a natural leader, Duma," I said.

He glanced at me, then frowned at the floor. "I told you how I was once branch president. I did other things too, things that have come back to haunt me after you showed up here. And then I listened to you read in our cell every night, and it made me remember. I remember why I joined the Church, what I felt."

He met my eyes. "Remember when the bombs came? And there were guards carrying the dead and people running? I was about to rush in that room, but a voice told me to stop. A *real* voice. It wasn't just in my head." His eyes turned, pleading. "Have you ever heard of that happening to someone?"

"Was it the Holy Ghost?"

"I don't know." He bit his dry lips. "I don't remember what that is."

"The Spirit—Holy Ghost—speaks to us from God. Sometimes the Spirit makes us feel peaceful and comforted. That's how He testifies of Christ. It is through the Holy Ghost that God helps us know something is right or good—it is what you felt when you decided to join the Church and be baptized. But it can also warn us of danger—or tell our hearts when we must repent and change. When we are baptized, we get the gift of the Holy Ghost. You were given that gift, Duma, when you were baptized. The Holy Ghost will be with you as long as you are being righteous and doing things that invite the Spirit."

"But I haven't been righteous," he said.

I thought about the last conversation we had in our cell, how Duma had said it was too late for him. "Have you been praying, Duma? Have you been asking God to forgive you?"

He looked down again and nodded. "Da, I tried to the other night."

"That is the beautiful thing about God. We try a little, and He meets us with open arms. He is not like you and me. He wants to forgive."

Duma nodded. "You say this, Stareyshina, but you don't know what I've done." He began to wipe his eyes with his sleeves.

My heart went out to him in a way it hadn't before. I realized I'd been angry at Duma since the first day I'd met him. Angry about the things he'd done. Angry about his attitude toward me. And even mad because I'd been sent to prison to find him—I was holding him responsible for things he had nothing to do with. I said a small prayer inside to move past those feelings and be able to forgive him.

"You're never so far away that the Lord can't reach you," I said, as much for my own benefit as Duma's.

"I see that is true." Duma took a deep breath, then mumbled at the ground, "Maybe that is why He sent you here."

His response touched me, showing more humility than I'd ever seen in him.

He looked up at me. "What is your plan? You know I saw the letter from your mission president. I couldn't read it, but I know he was giving you instructions."

I nodded slowly. "He said to escape if I get the opportunity and go to Kiev. Find the stake president there." I stopped, fear settling in my chest. "I have no plan."

Duma was quiet, but I could hear his mind working like the wheels of a machine, balancing, weighing, figuring.

I crossed my arms and tried to sound casual. "Have you heard from my old companion Kaufman lately? Did you ever write him back?"

Duma rubbed the shadow of blondish whiskers on his chin. "Nyet." He crossed his arms and blew out, and something told me he wasn't telling the truth.

"I'm still bothered by it," I admitted. "We were good friends."

Duma looked up, surprised. "Friends? Are you sure? How close of friends?"

I hesitated, not sure what he meant. "We were companions."

His eyes sparked. "Your accent is respectable, Stareyshina, but you are still undeniably American." He grinned. "Let me give you some advice: don't trust everyone you meet—especially the ones who are nice to you. I can guarantee Kaufman is not who you think he is."

His words confused me. Kaufman hadn't been just nice to me. He'd been real. I didn't doubt his friendship, but then I thought about the small locked box inside the Bible, and I suddenly had to know something. "Do you remember," I asked, "that first time you told me Kaufman had written? You told me one needed the Bible and the Book of Mormon together. What did you mean by that?"

Duma stared at my face as if trying to discern what I was really asking. Then he said, "If you ever get the Bible that goes with that Book of Mormon, I'll *show* you."

My heart began to hammer. "Why do you say *show*?"

He craned his neck to the mattress I'd been sleeping on, my scriptures in a neat stack on the floor. "Do you have it, Nil?"

Distrust entered my heart as quickly as a beaver dips under water. I saw him as a branch president, stealing tithing money from widows, and a man who hated stareyshiny. I couldn't trust him with whatever was inside the Bible—even if he could open it. He'd said so himself—don't trust everyone.

"Do I have what?" I asked.

He hesitated. I saw a confession beginning on his tongue, but he closed his mouth and shrugged. "The Bible is just as important as the Book of Mormon."

"Da," I nodded.

Trust was so hard to earn and so easily lost.

I THOUGHT ABOUT KAUFMAN A little, but survival took all of my effort. Nothing outside of food, water, and safety seemed to matter. Five days went by, and our water was gone. We were only allowed three cups a day, but we had misjudged how much one hundred men would need to drink. And now, from a meager three cups, we were down to nothing.

Every day I spent a majority of the time reading from the scriptures. It kept the men quiet and, therefore, safer. After my conversation with Duma, I hid my Bible in the closet with the supplies I'd found our first day. I started reading from the beginning of the Book of Mormon out loud to the men, and that was what we did the majority of the time. It was like I was with Egor again only this time there were dozens of men sitting around me, listening.

But thirst was becoming a major issue, and we were starving.

Maxim and his two men were sent out again as soon as it got dark. All night, we waited. In the morning, only one returned to tell us the other men were working on a plan, but we would need bartering supplies. We had nothing but shoes and supplies for making them.

He also told us that electricity and water were back on in the city, but something was still wrong with the sewage. And people in the city were getting sick.

That day, Duma worked on a plan to make shoes in the basement. That night, several men went upstairs with candles and found the shoe factory roughed up. But some supplies were still there. Tools, nails, leather, soles, laces, anything they could find and carry back downstairs. That night, primitive shoe making commenced.

The men were able to bring three fifty-gallon buckets and a cart of food, which Sergei planned out, divided, and then finally used to feed us.

I was hammering a crude table with Duma on our seventh day in the basement when he said, "We leave tonight. You and I together."

I glanced behind to see if anyone was listening. "Tonight?" I whispered.

He leaned against the table and waited until I met his eyes. "My sister was living in Horlivka as of last month. She might still be there if the war hasn't spread that far. She can help us find the stake president in Kiev."

"Why?" I asked. I continued to hammer at the table. I didn't want to seem overly eager or suspicious of him. I glanced up. "Why are you doing this for me?"

He met my eyes. "Because I prayed and asked God what I need to do to repent, and He told me to help you leave."

I opened my mouth, dumbfounded. Since when was God answering my prayers through Duma? "What about all these men? They need you."

He looked down at the table and shrugged. "They will be fine, if they follow my directions. I have people who can take over, who know what is going on. Sergei is running the food bartering already."

"How long do you think the men will have to stay down here? What will happen when all this is over?"

"I don't know." He began to push the heavy table over, and I helped him set it the rest of the way down. Panting, he said, "But I have a plan, and if the electricity comes on, it won't work. We need to escape tonight."

Duma told me Horlivka was northeast of Donetsk, about a forty-minute drive. Walking would take around nine hours, a whole night. We thought of taking a train or bus, but even if there were trains running, we didn't have any money readily available to take one and no papers if we were stopped, which could mean death or imprisonment or being forced to fight in the military.

Walking seemed the most logical—and illogical—choice.

"I don't like it," Sergei said, handing me an empty Coke bottle. We would be taking no water; the goal was to find it after we were out. "You have a better chance of survival in here."

"I need to trust the Lord, and this is what He is telling me to do." I put the bottle in the hand-sewn bag we had constructed from a threadbare coat. I buttoned the dark jacket I'd found in the closet, then stuffed my hat in the pockets of the dark pants.

Sergei rubbed the brown stubble on his thin cheeks as his eyes grew moist. "Live or die," he repeated. "Live or die, you are my brother." He reached out and held me in a tight embrace. "Thank you for coming to find me here."

When he let go, I couldn't hide my emotions from him. I wiped my eyes. "I wish I could take you with me, away from here."

"You have," he whispered. He picked up my Book of Mormon and handed it to me. It was our only set of scriptures in the basement. Sergei had gone to find the others in Father Michael's room and found the place torn apart; anything there had been destroyed. I stared at the book, thinking about all the places it had been, even that it had survived a bomb.

"You keep it," I said, handing it to him.

His eyes opened wide. "Are you sure?"

"I don't have room."

I wished I could leave my Bible with him too so the men could read it. But there was a secret surrounding it that felt unsafe. "You keep my book and share it with others. You will be the preacher when I'm gone." I picked up the Bible, looked up, and saw Duma watching me. I felt his eyes on it as I shoved it deep into my bag.

"You shaved," Sergei said. "Where did you find a razor?"

Duma shrugged. "I used the kitchen knife."

"Really?" Sergei slapped Duma's cheeks. "You did a very fine job."

Duma handed me a map. "One of the guys found this."

I folded it carefully, then slipped it in my coat pocket, where I could have it quickly and it wouldn't get smashed. I swung the bag onto my shoulder and turned back to Sergei. "Take care of these men. They need you."

"Will we ever see each other again?" he asked.

I hugged him one more time, moisture in my eyes, knowing I wouldn't. Even if I didn't escape and was caught, the chances I would be lucky enough to be sent back to the Donetsk prison were nonexistent.

Duma held up a fabric piece. "Here," he said. "Wrap these around your boots." He handed me some string.

"Your mind is a criminal work of art, Duma," I muttered.

He smirked as if he enjoyed the comment as he helped me hold the fabric in place while I tied the knots. Then I helped him do the same.

Sergei gave Duma a hug like he had me. "Take care. I will miss you, my friend."

Duma returned the hug. "You know what they say, 'Little thieves are hanged, but great ones escape.'"

Sergei laughed. "You always have a way of building yourself up at the expense of others."

"Remember what I taught you."

"Forgetting it would be death. And you take care of Nil."

Duma glanced at me, his face solemn. "I intend to."

Escaping from prison was easier than it should have been. Either Duma had timed it all just right, or people were confused about who should be coming and going from the prison. I followed Duma through the frigid darkness. It had been a long time since I'd been outside and even longer since I'd felt the nighttime cold. I pulled the warm beanie tighter on my head.

There was only a sliver of a moon, and with no lights on at the prison, we could barely see ten feet in front of us. Our boots didn't make the loud clunking sounds they normally did, thanks to Duma's fabric idea.

Softly, we tread across the short back-loading area until we neared the ten-foot-high chain-link fence. Coiled barbed wire ran the whole length, resting on top of the *Y* posts like a sleeping, coiled snake. We wouldn't be able to climb over it.

Duma walked the length of it. He stopped, and then after a second, I saw his hand make a movement for me to follow. As I neared him, I saw that one of the giant posts had been broken in half, causing the snake to droop, creating a two-foot by four-foot gap in the fence. This was how our guys had gone in and out.

Duma went first, and I crawled under after him. The ground on the other side of the concrete was solid, frozen mud. We scrambled up and followed the fence past some empty trucks. We saw no one, not even a soldier guarding, but in the far distance, we could hear sounds—sounds of movement and destruction. My mind wandered to thoughts of Ivan, Trofim, Gavriil, and Boris. Where were they now? Were they alive? Were they learning to fight? Would they kill each other?

We moved swiftly around the small military camp that took up the block on the west side of the prison. The next block looked as though it had been made up of homes, but now the cobblestone road was covered with debris of glass, pieces of roof, and fences.

We stuck to the shadows as silently as we could, getting farther away from the prison with each passing minute. After an hour of walking, Duma stopped in front of a house and began searching behind bushes.

"Are we going the right way?" I asked, warming my hands under my armpits.

Duma looked up sharply, then both ways down the street. "Shh, Stareyshina," he whispered. "This war doesn't care who it kills."

He moved to the next bush and, on his stomach, began searching under the low branches. I crouched on the ground next to him, feeling too tall and visible standing alone. This time, he pulled out a brown-wrapped package. He stuffed it in his coat-bag.

I wanted to ask what it was but didn't dare speak again.

"Let's find some water," Duma whispered. He stood and dusted himself off, and I wondered if he was keeping secrets from me. But I had no alternative but to trust him. I didn't know where I was going or how to operate in a war zone. Following him felt like the right thing.

For several blocks, we walked with no signs of electricity anywhere. A dark line of houses looked vacated and dead. One of the doors stood ajar; we could see its crooked angles and the spaces of deeper black. Slowly, quietly, we approached it. There were no sounds, so we stepped through the door. Debris was scattered through the house as if it had been bombed and ransacked.

The kitchen wasn't far from the door. The metal on the sink glowed under the moon and starlight. Duma turned the knob and water came flowing out. Without thinking, we both took turns drinking as much as possible under the faucet, feasting on it again and again. We pulled out our empty containers and filled them before turning it off.

My stomach hurt from fulness, and we both had to use the bathroom before we'd gone very far. We wandered along the dark street again. Another road, then another. The buildings became taller, and we saw no people, but we saw signs of fighting. Papers and large objects blocked our progress in the dark. There were cars overturned and military vehicles left to the side. We kept to the shadows, which seemed most of the city. I wondered how much of this town had no electricity or if the people had simply turned off the lights and left.

However, the train station's lights were lit up like an amusement park. We could see the blue lights from several blocks away. When we got nearer, Duma stopped in a deserted park across from it, under a tree still bare from the frigid winter but with enough branches to help us feel hidden.

"This is where we part ways," Duma said. "I have other things to do. Things you would complicate."

I backed up several feet. "This wasn't the plan. I thought we were walking to Horlivka together. How will I find your sister?"

The temperature seemed to drop as we stood still under the trees.

He set his bag down on what was left of the frozen grass. "Here," he said, stepping forward and handing me a piece of paper. "This is the address. Don't lose it."

Cautiously, I bent and placed it in my sock.

Duma tore open the brown package. There were two shirts—one white, one plaid—a tie, and a fur hat. There was a little bit of money, which he divided between us, and a bottle of alcohol. I stared at it, confused.

"These are for you." He handed me the plaid shirt and fur hat before pulling off his own coat and shirt and replacing them with the white shirt.

I set my bag on the ground in front of us and followed what he was doing. I had no alternative, which made me feel both angry and helpless since, clearly, Duma had had a different plan all along. "How do I look?" I whispered once I'd finished.

He laughed softly. "Like a czar. Here, get rid of these." He handed me our guard shirts, and I shoved them in a nearby trash can, along with the discarded paper. It took some willpower to do it. Throwing clothing away when it was so cold seemed foolish. But getting caught with those clothes could place us and mean dire consequences.

I walked back to our things and picked up the bottle of vodka on the ground. "What's this for?"

"Put it in your inner coat pocket. You never know when you'll need it."

"I don't drink; you know that."

"Da, the better it is to have it with you."

"All right. I could argue with that, but I won't. Where are you going?"

"I'm not sure yet. Could you tie this on me? It's been awhile." He handed me the tie.

I wrapped it around his neck and tucked it under his collar. It had been awhile since I'd tied one too, but my hands hadn't forgotten. "You don't know where you're going?" I asked, suspicious.

"I have an idea, but it's nothing you need to worry about." He pulled the beanie off his head and combed his short hair over. "How do *I* look?"

I shook my head, frustrated. This wasn't what we'd talked about.

"How do I look?" he repeated. "It's not every day you see me in a shirt and tie."

I stared at his hair with three weeks' growth since we'd been buzzed, his dark pants and blaring white shirt and smooth cheeks. I frowned. "Like a missionary."

My comment seemed to make him nervous. He hurried into his coat and pulled the beanie on tight.

"What are you hiding, Duma? I have to know I can trust you."

He stopped buttoning his coat. "Why, Stareyshina? Why do you need to trust me?"

Wasn't it obvious?

He stared at me, waiting, our breath coming out fast in the cold. I thought of those I'd trusted—Kaufman, President Meyers, Egor, Sergei. I even thought of Angela. *What a mistake that had been.*

I thought of those who didn't trust me.

Maybe the answer was not to trust anyone. Then I couldn't be hurt. I swallowed and held out my hand, more comfortable now with the thought of him leaving. It was better this way. "Good luck to you, brother."

He stepped forward and shook it. "And good luck to you." He didn't let go; it was as if he knew I was inwardly withdrawing. "Stick to the plan. No matter what. Find my sister, then head to Kiev."

"Da, I promise." Still, he didn't let go. "Of course I will stick to the plan. What other plan is there?"

He let go of my hand, satisfied. "We can't leave together. Give me a five-minute head start."

I nodded. I had no clock, so I would have to wait until it felt long enough. I watched him heft his bag on his shoulder with mingled feelings of regret. I would never see him again. He was the person I'd dreamed about—had I done what the Lord had wanted me to?

"Duma?" He turned and looked at me, and I felt lost on what to say, so I finally sputtered, "Thank you."

"It will be okay, Stareyshina," he said, giving me a crooked grin. He turned without another word. I watched him slink soundlessly across the park, a moving black shadow. Then I couldn't see him anymore.

It seemed even darker now. I decided it might be a good time to eat a little. Slowly, I opened my bag lying on the grass. I removed items, searching for the few potatoes and hard bread. There seemed to be more room than before. Was I missing something?

The Bible was gone.

I tore through the items again, with the same result. Had I dropped it?

I searched the ground. Carefully I reloaded my bag and lifted it to my shoulder. It was definitely lighter than it had been. There was only one answer: Duma had taken it.

I stared across the street at the lit-up train station and wondered what I should do.

Follow the plan, Duma had said.

Of course he would say that.

I HID IN THE SHADOWS near the train station, the lights illuminating the map so I could find where I was. It looked like if I stayed near the E50, it would take me north and slightly west to Horlivka. I looked at the towns around it, in case I went too far. I held my thumb up to the kilometers measurement in the corner and then held it up to the road. It was about forty kilometers, which was about twenty-five miles.

A clock above me said it was a little after ten o'clock. I stared at it, watching the hands move. It had been a long time since I'd seen a clock and known exactly what time it was.

I cut across the street and hurried into the shadows. I didn't see anyone, which made me feel nervous and vulnerable, though I heard a vehicle when I neared the E50. I was walking with trees on one side and an iron fence bordering a building on the other. I flattened myself against a tree and watched the military jeep drive by slowly, as if patrolling. It was the only patrol I'd seen all night, and I wondered if that was a good sign or bad.

I waited several minutes until I was sure it was gone, then turned onto the E50 highway and began walking northward. The night air grew even colder along the highway. I pulled the ear covers down on my fur hat. Necessity had to trump social expectations. I picked up my pace to keep my body warm with exertion. Each time a car passed along the highway, I got down in a ditch or hid behind a bush. They drove at reckless speeds, making me feel as though they were escaping danger, which made my adrenaline pump and kept me walking quickly.

I didn't know how far I'd gone when I neared what looked like a small bus stop. I collapsed on a bench and pulled out some water and one of the potatoes. I tried not to think of *if* I could walk all night in the freezing cold with little food and water. I'd been through worse. I would choose this over prison, over fighting in a war I didn't belong in. I tried to let that thought give me fuel and stood again, but my body made me sit. The exhaustion was too much.

Lord, please help me endure. Help me get to Horlivka. Help me find the strength I need.

I reached inside my coat to get the dead weight of the alcohol off me. Why was I even carrying it? The sound of a large vehicle made me stop, my heart hammering. I stayed where I was, hoping the truck or whatever it was would keep going. But my heart sank as I heard its engine slow and the brakes squeak.

A long bus pulled up, its door opening to me.

A middle-aged man in a blue uniform yelled out the bus door, "Hurry up, are you coming or not?"

Slowly, I stood. "Where are you going?"

"Spartak, Kashtanove, Kruta Balka, Krasnyi, P'yatykhatky, and end in Horlivka near the train station. Are you coming or not? This is not a round trip, only one way."

"Da," I walked over to the door.

"Where are you going?"

"Horlivka."

I counted out the money Duma had given me. I had just enough. The bus was two-thirds filled with people and almost all the way full of things. No one spoke. Some slept. One person moved a bag, and I sank into the empty seat facing forward. My eyes drooped with each passing kilometer. Kilometers I didn't have to walk. In less than an hour, I could be in Horlivka.

The bus only stopped if someone was sitting on a bus-stop bench. No one got off.

I woke with my head pressed against the cold window. I rubbed my eyes and saw an older woman watching me. She glared and mumbled, "*P'yanyy*," which meant "drunk."

"Where are we?" I asked her.

"P'yatykhatky," she said. "Where have you been?"

I ignored her sarcasm. "Have we passed Horlivka?"

"Nyet, that is next."

The bus slowed to a stop.

"Ozeryanivka!" the bus driver shouted.

No one got up, but the doors opened, and a man in a police uniform climbed inside and searched the bus from the entryway. I ducked my head behind the seat.

"Where are you coming from?" the officer asked.

"Donetsk."

"I'm looking for someone," I heard him say. "He is a convict who may have escaped from the Donetsk prison. I need to search your bus just like the others I've searched this week."

"What does he look like? Maybe he got off already."

"Perhaps. He's an American. A missionary."

I kept my head down, my heart racing. The police were looking for me? Why? What made me different from any other missing convict? It was almost like they'd been waiting for me—knew I'd escape. Knew where I was. I felt paranoid.

The older woman who had called me drunk yelled, "That's not a police uniform. My son runs the police force in Horlivka. I should report you."

I peeked out and stared at the man dressed in a black coat and slacks. He wore a matching officer hat with a star on the front. I couldn't tell if he was a genuine police officer or not. Thoughts of Kaufman's letter entered my mind—warnings, someone was trying to kill me. My heart hammered loudly in my chest.

"Now, babushka, don't make me arrest you for interfering with an investigation. It will only take a moment."

Trying to hide would only make it more obvious who I was. Maybe they would think I was asleep. I searched my brain for something I could use as a weapon. My hand closed around the bottle in my coat pocket. I made sure both my earflaps were down, then took a clump of dirt off my shoe and smeared it across my teeth and on my cheeks and chin.

I sat up and yawned. Without opening the bottle, I stuck it in my mouth, pretending to take a giant swig. I lazily blinked my eyes as if I were struggling to keep them open. I gave a small smile to the ceiling, enough to show my dirty teeth, then leaned my head against the back of the seat and closed my eyes.

"Drunk," the woman muttered, along with an oath.

I kept my eyes open a slit and saw the man searching each face. His gaze didn't even pause on mine. "He's not here. But he's dangerous. There may even be a reward if you find him."

"Bah, a reward?" the old woman muttered. "I've seen how they reward in this country."

The officer waved and shook his head at her, got off, and we began to move again. The next stop was Horlivka. I didn't want to get too far into the city center. The fewer people I talked to, the better. I pulled on the cord when we neared the bus stop to indicate I was getting off.

I was the only one who exited, the bus shutting its doors the second I cleared and pulling off. Silence met me all around. There was a small covered shelter at the bus stop. A man slept on the small bench. I glanced inside to see if there was a map and found one covering a small portion of the inner wall. I pulled out the piece of paper with the address from my sock and searched for the street on the map. I found it several kilometers away, but it was a straight shot with only a few street changes.

I memorized the names, my fingers aching in the frigid night air. When I'd finished, I set the heavy bottle of alcohol down next to the sleeping man. I wasn't sure if it had served the purpose Duma had envisioned or not, but I was done carrying it.

I headed for the shadows of the building. The roads were not vacant here in Horlivka, and I had to keep to the dark patches as much as possible. There were troops and civilians, making it easier to blend in. But there was also an edge of nervousness, as if everyone were walking on a tightrope, waiting.

I turned onto a road that went by a school. The fence was broken, debris scattered everywhere, as if a car had crashed into it. In the distance, I could hear the familiar sounds of gunfire. The air smelled of camping and fireworks.

I forced myself to keep to my chosen path, clinging even closer to the shadows. Whatever conflict had happened here had passed, but it had left evidence on the roadways. Pieces of clothing, mattress chunks, roof timbers, and dark stains were scattered on the road. A large bus lay discarded on its side, its windows smashed in. I didn't look too closely at the piles and shapes on the ground, spilling out of it and around it. I didn't need to. I knew what they were.

It was still dark as I reached the five-story apartment building with the address Duma had given me. I approached the outer door and saw that it was missing completely, torn from its hinges. I could no longer hear gunshots, but I wondered if everyone had deserted the building. I sat on the frozen dirt against a tree and tried to decide what to do.

It was too early to knock on someone's door, and I was worried about this next step. Duma had deserted me rather than come to his sister. Was this really his sister's home? Or was it all part of a setup?

Who did I trust?

I took a deep breath and kneeled. Early or not, I needed to act soon. Someone would find me. I bowed my head and said a silent prayer. I knew one person I could always trust. The answer came as Duma's words entered my head. *Stick to the plan.*

I shuddered in the cold, scared of what sticking to the plan might mean. I pulled the crumpled paper from my sock and looked at the numbers one more time. I had nothing and everything to lose.

I tried to move soundlessly as I walked up the stairs to the third story. Yellow lights lit the dark hall. The electricity worked here, at least; that was good.

The address was the first door next to the stairs. I faced it, then stared out the large window to my left. Along the horizon, I could see the blackness turning a lighter color of gray in the east. It was still too early. There was a possibility that no one would be awake and would be angry at being pulled out of bed. But a sense of urgency pressed at my chest. Someone was looking for me.

I pulled off my hat and stuffed it in my coat pocket, then combed through my hair with my fingers before knocking lightly on the worn white door. I counted to thirty and lifted my hand to knock again. This time, without a word, it opened three inches. I saw two eyes peek out from behind the chain-locked door.

I cleared my throat. "I'm looking for Duma's sister." I glanced at the paper again. "Anya." My voice sounded gruff from the cold air. She didn't answer, so I tried again. "Are you Duma's sister? Is this where she lives?"

"What's your name?" a quiet female voice asked.

I hesitated. She opened the door an inch more. The yellow light from the hall lit up half her face. "I know who you are. I saw you in the news. You're that stareyshina who was thrown into prison. What are you doing here?"

She didn't unlatch the door, but she opened it wider. The whites of her eyes were red and tired; her brown hair fell to the side in a messy brown braid. Even from the cracked door, I could tell she was much smaller than me. Anya was a common enough name in Ukraine. I'd never once thought I would know this one. But I did. Short, like the picture I'd seen her in. She looked exactly like Kaufman's Anya.

I took a step back. "I must have the wrong address. Sorry for disturbing you. Please—please don't tell anyone I was here. Please." I took another step back.

"Wait. You said my brother sent you. Duma? Is he all right?"

Despite her confirmation that she was indeed the Anya I was searching for, I couldn't make my feet move forward. "Da—I don't know. He sent me here, said you could help me get to Kiev."

Her eyes narrowed. "My brother hates stareyshiny. Why would he help you? Why didn't he come himself?"

They were good questions. I rubbed my head and stared at my cracked boots. "Your brother has changed." I met her eyes. "The prison was attacked, and we were living in the basement. We spoke of the scriptures and about the gospel of Jesus Christ. He desires repentance."

She narrowed her eyes. "A crow will never be a falcon."

Desperation and anger flared inside me. "Do you truly believe that? I've heard of you too, Anya. I was companions with Kaufman. You know him, don't you?"

She blinked at me. "What are you playing at? I won't be controlled by Kaufman—not through you, so you can go back to that prison you just left." She slammed the door shut.

I shoved my hands in my pockets and stared at the closed door. What now? There was no backup plan. Duma had assumed his sister would help me. I walked to the window and watched the beginnings of dawn, the sun revealing a frozen morning, the dew coating everything dusty-white.

I heard the door open and turned to look behind me. Anya peered through, her jaw set, the chain still in place. "You're still here."

"I have nowhere else to go. No other options."

She was quiet a moment, then said softer, "Is Kaufman blackmailing my brother? Kaufman told me he would help him. That is the only reason I went along with it."

I opened my mouth and closed it. "I'm confused. Your brother told me he doesn't know Kaufman. Why would Kaufman blackmail him?"

Her eyebrows lifted. "You said—you mean you were Kaufman's missionary companion before you were put in prison? What was your crime?"

"There is evidence that I stole a valuable ring from a museum—but I didn't." I took a deep breath. I needed Anya to trust me. I'd never make it to Kiev without food, water, and a place to rest, and she'd already seen me. She could tell the police. "Look, I'm sorry. You're right. I don't really know you.

I only recognized you from a picture Kaufman had. But you don't know me either. I'm from a small town in America. I was only here six weeks before I was thrown into prison. I just want to get home. Duma really did send me here for help."

"Why?" she whispered, swallowing.

I took a shot in the dark. "Maybe you're the only one he has left in this world who he can 100 percent trust."

She looked down, her cheeks pink. I wasn't sure if what I'd said was true—Duma had told me trust wasn't important. But maybe in forty years when he had lost everyone like Egor had, he would feel differently.

The echo of an explosion in the distance made me drop to the ground. I threw my arms around my head, my body tense. I heard her unlatch the chain, and the door creaked open. I wiped my forehead with my sleeve and shakily stood.

"Come," she said from the doorway. "It's better to talk inside."

ANYA PICKED UP A BAT as I cautiously walked into her apartment. She looked so vulnerable holding it that the movement was more comforting than intimidating. Her apartment was small and shabby, littered with papers and clothing. A bag sat open on an old couch that faced an ancient television placed against the wall. I looked around at the mess and wanted to ask her if she'd been robbed.

She answered my thoughts. "I'm leaving. Many people in the neighborhood have left—at least those with places they can go. It's not safe here."

She headed to a small white kitchen with yellow wallpaper and a small round table. She set the bat against the cupboards, then opened a fridge. "So, your name is Stareyshina Christensen?"

"Da, Neal Christensen," I said, watching her serve some food from a bowl onto a plate. The smell made my mouth water.

"Do you want me to warm it up?" she asked.

"That is for me?"

"You're probably starving. No point wasting it." She glanced at me with eyes that reminded me of Duma's, except for where his were a light, cool green, hers were a rich, warm brown. "Sit." She motioned to the table.

I took the seat on the far side, my arms folded as I watched her warm it in a small yellow microwave. "Do you live alone?"

Her shoulders tensed, and she gave me a long look but didn't answer. I sounded like I was trolling for information.

The microwave dinged, and she set a steaming plate in front of me. Rice, carrots, and some kind of meat—I closed my eyes and bowed my head. *Thank you, Lord.* When I opened them, she silently handed me a fork. My stomach growled loudly, and I tried not to burn my mouth as I took a bite. I hadn't had warm food in six months.

She began to pull things out of the fridge. The food on my plate was gone too quickly. I wished for more but instead walked my plate over to the sink. She turned to take it from me, but I said, "I can wash it."

"A man who does dishes? Where did you come from again?" She smiled briefly at me, and I felt my cheeks grow hot. She turned back to the fridge.

While I scrubbed the plate, I asked, "Where are you planning to go?"

Her voice was muffled in the fridge. "I haven't quite decided. Our branch president gave us addresses for church buildings in other cities. I just want to get away from the fighting. It looks as though all the east is under attack. But I have to make sure the orphanage is taken care of first."

I dried my hands on a towel nearby and turned to face her. "The orphanage? Is that where you work?"

She put the food in a backpack and zipped it up, then carried it to the door. "I volunteer there. I wish they could evacuate, but they have nowhere to go. The Russian separatists and Ukrainian military have taken over every government building and some of the churches, including our LDS meetinghouse. They've banned worship and are using it to house militants. I also heard from a friend in Donetsk that the church there was spray-painted with 'Children of Satan' and 'Yankee, go home.' No one is safe. We need to leave soon."

I held on to that word: *we*. "Am I going with you?"

Her eyes darted to the corner behind me, where she'd left the bat. "You said you need to get to Kiev?"

"My mission president told me to escape and get there if I can."

"Your mission president?"

"He believes I'm innocent. He's trying to help me."

Her eyes suddenly narrowed. "I believe you when you say my brother sent you. After all he's done, I still don't think he'd send someone here who would hurt me. But if you mess with me at all, I will not hesitate to turn you into the nearest military establishment, got it?"

I nodded. "I promise, I won't hurt you."

She swallowed and looked me up and down before nodding. "Kiev it is, then."

I let out a stabilizing breath, relief coursing through me. "Thank you, Anya." She didn't answer but turned back to the fridge. "So it's true, then," I said. "The mission is closed? All the missionaries went home?"

"The conflict is only along Eastern Ukraine. But yes, I think everyone has left from the Donetsk mission. Everyone but the missing missionary, of course."

"Missing missionary?"

"Da, from America. Stareyshina Tyson, I think was his name? From California?"

My ears began to ring. I sank into one of the kitchen chairs. *Brett is missing?* "When?"

"Five days ago. They think he was kidnapped." She glanced at me. "Did you know him?"

I rubbed my mouth with my hand. "Wow."

Another explosion sounded, this time shaking the building. I hit the ground and grabbed my head, my heart racing. I waited for the walls to cave in, for the smoke.

I felt something touch my hand. It was Anya's foot. "It's okay," she said. "We're okay."

I sat up and breathed in deeply. "Is it always like this? Have you been hit yet?"

"It hasn't been that loud before," she said.

I didn't want Anya to think I was a crazy, psycho convict. I scrambled to standing position. It didn't matter that Duma had discounted trust—I needed it. "Anya, I don't have any money, not any. I hate to ask for your help."

Her serious eyes met mine and softened. "Then how are you different from anyone else in Ukraine, huh? Let's get as much food as we can." She walked across the room and took my small handmade bag, dumping the contents on the couch. She studied what I'd brought and picked up things like my Coke bottle and potatoes.

She handed me a large backpack. The two of us raided her cupboards and drawers, packing anything edible. She didn't have much, but we took it all. We piled items into my small bag and a couple grocery-type bags. She took my uneaten potatoes and packed them with the food as well.

"We'll need warm clothes. I'm sure I can find something in the closet that would fit. My roommates left some things."

Wearing girl clothes might have bothered me seven months ago but not now. Clothing kept me from freezing. "I will do what you think is best."

She hesitated, then turned around. "It will probably take three days to get to Neper."

"That long?"

She picked up one of the bags of groceries and carried it to the door. "We will need to walk out of the city so we are undetected and get somewhere safer."

I nodded, remembering the signs of violence I'd seen through the streets and the bus lying on its side.

She came back over to the kitchen, grabbed her bat, and said, "Come with me."

Down a short hall were two bedrooms. She stood outside one of the rooms and instructed me to stand near the closet inside—her decision to trust only went so far.

I tried on several sweaters that made me look feminine and didn't cover my arms or my torso all the way. We had better luck in her roommate's bedroom with a large gray sweatshirt with the flag of Ukraine on it. I stared at the two stripes: yellow on the bottom, blue on the top, like prison stripes. She also found some sort of tiger-print stretchy pants she was sure would fit under my navy-blue pants.

I grabbed a yellow scarf. "Do you think this is too bright?" I asked, feeling it for warmth and thickness.

She shrugged. "Maybe it won't matter in the long run what we wear."

I met her eyes and swallowed. The people on the bus could have been wearing the color of night or a fluorescent orange bull's-eye. It hadn't made a difference. It hadn't even mattered if they were pro-Russian or Ukrainian.

She directed me to the bathroom. "I'm afraid people will recognize you. I think maybe no one will care right now with everything else going on, but, then, you can never be sure." She gave me a kind smile. "Your accent is good. Prison must be a good teacher?"

"Da." I rubbed the back of my neck. "Much too good in some ways."

She nodded, her eyes settling below my left eye where I knew my scar was. "I never would have suspected you were American. But your face within Mormon circles became quite well known after you were arrested." She took a step back. "You can shower, but be quick. We need to leave soon."

She shut the door, and I undressed and stared into the mirror above the sink. Even without the prison clothing, I looked like an ex-convict. I rubbed at the scar below my eye, which protruded in contrast to my hollow cheeks. I tried to picture how I'd looked before Ukraine, but there was no *before* Ukraine. How could there have been?

I tried to smile into the mirror at myself, but it felt and looked too unnatural. "No one will recognize me," I said. "I don't recognize myself."

I turned on the shower and felt the warm water run across my neck, my hands, down my elbows. Warm water was the most delicious thing I'd ever felt. I scrubbed every inch of me three times.

After the shower, I dressed and slipped the tiger pants on, which, embarrassingly, did fit. At least I would be wearing pants over the top of them.

I walked out of the bathroom, and Anya was already dressed in walking shoes and black pants, her coat a dark gray. She held out the largest backpack full of supplies, and I slipped it onto my shoulders. She adjusted the straps around me so it would be comfortable, then handed me my prison-made bag full of food.

She put on the other backpack and picked up a grocery bag. Before she shut the front door, I watched her pause and take in everything around her, saying goodbye. Then she locked it and shoved the key under the door.

"It was lucky I caught you before you left," I said as we headed down the stairwell.

She turned to look at me. "Luck, Stareyshina? I thought you believed in God."

IT WAS MIDMORNING AS WE set out. There were no cars or buses. It was like a dead town, reminding me of zombie movies. The orphanage was several kilometers away. I was afraid I'd have to walk by the bus again and see it in daylight, but Anya guided us on a safe route that showed little signs of destruction. Some of the buds were starting on the trees as tiny nubs at the ends of the bare branches.

We passed by a whole row of trees near the road, their bottom halves painted a stark white. "Why did they paint these?" I asked.

"They don't paint trees in America?"

"Not where I'm from."

"How strange," she said. "Never? I don't know why. They just do, every spring."

I stared at each one, marveling at the strangeness of it until we reached the last five trees, where some had streaks of red across the white. Debris covered the road and grass. The sight made my stomach queasy, and I stopped watching the trees.

The orphanage was a stone-white building, with a blue-painted iron fence surrounding it. First impression, it looked like a prison. Enough so that my palms began to sweat. Anya led me to the side, where a small, tree-covered park made it look slightly more inviting. There was a door there, where perhaps goods were delivered. She knocked several times before a middle-aged woman, nicely dressed, with curled dark hair, opened it partway. "Oh, good, Anya, it's only you." She stopped. "Who is with you?"

"Um, this is my friend." Anya opened her hand to me. Her hesitation gave me the common sense to think up a different name.

"Egor," I said, stepping forward, my hand out to shake hers. "It's nice to meet you." She shook it but didn't smile.

"This is Mrs. Panyakov."

"Are you with the army?" she asked me.

"Nyet," Anya shook her head. "He is a friend of my brother's. He is helping me leave town. We brought you supplies." She held up the bag, and I did the same.

She nodded and opened the door all the way. "Come in." She glanced behind us and through the park. "I had two men come by while you were gone, eyeing the place. I don't think they were Russian, but it's getting harder to tell. I hope they don't plan on setting up camp here or burning us to the ground like the Orthodox cathedral. Did you see it?"

Anya shook her head as Mrs. Panyakov shut the door firmly behind us.

"A bomb hit the building next to the cathedral, and the fire swept through the neighborhood. Lost. That church is older than this country. My friend was married in it. Such a shame." She clicked her tongue and walked down the hall.

"Is the orphanage evacuating?" I asked, following behind Anya.

"Where would we go? There are over one hundred children here." She shook her head. "Nyet, Anya has been helping us set up a small food storage in the basement, a place we can go if the fighting comes our way. And others have left things to help us."

Mrs. Panyakov led us down some stairs into what felt like a cellar. I set the backpack down next to a makeshift shelf, along with the other bags of groceries. She and Anya went through the backpack I'd been carrying, pulling out jars of preserves. Then she went down the storage shelf, picking out a few canned items and some potatoes. She distributed some supplies, cans of food, and blankets more evenly between our two bags, then handed the large backpack to me.

We trudged up the stairs, the backpack much lighter now. I followed the two women down a hall and into a room where several children sat at tables, eating. Anya set her bag next to my feet where we stood by the entrance, then she walked over to a group of girls, their dark hair all plaited in two braids, all matching one another. Anya held one of the braids up and smiled as each girl turned their head so she could admire them. One of the girls insisted Anya sit in front of her on the floor. She undid Anya's messy side-braid and combed it with her fingers.

Several of the children were watching me, and I realized how awkward I looked, standing there with a backpack on.

A missionary would talk to the children.

A prisoner wouldn't. They'd be afraid of a prisoner.

Which one was I?

I slipped the backpack off and set it by Anya's. Slowly, I walked to one of the tables and asked some of the boys if I could sit by them. One silently scooted over and ducked his black head.

"How is your meal?" I asked.

He took a bite and shrugged.

One of the other boys sitting across from us said, "They give us hot chocolate at Christmas."

"Do they? That's wonderful. I love hot chocolate."

"I do too," he said, rubbing at his brown freckles.

"What do you do for fun here?" I asked.

"We play dragon. I like to be the tail. And we play hide-n-seek when it gets dark and the loud booms start."

I nodded to show I knew what he meant. "I don't like that game very much."

"You sound strange," he said. "You say words differently."

"Do I?"

"Nick," a voice said behind me. It was Anya, her hair now in two braids, like the little girls. "Be polite. Maybe he hasn't been taught as well as you."

"I definitely have not," I said.

Anya seemed to find that funny. She patted me on the shoulder, and I knew it was time to go.

"It was nice to meet you young men. Thank you for sharing a seat," I said to the shy boy. I stood and followed Anya over to the doorway, where we hefted our bags over our shoulders.

"Goodbye, Dasha," Anya said, embracing Mrs. Panyakov.

"Where are you going?" Mrs. Panyakov asked, releasing her.

"I think I will settle in Neper. Maybe—"

An explosion sounded from somewhere nearby, making the building shake.

"Is it time for the hiding game?" Nick yelled loudly.

"Da, children, quickly, bring your food. Anya? Could you take them to the basement?" Anya nodded and grabbed several small children's hands. I did the same while Mrs. Panyakov ran up some stairs.

Gathering all the children to the basement took nearly ten minutes. The children had blankets and special items and wore thick sweaters and coats. It was a tight fit. They sat cross-legged on the cold cement floor, some on the laps of older children. Nick adjusted himself until he was right next to me and leaned against my shoulder.

Another bomb shook the ceiling, and the kids covered their ears and heads.

Anya grabbed a chapter book off the shelf, settled herself underneath the hanging lightbulb in the midst of some of the younger kids, and began reading. I watched her expressions and the way the children quieted down so they could hear her. I thought about the men I'd left behind in prison. Was Sergei reading to them? Were they still without water and plumbing? Were they safe and hidden?

It was several minutes before I realized she was reading *The Hobbit* by Tolkien. I hugged my knees and thought how Kaufman had nicknamed me Hobbit. But now I was a hobbit accused of stealing a ring. And who was Kaufman in all of this? Anya made it sound like Kaufman had hurt her. There was so much I didn't know and didn't understand, like why did Kaufman's scriptures have a little locked box? And why had he written Duma?

I was relieved when Mrs. Panyakov came down the stairs and said, "I can't hear any more fighting. I sent Andrii down the street to see what he can find out."

"Read some more, Anee," one of the girls with braids said.

"Da, please," more children said.

"I have read for so long I can't believe you haven't all grown beards!" She looked at me. "Maybe this man Egor knows some stories. He has lived in many places. Ask him if he has seen a castle. Or a dragon?"

"A dragon?" Nick asked, impressed.

I laughed. "Nyet, I have not seen big dragons, only small ones that hide under rocks and are blue."

"Blue? But do you know any *stories*?" the girl with braids asked.

I opened my mouth to say I wasn't a very good storyteller but then closed it. It was as if my life was on repeat—*The Hobbit* and now someone begging me to tell a story. My thoughts kept swirling around Kaufman. "All right," I conceded, "I will tell you my favorite story. It's about a pig. His name was Wilbur."

Mrs. Panyakov sat on the steps as I proceeded to tell them the story of *Charlotte's Web*. The children were quiet the whole time, as if I were telling the most exciting story in the world. I added as many details as I could remember about how much Fern wanted to save Wilbur from being eaten and how kind her dad was to let her keep him. I included all the characters: the goose family, the cow, the horse, the sheep, the rat, and, of course, the spider. When I finished, hands shot up in the air.

"Did her dad really let her keep him?" "Did they have enough food to keep a pig and all those animals?" "What happened to Wilbur's family?" "Did he miss them?"

And like American children, they wanted to know if spiders really could spin webs with words in them.

"Of course." I grinned. "Haven't you seen a spider before? They look very intelligent with their long legs. Think how much they could write if they chose. Maybe they are writing words that are their own language, ones we can't understand."

Anya stood and walked toward Mrs. Panyakov and the two of them went up the stairs.

"Tell us another story," Nick said.

"One about a princess," a girl said.

"Okay . . ." I tried to remember any princess stories I'd heard. I finally settled on Cinderella. My sister had liked the Disney movie. "Do you know this story?" I asked after starting it. Several children nodded. "Then I choose you to finish where I left off and then pass it to the next person to tell it, and then it will be your turn." I pointed at several of the older girls. "Take turns until it is finished."

I was eager to leave. I wanted to get to Kiev, to get home. I walked up the stairs and opened the door at the top without a sound. Anya was standing near Mrs. Panyakov, her back to me, speaking.

"This message changes everything. I need to get to Neper—"

Mrs. Panyakov cleared her throat, and Anya stopped talking. She turned, and I watched her hide a small note behind her back. She met my eyes briefly, then picked up two empty soda bottles and crossed the room to the sink.

Mrs. Panyakov turned toward her. "Please, Anya, consider staying—see reason. It's not safe, especially for a woman walking such a long distance. What if you're too late anyway?"

Anya shook her head. "I appreciate all you have already done for me. But I have to go."

Mrs. Panyakov folded her arms and slumped against the wall, clearly upset.

I shifted my feet. "Um, what did Andrii say?"

Mrs. Panyakov didn't look at me but stared out a window across from her. "He hasn't come back yet. I can hear the shooting. I shouldn't have told him to go."

"I think you should stay in the basement only if you hear gunshots," Anya said. "But when it's quiet, come up and get the kids warm. They'll get sick staying down there so long. Organize them all into teams and make a game of getting to the basement quickly. Today took too long. Maybe keep extra blankets and supplies near the door here so they are easy to grab but will stay warm. Olya and Sveta are capable of leading."

Mrs. Panyakov took a deep breath and nodded. "What will we do without you, Anya?"

"You'll be fine." Anya held the bottles, now full, and walked over to her. "I'm going to find out how I can help you better. Get supplies. Find someone who will listen and help us, maybe through my church."

"The Mormons?" Mrs. Panyakov looked stunned. "How can they help us?"

"They offer food, shelter, clothing, even jobs to a lot of people from war-torn countries. I will ask for help and see what our options are."

"You are just one person, Anya, out of millions."

Anya was definitely Duma's sister. She was willing and ready to organize and save an entire orphanage. And—I thought of the note she hid behind her back—she seemed to keep secrets.

"If it is hopeless, I will come back."

"Nyet. Don't come back. Stay safe."

Anya handed me one of the bottles before slipping her backpack on. I did the same.

"Tell the children we said goodbye," I said. "It was nice to meet you, Mrs. Panyakov."

She squeezed my hand. "Take care of her; please keep her safe. God bless you both."

I nodded. Mrs. Panyakov let go of my hand, worried creases deep across her forehead. We went out the same door we'd come in. I wasn't sure how long we'd been in the basement, but it looked like sunset would be in less than an hour. The gunshots sounded distant, but each blast filled me with anxiety. Anya held a map in front of her.

"So, we're going to Neper?" I asked. "Not Kiev."

She glanced up quickly and met my eyes. "Sorry, something's come up. Neper first, and then I will find a way to get you to Kiev."

I swallowed my frustration. Duma had said to stick to the plan and get to Kiev. But part of the plan was to go with his sister. I could try to make it on my own, with no money, as a runaway convict—or I could stay with Anya. My hand still felt warm where Mrs. Panyakov had pressed it. She was a good woman, and Anya was a Mormon who volunteered to help orphaned children. It was obvious I could trust her. So what if she had private information she didn't want to share? I was a stranger to her. Leaving her would be selfish, something a criminal would do, not a follower of Christ.

"Okay," I said at last. "Show me your plan." She held the map where I could see it and traced a route with her finger but said it would depend on where there was fighting. We decided to take it one street at a time and judge.

I had heard of Dnepropetrovsk—known as *Neper*—but it was outside my mission. Straight west from Horlivka, it would take a week or more to walk, but we hoped to not do that. Krasnoarmiis'k was maybe a three-day journey by foot. If necessary, we had enough provisions to do that but hoped to find a bus or train sooner or later that could take us to Neper. We would avoid the main highways and take dirt roads. She handed me a compass and said we would check it every few blocks.

We saw more people now as we headed west, but they kept their heads down and moved fast. They were going the same direction as us, so we took that as a good sign, that we were moving away from the fighting in the city. We tried not to draw attention to ourselves, sticking to the sides of buildings and under trees.

In Horlivka, the apartments were shorter, the houses small and run-down. As we neared the outskirts of town, there were no sidewalks and the roads turned to dirt. The dried mud rivulets in the road made us stumble in the dark.

We followed the road around a large reservoir, and then there was only blackness in front of us. There was a sign for the small town of Sukha Balka, and we could see a cluster of lights out in the distance. We had no way of knowing which cities or areas the military was taking over, so our plan was to stay away from the cities as much as possible.

We talked very little. It seemed safest that way. And it preserved our strength.

There were slight hills and bridges. The moon reflected off the streams, giving us an idea of how far the water lay beneath the bridges. In the country, the air carried with it a sharper, more defined coolness, as if it came from the ground as well as the sky. I could see trees and farmland. Sometimes I caught a whiff in the air of something I hadn't smelled in a long time—cow manure—but it was too dark to really know what was around us.

Somewhere in the night, Anya said, "I need to rest. Would it be okay to sleep for just a few hours?"

"You're the boss," I said.

We walked off the road and through some bushes. The grass was already starting to gather dew, but the dirt was dry. We ate a little, then pulled our blankets out and huddled under a large tree. I tightened my scarf and pushed my warm fur hat further down on my head. It seemed stupid not to sit close together, and she seemed to agree, so by default, we huddled side by side against the trunk of the fat tree, each wrapped in a separate blanket.

The tree behind us didn't bend at all. Its wood felt firm as iron. I ran my hand along the smooth surface.

"It's *hrab*, hornbeam," Anya said.

"*Hrab*," I repeated.

"Very hard trees. My mother had a cutting board made out of one."

I snuggled under my blanket. The cold air stung my eyes, but I could still look up and see a whole sky of stars. It was the first time I'd seen any stars in Ukraine. "This is beautiful," I breathed, craning my neck to see the entire sky. "I can't believe I'm looking at the same stars I used to only now I'm in Ukraine."

"After all you've been through, you're amazed at the stars?"

I chuckled, the sound foreign, but the fact it had come so naturally gave me hope it would not always be so hard. It was freezing, and I was tired, but sitting under the stars, miles from the prison and its foul smells and violence, made me feel something I hadn't experienced in a very long time. Freedom.

"Stareyshina," Anya said suddenly. "I don't know what you heard about me, but whatever Kaufman said or other missionaries told you—it's not true. I know what the mission rules are. I know you're not supposed to be out here with a girl, looking at stars past curfew. I respect those rules, and I expect those rules."

For someone so small and innocent-looking, she was rather blunt. I could feel my ears burning under my hat. Did she think I was coming on to her? "Well, you don't know me very well either. It's an honor you think after six months in prison I'm still living that high a standard. I haven't even shown you my tattoos yet."

She buried her face in her blanket and looked away.

Deep down, I was still smarting that I'd been released as a missionary. I sighed and knew I should explain myself in a more honest light. "Look, prison life was similar to mission life—strict curfew, limited diet, plenty of time for companionship study and personal study. I prayed a lot. Taught the gospel daily. But I was released as a full-time missionary when I got sentenced to twenty years in prison."

"You were released?"

"Da."

"Well, I'm still not that kind of girl."

"The kind who sits under trees and talks to ex-convicts?"

"Da, that type." She paused. "Does Kaufman know you're released?"

I raised my eyebrows. Kaufman again?

"I haven't heard from or seen Kaufman since I was arrested. He wrote Duma a letter in prison. But I never told your brother or anyone I was released. It didn't seem important."

Anya covered her cheeks with her hands and breathed in deeply through her nose. "Kaufman knows where Duma is?"

"Is that a problem?" I asked.

"Maybe." She continued to hold her face. "I hope he's safe."

I gauged her strange reaction and again thought of the stolen Bible. "Me too," I murmured.

We slept against the tree, sitting up and leaning into one another. The morning sun warmed us. I spread out on my back in a sleepy haze, and Anya stretched herself out away from me as we continued to sleep in the sun.

The sound of a car driving by woke me. I lay on my stomach and tried to get a handle on my surroundings. Anya was still asleep, her head under her blanket, a thin braid of hair sticking out. On her arm was a wristwatch. I leaned over and checked the time. Nine o'clock.

I kneeled and stretched up to see over the bushes that had blocked us from the road. We were at the top of a small hill, and underneath us was a little valley of green, some scattered houses, and a river. It was absolutely picturesque. I had never seen this beautiful side to Ukraine. It seemed a stark example of how much I didn't know about this country.

Slowly, I stood, my muscles stiff from our walk and the uncomfortable night. I wandered off to find a bush while Anya slept. When I returned, she was still asleep.

"Anya." I shook her. "We need to go."

She stretched both her arms out of the blanket. Her messy braids stood out at odd angles, and she yawned. "Ouch," she said with a hoarse voice. "I wasn't meant to sleep outdoors. I think every muscle in my body hurts."

I began to pack up my bedding. She wandered away, and I didn't question where she was going. I put my bedroll in my bag and found a jar of peaches she had brought from the pantry. I pried the lid open with a rock. When she returned, her hair was out of the braids and fell in brown waves.

We shared the peaches and packed up the rest of our stuff. "How many kilometers do you think we walked last night?" I asked.

"About twenty-five."

"How many miles is that?"

She shrugged, and I tried to estimate in my head, thinking about how a 5K was 3.1 miles. I decided we'd probably walked about fifteen miles.

If Anya was right and we'd gone twenty-five kilometers, we had around forty left, maybe more. Things sounded so much longer in kilometers.

I tied my coat around my backpack, the spring sun warm. As we began walking down the dirt road, I continually looked behind and in front of us, searching for vehicles.

Someone was looking for me.

We walked down the small hill. Cows crossed roads, and I breathed in the scent of farmland. Houses like I'd never seen before dotted the countryside, their roofs made of straw, as if they were straight from the fairy tales I'd read and watched growing up.

Chickens ran across the wild patches of grass in their yards. A farmer used his horse and wood cart to carry tools out to the field. It was as if I'd stepped back in time. I bent down and picked up some rich, black soil, heavy with moisture. As a missionary, would I have seen this? I felt blessed to be able to see it, to be outside in it.

We crossed a bridge and stopped near the ravine to rest under a tree. In the distance, I could see the remains of yellow wheat fields that met the blue sky. I couldn't stop staring at them. "If only all of Ukraine looked like this and the hills and the houses, I would never want to leave."

Anya looked up from the stump she'd found to sit on. "It is beautiful." She took a bite of the dried bread. "Like your shirt." I looked down at the sweatshirt of the Ukrainian flag: yellow on the bottom, blue on the top. "That is why the flag looks like that, didn't you know? The yellow is the fields of wheat; the blue is the sky."

I smiled grimly at it. "I thought it looked like prison bars."

"There are some good parts of Ukraine, da?"

I swallowed some food. "Da. Even in prison, there were some good parts of Ukraine." I drank the last of my water. I would need to refill it soon.

"Where is the closest city?" I asked.

"Novooleksandrivka. It doesn't look like a big village on the map. We can stop there for supplies."

I put my backpack on to show I was ready to go. She stood and struggled to get hers on, so I walked over and lifted it so she could slide it on her shoulders. "This weighs more than mine," I said. "What do you have in here?"

I put it on the ground and dug through it. She had several jars of food, which I removed and stuck in my own. My hands wrapped around a book, and I pulled it out and stared at the Book of Mormon in my hands. "You brought your scriptures?"

She looked down. "I know there was a lot to bring, but I didn't know if I could get one very easily wherever I end up."

I flipped through it and opened it to the back cover to make sure there were no hidden boxes. I examined the spine and checked every inch of it.

"What are you doing?"

"Nothing—never mind," I said, handing it to her. "Would you like me to carry it?"

She took it from me and replaced it in her backpack. "It's not a problem. You took the heaviest things."

We circled around the reservoir and went into the small town of Novoo- leksandrivka. It appeared untouched by military action, but who knew how long that would last. We saw an older woman outside, tending to a garden, a scarf tight around her head.

"Can we trouble you for some water?" Anya asked.

"Do as you like," the woman answered, her accent different from the one in the city. "There's a pump right there."

Anya showed me how to run the pump, then left me to fill the bottles. Filtered water was definitely a thing of the past.

"Has there been an invasion here yet?" Anya asked the woman.

"Nyet. And the Bear had best stay away if he knows what's best. Where have you come from? Are you escaping?"

I kept my head down, and Anya stumbled over her words, realizing the mistake of asking questions. "In the east. I lost my job at the factory because it was bombed."

The woman nodded sternly and warily. "They best stay away. We have nothing for them here."

"Thank you for the water," Anya said.

The woman patted Anya on the arm, and I felt her kindness. "Do you need a place to stay?"

Anya thanked her and told her we were going to keep traveling, use whatever daylight we had. I saw the woman look down at my boots and up at my face as I walked by, and I felt myself inwardly panic. The sooner I got to Kiev, the better.

Outside of Novooleksandrivka, we hit a fork in the road. Forks were always hard because we didn't know if we should go north or south. Anya checked the map, and we decided to head north, hoping it would take us toward the next town: Tymofiivka.

The sun began to set. My shoulders and feet ached, my boots worn from miles of use. The landscape became more rugged, more trees and forest than farmland. The map showed there was a large lake, but we stayed south of it.

Before the sun went down completely, we stopped to eat and got out our hats and scarves. I reached in Anya's bag and pulled out the Book of Mormon. I wanted to read a little bit before the sun was gone. I turned to Alma 37. I didn't even have to read the words to know what they said.

"Read out loud," Anya said.

"'O, remember, my son, and learn wisdom in thy youth; yea, learn in thy youth to keep the commandments of God. Yea, and cry unto God for all thy support.'" I stopped reading; my throat closed. I couldn't read it without thinking of Egor. I wiped at my eyes. "Sorry," I breathed. I handed her the book. "You better finish."

She read silently a few seconds while I took in deep breaths of cool air. Then she said, "'Counsel with the Lord in all thy doings, and he will direct thee for good; yea when thou liest down at night lie down unto the Lord, that he may watch over you in your sleep; and when thou risest in the morning let thy heart be full of thanks unto God; and if ye do these things, ye shall be lifted up at the last day.'"

The Lord had protected me so many times in the last six months that it was overwhelming to think about.

"We should pray," she whispered. "We haven't prayed at all."

I realized she was right.

"Will you say it?" she asked.

"Da," I said, surprised that she would ask me. I kneeled on the ground, and she joined me. I thanked the Lord for Anya's help and prayed for our safety and for Duma's safety and for Sergei and the men. I prayed for Mrs. Panyakov and the children, for my family, for Brett's safety, and his family back home. I also prayed for all of Ukraine to find peace, that the fighting would end soon.

When Anya said amen, I watched her wipe tears away, and she let me take her hand and help her up off the ground.

The sun would soon set, so we decided to continue walking to try to get as far as we could through the night. It looked like we were heading into a forest. The road began to incline, the ground became covered with snow, and the trees grew thick with pines and oaks. There were no more patches of farmland.

Dusk came and went, and the large trees hid the moon. It was hard to know what was around us. In the distance, I heard a howl that reminded me of coyotes back home.

"What kinds of animals are in Ukraine?" I asked casually.

Anya's steps slowed. "Are you trying to scare me?" she whispered.

"I only want to be prepared."

"I don't know—wolves? Maybe deer?"

"Wolves? Are you sure?"

"In school, we learned they have a large range—large enough to cross into Russia or Poland and cover all of Ukraine."

"But they're afraid of people, right?"

She shuddered. "I don't know. I have heard of wolf attacks. There are even stories of opposing soldiers having to stop midfight and join forces to fight off the wolves because they're attracted to the scent of blood." Her teeth began to chatter. "Maybe we should stop for the night."

I hesitated. I had never seen a wolf, but I'd once seen a bear eating a decomposing calf. I would get no sleep now. And it was hard to know what was around us—what if behind the trees, there was a drop-off? There was no way to know in the dark. "Let's keep going, just a bit longer."

As we walked, I strained my ears to hear any sounds of movement. The snow was wet, softened into mud, and our footprints sounded muted, the ground giving way to our feet.

Next to me, Anya slowed her pace, and I wondered if she was trying to tiptoe. "They think wolves developed a taste for people during the black plague. The bodies were taken to the outskirts of town, and the wolves feasted on them. They think they actually developed a genetic taste for it."

I tried to walk faster, hoping she'd keep up. I heard her behind me. "And people can die from the bite of a rabid wolf sooner than they can get help because the disease reaches the brain almost immediately."

"I don't really think we should talk about this."

"And then there's the fact that wolves begin eating before their prey is fully dead."

I stopped walking and turned to face her. "Stop talking."

"I'm sorry," she whispered. "I can't help it. Wolves also weigh up to two hundred pounds," she squeaked.

I rubbed my face with my hands.

"How much do you weigh?" she whispered.

I blew out. "Not two hundred pounds."

"Me either."

"Enough. We're going to be okay. How about you say a prayer?"

"Okay," she said. She offered a frightened but faithful plea for help. I said amen and then, a few minutes later, asked, "Do you feel better?"

"Da," she said and reached for my hand. The motion surprised me, and I felt myself tense, but after a minute, I noticed she stayed with me much better when I was holding on to her. She felt warm and made me feel less worried.

After a time, I smelled firewood burning. Searching the horizon, I saw smoke rising above the trees. "A chimney," I said, pointing at it. We stayed along the road, and eventually a smaller road emerged through the woods, connecting with the one we were on. We walked down the smaller road and reached an opening in the trees, just big enough for the house, garden, and small barn.

"Here," I whispered, staying near the trees. There was a spot surrounded by bushes, but it was big enough for us to both sleep in. "Let's just stay here, close to the house."

"Nyet," Anya whispered back. "In the mud and snow?"

"I don't want to trespass," I said.

"I'm not sleeping where a wolf can pick me off like some black-plague body."

I stuck my tongue out in disgust. "You've thought too much about it."

We followed the shadows of the trees until we reached the far side near the barn. "Let's sleep in here," I said.

She hesitated. "Why don't we just knock on the door and ask if we can sleep inside the house?"

"Do you think that's safe?" I asked, fear rushing through my veins.

"Not everyone in Ukraine is like the people you met in prison."

"Da—I know—I'm sure, but someone is looking for me." I hesitated to tell her more, worried she'd regret helping me. "Isn't it best if we avoid people? So they can't find out where I've been?"

"Perhaps you're right," Anya consented. She stood behind me as I tried the large wooden latch. I prayed it wouldn't squeak as I gently pushed it open.

It did, like all barn doors do.

The scent of whatever lived inside was strong. I heard the whinny of a horse, and things around us shifted. There were two windows, one on each side wall, letting in a little light.

Anya gripped my upper arm with both hands.

As my eyes adjusted to the darkness, I could make out a couple of enclosures, which was good to see—then I knew the animals weren't just wandering about free. The ground was completely covered in straw. I tried to shut the door as quietly as I could.

I guided Anya to the left of the door, where we would be hidden from immediate sight. We sat against the wall, and I took a deep breath of horse and straw and sighed. Anya leaned in closer to me. "Your sigh sounds like you are happy in here."

"Da. This is the smell of home."

"Home? I thought America was a civilized country, with homes and hot water, where everyone drives cars and owns fancy computers and cell phones."

I smiled, my eyes closed. "Da, I had those things. But we also had a barn and horses and hundreds of cows. We were farmers."

She shifted in the straw. "Everyone in America must be rich."

"Da, but they don't know it. What did your parents do?" I asked to change the subject.

"My dad worked in the mine in Horlivka—until he passed away. They said it was his lungs. There was a fire. He was never the same after. Mama was a seamstress."

"Did she volunteer at the orphanage like you?"

"Nyet." She was quiet. "I started volunteering only because, well, through church, we helped there sometimes, but my parents were gone. Duma took care of me, but I was still an orphan, and I knew how those children felt. I left and moved to Kramatorsk to get a job but went back to Horlivka when things . . . didn't work out. Dasha helped me find a job, has always treated me like I was one of her orphans."

I wondered if the thing that hadn't worked out in Kramatorsk had to do with her and Stareyshina Johnson, but I knew it was none of my business. So I asked, "Are you planning on going back to Horlivka?"

She shivered, her teeth chattering. "There is nothing for me there—not anymore. I don't have a job at the clothing factory. The entire store is gone, all the supplies ransacked."

"Here." I opened a bag and pulled out a blanket. I tucked it around her tightly, then leaned against the barn wall again. It was warmer in here, the bodies of closed-in animals making me feel perfectly comfortable.

"Thank you," Anya said, pulling the blanket up to her chin. "I liked your story about the pig last night." I could hear the smile in her voice. "I kept thinking I could never see a Ukrainian man doing this—telling a story to all these children in a basement in the middle of a war."

"It doesn't seem so remarkable, telling stories to a bunch of bored kids in a basement. You were doing a fine job reading *The Hobbit*. Is that a popular book in Ukraine?"

"Da. Everyone knows Tolkien in Ukraine. I studied it in school. You seem less like a prisoner and more like a—" She stopped, and I held my breath. I wanted her to say it, to finish her thought, and then she did. "A stareyshina."

I chuckled quietly. "That's good to hear. It would be a bad thing to travel this far with someone who seemed more like a convict."

"Maybe it's because you are American?" she asked. "I have noticed the missionaries from America are very friendly. They like to laugh; they sometimes act like children themselves. Are all Americans like that?"

Her words were sounding less complimentary. "I don't know. America is so different. Maybe it's easier to be lighthearted. They don't have so much to worry about as you, especially when your country is in the midst of civil war."

She nodded and said quietly, "Da, maybe that is true. But despite what you have experienced here, Ukrainians are friendly in their own way. We are very loyal to our close friends; we sacrifice for others, even when we have nothing."

"I know what you say to be true," I said. "Especially the members of the Church in this country. They have gone without food to pay their tithing, to feed missionaries, to give to other members in need. You yourself have given me a shower, warm food, and clothing and are walking this great distance with me."

She smiled and seemed pleased by what I'd said.

I smelled the straw and animals and thought how blessed I was. I was grateful to be sleeping in a barn because I knew the alternatives of where I could be, proof that my experiences in Ukraine had changed me.

I thought of Sergei and worried that perhaps the power and water would never be working in the prison. With the city in limbo and government officials removed, who would care to fix it?

I cleared my throat in an effort to distract myself. "In the orphanage, you reminded me a lot of Duma. He organized a basement of one hundred men—food, water, beds, toilet. Are you both natural-born leaders?"

She gave a short laugh. "I suppose we both have a stubborn streak. So you were in a basement?"

I nodded. "We were hiding after the bombs hit the building. There was no water or electricity. We were just trying to survive." Thoughts intruded of Boris and Gavriil, who had joined the war, and the bus turned over with people strewn across the road. "But we were the lucky ones," I whispered.

"The lucky ones?"

I turned my gaze to her wide eyes, close to mine in the dark, but I could think of nothing to say but, "I feel lucky."

I hadn't meant it as a pickup line, but there it was, floating between us. I felt her breath hitch, and we stared at each other, her eyes inches away from mine. There was a charge that radiated through me, and I knew this was the moment in the movies when the boy kissed the girl. My heart was beating loud enough that I was sure she could hear it. No moment could be more perfect than in this warm barn, protected and alone.

And I wasn't a missionary anymore.

I could kiss her, and it would be totally legal.

But inside, I was still a missionary.

I looked away, breaking the trance, and stared hard at a small cut on the back of my hand. My heart was still thudding obnoxiously, as if I'd just run a mile. I couldn't believe what I'd been about to do—and part of me was still wishing I had.

But I came to Ukraine for one reason, and that was to be a missionary. That reason hadn't changed, even if I had been released. I hadn't realized until now that no matter what I'd been through, I was still a worthy LDS missionary. And being a missionary was what I desired more than anything else.

I felt Anya shift in her blanket, pulling it tighter around her. Then she settled next to me, her head resting against my shoulder.

THE SOUND OF A DEEP moo woke me several hours later. I was lying curled up in the straw next to Anya. Her hair was inches from my face. I leaned forward and inhaled for a moment. I just knew it would smell like shampoo and alfalfa fields—and it did.

I remembered the almost-kiss and felt such a relief spread over me that nothing had happened, that we had nothing to feel awkward about. The focus could remain on getting home. The faint glow of sun filled the windows, and I heard a new sound of a door shutting somewhere. I sat up, and again, the cow mooed. She was tied to a post in the corner with a rope, her udders painfully large.

It was milking time. My heart began to hammer.

"Anya," I shook her. "We need to leave—now."

She kneeled up sleepily, and I pulled her to her feet and told her to be quiet as we waited.

Wolves or not, why had we hid here?

I was trying to remember the house in proportion to the barn, taking into account each step and how long it would take until the farmer reached us. Anya squeezed my arm until it was painful, but I didn't move. I never heard the footsteps approach, but the door squeaked open, and Anya and I both jumped.

A boy around the age of eight or nine walked in, holding a lantern and bucket. He walked to the far corner, leaving the door open. The fresh, cool air hit us, and Anya and I moved around the door as quietly as we could. We slipped out and began to run back down the road we'd come in on, unsure if we'd been spotted or not.

I turned off into the woods, and we trampled over weeds and brush, not looking behind us until Anya stopped, breathless, holding her side, and said she needed a break.

"That was too close," I said, my heart thumping wildly.

"Did he see us?" she asked.

I turned and met her eyes in the dim morning light, the sun casting gold streaks through the pines. Her black beanie was pulled tight, and pieces of straw stuck out from masses of brown hair gathered around her shoulders. I pulled one of the bigger pieces of straw out and handed it to her. She looked down at it, her long, dark eyelashes against her cheek.

I automatically reached for her hand and began walking through the woods again. My pulse began to slow, but the senses in my hand tingled where my skin met hers. When we reached the road, I dropped her hand and stuffed mine in my pockets. I didn't dare look at her.

The sound of a car interrupted all thoughts, and we hurried back into the trees and got down low behind some shrubs and waited. A dated, rust-red car slowly inched its way down the road. It stopped near the path to the house, and I got down even lower. The car turned off toward the house and barn we'd slept in.

My breath came in sharp. "He's following our footsteps. It will only take so long before they can see we left and where we might be."

Anya gasped. "What should we do?"

"We've got to cross the road and throw them off track."

There was nothing to do but run across and hope the ground was too frozen to show our prints. We walked behind some shrubs. Then Anya tripped, noticing too late that it was a body she had hit.

I helped her to her feet, but three men got up quickly and pointed their guns at us. I put my hands in the air, and Anya followed my example.

"We don't want trouble," I said.

"Nil?" The biggest one pulled his black beanie off, and I saw the familiar bald head I'd looked at all those months in our cell and on the assembly line.

"Ivan?" I asked.

He ran and threw his arms around me and laughed. "Nil! What are you doing all the way up here?"

"I got away—we were all hiding in the basement of the prison with no food or power . . . What are you doing here, so far from Donetsk?" I immediately regretted my question. The men's eyes shifted among one another.

Ivan blew out. "It has been rough for me too. There are some things a man can do, and some things he cannot."

I thought about what Father Michael had said, what he'd predicted for those who had joined the fighting. "Where is Trofim?" I asked.

Ivan shook his head. "He did not make it." He breathed in deeply. "People who refuse to fight are killed. It's horrible, this war."

I nodded, feeling uneasy.

Ivan frowned and nodded. "I couldn't shoot them. Not Boris—not the others. I could not throw the grenades at the churches. They are looking for us, I'm sure. We've been careful, but it can only help so much." Ivan looked around me. "Who is this with you? She seems to want an introduction."

Anya blushed and took a step back.

"This is Anya. She's Duma's sister."

"Duma?" His eyes narrowed. "Da, Duma knew what he was doing, I'll give him that." He pointed a finger at her and sneered. "And you're the one who sent him the book—the one like Nil's? The one he marked up and sent out to some holy men. Said he was going to make a lot of money on that deal. Did it work out for him?"

My ears began to ring, as Anya stared blankly back at him.

He continued. "I know things—things that can hurt him."

The sound of a car made us all drop and scramble behind bushes. The same rust-red car moved down the road. We didn't dare breathe until it was out of sight. Slowly, we stood.

"Do you think that car is following our tracks?" I asked.

"Your—?" Ivan looked away from me and swore, then grabbed me by my coat. "If they find me because of you and your tracks, I'll—I'll kill you."

I pried my coat away from his hands. "They're gone. A boy might have seen us—they'll never think it was you."

"But you brought them here to our forest. They'll start combing the woods now, thinking it's a good place for traitors to hide."

I took a step back. "We'll get out of here. They'll find us first and make sure it was us they've been following."

"*Yourself*, you mean." He looked over at Anya, and I felt my heart drop. The blood drained from her face, and she backed up. He faced me. "But I know you won't go to them—you're running like me. Thanks for the girl. She'll come in handy."

"Nyet." My hands began to twitch. "I'm not leaving without her."

Ivan turned his body to punch me, but I ducked and rolled away. I shook off my backpack and stood. I didn't have to tell Anya to run. She took off, but Ivan's two thugs were faster. They brought her back, each holding an arm while she struggled.

Ivan laughed. "There's not much to her. I wager she is worth something to Duma though. And I'd like to settle our score."

I took deep breaths, my body tense. "Leave her alone."

"Ah, this girl is more than Duma's sister to you, is she? I'll be gentle with her."

"Ivan, I thought we were friends."

"Friends?" Ivan laughed loudly, his voice echoing off the trees. "Prison friends? The only reason no one messed with you was because of Duma." He turned his back and faced Anya, who shrank under his gaze.

Instinctively, I reached forward and grabbed for the gun in his holster. He spun and tried to pry me off his leg, then began pounding me with his fists. I held on until I had the gun out. He grabbed me, and I flew through the air, landing hard several feet away. I grasped at my side, my breathing labored, but I managed to roll over and point the gun at him.

He stopped moving, his face livid. The thugs hadn't moved a muscle, still holding tight to Anya.

I felt something wet on my face and knew it was blood, but I ignored it and kept the gun pointed at Ivan. He took a step toward me, his hands in the air. "I know you'd never shoot me. Not a religious man like you. You probably don't even know how to use that."

The blast I fired into the air hurt my ears, and he jumped back, his hands over his head. "You idiot!" he yelled. "They will hear you shoot!"

I scrambled up, still holding the gun. "Let go of her now! Or I shoot again!" The men hesitated, so I yelled again. "Now!" I knew I had only so much time before they realized they outnumbered us, they were bigger, and they had Anya to bargain with.

They dropped her, and she ran until she stood behind me.

"I'm leaving. Don't follow me. I don't turn you in; you don't turn me in. The law of the prison, da?"

Ivan glared, but he nodded.

I didn't wait for any more confirmation than that. Anya and I sprinted toward the road, Anya still in her backpack, mine still on the ground at Ivan's feet. We ran until my chest felt like it was on fire and there was enough distance we could rest. I stopped, panting heavily. Behind us, I could see we'd left footprints and some drops of blood where I stood.

I stared at the black gun in my hands, probably military issued. What if someone caught us and it incriminated me further? It suddenly felt too heavy, and I threw it in some nearby bushes.

My head hurt near my hairline on my right side, and I probed it gently with my fingers. I winced and stared at the red smears across my fingers. I went to touch it again, but Anya knocked my hand away.

"Don't do that," she said. "Let's keep walking and find a better place."

We stuck to the edge of the woods, where our footprints wouldn't show, to hide from the car as well as Ivan and his thugs. Soon, the trees receded and farmland came up to meet the pines. I listened for sounds of cars or walking, but all was silent.

I touched my head again. "Hopefully there are no wolves hunting this morning?"

Anya smirked. "They're probably hiding from the monsters in the woods."

She took my arm and led me to a rock, gently pushing me down. "Let me help you." She pulled the bottle of water out of her bag. It was nearly empty, which had been a blessing in our escape. I sat still and watched as she unwound the scarf from my neck. She poured a little of her water on the very tip and scrubbed my face, starting at my chin and moving up my cheek until she reached the spot near my hairline where it was cut.

Again, she wet my scarf. Her hand shook as she pressed it on the spot. It stung, and I winced. She held it there for a few moments, and then began dabbing at it.

"It's not too deep. I think it's stopped bleeding. Just don't touch it with your dirty hands," she said.

I held my hands out and noticed the mud caked under each nail, then tried to hide them.

She continued to dab at my wound. "You were very brave. I thought you might leave me back there. Your friend gave you an opportunity, but you didn't take it."

"I've had a lot of opportunities to leave you," I said, "but I haven't." I shifted on the rock, moving the scarf. Again, I flinched, the pain throbbing like a heartbeat there. "And he's not my friend. I think he made that clear."

She handed me the scarf, and I held it to my own head while she moved to dig through her backpack. When she came back, she was holding a white piece of cloth that looked like a handkerchief. She tied it around my head. "Sometimes friends aren't who we think they are."

She stared at me for several seconds, and I wondered who else she might be talking about—Duma? Kaufman? Johnson? Herself?

She straightened and walked back over to her bag. "It surprised me when you fought back like you did. Did you learn how to fight in prison?"

I thought of telling her Kaufman had been the first one to show me how to throw a punch in a hallway, but I worried it would influence her feelings about me. "I think it was just a reflex," I said.

She sighed heavily. "I don't think I've ever prayed so hard in my life." She bent down for her backpack, but I walked over and pulled it gently from her hands. I adjusted the straps, then slipped it on my own back. I was grateful we hadn't lost both of the backpacks. We at least had some food and a blanket. Anya offered to carry the water bottle.

The sun hid behind clouds the rest of the day. We varied our route, and instead of walking directly into the nearest city, we walked south of it, into more farmland. The plan was to go into Hrodivka and catch a bus to Krasnoarmiisk and, from there, a train to Neper.

My mind continually went back to what Ivan had said about black-mailing. I'd always felt Duma had wielded some kind of power over our cell, but it bothered me to learn he actually had. It made me distrust him even more.

"Anya, what book was Ivan talking about? The one you sent your brother."

She bit her lip. "I sent him a *Kniga Mormona* a couple years ago, but I don't know what your cellmate was talking about—about it being a scheme to make money."

"He said he sent it to some holy men. Who were those holy men?"

"Duma never said anything to me. He never does," she said quietly.

Something in her tone made me quit asking questions, but my brain wouldn't stop turning it over. I remembered the markings in the Book of Mormon that had correlated with the Bible and the lock. Someone had dressed like me—a missionary—and stolen a ring. Someone had intended to frame me.

A ring could make someone a lot of money. Rings were very small, small enough to fit in a tiny box in the back of a Bible.

And Duma had stolen it from me.

I shoved both hands in my pockets and kept a chaste distance between Anya and me as we marched steadily onward toward the small village of Hrodivka. A few cars passed on the dirt road that led through town, but they didn't seem to notice or care about us.

We saw horses pulling carts out to pastures and people in yards, raking the thawing dirt. A woman pushed her scarf further back on her forehead to see us better, her chickens clucking noisily around her ankles. I kept my head down, but Anya said, "Good afternoon."

The map showed a bus stop near the center of town. We walked past a small, white church with a cross. It looked clean and bright, like it had been newly painted. A short iron fence surrounded the property, along with a couple large trees.

Everything looked untouched from war.

Across from the church, there was a bench and a sign indicating it was a bus stop. But there were no times listing when it stopped, typical of most the bus stops I'd seen in Kramatorsk. I sat, my feet aching, but Anya paced back and forth in front of me, constantly checking her watch.

After several minutes of watching her, I asked, "Are you worried about missing the bus?"

"No. Yes." She looked at me with a pinched smile. She sat next to me, still distracted. She pulled her beanie off. Her hands shook as she braided her hair to the side. "Maybe this was a bad idea. Maybe we should have gone straight to Kiev."

"Why?"

She wound an elastic band around the end of her hair. "Because I'm afraid we are too late." She bit her lip and stared into my eyes. "You have been a good friend. You have risked your life for me. And I've not been honest with you."

My body tensed. She shifted so she was facing me on the bench; her brown eyes stared into mine. "I don't trust people very easily—I am careful—but I trusted someone before you came, someone we both know. I—I wasn't going to tell you, but what that man in the woods said about Duma confused me. Maybe it's better not to keep secrets, even when you're told to, even if you think it will help someone."

The sound of an engine caused us both to jump and lean toward the sound. A marshrutka bus came slowly through the town, black smoke puffing out the back.

Anya stood and waved her arms, anxious to be seen.

The side door opened, and the bus driver—a man with a long black beard—asked, "Where are you going?"

"Krasnoarmiisk," Anya answered for us.

People slid over for us, and we climbed in. Anya handed our money forward through several hands until it reached the driver. As the bus pulled away, I stared at the small church across the street, its slanted blue roof and shutters, and wondered how long it would take before they destroyed this place too.

Anya leaned toward me, her face inches from my ear. "I got a message at the orphanage," she whispered. "Kaufman has your missionary friend—Stareyshina Tyson. He's being held hostage."

40

My heart pounded against my ribs. "Why didn't you tell me?" I kept my head forward and tried to keep my voice level. The bus was full, and everyone could hear us.

She sniffed, and I realized after a few seconds that she was crying. She was curled toward the window, her beanie a knitted mushroom ballooning as she buried her head in her arms.

I searched the passengers, wondering if we were safe. Older women in scarves, men in fur hats, even children who didn't make a peep, all wearing the somber expressions I'd grown accustomed to.

I carefully slid my arm behind Anya to look like we were simply having a lover's quarrel. "Why does Kaufman have him?" I whispered.

She wiped her eyes and whispered in my ear. "He wants to make sure you go to Neper. I'm to meet him in a fishing warehouse with you. I don't know why. He threatened the orphanage if I don't bring you, and the thought of all those children. I—I didn't know what to do."

"Did you tell Mrs. Panyakov about this?"

She looked up at me with her tear-streaked face and sniffed. "Nyet. I didn't want her to worry. I told her I needed to help a friend. He said not to tell you. Was I wrong to?"

I didn't answer, but whatever she saw on my expression made her face pinch as she nodded vigorously and turned back to the window. Her shoulders shook with new tears.

"Stop, Anya," I whispered, massaging her neck with my thumb. "Just explain. I'm not angry. I'm confused. It doesn't make sense that Kaufman kidnapped Stareyshina Tyson. He was my friend—a good missionary."

She turned sharply to look at me. "Another friend that has fooled you, apparently. Would a good man tell me to write Stareyshina Johnson letters to get him transferred? Or to lie to you?" She shook her head. "I thought he was kind at first. I was friends with him and Jinya and Johnson. On p-days, we would meet places—at restaurants, museums, hiking spots, or somewhere to play chess. I went to their English classes. I was not in love with Johnson romantically. I knew they would not be here forever. I didn't want to write those letters. I knew it was wrong to say those things to a missionary—and to lie. Kaufman told me I had to, or he would tell the branch president and everyone what Duma had done and what I—" She swallowed and looked away.

"Tell me," I whispered.

Her face turned red, but she met my eyes. "I—I helped Duma once. I didn't know I was, but Kaufman somehow knew." Her eyes filled with tears. "I probably should be in prison too."

"No," I said firmly. I picked up her hand. "No. Prison is not for you. Let's not talk of this anymore." I squeezed my eyes shut, remembering the pain of prison. "There are men there who have done *nothing*—I did nothing. Just say we all paid that price for you."

The man in front of me shifted in his seat, and I realized what I'd just admitted to on a bus full of people. I nervously scanned the crowd, but no one seemed to be paying us much attention. A woman crying on a bus was probably not newsworthy in Ukraine at the moment.

I decided it was best to keep quiet a few minutes. I needed to think about the things Anya had said anyway. Kaufman kidnapped Brett? Forced Anya to write Johnson? Kaufman had acted strangely when it had come to Anya, it was true. But I had thought it was because he liked her. Maybe there were things I had misunderstood.

I leaned in close to her so the man in front of us wouldn't hear. "This doesn't make sense. Why does he have him?"

She shook her head and stared out the window. "I didn't bring the note, but it said you need your Bible. I noticed you didn't have one, so I brought my scriptures."

A sudden coldness swept through me. I swallowed and tried to fight the thoughts clicking into place. But the evidence was there. I was in prison for stealing, not with circumstantial hearsay evidence but with *video* of me stealing a ring, with my clothes, with my name badge.

The story of the hobbit and the ring—was it all a joke to him? Was it his way of teasing me, the whole time knowing he would steal a ring and frame me?

I'd been there in lessons and felt the Spirit. I'd discussed gospel principles next to an open oven in a freezing apartment, and Kaufman had borne testimony about the plan of salvation, the plan of happiness. He'd made me eggs and bought me waffles. He'd cared about my relationship with Tyson. Why would he go through all of that to pin a stolen ring on me?

I swallowed, fighting the urge to either cry or vomit as the bus bumped over the rough dirt road, making its way to Krasnoarmiisk.

Anya touched my shoulder. "We should have gone to Kiev. We should have changed our plans. We still can."

I nodded and clenched my jaw together, not sure what to think anymore. Brett was being held hostage because Kaufman wanted me, with a Bible—that I no longer had.

It didn't take more than a couple hours for the bus to drop us at the Krasnoarmiisk train station. Anya went to use the restroom, and I waited outside on a bench, playing out our options in my mind, fidgeting with the buttons on my coat, constantly nervous for Brett.

I waited ten minutes, twenty. When she didn't come out, I asked a woman to go in and look for her. She returned saying no one by that description was in there. Panic filled me as I searched the station. I walked the length of the building outside and in back. I looked up and down the train tracks.

Nothing.

I crumpled onto a bench outside. Maybe she was looking for me too. Or maybe she had taken off and left me. Why? I pressed my fingers to my eyes, helplessness washing over me. I had no money to buy a train ticket. How long would it take me to walk to Neper? To Kiev? I still had the backpack with some supplies.

A man came up and sat next to me. His beanie was black, like many others. His dark beard hid most of his face, but I recognized his coat and realized he was the man who had been sitting in front of me on the bus. He held a newspaper in front of him, and without looking up from it or uttering a single word, he handed me a train ticket and a note.

I took it. "What's this?"

He looked up at me, his eyes dark. "I was told to give it to you. I'm to be your escort."

With shaky hands, I read the note written in English. *She's fine for now. Get off at the stop where the lake narrows, before the bridge. Look for the old fishing factory. Best have the ring, Hobbit.*

41

MY EYES STAYED GLUED TO the landscape swirling past as the train barreled toward Neper. My escort sat a few rows behind me, which I preferred to having to be near him. He must have known I would go. That I wouldn't abandon Anya. Inside, I kept praying that the Lord would spare us.

I could see the spot off in the distance where Kaufman meant for me to get off. The lake became narrower, a bridge crossing it. Someone tapped me on the back; I turned and saw it was my escort now sitting behind me. The train slowed, and I knew this next stop was ours.

Clouds had dropped rain, and the air was filled with cold moisture as we walked down the dark cobblestone street. I didn't try to talk with the man, and he didn't offer any conversation.

We reached a building with some large metal doors. He stopped walking. "Go in. They're expecting you." The door squeaked loudly, reminding me of my cell in Kramatorsk. Inside, it was an empty black. I hesitated and looked back at the man. His back was to the door, and he was lighting up a cigarette.

I could jump him. We were a similar size, and he wouldn't expect it. Then what? What good would it do? The cold metal bit through my fingers.

He turned and looked at me. His eyes narrowed. "Having second thoughts?"

I glanced into the darkness. "Are you sure this is the right way?"

He smirked, his dark eyes crinkling at the sides. He dropped the cigarette and pulled a gun from his pocket. "I can escort you in, if you'd like, or you can go yourself."

I turned and backed into the dark but didn't shut the door. I stared at him from the dimness and saw him searching without seeing me. He looked unsettled as he stared at the blackness and moved cautiously forward, his gun in front of him. He reached slowly in for the handle of the door, trying to stay outside of the shadows as much as possible.

I knew what I had to do, but it scared me. I waited until it felt right, then grabbed his wrist and bent it the wrong way, catching the gun with my other hand. He swung a fist wildly, but I kicked him hard in the stomach, before slamming the door.

I leaned my face against the cold, dark metal and waited for him to try to come in. I could only hear and feel my breath heavy against the door, filling me with shame. The gun felt hot in my hands. I closed my eyes. *Dear Lord, please forgive me. I need to find Anya and Brett. If it's my time to go, I'm ready, but if there's a chance I can live through this, please guide me. Help me have wisdom and love and not do stupid things.*

I took several deep breaths. I needed to stay focused. I opened my eyes and looked behind me. There was a long hall, and at the end were lights. I walked as quietly as I could until I was standing at the edge of what looked like a giant warehouse.

Kaufman stood leaning against a metal rail about twenty feet in the air. About six feet to the left was the massive form of Brett in a white shirt and tie, name badge pinned to his shirt. His hands were tied behind his back. His eyes were wide with fear.

And six feet to the right was Anya, her hands tied to the rail in front of her, her mouth gagged. When I saw her, my heart felt instant pain.

I walked into the light, and Kaufman held his hands up and yelled in English, "Don't walk any closer or she dies." I stopped, the gun hanging limply at my side. "There is another gun you can't see aimed at your head. Believe me."

I looked around but saw only boxes and doors. I turned back to face Kaufman. He looked pale and sickly. Much thinner than I remembered him, his face sallow, with dark circles framing his eyes.

"So, you came, Hobbit."

He'd chosen to speak in English, so I did too. "You didn't give me much choice."

Brett straightened beside him, and I saw Kaufman shift too. I fingered the grooves on the wrist of my hand holding the gun, the scars still there after all these months, and my heart hurt for Brett. How could Kaufman do this?

"Did you bring the ring?" His hand shook as he pointed at a rope hanging nearby. "Place the ring in that basket, and I'll pull it up."

I moved toward it slowly. "Are you going to release Anya and Brett? That was the deal, right? The ring for them? How can I trust you?"

"That's just it, isn't it?" he said, spreading his arms wide. "It's so hard to know who to trust."

I stopped walking. "Trust," I echoed.

He dropped his hands. "Please," he said and closed his eyes. "Please put the ring in the basket and walk away."

I'd never seen Kaufman act like this—look like this. He'd always seemed so cool and collected. This should be his victory moment, but he looked as if he might fall apart. He wasn't the same person I'd left in Kramatorsk.

"You used me. You used Anya. Now you're using Brett? I don't get it. This isn't the Kaufman I knew."

He rubbed the bar in front of him and smiled at it. Brett moved his arms, trying to get free. His body looked as if it was in pain, and a look of panic crossed Kaufman's face.

I remembered my first day in prison and how I'd felt around Egor, the guards. The distrust and fear. I could see it in Kaufman now. He was afraid—he'd been taught to fear something—someone. Sadness and pity washed through me. I began moving forward again. "Why are you doing this?"

"You're such a *frog*, Christensen." I stopped walking. "People change; isn't that a good enough reason? It's your turn to not trust the *dragon*."

The *frog* and the *dragon*? Decoded, the message was, "Don't trust Brett"— my personal dragon. My eyes darted between the two of them. Brett was handcuffed—he was the one hurt and in trouble—not Kaufman. Was this another trick?

Kaufman looked directly at me. "Put it in the basket."

"I don't have the ring."

He straightened. He began to perspire; beads of sweat appeared around his temples, and he wiped them with his shirtsleeve. "Then why did you come?"

My eyes shifted to Brett. From his stoic stance, Brett moved his lips, but he wouldn't meet my eyes.

"Do you know where the ring is?" Kaufman asked.

"I have a good idea where," I said, my voice suddenly hoarse.

Again, Brett's lips moved, but Kaufman was the one who spoke out loud. He held the rail, his head down, not looking at me. "Then tell me and your two friends live." He looked like he wanted to sit, as if he was exhausted from standing.

Why was Brett telling Kaufman what to say? I held the gun tighter against my leg.

Anya's eyes were swollen, and tears fell down her face, but she met my eyes, then stared directly at Brett before meeting my eyes again. The letters, the messages, whatever Kaufman had been guilty of, it was clear she was directing me to Brett as the dangerous one.

I found my voice. "First, I—I need to tell Brett something."

Kaufman raised his head and looked at Brett. Prison had taught me many new rules. One was understanding who was in charge. And it was clear Kaufman was getting permission, not giving it.

"Okay. Say it," Kaufman said wearily.

"I want to know if you've forgiven me, Brett?"

At last Brett met my eyes. He cleared his throat. "Of course, Neal."

"When I was in prison, I saw firsthand what I put you through. You were right; it's the worst feeling in the world to be accused of something you didn't do. No one deserves to feel that way. I'm truly sorry."

He swallowed and nodded, never looking at Kaufman, never worried about opening his mouth. Clearly, he'd never been hit by his abductors. "Absolutely." He blinked several times. "Just give Kaufman what he wants. I want to go home. Please, Neal."

I nodded. "Thanks, I'm glad you can overlook our past."

Brett nodded, then gave a tight smile. He actually smiled. My insides froze, and I was afraid for a second that he would read the distrust in my eyes. He seemed to recall he was playing the part of captive and dropped his head.

Brett?

I cleared my throat. "Let them go, Kaufman. I'll tell you, but not until you take me as hostage and let them go."

"Just tell me where the ring is," Kaufman said. "Then everything will be okay." But he didn't look like it would be.

"You were always such a prince, Kaufman. Always the hero. Always trying to save the day." I began walking forward. Kaufman looked at me; his eyes were tired, but I could tell he was listening. "But you don't have a sword now."

With his eyes only, he looked sideways at Brett.

Brett has the weapon.

As long as I kept Kaufman talking, maybe we could think of something, maybe we could find a way out of this mess.

Kaufman smiled at me. "Oh, I have a sword. And it's a big one."

Kaufman was braver than I'd ever given him credit for. "I could shoot you," I said.

"Do it," Brett said, but he swallowed guiltily.

I held up the gun, disappointment filling my chest. How could Brett do this? I pretended to hesitate. I tried to look afraid, which wasn't too hard.

"Just let them go, Kaufman. I don't want to kill you. I'm not like you."

"Tell me where the ring is." He crossed his arms. "My patience is growing thin."

I lowered the gun. "Growing thin? That's a weird thing to say. Shouldn't it be *melting* thin or *shrinking* thin? *Growing* thin just seems like an oxymoron."

"An oxymoron? You listened in English class after all, then, did you?"

"Shut up!" Brett screamed, stunning us to silence. One of his hands held a gun behind his back. He twisted and pointed it at me. "I can't stand all this chatter. I—I don't have the patience for it. Drop it, Neal."

I carefully held the gun in front of me and set it on the ground. Kaufman rushed to shield Anya with his body, and I saw him tugging at her ropes, but Brett just stared at me, frozen.

"Brett, calm down," I said, holding my hands in the air.

"Kick it."

I kicked the gun away. It slid across the floor and landed behind some boxes.

Brett glared at me. He punctuated each word. "Tell me where the ring is."

"Why are you doing this, Brett? This isn't like you."

He shook his head. "It hurts, doesn't it—getting stabbed in the back. Thinking someone is your friend and then they are holding a gun at you? Thinking you are off scot-free and then wham—caught."

"You did this to me?"

"I didn't have to, Neal; you did it to yourself. You lied to me. You're behind all of this. You stole that ring. I'm not going to let you get away with it. No one will care that you died in an old fishing factory in the middle of Ukraine. No one can trust you. I know you wrote your family and my mom and told them what you did to me."

"Yes, I did. It was part of my repentance process—"

Brett laughed, but he didn't sound amused. I noticed Kaufman and Anya scrambling toward the stairs. Brett seemed too focused on me to care.

"You mock those words. You mock the Savior! What we stand for! You only did it to gather sympathy—to look sincere. Tell me, how long did you know you were going to steal something here? I know your family is hurting for money, but this? I can't understand it. I could never understand you. You were so self-righteous through high school. You went to seminary, Scouts, church every Sunday—and yet, here you are. You never cared about me. You don't care about anyone but yourself."

I felt dizzy. My body buzzed with anger. "I didn't steal that ring. I went to prison for it—wrongly. If anyone could understand how that feels, it's you, Brett."

I heard a door shut behind me. Carefully, I turned to see who was there. Jinya, our housekeeper, stepped into the light. His hair was cut short, combed to the side like I'd last seen him. He wore a white shirt, a tie, and a missionary name badge. He held a gun casually at his side.

He spoke quickly in Russian. "Stareyshina Christensen, this has been a happy reunion, da?"

My adrenaline was pumping, and my thoughts were getting fuzzy. Kaufman to Brett to Jinya—it was too quick to process. I didn't dare say anything. I didn't know what to say. Two guns against me—I didn't have a chance.

"You probably don't understand a thing I'm saying if your Russian is as bad as when I last saw you. I'm glad you stole the gun from Dmitry. I was hoping you would. He's so slow at things like that. I had visions of you coming in here and shooting Kaufman and rushing out with Stareyshina Tyson. That would have saved me a lot of trouble. Tell me, do you like my outfit?" He rocked back on his feet, clearly wanting me to admire him.

I glanced over his clothes, my eyes settling on his name badge. *It was mine.* The tie was also mine, and as I looked him over, I recognized the pants, even the shoes.

My stomach churned. Months of pain seemed to surface as I stared at him wearing my clothes. I willed myself to stay calm, but my hands were shaking. "It was you. You're the one who stole the ring on the video."

His smile widened. "You understand me? Good. Your time in prison with Duma was not wasted. Where is the Bible?"

I shoved my hands into my pockets and breathed deeply. "I don't have it."

"Well, I know you *did*." He scoffed and gave me a contemptuous look. "Who takes their scriptures with them to prison anyway?"

"Oh, they're very popular there," I said. "But maybe you'll get to see for yourself one day, da?"

His expression darkened. "Don't play with me. I will shoot you. Maybe you stole my Bible on purpose."

I shook my head. "I'm not like you. I don't steal people's things. And your Bible's value isn't because you hid a ring inside it. It's because of the light and comfort it brings to those who suffer."

He smirked. "I chose the right stareyshina. I needed someone new, someone too stupid to understand. It helped that we looked like each other. It was either you or Stareyshina Tyson, and *you* were the obvious choice. But you were not supposed to end up with my Bible. I really didn't think you and Kaufman would be coming home that night—I paid someone to make sure you didn't. You caught me by surprise, and I had to sneak out of your apartment before I could grab it. I barely had time to turn off the light before you came barging in. I called the police to speed up your arrest. But when I came in later to get it, it was gone" He shook his head. "You took it to prison."

He glared as though it still made him angry after all these months, and he raised the gun. "Did Duma tell you? About his mother? Oh, I would have loved to see his face when he discovered you were a stareyshina."

"How do you know Duma?" I asked, panicked at seeing the gun pointed at me.

He sneered, enjoying my question. "I met him while he was serving as branch president. I was a stareyshina when he stole the tithing money. Duma is smart. It was good I put him in prison when I did; otherwise, I would have had to share the ring with him. It was his plan, stealing something small and storing it in scriptures." He smirked. "Pity you didn't know he was the reason you were behind bars. Maybe you could have paid him back, eh?"

"Kaufman wrote him. He never said it was you."

Jinya grinned. "It was Kaufman. Kaufman always does what I ask him to." He looked over where Kaufman was standing alone at the bottom of the stairs. He narrowed his eyes at Jinya but made no comment.

I carefully glanced around for Anya. I met Kaufman's eyes, but he kept a blank face.

"Tell me, does Duma have your Bible now? Did he tell you he wanted to read it? And you are so stupid you believed him and handed it over."

"Drop the gun!" Kaufman yelled. He was standing near a stack of cardboard boxes now with the gun I'd kicked away. He had it pointed at Jinya.

Jinya's confidence didn't falter. He glanced up, and I followed his gaze to Brett, leaning against the railing, watching us. Brett didn't move.

"*You* drop the gun," Jinya said. "I don't believe you want me to kill this companion of yours, but you know I will. Come, dog. Do as I say. Drop it."

The man I'd stolen the gun from came out of the shadows behind Jinya, a new gun pointed at Kaufman.

Kaufman threw the gun on the ground. It clattered across the concrete.

"Move. Both of you stand together where I can see and shoot you both at the same time. My own personal firing squad." He laughed again. "I like that." He paused. "Where's the girl?" He looked up at Brett and yelled it louder, "Where's the girl?"

Brett shrugged, still leaning in the same position.

"What use are you, Tyson? You let people get away? You can sleep in Kaufman's room tonight."

Brett responded with a withering look, straightened, and walked down the steps. He met my eyes, and I shook my head, disappointment filling every crack in me.

Kaufman walked across the room until he and I were nearly touching. I remembered how desperate Kaufman had been to talk with Anya; how she'd said Kaufman had used her. He deserved answers from Jinya too.

"Did you tell Anya to write Johnson too?" I asked Jinya. "Or was that another duty Kaufman performed for you?"

Jinya rubbed his chin. "Ah, so you know about that. You and Anya spent a lot of time together, I think. And since you are *American*, she probably didn't even have to work to make you fall in love with her, just like Johnson, just like Kaufman."

"Kaufman isn't American."

"I've never even eaten at a McDonald's," Kaufman said.

"Really?" I looked at him, and he shrugged. "How could you avoid it? They're all over the place."

"My mum said it was pig food."

"Pig food," I repeated, pondering. "We fed our pigs scraps of moldy leftovers. I never thought of going to town and actually purchasing a burger for them."

"Da!" Jinya yelled. My head jerked to the front. A vein in his neck bulged purple. "I am the one who told Anya to write Johnson! Okay? You don't even act like a gun is pointed at your heads. You don't think I'll kill you?"

My throat went dry. I knew he could kill us, but I refused to think about it. I had been through too much. "Why did you want Johnson gone?" I asked.

He took a breath, and his face returned to a more normal shade. Clearly, he'd been waiting a long time to have an audience for his story. "Johnson caught me doing something I shouldn't—we'll just leave it at that. And if anyone found out, I'd lose my position as housekeeper for you two holy men, and then I wouldn't have access to your clothing anymore, and my plan to steal that ring would never work. Anya was more than willing once I told her the price."

My blood pressure rose. "You forced her to do something she didn't want to do—not just with Johnson. You made her come here too. For what? A stupid ring?"

"A *$5 million* ring. Now, this is the last time, Stareyshina. Tell me where it is."

"I don't know."

He clicked his tongue. "You'll have to do better than that. But I'm tired of holding this gun, and I have to go fetch Anya now. Take them, Dmitry. We'll find a way to get information out of Christensen—we've already practiced our methods on Kaufman," he said, chuckling darkly, "and they seemed to work well enough."

Kaufman set his hand on my upper arm for support. He looked so much thinner up close, as if he'd lost as much weight as I had, maybe even more.

We were led to the back of the warehouse where some small closets and storage rooms lined a back wall. Dmitry opened one of the wooden doors and waited outside it, keeping his distance from us. His arm was wrapped at the wrist with a bandage where I'd twisted the gun away. I glanced at it, and he glared as if he wished to shoot me on the spot.

The room was small, with a twin mattress using up over half the space. A little light came through a partially boarded-up window, and I could feel a damp, icy breeze wafting through it. Various magazines and books were scattered across the mattress. It smelled of fish and urine. I breathed through my mouth.

Dmitry locked the door behind us.

Kaufman sat on the mattress and pulled his knees up to his chin, but I would not be sealed up again. I banged on the door. "Brett! Jinya! Open this!" I heard laughter behind my fist.

I turned toward Kaufman. He was running his fingers through his white hair. "Would you like to sit?" he asked in English.

I responded in Russian. "How long have you been here?"

His forehead wrinkled, and he switched to Russian. "Three months?"

"Three months? That long?"

He shook his head and smiled. "Wow, your Russian is amazing. It's like you're a different person than I knew before."

I smiled briefly. "Not the type who would jump in a dumpster out of fear?"

"No, very much the type who would." His eyes traveled down my clothes. "But not out of fear." I looked down at my shirt, tattered and dirt-covered from days of wear.

I met his eyes, and we smiled; a feeling of momentary calm washed over me. I had missed my friend, my companion.

I touched a spot of blood on the bottom edge of my shirt and wondered if Anya was safe. Had she made a break? I turned my face to the door and tried to listen for sounds that would give me a clue. Everything was quiet.

"These aren't my clothes," Kaufman said, and I turned my attention back to him. "They forced me to shower today and gave me these. It was the first shower I've had. I spent the entire time drinking the water, finally getting my fill of it."

The thought made me sick. He blinked up at me, and I saw tears gathering at the corners of his eyes. He wiped them as I sat next to him on the mattress.

"What happened? I thought you went home."

"I did," Kaufman said. "January, I started up at the university, a couple hours from my parents' home. Jinya called me up one day. I met him at a small café, far from my flat on the other side of town. He told me he had something to give me from Anya." He shook his head. "I think he was amusing himself because I would have gone to meet him even without the promise of a gift from her. I would have gone just to see Jinya." He added sadly, "I thought we were friends."

"It's hard to know who is a true friend," I whispered.

Kaufman wiped his forehead and swallowed. "He wanted the Bible. I, of course, didn't know what he meant. He forced me outside with a gun, put me in his trunk. I should have told him to shoot me there. No one knows I'm here. No one knows I'm missing. He hacked my email so he can write my parents. They think I'm in Bolivia, helping refugees. He even sends them pictures. I think he enjoys it. It's just a game to him."

Words failed me. I couldn't imagine anything viler. "He's—he's a monster. I can't believe Brett has gone along with this. Why did Jinya bring you all the way back to Ukraine? How did he even manage it?"

"He bought me a ticket and threatened to kill my parents. He had a fake passport with a different name and everything. At first, I thought I would come here, do a thing for him, and then he would let me leave. Then I thought he was kidnapping me for money—and then I thought he just wanted to keep me silent because maybe I knew too much.

"But yesterday they made me write a note to you to get you to come here. I thought you were still in prison. They assured me if you came, they would let me go. That's why I signed it like I did—with Hobbit. Then you would know it was from me. And then they would let me go." He covered his face with his hands and began to cry. I had seen men cry in prison. I'd even done it myself. But I'd never had to be in prison alone like Kaufman had, with no hope. I put an arm around his shoulders and held him tight.

"I'm sorry," he gasped. "I was so selfish."

I looked around the room and filth. "You don't have anything to be sorry for. Jinya is at fault here—not you. He did this to you, and he did this to me." I rubbed his back while he wiped his eyes. I couldn't believe I was here with Kaufman, locked up. After all the months of injustice and dulled hopelessness, sitting here with Kaufman was almost beyond comprehension.

He began to chuckle, his shoulders shaking.

"What's so funny?" I asked, dropping my arm.

"Us." He shook his head. "They say coming home from a mission is hard; it can haunt you. I wasn't expecting this. This is truly something else."

I shook my head and heaved a sigh, feeling miserable.

"To tell the truth, Hobbit, the last few weeks of the mission weren't much of a picnic. I was transferred to Donetsk for my own safety. It ate at me every day, wondering if you were okay. President asked if I wanted to go home, but I said no. I didn't leave until I learned you'd had your trial and you'd be staying in Ukraine. I didn't expect that. I knew you couldn't have stolen that ring. You couldn't cross the street without holding my hand."

I laughed. "That isn't even an exaggeration."

"I'm glad you had Anya." He wiggled his eyebrows. "I wager her hands are softer."

I felt my face grow hot, and I pushed Kaufman's shoulder gently. It felt lighter than it should.

"It finally made a bit of sense today," he said. "I'm the villain. I'm the one who is supposed to be doing these crimes Jinya has done. No wonder Anya was so cold before she left. I'm sure Jinya will find a way to pin Brett's kidnapping on me too—even though it's the other way around."

"They can't get away with this. What do you think they plan to do?"

He cleared his throat and picked at the cuffs on his sleeves. "Torture you for information."

I swallowed and tried to still my heart. "It wouldn't be the first time," I said quietly.

He took in a shaky breath. "How did you live like this for six months? I would be insane. I'm not even sure how sane I am now. How did you do it?"

"I've never had to endure what you have. At least my parents know where I am."

Again, I wrapped my arm around Kaufman's shoulders. I wanted to comfort him, take away all his suffering. "Jinya is a fool," I said. "He thinks the scriptures are valuable because of a ring. He doesn't realize their true worth. They were my lifeline in prison. He will never know the peace and confidence that comes from having God as your companion. God didn't abandon me in prison. He hasn't abandoned us now. He helped me escape war. He brought me here to find you. I have been preserved by the Lord. Me here is proof of His love and concern for you and that He will win—we will get out of here."

Kaufman took in a shaky breath and wiped his eyes again. "Thank you," he whispered. "Thank you."

WE LEANED AGAINST THE WALL, waiting. It felt like hours had gone by; the cracks in the boarded window were dark. The only light came from the space under our door. I was exhausted, but sleep wouldn't come, not while I was locked in a cell with Kaufman in a place neither of us should be.

"Is Ukraine really invaded? I heard Jinya mention it once."

"Da," I said sadly. "I've never seen anything like it. Some areas are complete chaos. People are leaving the cities. The Donetsk mission is closed."

"All the missionaries are gone?"

"Da, President Meyers left me a letter. He said if I could escape, I should. He left information with the stake president in Kiev."

"He wanted you to escape?"

"I think he saw it was going to be a hopeless situation for me, stuck in limbo under a new government—and he believes I'm innocent. Someone helped me escape. Duma—Anya's brother—he was in the prison with me. Did you know him?"

"No, but Jinya had me write a letter to him."

I swallowed. "Da, I saw it."

He made a *tsk* sound. "Anya Mishkin. I warned you about her, didn't I?"

"Why is it you always want to talk about girls?"

"And why is it you never want to?"

I smiled. I'd experienced multiple disappointments in the last twelve hours, but discovering Kaufman's innocence was pure joy, and being with him again was healing. "You did warn me to never underestimate the girls here. I assure you, I never did. You, on the other hand—tell me again, how did we end up in that dumpster?"

He chuckled. "You know she'll turn into a babushka."

"Hmm," I said, pausing to think about it. "I don't think that would be such a bad thing anymore. Babushkas have nice knees, I hear."

He laughed loudly, throwing his head back.

It was so good to be with him, like Alma must have felt when he happened upon the sons of Mosiah—after all they'd been through as missionaries, with their trials and successes—to just enjoy being together again.

My fingers found the dried spot of blood on my shirt, and I rubbed it. "Kaufman." I hesitated, then asked, "Did you really like Anya? I know you told me you didn't—but I saw you saved the note with her picture."

"The note she probably didn't write since Jinya gave it to Berg to get us in trouble. Why? Do you like her?" He grinned his familiar teasing smile.

I stared at my hands and picked at some dead skin. "I don't know. She was a good companion—like you. Do you remember the waffles we ate?"

"Oh, don't—please."

"They have haunted me every day I've been in prison."

Kaufman moaned. "My stomach is truly going to implode on itself. Do you remember your burnt eggs?"

"I would even eat those right now," I muttered, my stomach growling.

"Agreed, mate."

I sighed. "I hope she is okay. Maybe she will get help? But really, I'd like her to stay far away from this place."

"Can't stop thinking about her? Sounds like love to me."

I shoved him lightly, and he elbowed my hand. "Stop it, Hobbit. You will not intimidate me with your meaty, boot-building hands. Come." He knelt on the mattress. "Will you pray with me? Let's pray for Anya, and let's pray for deliverance."

***

Sometime in the night, I heard a woman's scream. Kaufman and I were asleep on the mattress. We'd had no dinner, no water. No one had checked on us.

I sat up, panicked. "Anya?" I whispered.

The cracks through the boarded window made it impossible to tell what time it might be. Again, I heard the scream, but this time, I heard snickers too. Kaufman scrambled off the bed next to me, and I knew my torture was beginning.

The door opened, the light from the hall blinding me. I saw the outlines of two men walk in holding some kind of sound device.

"Does that sound familiar?" Jinya asked.

"Nyet," I lied. "What do you want?"

"You know what we want," Jinya said. "Tell us where the ring is, or you will be hearing that scream again but in person."

"You'll have to shoot me first," I said.

I heard a thwack, then Dmitry dropped to the ground in front of us. The CD player he'd been holding clamored across the floor, the top breaking off. A larger outline filled the doorway—Brett.

"You shouldn't have done that, Stareyshina," Jinya said, his voice calm but full of rage.

Brett looked prepared to tackle him, but I knew Jinya would have a weapon. I jumped forward at the same time Jinya was reaching behind him, and I grabbed his ankles, and he stumbled. Brett punched him across the face. Jinya fell on the ground, and Brett grabbed his gun.

Kaufman and I scrambled around the men. Jinya rolled over and made an attempt to crawl after us, but Brett pushed him roughly into the room and slammed the door shut, leaving Dmitry and Jinya locked in our cell.

Brett rubbed his knuckles and took deep breaths, his eyes wide.

Kaufman and I leaned against the wall, also breathing heavily. Then I stared warily at Brett and the gun in his hand.

"He was a jerk." Brett swallowed. "I didn't know you were innocent. Until yesterday, I only knew what Jinya told me. He cleaned your house, was friends with Kaufman—I just assumed he was right about you."

"Even when he kidnapped Kaufman?"

Brett rubbed his head, his tie askew. "I've only been here a week. I didn't even know Kaufman was here until yesterday when Jinya told me the plan to trick you. I just assumed Kaufman had been after the ring too—on your team, Neal. I know it was wrong. Everything about it felt so wrong. But Jinya told me you'd escaped and were coming here with the ring. I—I wanted to help stop you. Jinya told me he would pay me, that he was working with the police. And," he swallowed and looked away. "I wanted revenge. I didn't want you to get away with it.

"But I sat outside your door during the night and listened to you and Kaufman talking. I was on the wrong team. My family must be so worried. I can't believe I willingly walked into this."

"Sometimes we make mistakes," I said, staring at him. "Big ones—ones we wish we could undo."

He swallowed and nodded at me. I narrowed the gap between us and embraced Brett. His large frame shook as he squeezed me back. This wasn't the mission either of us had prepared for.

He released me and wiped his eyes with the bottom of his white shirt. Sharp, angry knocks on the door shocked us into motion. "Jinya has other guys guarding buildings around here, but maybe I can smuggle you out. We have to leave now," Brett said.

We followed him down a hall, then he opened the door leading to a small parking lot. Light was beginning to warm the sky. I grabbed his arm. "Wait. Is Anya really here? We can't leave her."

Brett shook his head and whispered, "I don't know what happened to her. Jinya was pretty angry that she got away. Come on, we have to hurry."

Brett led us to a small white truck that reminded me of a U-Haul, only miniature. He opened the back so we could jump inside, then started the engine. Kaufman and I sat in total darkness with our backs against the wall.

The truck jostled us back and forth as we pulled out of the parking lot. It swung wildly one direction, then the other as the cobblestone road I'd walked on the day before vibrated us until my teeth hurt. We hadn't been driving long when I heard sirens. The truck slowed, the bumps evening out until the truck finally stopped.

I could feel my heart thrumming like a caught rabbit. Kaufman said one of his choice English swear words while I held my breath, afraid the smallest sound would give us away.

I'd been caught by police before. It wouldn't end well. Brett was supposedly kidnapped, I was an ex-convict, and Kaufman was supposed to be in Bolivia. And none of us was from Ukraine. Maybe we'd all be going to prison.

Or maybe just me again.

It seemed my lot in mission life. Tears welled up in my eyes, and I felt one slide down my cheek. I didn't wipe it, just held perfectly still, waiting. I imagined going back to a dark room with a blinding light, being chained and beaten, and then having to live a life behind bars. Never seeing my family or riding a horse again. Never eating my mom's homemade bread or going to church. Never getting married, having kids. No choice in how I wanted to live the rest of my life. My gut ached with fear and longing.

I will be with you, a voice said, piercing my mind and heart.

I knew that voice, and I trusted my Maker. I covered my eyes with my hands and took in several deep breaths. I felt my anxiety ebb away, replaced by a light burning inside that everything would be okay. The Lord would not leave me comfortless. I always had a choice, no matter what happened, and I chose the Lord.

Voices began to sound outside the back door of the van. I heard a jangle of keys and a tugging on the lock. Kaufman and I simultaneously scooted farther into the back, where the shadows might hide us. The door flung open, light and dampness flooding in.

I lifted my arm to shield my face. Maybe they wouldn't recognize me.

"Stareyshina Kaufman?" a man's voice asked. "What are you doing here?"

I opened my eyes to see the familiar face of President Meyers helping Kaufman up into standing position. Kaufman embraced him and began to cry. Unsteadily, I got to my feet and took several steps forward.

President turned and met me with a hug too. "Neal," he said in my ear. "You made it. Duma was right, thank the Lord. He said this van might be you. I'm glad we listened."

I stared at my reflection in the bathroom mirror in the Kiev mission president's home. It had been six nights since I'd slept with a hundred dirty prisoners in a freezing basement, and now I was showered and wearing deodorant, pressed and clean clothes, and fresh garments, and I was about to have my exit interview. President and Sister Volkov were letting President Meyers, Brett, and me stay there as we prepared to fly home to America. Less than twenty hours from now, I would be home with my family.

I ran a hand through the new haircut Sister Volkov had given me this morning. The same scars were there since the last time I'd looked, plus one more wound along my hairline from my run-in with Ivan just two days ago.

Last night, Kaufman had left. His father had come immediately when he'd heard what had happened. He met us in Kiev at the airport drop-off when we arrived late that night. He was tall, thin, and blond, and I could imagine Kaufman looking very much like him in thirty years—but perhaps the last three months had narrowed that gap. He was planning to take Kaufman directly to the hospital in London.

When it was time to say goodbye, I gave Kaufman one last hug. He clung on to me tightly. Tears streamed down our faces, and I couldn't let go, not until his dad put a kind hand on Kaufman's shoulder and transferred the hug to himself. Kaufman gripped him, sobbing, and his dad said they would call us when they arrived in London. I stood shaking and wiping my eyes until Brett put an arm around my shoulders and helped me back into the van.

Watching Kaufman and his dad reminded me of what would be waiting for me at home. I touched the tender side of my forehead, swollen and bruised, my wound a bit raw-looking. I would probably need to go to a doctor when I got home. My parents would see my thin body and scars, proof of extreme adversity, of brutality, and unfair treatment. I wouldn't be able to shield them from it. Even my mom—the perpetual optimist—wouldn't think they were just paper cuts from reading my scriptures. I worried how that reality would affect her.

But I was more worried about my dad. Would he blame the Church? Would it affect his slowly growing testimony? What could I tell him?

I hoped he would accept the brutality more easily. We lived on a ranch, where life and death, seasons, changes, hardships made us who we were. I stared at the lump below my eye. The scars were more than signs of harsh treatment; they were proof that the Lord had spared me. When I looked at them, I remembered the dark times when Christ had lifted my burdens and helped me walk.

They showed me who I belonged to.

They were my brands.

Would I be able to explain to my dad how those scars had built my conviction in Christ?

I shut the bathroom door quietly and walked down the hall to the office President had said he'd be in. The door was shut. From where I stood, I could see the living room, and I recognized someone sitting on the couch.

It was Duma.

I hadn't spoken with him or Anya yesterday in all the commotion. Authorities had taken us to a building where our statements had been recorded regarding everything that had happened. Jinya and Dmitry had been arrested. I didn't know what would happen to them, but the thing that made the biggest difference was when Duma unlocked the Bible in front of the authorities and handed the ring over.

That was what had truly freed me.

Duma had stared at me the entire time, his eyes somber and afraid, and I was struck by the feeling that I'd let him down. That after all I'd been through, I hadn't done enough for the person I'd been sent here to find. He'd given me liberty in the end—I had only given him suspicion and doubt.

We'd left Anya and Duma and rushed to Kiev to get Kaufman on his flight home.

As we'd driven, President had told us how Duma had shown up in Kiev at Stake President Warren's home, wearing a white shirt and tie. President Meyers had also been in Kiev at the time, staying at President Volkov's home.

With Brett missing and their mission being dissolved, President Meyers had stayed back to try to help.

Duma told President Warren I was in trouble, and he immediately contacted President Meyers. He also told them what he knew about Jinya and how he suspected he was behind the whole thing.

When they searched for Jinya, they found he'd moved several months ago. Brother Kuznetsov, the branch president in Kramatorsk, said he would ask if anyone in the branch had seen him. Sister Smirnov reported the last time she'd seen Jinya was the day the other missionaries had been evacuating by train. He was with Brett.

That was all the information they'd had to go by, but then Brother Kuznetsov had contacted President Meyers again. Anya had called him with information regarding Neal, Brett, Jinya, and Kaufman. President joined trusted authorities to try to find which fishing warehouse it was. There were so many buildings, and Anya could give them only the general area.

Duma and Anya had been sitting in a car parked at the curb with President Meyers and an officer at 7:00 a.m. when our moving van had pulled out of a nearby parking lot. Duma was the one who had said to follow it. Later, he told President it was the way Brett had hesitated, driving on the right side of the road first, then swinging quickly to the left.

Now Duma was here.

He sat in the living room, his hands pressed tightly together, the tattoo on his neck partially hidden by his coat. There was nervousness etched on his face that I'd never seen in prison.

He stood as I came near, and I reached out a hand to shake his. "I was hoping I'd get to see you before I left. Where are you and Anya staying?"

"At President Warren's home." Duma placed his hands on his hips and blew out. "I'm sorry, Nil. You probably wonder how I knew how to open that Bible."

I shook my head. "I stopped marveling at your quick brain long ago. I'm just glad you knew how to."

Duma didn't smile. He fidgeted, then sat down.

I decided to make it easier for him. "Jinya told me the Bible was your idea. And Ivan mentioned it too. We came across him in the woods."

"Da," he said, his eyes darting from me to his clasped hands. "My sister told me about that and how you protected her. It would have been all my fault if she'd died."

I sat next to him on the couch.

He shook his head. "I knew the first time I looked at your *Kniga Mormona* that it was Jinya who had put you in prison, because it was the same one I'd marked up and sent back to him. We had discussed a Bible with a lock in the back, able to hold something small. The two would work together. The Bible would have the combination lock, and the *Kniga Mormona* would hold the code to get in. Did you ever suspect the two worked together?"

I shrugged. "I never could figure out the code or how to open it, and I don't think I wanted to know. I just wanted to go home. I just wanted people not to get hurt by it or have it incriminate me. That's why I kept it instead of leaving it in prison."

"Were you worried I'd stolen it?" He didn't smile, and I could tell he really felt bad—perhaps for the first time in his life.

I smiled. "A little. But I was also worried it would get you in trouble. You saved us. You're the reason I'm going home, Duma."

He stared at his hands. "It's the least I could do after putting you in prison to begin with."

"Nyet. Jinya made that choice. You're not to be blamed for what he did."

Again, Duma began to fidget, drumming his fingers against his knee. "Jinya is the one who made me branch president, you know. It was in a small city called Alchevs'k. I thought he had poor judgment, but really, he recognized a fellow scoundrel. We spent a lot of time talking about things. We were in direct opposition to God.

"I deserved to go to prison. My heart was closed, like a hard rock, until I saw you with that *Kniga Mormona* and saw what the consequences of my actions were, how they affected other people, other families. You were innocent. You had done nothing and were suffering, but you didn't blame God like I had. You didn't shut Him away but clung to Him like a friend."

Duma cleared his throat and pinched the bridge of his nose, clearly emotional. "Slowly, every day, you began to break that stone in my heart until it cracked down the middle and God was finally able to speak to me again. I have done many things I regret. I have many things I need to repent of. President Warren is helping me."

I blinked, my heart full. "Will you have to go back to prison?"

"I'm free." He raised both eyebrows and stared as if he still couldn't believe it. "The government acquitted me as a reward for the ring. Your President Meyers helped me with that. He is a very generous man. And not just with his socks." Duma grinned, and I laughed at the memory of those fresh, beautiful socks.

"He truly is," I said.

"I will be staying here in Kiev, working with the bishop and stake president. They are giving Anya and me jobs to help with the war relief." He swallowed and stared at his hands. "Will you forgive me, Nil? I know I have not always been kind to you."

I reached out and touched his shoulder. "I know you think I am a foolish American who trusts too easily, but I have always cared about you, Duma. And now I owe you everything. You helped me escape, you rescued us, then you produced evidence that freed me. I am proud to call you my friend. And watching you come to the Savior . . ." I shook my head, my emotions on the surface. "It makes all I have been through worth it if it meant finding you." My eyes filled with tears, and I had to bow my head and wipe them because I realized I meant it.

I'd found the lost man, and I'd freed him.

"God truly sent me to you. He must have a great work for you to do. I never knew God could care about one man so much until I came on my mission. And not just you—He has shown His love for me again and again."

Duma rubbed his hands over his face and cleared his throat. He looked over at me, his eyes red. "You will always be my brother, no matter where you go."

President Meyers opened his office door, and Anya stepped out. My mouth suddenly went very dry. She was wearing a long white dress with a flowered belt, her hair smooth and straight. She shook President's hand, then glanced shyly toward me.

"I heard about the barn," Duma said, causing me to jump.

I glanced at him. "What do you mean?"

He gave a tight-lipped nod. "I'm watching you." He patted me on the back. "Brother."

She began to walk toward us, so I quickly crawled off the couch and smoothed down my tie.

"President Meyers is helping me go to BYU in the fall," she said in broken English. She grinned at President Meyers next to her, and he returned the smile.

"Wow," I breathed. She'd be in America. "That's fantastic!" I said in English.

Her eyes sparkled at my reaction, and she switched to Russian. "Is California far from Provo?"

"No—it's close. Like Kiev to Donetsk."

"Oh." She looked disappointed.

"Well—it's closer than Ukraine to California. I have a car. I will visit, I promise."

She dipped her head and smiled, and my heart soared higher than forty thousand feet. She dug into her bag and pulled out a paper and pen. "Will you write your address, email, and phone number?"

I jotted them down as neatly as I could, my heart hammering the whole time. It suddenly seemed a small miracle I had survived three days alone with her and managed not to pass out. I handed it back and shoved my shaking hands into my pockets.

"How is the orphanage? Have you sent word to Mrs. Panyakov?"

She nodded, her face more serious. "They are fine, except for Andrii. They found him dead in the street."

I opened my mouth, shocked. "I'm so sorry," I said. I felt my face burn with sorrow and the injustice that so many innocent people could be killed.

"I am helping them through the Church. The fighting has moved to other parts of the city, so I think they will be okay. But I still worry for them."

President came and stood next to me. "This war has been brutal. Every day, I hear of more horrors. Members' homes that have been destroyed. Churches burned. I pray it ends soon."

"How do you deal with it?" Anya whispered. "'The horrors,' as you put it? How did you survive the not knowing about Nil and Stareyshina Tyson and Kaufman?"

President dropped his head, examining the floor for several seconds before lifting his gaze. His eyes were wet. "I suppose the not knowing is its own form of torture. But I know who wins the true war—the war between right and wrong. I know who knows all. And that He is aware of all. I have had to trust that He can take care of it and will guide me to help others. And He has done that again and again. I've trusted in Him, and I will continue to trust."

"How do you forgive?" I asked, my collar hot around my neck. "How do you forgive Jinya for what he did to Kaufman? For what he did to me?"

President blinked moistness out of his eyes and focused on me. "It's all about love, Neal. The answer is always love. Pray that Christ will share some of that love for others with you. That is what I have to do—it's the only way I can get through any of this."

I understood. I had already experienced what he was talking about. I had an even greater respect for President Meyers for all he was dealing with.

Anya sniffed and wiped her eyes, affected by President's words. I studied her, thinking once more how beautiful she was. Just her presence made me feel calm, uplifted. The giddy feeling in my stomach returned thinking about seeing her in America.

"Neal? Are you ready?" President asked. "We have a plane to catch soon."

Anya gave me a hasty hug goodbye, and I breathed in the smell of her hair before she let go. She lifted one finger and gently touched the cut at my hairline, her eyes full of concern. "You were brave in the warehouse. I never got to tell you."

"Thank you." Chills went through me, remembering how close we'd come to harm.

"Goodbye," Duma said, stepping between us. He squeezed me tightly, and I returned the hug while smiling at Anya. She clasped her hands together at her chin and grinned at us. I could imagine how happy she was to be with Duma again—and to know he was free.

I patted Duma on the back as he released me. "I'll miss you both," I said. "Write me."

Duma winked and opened the front door, and Anya turned to follow but then suddenly spun around and returned to plant a kiss on my cheek. I grinned, my face on fire where she'd touched it with her lips.

She waved at me and President before she followed Duma out and shut the door.

I sighed loudly, then rotated to look at my mission president. He raised one eyebrow. "That's the most unusual beginning to an exit interview with a missionary I've ever had. Will every interview require a confession?"

"Not this time," I said. Both his eyebrows rose. "Well, maybe just a few things. It's all about love though, right? Like you said?"

"You'd better step into my office."

I slunk over to his door, and he smiled. "Don't look so glum. I'll try to speed up her process to BYU. Looks like your dog, Pal, has some competition."

44

Six weeks later . . .

I STRETCHED MY ARMS ABOVE my head.

"Wait. Why are you doing that?" Brett asked. He held his ankle, his leg bent behind him to stretch his thigh. "You're not going to be running with your hands. Or is that in your skill set?"

I rolled my eyes and said in Russian, "I'm just stretching everything so I hurt less when you smear me across the sagebrush."

He leaned down to touch his toes and squinted up at me. In Russian, he said, "No matter how hard you try, the bull will never give you milk."

I laughed. "Never gets old."

"Never," he agreed.

"Are you boys planning on running anytime this year?" my mom asked from the front lawn. She was carrying eggs from our chicken coop into the house. "I thought Brett was trying out for Boise State tomorrow."

He grinned. "Yes, ma'am. But we're not doing this for me. This is to help your son get some lean meat on those bare bones. He was lounging around for six months on some sort of liquid diet."

I switched to Russian. "You mean, making boots, starved, and tortured every single day."

"Don't get technical with me," he replied in Russian.

I glanced at my mom, and she waved a hand and grinned before going inside.

"Are you worried about tomorrow?" I asked and copied the stretches Brett was doing.

"No way. The assistant coach is from Vinnytsia. I've so nailed it."

"All things work together for our good?"

He grinned and stretched his other thigh. "Have you decided where you're going to school?"

I shrugged. I was still learning to speak English and sleep in a real bed. "I think I'm going to stick around here and help my dad through the summer. Then maybe I'll start looking."

"I hear BYU is nice," Brett said, his face full of mischief. "Has she called you lately?"

I stared at my feet and tried to focus on flexing my shins. "Maybe."

"She called again last night, didn't she? Didn't she?" He jumped up and made a touchdown gesture. "Whew! That's what I'm talking about—boom baby!"

I laughed. "You're way more excited about this than you need to be." But I felt my face get hot, thinking about Anya and our friendship.

He shrugged. "I'm just practicing what my touchdown move is going to look like when I run the ball over the line. I was thinking something like this." He jumped again and pumped his fists in the air.

I tried to mimic it, and he said, "Um, no . . . okay. When you do it, see, I have to rethink the whole process." He laughed and shoved me. "Race you down to the end of the road."

I groaned. "Go easy on me."

I followed him down the long dirt road that connected my house to the highway a mile away. Brett could have run circles around me, but he didn't; he stayed close by and let me set the pace. Since we'd started running, I could feel my body getting stronger, and the extra energy output made it easier to sleep at night when my mind wanted to wander to prison cells and overturned buses.

For a long time, we just ran, my thoughts far away. Duma had emailed me about the prison in Donetsk. It didn't look good. It was sitting in the middle of a war zone. One side of the fence had "Glory to Ukraine" written on it; the other side flew the People's Republic (*DPR*) flags, the shells continually flying from both sides. Sickness had spread through the prisoners in the damp basement, and Duma said they were worried about dysentery. He'd found a way to set up a supply spot the prisoners regularly visited for medicine and food. They were totally self-reliant now—no Ukrainian authorities or Russian separatists delivered anything to them. They were forgotten in the crisis happening all around them. I knew how helpless that could feel.

Brett interrupted my thoughts. "I want to tell you something. It's been weighing on my mind, and since I'll be leaving tomorrow, I just want to say it." He was quiet, and for a while, it was just the sound of our feet hitting the dirt. Then he said, "You know I wasn't ever going to shoot you, right?"

His question was abrupt, and it took me to a place I didn't want to go. Seeing Kaufman again on that balcony, knowing what he'd been through, was still too hard to think about some days.

"I don't know if Jinya thought I would—and that bugs me. It eats at me, wondering why he would think I'm that person. I know I could never do that, no matter what, even if you did steal that ring and I had to be the one to stop you."

"I know you wouldn't," I said. "Who you are, your testimony, is something Jinya can't take away from you. No one can. Not man or prison. Don't let it bother you. I don't even think about it."

At least, I tried not to.

"Thanks, man," he said, and my throat felt tight hearing him say it, thinking about how far we'd come.

We ran to the end of the road and back. The last hundred yards, Brett sprinted, ending them by jumping the small fence surrounding the front yard. My mom had been watering flowers nearby and clapped her gloved hands.

"Show off!" I yelled, walking through the gate, holding my side.

My mom removed her gardening gloves and brought a plate of cookies over to Brett.

Brett took one off the plate and held it up. "Impressing the ladies is never a waste of time."

I shook my head. "That's my mom you're flirting with."

My dad came around the side of the house, holding a shovel, Pal at his heels. Dad took off his hat, his light-brown hair graying around the edges. "He's got good taste," he said. He took a cookie from my mom and kissed her. Pal ran over and gave my sweaty legs affectionate licks.

The sound of a car coming up the road made me turn. A short, tan Toyota truck came over the last hill.

"Is that Bishop Hendricks? Again? That's three Saturdays in a row," I said. I glanced over my shoulder at my parents, but my dad was already waving and walking up to the cement carport. Bishop had driven my parents to Reno to pick me up at the airport. It was as if they had a new best friend. Bishop had embraced me in a way I'd never felt from him before.

I knew it might be awkward when I got home, people knowing what I'd done to Brett and then the whole being arrested and thrown into prison.

Not to mention I'd been out on my mission less than a year. But it was nice that I wasn't by myself in that—Brett had come home early too. Sometimes I wondered if he'd refused a reassignment just for me, so I wouldn't be alone. The idea filled me with gratitude and love. He checked on me every day, and I knew he'd jump anyone who so much as looked at me wrong.

Bishop walked with my dad over to the grass, then shook my mom's hand, Brett's, and mine. My mom offered him a cookie.

My dad turned to me and said, "Son, can I speak to you a minute in the house?"

I followed him up the steps and let the screen door slam behind me—I'd missed that sound. He dusted his pants off before sitting on the couch. I took a seat on the nearby love seat, my sweaty shirt sticking to my back.

"I have something important I want to talk to you about," he said. He swallowed and looked at his hands. "It's hard for me to talk about what we felt—experienced—with you gone." He cleared his throat, and I saw all the things he didn't say—the fear that I'd never come home, that they'd never see me again. I'd felt those same things, but seeing them from my dad's perspective always scared me more.

"I did a lot of soul-searching and praying. People from church really came through. You don't know this, because I didn't want your mom to say anything, but I made a choice the week you left to start taking the missionary lessons. I wanted to know what you were teaching and imagine it better."

Again, he swallowed. "Those lessons saved me. Crying with those elders is more crying than I've done my whole life." He laughed, and I returned the smile through my moist eyes.

"I've chosen to get baptized. I actually decided before you came home, but I kept hoping—" He stopped, and I saw his eyes had filled with tears.

I'd seen my dad cry only once, and it had been because he had to put his favorite horse down.

He wiped his eyes. "I kept hoping—" Again, he got stuck on that word. He took a deep breath. "I kept praying you'd come home and get to be the one to do it. I didn't want to rush you with all you've been through, but if you're willing, I'd like to set the date and make it official. Would you baptize me, Saturday, June 22?"

I blinked my eyes. "Da—yes—I can't believe it, Dad—I'm so happy."

He reached out and cuffed my chin like he used to when I was a kid. His thumb moved across the scar on my cheek, and he rubbed it silently a second. "Thank you," he said, his eyes becoming moist again. "Thank you for enduring so much, for being strong. Your mission changed us all, didn't it?"

I sniffed. "Thank you for always being my hero, Dad, and teaching me so much. I thought about you all the time in Ukraine." I glanced down at my Nike's. "You'll be my first baptism." The thought made me somber and grateful at the same time. There was no one I'd rather baptize."

He rubbed my shoulder. "Next stop: temple."

I felt completely overwhelmed at the thought and patted his hand on my shoulder. We stood, and I followed him to the door. "I'll tell the bishop it's official."

I watched from the porch as my dad told Bishop the news. Brett grinned and shook my dad's hand. My mom hugged and kissed him on the cheek. I took a deep breath and watched them all, my heart full and utterly amazed.

A scripture came to mind, one of the many I'd studied all those months ago in the dark cell with Egor—2 Nephi 28:30: *"I will give unto the children of men line upon line, precept upon precept, here a little and there a little; and blessed are those who hearken unto my precepts . . . for they shall learn wisdom; for unto him that receiveth I will give more."*

ABOUT THE AUTHOR

ROBBIN JENSEN PETERSON EARNED HER degree in English literature from Utah State University in 2002 after attending Snow College. She is the author of *Going Home* and lives in California. If she had to choose between the silence of a prison cell or a house full of noisy children, it would be a toss-up some days—both sound amazing.

You can find her on Facebook at Robbin J Peterson Author or on her website at www.robbinpeterson.com